Hollywood Wives
The New Generation

Jackie Collins

Hollywood
Wives
The New Generation

SIMON & SCHUSTER
A VIACOM COMPANY

First published in Great Britain by Simon & Schuster UK Ltd, 2001
A Viacom Company

3 5 7 9 10 8 6 4 2

Simon & Schuster UK Ltd
Africa House
64-78 Kingsway
London WC2B 6AH

www.simonsays.co.uk

Simon & Schuster Australia
Sydney

A CIP catalogue record for this book is available from the British Library

ISBN 0-7432-0855-2

This book is a work of fiction. Names, characters, places and incidents are
either a product of the author's imagination or are used fictitiously. Any
resemblance to actual people living or dead, events or locales is entirely
coincidental.

Typeset by SX Composing DTP, Rayleigh Essex
Printed and bound in Great Britain by
Butler & Tanner Ltd, Frome and London

For all the Hollywood Wives
Old and new . . . male and female . . .
Gay and straight . . .
A constant source of inspiration!

And for Arnold Kopelson,
who told me much more than I
ever wanted to know!

And for my darling Frank,
Always

Prologue

Eric Vernon walked into Sam's Place, a seedy topless bar in the valley, and immediately fixed his gaze on Arliss Shepherd.

Arliss was not a pretty sight as he leaned against the bar, nursing a half-full bottle of beer. Long-faced with pale, pock-marked skin, and lank, shoulder-length yellow hair, he was skinny as a starving coyote and just as skittish. Nervous habits surrounded him – he chewed his straggly hair, picked his teeth, rarely changed his underwear, and smelled of stale onions.

In spite of his shortcomings, Arliss was not lacking in friends: a group of similar misfits hung out at Sam's Place, with Arliss leading the pack. Sam, an obese man famous for only having one ball, ran his bar like a friendly club for losers. Regulars included Davey 'The Animal', Little Joe, and Big Mark Johansson. They were a motley crew, drawing solace from each other's company and the fact that there was strength in numbers. Together they could kick ass. Alone they were useless, nothing more than a bunch of loud-mouthed failures. Which, as far as Eric Vernon was concerned, was a good thing, because men with no self-esteem were far easier to manipulate than men with balls. He'd discovered that in prison when he was doing time for manslaughter.

Manslaughter my ass, Eric thought as he approached Arliss at the bar. *I hit the scumbag with a two-by-four until he dropped dead in front of me. And not a moment too soon.*

Eric Vernon was a nondescript man of medium height and slight build, with bland features and sandy brown hair cut short. He had the kind of face that blended in – the kind of face that nobody ever remembered.

Except that skanky bitch remembered me all right, he thought sourly. *Oh, yes, she remembered me so well that I served six miserable years in prison because of her.*

The first thing he'd done when he'd got out of the joint was taken care of her. Smashed her pointy face until it was no more than pulp. Then he'd burned her house down.

The best revenge is deadly. Eric had learned that at an early age.

Immediately after dealing with the tattling bitch he'd adopted a new identity and moved to California, eventually settling in L.A. where he'd taken a job with a computer company – a skill he'd mastered in jail.

All this had taken place two years earlier, and no one had ever questioned who he was or where he came from. Which is exactly the way he'd planned it.

A person does not sit in jail for six stinking years without making plans. And Eric had an agenda, an agenda he was getting ready to pursue.

Chapter One

'**Y**ou look *fantastic!*'
      'You think?'
      'I *know.*'
      Lissa Roman narrowed her eyes as she studied her reflection in the large, lightbulb-studded makeup mirror. She saw perfection, and so she should, considering she worked like a long-haul truck driver to look as good as she did. And it wasn't easy. It took real dedication and non-stop action. Yoga, Pilates, starvation, ice-cold showers, Brazilian waxing, hair colouring, jogging, swimming, weight training, fasting, aerobics, spinning – you name it, Lissa did it. Everything except plastic surgery. She was too scared of the knife. Too petrified that the surgeon would make her look like somebody else – take away her identity, her personality. She had seen it happen to numerous people in Hollywood, men *and* women. Besides, she was only forty – younger than Madonna and Sharon Stone, for God's sake. And, anyway, she didn't need it.
      'You're *sure* I look as good as it gets?' she questioned, forcing Fabio, her faithful makeup and hair artist, to repeat his compliments.
      'Divine. Beautiful. The works,' Fabio assured her, tossing back his luxuriant mane of expensive hair extensions.
      And he meant every word of it, because although Lissa

Roman was not a classic beauty, she had that indiscernible something that made her a superstar. It was a combination of blatant sex appeal, fiery energy and a body to die for. Not to mention blazing blue eyes, high cheekbones, and full, pouty lips. Fabio *loved* basking in her aura.

'All thanks to you and your magic fingers,' Lissa murmured, smoothing her shoulder-length platinum hair.

'That's what Teddy told me last night,' Fabio said, with a self-satisfied smirk.

'Lucky you,' Lissa said, rising from the makeup chair.

'No,' Fabio said, wagging a beringed finger at her. 'Lucky *Teddy*.'

'You have some ego!' Lissa teased, heading for the door.

'*Almost* as big as yours,' Fabio retorted crisply, following her out to the studio where the photographer from *Maxim* magazine waited.

Lissa and Fabio had worked together for eight years and enjoyed an excellent relationship. Fabio actually *liked* Lissa Roman. For someone of her stature she was not an egocentric bitch. She was warm and friendly and quite funny at times. Of course, she had appalling taste in men – but living in Hollywood there was hardly a vast pool of eligible men to choose from. And as far as Fabio was concerned, all the good ones were gay – thank *God*!

Her second husband, Antonio, the man who'd fathered her only child, sounded the best of all. Not that Fabio had ever met him, but he'd seen photos, and Antonio was a magnificent specimen: all dark sexy eyes, impressive physique, and broodingly handsome features. Fabio often wondered why she'd let that one slip away.

'Antonio had a wandering cock,' was Lissa's only explanation.

Fabio didn't get why straight people were so uptight about sex. After all, sometimes a wandering cock could be a good thing.

* * *

Nicci Stone gazed unblinkingly at her kickboxing instructor's crotch. It was quite a package, and so was he. His name was Bjorn, and he was tall and blond in the Nordic style, with subtle muscles and sinewy bronzed thighs. He was over six feet tall with large Chiclet teeth and a gleaming smile.

I bet he gives great tongue, Nicci thought, with a secretive smile. *He's Scandinavian. Scandinavian men rock.*

Not that she'd had that many. Sven, the Swedish facialist. Marl, the Danish rock 'n' roller. And Lusti, the Norwegian personal trainer. Actually, that was a lot. Enough to make her realize that European men were far more inventive in bed than their American counterparts.

She wondered how Bjorn, with his quite commendable package, would stack up. Maybe she should give him a try . . .

No! a stern voice in the back of her head commanded. *You are currently engaged and there will be no more screwing around.*

Damn! Who came up with *that* rule?

Mommy, of course. Lissa Roman, mega movie star, singer and legendary sex symbol – currently on her fourth husband.

Yeah. That's right. Four.

Nicci hoped it was Lissa's lucky number. The next wedding was *hers*, and she did not take kindly to competition, even though she had lived with it forever.

Growing up with Lissa Roman as your mother was no day trip to Disneyland. Whenever possible, Nicci had kept the identity of her famous mom a deep, dark secret. Although keeping it to herself never lasted long, because somebody always managed to find out – blowing her chance of a normal (*what's that anyway?*) relationship.

Nicci was, at nineteen, a spirited kind of beauty. Unlike

her mother's platinum blond sexiness, Nicci had inherited her exotic gypsy looks from Antonio Miguel Stone, her Spanish father – Lissa's husband number two – a drop-dead handsome philanderer with no money to speak of and a somewhat shaky pedigree. His mother, Nicci's grandma, was supposedly a third cousin to the King of Spain – although they'd never been invited to tea.

Nicci knew the story. Lissa had fallen for Antonio when he'd arrived in Hollywood to liaise with a gorgeous redhead. Five days after their first meeting, the redhead was history, and Lissa and Antonio were on their way to Vegas in a chartered plane where, after two days of gambling and incredible sex, they'd got married.

Nine months after that, Nicci was born.

One passion-filled year later, Lissa caught Antonio cheating with her so-called best friend and promptly divorced him. Shortly after that he'd returned to Europe to continue his career as an ace playboy and sometime racing-car driver, roaming around the best resorts and the most beautiful women.

At age ten Nicci had started demanding to know more about her father – a man she had only seen pictures of. Reluctantly Lissa had instructed her lawyer to contact her ex and remind him that he had a daughter. Surprisingly, over the next few summers, Antonio had rallied and sent for the little girl. Nicci's visits were a big success. She was pretty, sassy and smart, and Antonio was quite entranced. So much so, that over the following years she began spending months at a time with her charismatic dad, until, at age fifteen, she dropped out of Beverly Hills High School and enrolled at the American school in Madrid. Lissa didn't seem to mind. Lissa had a career to take care of.

Nicci was thrilled, freedom at last! She soon discovered that Antonio was far more exciting to live with than her mom. He acted more like an older brother than a father figure, full of devilish doings. He taught her what he considered to be all the good things in life – such as how to smoke pot, drink martinis without getting too wasted, and handle men with the right combination of flattery and disinterest. One of his many exotic girlfriends had given her a crash course in birth control. How cool was *that*? What more could a young, eager-to-learn teenager ask for?

By the time Nicci was sixteen she was wise way beyond her years, certainly wise enough to realize that her father was incorrigible – a bad boy with a fun-loving disposition and a big heart. He adored his daughter, she was his one link to normality. And Nicci adored him back, even though she knew he was a rogue and somewhat spineless. So what? He was her dad and she loved him.

The only downside to living with Antonio was his mother, Adela, a fierce-faced woman who dressed only in black and screamed at her son whenever the opportunity arose. Antonio didn't seem to mind, he gave as good as he got, raising his voice back with no concern about anyone listening. Nicci soon realized it was a game between the two of them. A competition. Their deal was who could scream the longest and loudest. Grandma always won. Grandma was a determined woman. She was also the keeper of the family money, and much to Antonio's annoyance, she doled it out on *her* terms.

Adela owned the house they inhabited in Madrid, plus a luxurious villa in Marbella, both properties left to her by her late husband who'd suffered a fatal heart attack when Antonio was only ten. Since that time Adela had drummed it into her handsome son that he was now the man in the family, and therefore had to look after her. Then she'd promptly sent him off to a military academy, where he'd had the crap beaten out of him on a regular basis.

When Antonio had finally got out, he was ready to party, and in spite of Adela's objections, party he did, winging his way across Europe bedding a constant procession of sleek women. Along the way he'd become interested in racing cars. As soon as Adela found out, she'd thrown a fit. To appease her, Antonio made it a hobby instead of a career, a move he'd always regretted.

Now he split his time between his mother's two residences, carefully planning to be wherever she wasn't.

Adela was no push-over – she kept tabs on her son. She considered it enough that he'd married a cheap American movie star when he'd ventured out of her range, and she certainly had no intention of allowing that kind of madness to happen again.

Nicci had a strained relationship with her strict grandmother. Adela professed to care for her half-American granddaughter, but at the same time she was forever disapproving of Nicci's behaviour. Nicci soon learned how to deal with her – whenever the criticism and muttering got too much to take, she flew back to L.A. and hard-working Lissa, who was so caught up in her career that she didn't seem to mind *what* Nicci did.

And Nicci did plenty – for she had inherited her mother's passion for breaking barriers and her father's wild ways. She was into experimenting, seeing how far she could go without actually doing IT. In spite of her lessons in birth control, she was nervous about going all the way – that is, until back in Europe she met Carlos, Antonio's distant cousin.

She was seventeen and ready for the big deal.

Carlos was twenty-five, self-assured and extremely good-looking.

It didn't take him long to break down her inhibitions, and then, shortly after, to break her heart.

Unfortunately, like his cousin, Carlos was a serial philanderer who could not resist a pretty face. Furious and hurt by his rejection, Nicci had travelled the revenge route, jumping into bed with as many men as possible, while harbouring the vain hope that Carlos would become hopelessly jealous and beg her to come back to him.

He didn't.

With a great deal of prompting from his mother, Antonio eventually got on her case, pointing out that if she wasn't careful, people would start calling her a slut and a whore.

'And what are *you?*' she'd yelled at her father – a man who found it impossible to keep it in his pants. 'A goddamn *virgin?*'

'No. I am a man,' he'd replied, with a small, superior smile. 'And men can do anything.'

They'd argued bitterly for most of the night, both saying things they would grow to regret.

The next morning Nicci had boarded a plane to L.A. and had not been back to Europe since.

That had been almost two years ago, and now she was engaged she couldn't help wondering if she should call Antonio and tell him. 'Hi, Daddy,' she'd say sweetly. 'I'm no longer a slut and a whore. Will you come to my wedding and give me away?'

Mr Double Standard. He should've called her, and he never had. Oh, well, Lissa had always claimed Antonio was a big disappointment; perhaps she was right.

Nevertheless, Nicci still loved him, although she certainly did not respect him, for his casual way with women had coloured her view of all men, forcing her to adopt the motto *Use them before they use you.* Until now she'd run her life that way, unlike dear old Mom, who kept falling in love or lust – depending on how one looked at it.

Nicci admired the professionalism and achievements of her mother. However, she did not feel particularly close to her. How could she, when Lissa always seemed to put her career first, love life second, and trailing a poor third, came

Nicci, her only child, to whom she'd given birth when she was twenty and on the brink of becoming very famous indeed?

Nicci often considered it a good thing that Lissa had not had more children: she was hardly mother material.

No, Lissa Roman was a true superstar, destined to be worshipped by millions.

Lissa Roman worked a camera like nobody else. She had all her moves down, and enjoyed making love to the lens. Creating dynamic photographs was one of her strengths, and the camera adored her.

Hard work had never bothered Lissa. In fact, hard work was the way her parents – a strict, Midwestern couple – had raised her. 'Work hard and don't expect no thanks,' her father had drilled into her. He was an austere man incapable of giving affection. She'd worked her brains out at school, achieving top grades, and getting no words of praise from her distant parents. Even when she was voted top of her class, they'd refused to acknowledge that she'd achieved anything. Finally, at sixteen, after a horrible fight with them, she'd run away to New York with her high-school boyfriend and never gone back. As far as she knew, they'd never come looking, and she didn't give a damn.

'Do you need anything, honey-child?' Fabio asked, standing on the sidelines sipping green tea from a leopard-print mug.

'Put on the Nelly Furtado CD,' she requested. 'Track four, 'Legend'. I can't get enough of that song.'

She always made sure to bring a selection of favourite CDs to every session. Today it was Nelly, Sade, and Marc Anthony. She was very into soul and Latin sounds and was currently planning her own CD which would incorporate plenty of both. She was also working on a book, sitting with a ghost writer whenever she had the time to produce a glossy coffee-table book to be titled *A Week in the Life of Lissa* . . .

Like Madonna and Cher, she was known by one name.

Apart from the CD and the book, there was also a movie she might do, a remake of *Gentlemen Prefer Blondes*. Nothing signed yet, she was waiting for the right script. And in her immediate future was a one night stand in Vegas at the opening of an incredibly lavish new hotel, the Desert Millennium Princess, which would pay her three million dollars for the pleasure of her company for one night only. Quite an achievement. And then there was her daughter's upcoming wedding, which Nicci had assured her she could deal with herself.

So Lissa was extremely busy, but not too busy to contemplate her fourth divorce. Currently she was married to Gregg Lynch, a ten-years-younger-than-her singer-songwriter. And thank God her lawyer had insisted that he sign an iron-clad pre-nuptial agreement, because lately she'd begun to suspect that Gregg was composing his love songs elsewhere. And not only that, but over the last six months he'd started showering her with mental abuse.

His constant nagging about things she supposedly did wrong were beginning to get her down. There were times he would pick on the smallest detail and yell at her endlessly. Other times he would berate her for not recording *his* songs, accusing her manager and agent of forming a vendetta against him. He'd tried to persuade her to fire them both. 'Can't you see that they're stealing from you,' he'd yell, 'and you're too dumb and stupid to notice?'

He distrusted her business manager. Loathed her lawyer. Hated her yoga teacher. Criticized her friends. In fact, anyone who worked for her was on his shit list.

She ignored his insults, because she knew that deep down he didn't mean it. And whenever he indulged in one of his temper tantrums, he always apologized later. She also

11

understood *why* he was so super-critical. He was furious that he'd never made it, and because of that he was forced to take his frustration and anger out on *someone*, and since she was the closest person to him, that someone was her.

The big problem was that she was never quite sure who she was going to wake up next to – the good or the bad Gregg. Unfortunately they now seemed to exist side by side.

She couldn't stand him when he was in one of his bad moods. Loved him when he was mellow and caring and supportive – qualities that were fast vanishing.

Lissa was prepared to put up with a lot – she knew from past experience that there was no such animal as the perfect man – but the one thing she refused to stand for was infidelity. The moment she suspected that might be happening, it was time to move on. No Hillary Clinton was she, and lately she'd been recognizing the signs only too well. All-night meetings, a renewed interest in his personal appearance, taking one shower a day too many, and developing a paranoid attachment to his cellphone.

As soon as Gregg started exhibiting the symptoms, she'd called the Robbins-Scorsinni Private Investigation Agency and requested forty-eight-hour surveillance. She'd used the agency on other occasions and they'd never failed her.

It was so depressing that it had to come to this again. Why was it that she had yet to marry a man who could keep it in his pants?

Nelly Furtado crooned over the sound system. Lissa licked her already glossy lips while Fabio fussed with her hair.

'Will we be finished soon?' she asked Max, her publicist, who was hovering on the sidelines with a group of people from the magazine.

'Any time you want,' Max said, a short, cigar-smoking

man who wore flamboyant suits, and had a different bow-tie for every day of the month.

'One more roll,' the photographer begged. He was young, in awe, and excellent at what he did.

Lissa was always open to young and excellent: it kept her career edgy and fresh.

Throwing her head back, she struck a pose, honouring the camera with a true-to-form provocative gaze. Parted lips, half-closed diamond blue eyes, an expression of sexual yearning.

Lissa Roman gave great sex. It always paid off.

Kickboxing class over – a virtual feast of kicking, punching and sparring – Nicci hurried into the dressing room, took a quick shower and changed into shorts and a stomach-baring T-shirt: all the better to show off her killer abs, glowing tan and recent navel piercing. Then she stared in the mirror for a moment, which reminded her that she'd certainly inherited Antonio's looks. Rich, dark brown hair cropped like a gamin, with long bangs falling into her huge brown eyes, which were fringed with impossibly long, silky, midnight black lashes. Long legs and a lithe, lean body. Her over-full, sexy lips and high cheekbones were the only clue that she was Lissa Roman's daughter.

Yes, she decided, she was definitely going to call Antonio. He *had* to come to her wedding. He was her father, after all, and she needed him beside her on the most important day of her life. It wasn't like she had any other family – Lissa's parents were forbidden territory, although she'd always harboured a secret desire to contact them, see if they were as strict and unloving as Lissa said.

Grabbing her bag, she headed for the car park, where she climbed behind the wheel of her gleaming silver sports BMW, an engagement present from her fiancé, Evan.

Ah . . . Evan, she thought fondly. A goer. A doer. A man

with a mission. Thirty years old and already a self-made millionaire from a string of off-beat comedy movies he'd co-written and co-produced with his brother, Brian.

So intently was Nicci thinking about Evan, that she did not notice the dusty brown van pull away from the kerb and fall in behind her car as she left the parking lot and hit Sunset.

Evan and Brian Richter. A younger, hipper version of the Farrelly brothers. Their rise to power had been meteoric – six movies in five years, all of them box-office smashes.

Nicci had met Evan at the dog park on the top of Mulholland. She'd been walking her then boyfriend's Great Dane, and Evan had been trying to control a couple of crazed, large German shepherd puppies, who were intent on running riot and attacking as many other dogs as possible. Coolly assessing the situation, she'd gone up to him, grabbed the leashes out of his helpless hand, chased down both puppies and collared them firmly.

'Here,' she'd said brusquely, delivering the two German shepherds back to Evan. 'I suggest you hire a trainer.'

'How much?' he'd asked, all spiky brown hair, lanky limbs and comic-book features.

'How much what?' she'd answered haughtily.

'How much'll *you* charge to do it?'

A disdainful look. 'You can't afford me.'

A crooked grin. 'Wanna bet?'

What the hell? She had no job to speak of and he seemed vaguely legitimate. 'A thousand a week. Cash,' she'd said, challenging him.

No challenge was too big for Evan Richter. 'When can you start?' he'd said, admiring her spunky attitude.

And that's how it all began. A casual meeting, with neither of them knowing anything about each other. He'd only kept the dogs a few weeks because they were messing up his impeccable house, but by that time Nicci and he were quite inseparable.

That had been five months ago and now they were due to be married in six weeks and she had a wedding to organize with no help from Lissa, whose only suggestion had been to hire a wedding planner.

Nicci sighed. Naturally she loved Evan. Sort of. Well, he made her laugh, didn't treat her badly and gave great head. He could also handle the fact that she had a famous mom, which freaked most guys out. That should be enough to sustain a long and fruitful marriage . . . shouldn't it?

Yes. Except there was one tiny little drawback. Very small. Extremely insignificant.

Nicci loved his brother too.

And sometimes she wasn't sure which one of the Richter brothers she loved the most.

Chapter Two

Lissa Roman had three best female friends, plus one token male. They called themselves the New Hollywood Wives, and tried to get together at least once a month, which wasn't easy, because they were all exceptionally busy – except James, who played house-husband to his black male lover, Hollywood music mogul, Claude St Lucia.

'Look at you ladies go,' James was inclined to say, raising his well-groomed eyebrows. 'Why not play it like me and do absolutely nothing? It's so much *easier*.'

James was tall and English, with dark blond hair worn a tad too long, and fine aristocratic features. He was extremely lazy, and a loyal friend who could be relied upon to listen to all their problems, and between the four women that meant a lot of problems.

Lissa never felt the need to visit a shrink, she had James to depend on, although she didn't tell him *everything*, and she certainly wasn't about to reveal her suspicions about Gregg.

Today they were meeting at Mister Chow's – a long time popular hang-out on Camden Drive.

Lissa got there first, safely delivered by her permanent driver, Chuck, a large, bald black man, who doubled as her bodyguard. She'd learned the hard way that she couldn't be too careful. She'd had her share of stalkers, freaks and over-zealous fans. Caution was second nature to her now.

Then James walked in, debonair as usual in a casual Armani sports jacket and perfectly pressed jeans. James loved clothes, Claude loved buying them for him.

Taylor Singer arrived next. Taylor was a tall, striking woman in her mid-thirties, with cat-like green eyes, long wavy hair, and well-defined features. She was married to Lawrence Singer, mega Oscar-winning writer-director-producer. Taylor was an actress who had plans to direct and star in her own project, a movie she'd been developing and talking about for two years. So far it hadn't happened, but with steely determination, and a great deal of help from her powerful husband, she was sure it was about to.

She was followed by Stella Rossiter, a short, dynamic blonde, who produced movies with her husband, Seth, a man thirty years older than his pretty, smart-mouthed third wife. Together they were a well-respected, powerhouse couple who consistently made hit films.

Stella was pregnant. Well, actually *she* wasn't - she was far too busy to put up with the inconvenience of pregnancy so a mix of *her* eggs and Seth's sperm had been fertilized and implanted in a surrogate mother. Stella was delighted to inform anyone who would listen that they were about to give birth to twins. Seth's three adult children from his two former marriages were not thrilled. Nor were his ex-wives.

And finally, in strolled Kyndra, sultry queen of the divas, making her usual late entrance.

Lissa glanced pointedly at her watch. 'What is *this*? Black time?' she demanded good-naturedly.

'Oh, honey,' Kyndra answered in her low-down smoky voice. 'You all would *still* be sittin' here come midnight if this was black time!'

Everyone laughed, while Kyndra settled into her seat. She was a voluptuous woman, with a huge bosom, long Tina Turner legs, and clouds of thick, dark curls surrounding a strong sexual face. She'd been married for twenty-four years to Norio Domingo, one of the most successful record producers in the music business. 'Come tomorrow, Norio and I are in the recording studio,' Kyndra drawled, 'an' that's the last you'll see of us until our party. So get this mama a lychee martini an' let's *dish*!'

It was Lissa's lunch, so she signalled to the waiter, ordered drinks and all kinds of tempting starters from chopped seaweed to honey spare-ribs. The food would probably sit there, as everyone – including James – seemed to be on a permanent diet. But it was a good idea to have it on the table just in case anyone was in an eating mood.

'You're on, James,' Lissa said, turning to her best male friend. 'You *always* know everything first, so let's hear the latest.' Not that she was interested, gossip wasn't her thing, but she needed *something* to take her mind off what she was doing later.

'Well . . .' James said, a knowledgeable glint in his slate grey eyes. 'Did anyone *hear* about Ricky M and the two French models?'

'Even better,' Stella interrupted. 'I went to one of those "how to give the perfect blow job" parties. Talk about bizarre.'

'*I* went to one of those,' Taylor said enthusiastically. 'Rubber cocks straight out of the dishwasher! And some funny little ex-nurse who tried to instruct everyone how to do it. Can you imagine!'

'Pu-lease,' James said. 'It's far too early for this kind of crude nonsense.'

'Ladies,' Kyndra intoned, 'if you don't know how to give the perfect BJ by this time, then I suggest you pack on up and get your skinny white asses back to where you came from!'

And after that it was all systems go.

*   *   *

Driving fast, with one hand on the steering wheel, the other clutching her cellphone, Nicci reached Evan on location in Arizona, where he was shooting his latest movie. 'Busy?' she asked briskly.

'Busy missing you,' he replied.

'How come you always know the right thing to say?' she said, pleased to hear he was missing her.

'Practice.'

'I hate the thought of practice,' she said, screeching to a halt at a red light.

'Huh?'

'Practice means there's been other women. I *hate* the thought of other women.'

'No other women,' Evan said solemnly. 'I was a virgin before you. All I did was jack off.'

'Ugh! I'd sooner there were other women!' She laughed, ignoring the man in the Toyota behind her who was busy giving her the finger on account of her abrupt stop.

'No pleasing you today,' Evan said lightly.

'I'm planning on phoning my dad,' she announced, groping for a cigarette in her purse.

'What? To tell him I jack off?'

'You're weird,' she said, laughing.

'I am,' he agreed. 'But you knew that.'

'Uh . . . how's Brian?' she asked casually, lighting up.

'An asshole as usual.'

'So things are normal.'

'You could say that.'

The light changed to green and she shot away, driving too fast as usual. 'E-mail me your undying devotion.'

'I already have.'

'Miss you,' she said. 'Call me later.'

'Of course.'

She clicked off, a smile on her face. Evan always made

her smile, which is more than she could say for most of the men she'd been involved with. Carlos had possessed no sense of humour at all. Looking back, she had no clue what she'd seen in him – apart from his smooth looks and incredible prowess in bed. Hmm . . . two qualities that shouldn't count, but definitely did. Sensational sex was hard to come by.

Evan was good in bed. Obliging and considerate. But no way was he wild.

Nicci had a strong suspicion that Brian was the wild one in the family. She also had a nagging itch to find out.

No! she told herself sternly. *Stop thinking that way. It's Evan you're marrying. Not Brian, who comes on to every woman who breathes, and is certainly not faithful and trustworthy like his brother.*

Cutting off a white Mercedes driven by a grey-haired lech, she pulled up in front of Starbucks and hurried inside.

Skipping to the front of the line, she winked at the lanky guy behind the counter – a wannabe actor with bright red hair and crooked teeth. Since he knew her, she didn't have to tell him her order. 'What's happenin', Freddy?' she asked, reaching for a cookie on the glass-topped counter.

'Courteney Cox was in,' he confided.

'Cool.'

'She's a babe.'

'*And* taken.'

'I can look, can't I?' Freddy said hopefully.

'When you make it big, you can do more than look.'

'Encouragement,' Freddy said, grinning. 'You spur me on.'

Freddy had no idea who she was, which was good, because Nicci had never traded on being Lissa Roman's daughter. The less people knew, the better. After all, it wasn't as if she had any desire to be an actress or a singer. Truth was, she hadn't decided *what* she wanted to do. She'd dabbled in a few jobs, just like she'd dabbled in a few drugs. Nicci was an adventurer, anxious to cover every experience.

Recently Evan had suggested that since she obviously had no intention of going to college, and was currently without a job, she might be interested in working with him.

'What as? A gofer?' she'd asked suspiciously.

'Oh, yeah,' he'd answered sarcastically. 'I can see *you* running errands for people.'

'Then *what?*'

'Hang out on the set – see what gets your adrenaline going.'

'*You* get my adrenaline going,' she'd said warmly.

'That's why I love you.'

'You love me 'cause we have great sex,' she'd joked.

'I love you 'cause you're the only woman I can ever imagine spending more than five minutes with.'

And this was true, because Evan did not have a long, complicated romantic history like Brian. According to Evan, he'd had no serious attachments before her. And that made her feel very special.

I'm getting married, she thought, as she left Starbucks, clutching her coffee. *Guess that means no more adventures.*

Evan had requested a traditional wedding. She'd sort of entertained the idea of running off to Vegas and getting hitched by some kind of Elvis impersonator, but Evan was having none of it. 'A runaway wedding would break my mom's heart,' he'd said.

He had a mom! How normal. A widowed mom who lived in New York. They'd flown to New York so that she could meet Nicci. Somehow Nicci had imagined a little old lady in Easy Spirit shoes who wore fluffy angora sweaters and kept cats. No such luck, Lynda Richter had turned out to be a tall, big-boned woman clad in Escada and diamonds – purchased for her by her sons – with teeth the size of baby tombstones and plenty of overbearing attitude.

Nicci felt quite intimidated by her – especially after she got back to L.A. and had to endure a daily phone call checking up on wedding preparations. 'Have you ordered the cake? The band? Double-checked the place settings? Decided on the flowers? Hired the preacher? Booked a photographer? Chosen your dress? Chosen your *bridesmaids'* dresses? What are you waiting for, dear? YOUR WEDDING IS IN SIX WEEKS.'

Nicci dreaded Lynda's daily phone call. Usually she let her voice-mail pick up, but she soon grew annoyed that she was prevented from answering her own phone.

She'd tried to talk to Evan about it, but, typical male, Evan thought his darling mommy could do no wrong and refused to listen to any form of criticism concerning her.

The saviour was that Lynda Richter resided in New York. Nicci didn't think she could have handled it if Lynda had lived around the corner. What a nightmare *that* would've been. Besides, she resented Lynda butting in as if she was a ditzy airhead. She was perfectly capable of planning her own wedding, and had everything under control.

Well . . . almost.

She'd booked the venue – a gorgeous bluff situated in Palos Verdes overlooking the Pacific Ocean. The ceremony and reception would take place outside at sunset. Not exactly as traditional as Evan expected, but it would be so romantic. And the woman who ran the place had assured her she could organize whatever Nicci required.

So. . . all she had to do was figure out what she required.

Lynda's list ran through her head like an unrelenting mantra – dress, cake, band, bridesmaids . . . Bridesmaids! God! How traditional was *that*?

Evan was having a best man and six groomsmen, so he'd insisted she have bridesmaids. *Probably so the groomsmen can get laid*, she thought dourly.

The truth was that she was not a girly girl – most of her friends were male. After much thought she'd managed to come up with six suitable candidates. Now all she had to do was get them fitted for dresses. She was well aware that she'd left it horribly late, although her maid-of-honour, who was also her best friend, Saffron Domingo, had offered to help.

Hmm . . . Saffron was hardly the most reliable person in the world. Like Nicci, Saffron was a free spirit with not much idea about tradition. The daughter of Kyndra, a diva-style black singer, and Norio Domingo, an eccentric white record producer from Colombia, Saffron was a girl who lived by her own rules. Although she was only nineteen, she had a three-year-old daughter, Lulu, to whom Nicci was godmother. Lulu's time was divided between living with Saffron in her modest Westwood house, and visiting her daddy, famous NBA player, Bronson Livingston, who resided in a huge mansion in a gated community with his second wife and three children – all from different women.

Nicci hated Bronson: in her eyes he was a big, stupid sports star with a giant ego who'd taken advantage of her best friend. And the kicker was he paid minimal child support, and Saffron refused to take him to court to get more.

Nicci hated him because he'd stolen Saffron's youth, and the sad thing was that she'd never get it back.

'I have to go,' Lissa said, clicking her fingers for the check. 'It's been memorable, as usual.'

'Honey, when I'm around it's always memorable,' drawled Kyndra, producing a solid gold compact and applying an over-abundance of purple lip gloss. 'Now don't forget, my anniversary party is coming up soon, and I expect to see you all there.'

'Wouldn't miss it,' everyone chorused.

'I'm not certain Larry will make it,' Taylor said, her green eyes darting around the restaurant to ascertain if there was anyone important she should say hello to. 'He's in discussion on a big project with James Woods, Harrison Ford and Nick Angel. You know Larry when he immerses himself.'

'I'd love to do a movie with Larry,' Lissa said wistfully, reaching for her purse.

'I believe there *is* a strong female role,' Taylor said thoughtfully. 'Once they're set, they'll be starting auditions.'

'Oh, *sure*,' Stella said, laughing derisively. 'Like *Lissa* would audition.'

'For Larry, I might,' Lissa said, handing the waiter her credit card. 'After all, he and Spielberg *are* the two finest directors around.'

'I prefer them more cutting edge myself,' Stella remarked, 'such as Guy Ritchie or Sam Mendes.'

'*American Beauty*, an American classic.' James sighed reverently. 'Claude and I saw it four times.'

'Really?' Taylor said, with a bitchy edge. 'And which one of you had the hots for Kevin Spacey?'

'*Pu-lease,*' James drawled. 'He's hardly my type.'

'*Everyone*'s your type,' Kyndra joked.

James shot her an 'I do not appreciate jokes at my expense' look.

'Personally I preferred *Snatch*,' Lissa said. 'Guy Ritchie has amazing style.'

'*We*'re using an excellent director on *our* new project,' Stella said, picking a lychee from a dish set in the middle of the table. 'A young English guy who's shot several award-winning television commercials.'

'Lots of luck, dear,' James interjected. 'TV directors are notorious for going way over budget – *especially* the English. Claude says they're not worth the hype.'

'Nobody's going over budget with Seth and me on his case,' Stella boasted. 'We know how to kick *major* ass.'

'*Such* a lady,' James murmured.

'Just like you, dear,' Stella retaliated.

Laughter all around.

The waiter returned with Lissa's credit card. She signed the check and got up to leave.

'Where're you rushing off to, anyway?' Kyndra asked.

Lissa decided there was no reason to tell them that she had a meeting with a private investigator. It was embarrassing enough that divorce number four might be lurking on the horizon – why tip it before it happened?

Not that any of them particularly liked Gregg. Even before she'd married him her friends had warned her. Kyndra had accused him of being a user; Taylor commented he hit on other women when he wasn't with her; and Stella observed that he seemed to be extremely needy. How right they all were.

Nobody had mentioned that, apart from being a user, a flirt and needy, he was also stone-cold broke and had been going through her money at the speed of sound. He'd lost over a million dollars on the stock market, and that was just the beginning.

No more, because she was sure that the private investigator she'd hired would come up with plenty of incriminating evidence.

Call it woman's instinct, but she knew that marriage number four was definitely over.

Shortly after Lissa left the restaurant, Taylor announced she had a meeting with her writer and had to rush.

'Jesus!' Stella exclaimed. 'How long have you been working on this script of yours now?'

'Too long,' Taylor said, with a grimace. 'And I'm *still* stuck in development hell.'

'Surely Larry can help?' James asked.

Yes, Taylor thought grimly. *He can and he will.*

When she'd first got involved with the project, she

hadn't imagined that she'd require her husband's assistance. She'd been determined to prove to Hollywood that there was more than *one* talent in the family, that she was quite capable of getting a movie off the ground by herself.

The truth was that – dammit – she couldn't. Hollywood was basically a boys' town, and even though she was married to one of the boys, when she was out there operating on her own, it didn't make any difference.

This was infuriating, because more than anything Taylor craved recognition and her own identity. Hollywood knew her as Mrs Lawrence Singer, the wife of an extraordinarily multi-talented man who had three Oscars on his mantel and numerous other awards. A man who was well respected and well liked. And just because she was his wife (second), so was she.

Larry was, at fifty, only a mere sixteen years older than her – hardly an age-gap in Hollywood circles, where the norm was at least twenty years.

Successful men usually dumped their first wives within several years of making it big. Then they married the second much younger wife, and started another family, claiming that they would now be able to spend quality time with their new offspring – conveniently forgetting how much this self-serving statement pissed off their original children.

Stella's husband, Seth, was a classic example.

Taylor had decided that children were not on her agenda for now. First, a kick-ass career, then maybe a kid or two. It wasn't as if Larry was desperate – the one time they'd discussed it, he'd told her he didn't care either way. He had a teenage daughter from his first marriage, and fortunately the girl resided in Hawaii with her mother, so Taylor hardly ever saw her.

She and Larry had been married for five years. They'd lived together for eighteen months before he'd got his divorce – a divorce that had cost him millions, but he hadn't seemed to mind. Taylor *had* minded. Especially when his lawyers stepped in and suggested that *she* sign a pre-nuptial. She'd moved out of his house in a rage, and not spoken to him for days. Her behaviour paid off. He'd begged her forgiveness and the pre-nup was never mentioned again.

They'd met on one of his movies. She'd had a small role and he was king of the set. She'd gone after him from day one. Married or not, Larry Singer was destined to be her ticket to ride on *all* the roundabouts.

Tracking him was easy – especially for an experienced player like Taylor, who'd been knocking around Hollywood for several years, snagging small roles in theatrical movies and starring in a couple of failed sit-coms.

Taylor was an ex-cheerleader who'd come to Hollywood after winning a beauty pageant. Once there, she'd managed to fuck her way to the middle.

Larry was an extraordinarily talented, rather plain man who'd never explored his sexual potential.

Taylor had helped him make the trip.

Now it was his turn to help her.

She had a script that was almost right, and so it should be: she'd been working on it for long enough, hiring and firing a succession of writers. When the script was exactly the way she wanted it, she planned on directing *and* playing the lead role of a strong woman. So far three studios had passed, and finally she'd been forced to ask Larry to come to her aid. With his kind of clout they both knew he could get anything done.

Pending script approval, he'd set up a deal for her at Orpheus Studios. God knows what he'd promised them to make the deal. She didn't know and she didn't care. It was her turn to shine. Her turn to get the recognition. She'd given up her acting career for Larry, and now it was time to get it back on track.

She stood outside the restaurant waiting for the valet to bring her car – a metallic blue Jaguar that Larry had given her on her last birthday.

In her mind she was just as talented as her famous husband, and it was about time the world realized it.

Chapter Three

'We gotta plan your bachelor party,' Brian Richter remarked, as he finished rolling a joint. 'Or rather *I* do. All you gotta do is gimme a night, and leave everything else to me.'

'No party,' Evan Richter answered stubbornly. They were sitting around a long table covered with scribbled-on script pages in a hotel room in Arizona, where they were on location for their current movie, *Space Blond*.

'Why not?' Brian said, lighting up the rolled joint.

'I've been a bachelor forever,' Evan said, annoyed that he had to explain. 'Did enough partying to last a lifetime, so what've *I* got to prove?'

'You gotta be shittin' me?' Brian said, with a disgusted look. 'Bachelor parties are the only sane reason for getting married. If you're gonna lock yourself up in pussy prison, you may as well fuck your balls off before your old lady *cuts* 'em off.'

'You're sick,' Evan muttered.

'No. *I'm* normal,' Brian retorted, dragging deeply on his joint. '*You're* the fucked-up member of the family.'

'It's a tragedy we weren't separated at birth,' Evan muttered, wishing it were so.

'That would've suited me just fine,' Brian retorted. 'And I'm sure Mom wouldn't've minded.'

The Richter brothers. Fraternal twins. Totally unalike physically. Evan, quirky and nice-looking, but no hunk with his spiky brown hair and lanky frame. Whereas Brian was all piercing blue eyes, beach-blond shaggy hair and a hard body. In spite of Brian's bad-boy habits – which included gambling, drinking too much, drugging a lot, and indiscriminately sleeping with a variety of nubile females – he was in excellent shape.

The Richter brothers. Hot properties in Hollywood. Hot and unpredictable. Some thought Evan was the one with all the talent because he appeared to be more serious than Brian. But Brian was the one with the best ideas. And Brian was the one who came up with the main story line and wrote most of the scripts. While Evan kept it all together, handled the financial aspects, could unfailingly close any deal, and made sure their movies came in on time and usually under budget.

The Richter brothers were always arguing. It amazed everyone who came in contact with them how they were able to maintain such a successful working relationship. Bicker, bicker, bicker. Day and night they went at it.

Often they threatened to dissolve their partnership and go their separate ways. But usually sanity prevailed, because why mess with something that was making them both more money than they could ever have imagined?

'How *is* dear little Nicci?' Brian asked sarcastically. 'Still calling you six times a day?'

'We alternate,' Evan muttered, wondering why he was even bothering to explain.

'Bullshit,' Brian said disbelievingly.

'How come you're always on her case?' Evan responded, frowning.

''Cause she's nothing but a needy kid.'

Evan glared at his brother. 'Like *you* date adults,' he said.

'I *date* 'em, don't marry 'em,' Brian pointed out. 'Marriage is for old people who can't get it up.'

Fortunately, Teena, their script assistant, rushed into the room, speaking into a cellphone. Short and in her thirties, she was an eccentric-looking woman with hair like straw, decorated with various coloured clips and slides, plus a bold blue streak. Her round face was made more so by the addition of huge wire-rimmed glasses, and she had a prominent snub nose.

'What's up?' Evan said, happy for the interruption, because he was not about to get into a discussion about why he was marrying Nicci with his sex-crazed brother. It was none of his business.

'Everything,' Teena said, clicking off the phone and rolling her purple-shadowed eyes. 'Abbey doesn't care for her new lines. Harry is under the impression that his trailer is smaller than hers. And Chris can't handle it. He's apparently gone into a funk. We'd better get over to the location, pronto.'

Abbey Christian – a leggy twenty-two-year-old natural blonde, with a smile that could light up Christmas. Star of their latest movie. Major player. Major coke-head.

Harry Bello – big-deal comedy actor supreme. Rubber-faced and coming up to fifty. Paranoid about getting older and quite certain that Abbey was receiving better treatment than he was.

Chris Fortune. Boy-wonder director. The same age as Abbey and somewhat intimidated by his two stars – even though he'd directed the big sleeper hit of the previous summer.

'Freakin' actors,' Brian grumbled, exhaling smoke. 'We should be making *animated* movies.'

'You finally came up with a decent idea,' Evan said. 'No more over-the-top salaries.'

'Please, guys, let's move it,' Teena urged, almost jumping

up and down with agitation. 'Abbey won't come out of her trailer. Harry's sulking. And Chris is heading for a panic attack. We *must* get over there.'

'Let's go,' Brian said, carefully preserving his joint in a Kleenex for later. 'Nothing like a view of Abbey's tits to wake me up in the morning.'

'Remember,' Evan said ominously, 'no fucking our star until the movie wraps.'

'Hey,' Brian said innocently, 'I can look, can't I?'

Lissa Roman went to great lengths to keep her private life private. Which was not easy considering she lived under constant media scrutiny. Danny, her assistant, was a big help. Earlier that day she'd instructed him to hire a car, leave it in the parking lot at Saks, and give her the ticket. He'd done so, no questions asked.

After lunch, she'd had Chuck drop her off at Barneys, instructed him to come back in two hours, walked across to Saks, got into the rented car and driven out to the valley. There was no way she planned to alert Gregg to what was going on, or anyone else for that matter. This was *her* business, and when Lissa wanted to keep something private, she knew how to do it.

Anyway, she was quite capable of driving to the valley on her own. She didn't need security, just a pair of dark glasses and a baseball cap to hide her tell-tale platinum hair. Besides, it was an adventure doing something on her own for a change.

She put on talk radio and listened to the various call-ins, which was always a trip, until finally she arrived at the Robbins-Scorsinni offices on Ventura, where she was greeted by a plump, middle-aged Asian assistant in a flowered pant suit. The offices were old and kind of run-down, but Lissa felt quite comfortable. She wasn't looking for one of those hotshot Hollywood PI agencies that knew everyone's business. This low-key place suited her fine.

Quincy Robbins, who ran the private investigation/security agency with his partner, Michael Scorsinni, was a pleasant, reliable man, whom Lissa had used on several other occasions for various matters. His partner and himself were ex-New York detectives, and that made her feel secure. When she'd moved into her house several years ago, she'd hired Quincy to be her chief security adviser. She'd never met his partner, but she knew that his reputation was also stellar.

'Take a seat, please,' the Asian woman said, with a gummy smile, revealing a row of uneven teeth. 'I am Mai Lee. Michael will be with you soon.'

'I'm not here to see Michael,' Lissa said, anxious to get this over with. 'Quincy is expecting me.'

'Nobody contacted you?' Mai Lee said, sounding surprised.

'Not that I know of.'

'Oh dear,' Mai Lee said, now highly embarrassed. 'I think *I* was supposed to call you.'

'About what?' Lissa said, fast losing her patience.

'Quincy's laid up at home,' Mai Lee said, fluttering her hands. 'He broke his leg.'

'You've *got* to be kidding?'

'I'm afraid it's true.'

'*When* did this happen?'

'A few days ago. But not to worry, Michael took over your case. You'll be happy with Michael, he is most capable.'

Lissa stood up. 'I always deal with Quincy,' she said tightly. 'This could've waited if I'd known he wasn't available.'

'My fault,' Mai Lee said, now taking full responsibility. 'I was supposed to explain. You see, Quincy didn't seem to think you would *want* to wait.'

Lissa wondered how much Mai Lee knew. This was so

embarrassing, she could see the headlines now – *LISSA ROMAN CATCHES ANOTHER CHEATING HUSBAND.*

'Oh, God!' She sighed, realizing there was nothing she could do at this late stage. 'I suppose I'll have to see Michael. Where is he?'

'Sorry,' Mai Lee said apologetically. 'He's out of the office right now.'

This was ridiculous. She'd driven all the way out to the valley, and now she was getting a run-around. 'Are you telling me that you expect me to sit here and wait?' she said sharply. It wasn't often she played the star, but one perk of star treatment was never having to wait.

'He'll be back soon,' Mai Lee volunteered. 'Very soon.'

'Unbelievable!' Lissa muttered irritably. 'I drove over here especially.'

'There's plenty of magazines,' Mai Lee offered soothingly. 'Why don't you sit down and relax?'

Why don't you *shove it up your ass?* Lissa wanted to say, but she didn't. That would have been mean and petty, and one thing she was always careful about was preserving a good public image.

I'm nervous, she thought. *I'm nervous because even though I know for sure that Gregg's screwing around, it's still difficult to deal with.* At least Quincy – big, black, comfortable Quincy – would have held her hand and said, 'Listen, this is something you're not gonna want to hear, but these are the facts.'

Now she had to hear it from a stranger.

Well, not exactly a stranger, Quincy had often mentioned his partner's name. 'My friend, Michael,' he'd always say. 'You should've seen us when we were detectives together in New York. Michael got shot, nearly bought it. You'll like him. He's one of the good guys.'

And yet, over the years, she'd never met him.

She sat down, picked up a magazine and flipped the pages impatiently, until suddenly the door was pushed open and a tall man strode in.

'Michael,' Mai Lee said, jumping up, 'Ms Roman is here.'

He walked right over to her. 'Sorry to have kept you waiting,' he said. 'Quincy insisted I shouldn't make you wait, but it was unavoidable. I'm really sorry,' he added, giving her a long, sincere stare.

He had the blackest eyes she'd ever seen, thick jet hair, and dark olive skin – with a two-day stubble. He was handsome, with a dangerous edge – an irresistible combination.

So this is Michael Scorsinni, she thought. *Quincy never told me he looked like a movie star – only better.*

'Uh . . . hi,' she said, and wondered if this might turn out to be easier than she'd thought.

Chapter Four

'How's everything?' Eric Vernon said, sliding onto a bar stool next to Arliss Shepherd.

Arliss bobbed his head several times. Eric Vernon made him fidgety, he couldn't figure out what the man was after. No one kept on buying drinks unless they were after *some*thing.

'Another beer?' Eric offered.

Arliss bobbed his head again. Rule one. Never turn down a free drink, even though he still had a half-full bottle clutched in his hand.

'Pattie,' Eric said, snapping his fingers to attract the attention of a half-clad woman with a lopsided boob job, who toiled behind the scuffed wooden bar. 'Another bottle for my friend.' He patted Arliss on the shoulder. 'Been thinking about you,' he said.

'You have?' Arliss replied, stifling a fast-rising burp.

'I was remembering that conversation we had the other night.'

Arliss scratched his head. If the conversation wasn't about tits and ass, he did not retain it.

'Yes,' Eric continued, thinking that Arliss Shepherd smelled like a Mexican meal left out in the sun for a week. Putrid. But since he wasn't about to hire him for his good hygiene, who cared if he stank? 'I was thinking 'bout how you said you hated your job.'

'I do,' Arliss agreed, nodding furiously. 'I certainly do.'

And who wouldn't? He was the caretaker of a big old building filled with nothing but rats and roaches and memories of the time it was a flourishing dress company. Why the owners needed a caretaker in a place they'd been threatening to pull down for years, was beyond him. In the meantime, it was his job to keep the transients out and the place protected.

Protected from what? Who knew? Who cared?

He'd fashioned himself a makeshift apartment in the basement, and he didn't have to answer to anyone – except the snotty-nosed son of the owner, who put in an occasional appearance.

Still, what kind of an existence was it to be shut up in a deserted old building all day and most of the night? Arliss wished for something better, although deep down he knew there wasn't anything better. He had no qualifications, he could barely read, he was fortunate to have any kind of job at all. However, it certainly didn't stop him from complaining, which – after several beers too many – he'd obviously been doing to this Eric Vernon character.

Pattie slid a cold bottle of Heineken in front of him while shooting Eric a flirtatious sideways glance. This infuriated Arliss, because he'd been trying to get her to pay attention to him for months.

'She'll give ya crabs,' he muttered to Eric, as Pattie sashayed off.

Eric got it immediately. 'Not interested,' he said abruptly.

Why not? Arliss thought. *You one of them faggot freaks?* Prudently, he kept his thoughts to himself. If Eric Vernon was a fag it was none of his business as long as the man kept on buying. He lifted the cold bottle of beer to his lips. 'You married?' he asked.

'No,' Eric replied. 'Are you?' He asked the question

even though he already knew the answer. He knew everything about Arliss Shepherd that needed knowing.

Arliss shook his greasy head. 'I'm stupid, not soft,' he said scornfully. 'Wimmen give a man nothin' but trouble.'

'Right,' Eric agreed, his small, sharp eyes checking out the bar.

'Course, they're all right for some things,' Arliss added, with a lewd wink.

Eric had endured enough small-talk, weeks of it in fact. What he needed now was action. Leaning closer to Arliss, almost recoiling from the stink, he said, 'How would you like to make some *real* money?'

Arliss's narrow face brightened. Real money. Who wouldn't want to make a score? If he had real money he could buy himself a better life. 'How'd I do that?' he asked, trying not to sound too eager.

'By co-operating on something and keeping your mouth shut.'

'Somethin' legal?' Arliss said suspiciously.

'If it means big bucks, do you care?' Eric shot back. He knew Arliss had done time for petty burglary so he would not be averse to criminal activities.

'How big *are* the bucks?' Arliss ventured.

'Enough to keep everyone happy,' Eric said, tapping his fingers on the bar. 'I need to put together a team I can trust.'

'What kinda team?'

'I've been watching you and your friends. You all seem pretty tight.'

Arliss did not take kindly to the thought that Eric had been spying on them. Davey and Joe, and especially Big Mark, would not like it either. Big Mark could crush this guy's ass if Arliss gave him the word. Mark was the strong one in the group. He worked as a bouncer at a club on the strip, and according to Mark, not a night passed unless he split some asshole's lip or broke a nose or two.

'We're tight all right,' Arliss said stiffly. 'Tight enough not to need any intruders.'

'Don't get me wrong,' Eric said quickly, 'I'm looking for a few guys who can handle themselves in any situation *and* make big money doing it.'

'Doin' what?' Arliss asked, blinking rapidly.

'It doesn't matter,' Eric said, backing off. 'I sense you're not interested.'

'Didn't say that,' Arliss growled. 'If it means big bucks, I could be ready t' do anythin'.'

'Anything, huh?' Eric said, giving him an appraising look.

'Short of murder,' Arliss added, with a nervous cackle.

'And even murder has a price, doesn't it?' Eric said mildly.

Arliss nodded, he couldn't help himself.

It was then that Eric knew he had found the right man.

It never occurred to Eric that he could fail at the scam he was shortly to put into motion. Failure was not a word in his vocabulary. Failure was his past, and he was *never* revisiting his miserable past.

Two months previously he'd been sent to some big movie star's Bel Air mansion to do some work on her computers – upgrading, Mr Hailey, his boss, had informed him. Usually Mr Hailey took care of all the famous clients, but recently he had been undergoing a punishing course of chemo treatments and was losing his hair, so he'd started sending Eric out on the more high-profile jobs.

Mr Hailey trusted Eric, who was quiet, always on time and did his job well. And then, of course, there were Eric's forged references attesting to his diligence and honesty. Those references had landed him the job.

How easy it was to clean the slate and start afresh. How simple it was to fool people.

So one fine morning Eric had set off to the movie star's Bel Air mansion, pressed the buzzer at the bottom of a long, winding driveway, and when the gates opened, had driven up to the house.

He was greeted by her assistant, a gregarious gay man with a halo of curly auburn hair and matching beard. He introduced himself as Danny and led Eric into the office.

'This is her *home* office,' Danny said. 'Her *production* offices are at Universal. I work *here*.' A conspiratorial wink. 'Lucky *me*!'

Eric had no idea who the celebrity was. He didn't watch TV or go to the movies, and he certainly didn't buy CDs or attend concerts. The walls of her office – covered in framed posters and photographs – soon clued him in. He recognized her as that slutty blonde who wore revealing outfits and sang controversial sexy songs. He recognized her because the con in the cell next to him had her picture pinned to his wall and had christened her 'Queen of the Wankers'. Lissa Roman, that was her name.

So here he was in the office of 'Queen of the Wankers,' and he didn't give a damn because Eric didn't like women, and he liked famous, rich ones even less.

'Madam is not around today,' Danny announced.

As if Eric cared. The last thing he needed was to check out some overblown movie star tramp.

'The princess is working on her new video,' Danny volunteered. 'It'll be amazing as usual.'

'Mmm . . .' Eric said, heading towards the two computers. 'What needs doing here?'

'Sometimes Miz Roman enjoys dropping into chat rooms,' Danny confided. 'Naturally she uses an alias, but she likes to visit, and right now she's not getting connected quickly enough, so I was told you could do something.'

'The phone company has to install a DSL line,' Eric said gruffly. 'Then I can fix it so that everything happens faster.

After the phone company's done their work, I'll come back.'

'I don't understand this chat-room obsession some people have,' Danny said, pursing his lips. 'Me, I'm bored by them. All those fifty-year-old men pretending to be twelve-year-old boys.' A sly giggle and a provocative glance. 'Naughty, naughty!'

Faggot, Eric thought. *I don't want to hear about what you do in your spare time.*

'Ms Roman's husband wishes to update some of their equipment,' Danny continued. 'He was thinking of a new photo scanner, and perhaps the latest flat-screen computer. We'd like suggestions and price quotes.'

Eric nodded, checking out the equipment.

A week later he returned with several new items.

This time Danny greeted him like a long-lost friend. '*So* good to see you again,' Danny gushed. 'Has life been treating you well?'

Eric barely nodded, and immediately went to work installing the new equipment, tuning out Danny's annoying chatter.

Why should some people have everything and he nothing? Oh yes, he had a job, a van, and a small rented one-room apartment, but that was about it. Why couldn't *he* enjoy the luxuries that all these rich people seemed to possess? Why couldn't *he* be living in a mansion with a swimming pool and several luxury cars in the driveway?

Exactly what had this Lissa Roman bitch done to deserve such recognition anyway? Sung some slutty songs and exhibited her body in a few commercial movies. Any little tramp could do that.

And then Lissa Roman herself put in an appearance. The woman had porcelain skin, white blonde hair, ruby red lips and a welcoming smile which revealed small sharp teeth. 'I'm so glad you're doing this,' she said, in a low throaty voice. 'Would you like a copy of my latest CD – maybe for your wife or someone?'

'What?' he said, frowning.

She looked a little taken aback that he hadn't jumped.

At that moment it occurred to him that Lissa Roman thought everyone loved her. Well, she was wrong. She was standing in a room with someone who couldn't give a rat's ass.

Danny obligingly handed her one of her CDs and a pen. She turned to Eric with a bright smile. 'To whom shall I sign it?' she asked.

'Eric,' he muttered, watching her carefully.

She signed the CD with a flourish and handed it to him. She'd written *To Eric – with love, Lissa Roman.*

'Want me to explain how this new scanner works?' he asked, shoving the CD in his back pocket to be thrown away later.

'No,' she said, shaking her platinum head. 'Danny will fill me in. Nice meeting you, Eric.' And she left the room, leaving behind a trail of exotic perfume.

'Isn't she a treat?' Danny enthused, when she'd gone.

Eric grunted. He didn't find her a treat at all.

'She's *so* nice to everyone,' Danny said reverently. 'Such a *lady.*'

Lady, my ass, Eric thought, as he continued working. And then he noticed the two trade papers casually laid out on Danny's desk. *Variety* and the *Hollywood Reporter.* They both sported stories on the front page about Lissa Roman. Danny had outlined the pieces in thick red pen, ready to put in her scrapbook.

As he worked, Eric managed to read the headlines. *Lissa Roman Inks Three Million Dollar Deal For One Night's Work at Millennium Desert Princess Hotel.*

Three million dollars. Eric was in shock. That amount of money could buy him everything he'd always craved. And this blonde bitch was making it in one night.

He managed to scan the other headline. She was opening a new hotel in Vegas for which they were paying her three million big ones. Jesus!

Then it came to him in a flash. What if he *kidnapped* her and held her for *ransom*? Would her record company pay? Would her movie bosses cough up? Or would the cops come down so hard that they'd find her before he could collect the ransom?

Back at the office he looked her up on the Internet. There were over eight hundred sites devoted to her. He clicked onto several of the main ones, and found out more than he ever wanted to know.

She was very, very famous. Too famous.

She'd made seven movies. Released ten best-selling CDs. Appeared on over a thousand magazine covers. Been married four times.

How did he go about kidnapping someone with such a high profile? This obviously needed meticulous planning.

Over the next few weeks he spent all his spare time following her, soon discovering she was an extremely well-protected woman who never went anywhere by herself. She was always accompanied by a publicist, a driver, sometimes guards, and often her husband – a muscle-bound man who never appeared to work.

Eric realized that kidnapping Lissa Roman was not going to be an easy task.

He decided that befriending Danny – her loyal assistant – might be a good plan. So he called him up, reminded Danny who he was, and suggested they meet for a drink.

Danny agreed, and they met at a gay bar on Santa Monica Boulevard.

'My boyfriend would be livid if he suspected I was stepping out on him,' Danny said archly. 'However, he's away in Seattle for the weekend, so no harm.'

Eric knew exactly how to deal with fags – after all, he'd

been incarcerated with a whole bunch of them for six long, miserable years. He proceeded to get Danny good and drunk, then questioned him, finding out everything he wanted to know.

By the end of the evening he had his answer.

Lissa Roman had a daughter, Nicci, who did not live with her. *Nicci* was the one he should be targeting. Nicci was the perfect victim.

And from that moment on, Nicci had become his obsession.

Chapter Five

'C an you meet me for lunch?' Nicci said on her cellphone, still driving.

'I'm not eating,' Saffron replied.

'Why?'

''Cause I'm fat.'

'You're a size four,' Nicci pointed out.

'I'm zeroing in on a size two.'

'Get a life, girl.'

'Have you *seen* Calista Flockhart and Lara Flynn Boyle? That's my goal.'

'Oh, to be white and skinny,' Nicci said scathingly, glancing at a passing stud on a Harley, while almost back-ending an uptight face-lift in a cream Bentley. 'Anyway, you *have* to meet me for lunch, it's urgent.'

'Does it concern a pre-nup?'

'*What* pre-nup?'

'The one he's gonna make you sign.'

'Evan will *not* make me sign anything,' Nicci said haughtily. 'I think you're forgetting we're in love.'

'Ha!' Saffron exclaimed rudely. 'So were Sly Stallone and Michael Douglas at one time, an' look what happened to *them*. Man, did *they* get a blast of the first-wife blues!' A beat. 'Evan's lawyer will *never* let him marry you without a pre-nup. So get ready.'

Nicci realized there was no use arguing with Saffron when she was on a roll. 'Meet me at Fred Segal's in half an hour,' she said. 'And try not to be late.'

'Only if you *promise* you'll let no food pass my lips.'

'Deal.'

'See ya.'

Nicci had decided to hand over responsibility for the bridesmaids' dresses to Saffron. She could handle it, she had nothing else to do.

It did not occur to Nicci that she had nothing else to do either. That wasn't the point.

Reaching for a cigarette she zoomed off down Melrose.

Taylor Singer parked on the street in Venice, reluctantly, because she was a valet-parker addict and hated having to walk anywhere. Locking her Jaguar, she headed down a narrow side-street that led directly to the beach.

Christ! she thought. *If my car is stolen, how do I explain what I'm doing in this seedy neighbourhood?*

No explanations necessary. Larry trusted her. He loved her. He would *never* believe she would betray him.

Yet that's exactly what she was doing. Betraying him big time. She simply couldn't help herself.

Her high heels clicked along the street until she reached the entrance to a run-down apartment complex painted a particularly sickening shade of orange. Producing a key from her Hermès Kelly bag, she let herself in the side door, which led to an open overgrown courtyard. There were four apartments in the complex, and she headed to the furthest one. The door was open. Oliver was expecting her. Her skin began tingling in anticipation.

Oliver Rock. Twenty-two years old. A long-haired, skinny screenwriter who'd yet to sell a script.

Oliver Rock. Her first cheat.

He'd been recommended to her by an agent who'd

suggested her script needed to appeal to a younger audience. 'Go see Oliver,' the agent had said. 'He's gonna be big. Get in at the beginning.'

She'd got in all right. She'd been getting in for three weeks and she couldn't get enough of him.

She entered the small, messy apartment. The living room smelled of cat piss and pot, even though the windows, which overlooked the ocean, were wide open. A word-processor stood on a rickety wooden table. Loud rap played on the compact sound system.

Taylor took a deep breath, shut the door behind her and locked it. 'Oliver?' she called.

No answer.

Shrugging off her jacket, she put down her bag and stepped out of her shoes. Then she unzipped her skirt, unbuttoned her blouse, and walked into the bedroom.

Oliver was sprawled on a mattress on the floor, asleep. He didn't believe in traditional sleeping arrangements, or maybe he couldn't afford a proper bed. She didn't know and she didn't care. Conversation was not their strong suit.

For six years she'd been faithful to a man who was not a sexual being. Larry tried, but in the sex stakes he was a loser. Now, with Oliver, she'd finally found her sexual soulmate.

And even though it was dangerous beyond her control, she was totally helpless, and there was absolutely nothing she could do about it.

Nicci was already settled at an outdoor table when Saffron turned up half an hour late. Saffron was an exotic treat with her finely chiselled features, milk-chocolate skin, gold nose-ring, long black dreadlocks and sinuous body. Heads swivelled to watch her as she wafted to the table.

'Greetings, O Pale One,' Saffron said, oblivious to the stares. 'You been considering what I said?'

'No,' Nicci retorted. 'And I am like *so not* pale. I've got the best tan I've ever had.'

'Bad for the skin, all that lying out burning your body,' Saffron remarked, sitting down.

'Fine for you to say with your natural year-round sun-tan thing going.'

'Wanna swap?' Saffron said, amused.

'Wanna get serious?' Nicci retorted.

Saffron stretched sensuously, almost causing a business-man at the next table to choke on his steak. 'Tell me what's on your mind,' she said.

'I need you to take care of the bridesmaids' dresses,' Nicci said crisply. 'Y'know, order them, like get them made in time, see that they fit. All that kind of stuff.'

'*Me?*'

'No,' Nicci said, rolling her eyes in exasperation. 'That guy sitting over there.'

'Isn't your *mom* supposed to be taking care of all the details?' Saffron said, reaching for a bread roll.

'My *mom* is taking care of the bills,' Nicci said, slapping her friend's hand away from the bread. 'And I have like a thousand other things to organize. So *please*, Saffy, do me this one minor favour.'

'Hmm . . . I suppose if you like *insist*,' Saffron said. 'But only if you call the waiter over right *now* before I *starve* to death.'

'I thought you weren't eating.'

'If I'm working then I'm eating,' Saffron said, picking up the menu. 'Spaghetti and meatballs. Yum. And carrot cake for dessert. Girl, I need all the energy I can get.'

'You're amazing.'

'I know,' Saffron agreed, with a Cheshire-cat grin.

They'd been friends since childhood, sharing the common bond of very famous mothers. And since their mothers were also good friends, they'd got to spend plenty of time together. Saffron had even visited Nicci when she'd lived in Spain. They'd had a fine time running riot with no adults to tell them what not to do.

'Whassup?' Saffron asked. 'Anything I should know about?'

Nicci shrugged. 'I'm getting married. Isn't that enough?'

Lissa found herself sitting up straighter. 'So, I finally get to meet you,' she said. 'Quincy's talked about you a lot.'

'Quincy loves telling stories from the old days,' Michael said, with a wry grin. 'Like how I got shot, huh?'

'I think he told me about that,' she murmured, continuing to check him out. Damn! He was good-looking. She'd worked with plenty of handsome actors, but this guy was exceptional.

'Let's go in my office,' he suggested, rubbing his faintly stubbled chin.

She got up and followed him into a big, comfortable room next to Quincy's. There was a worn leather desk, two chairs, a TV and stereo equipment. A framed print of a classic Ferrari hung on the wall next to a black-and-white picture of him and Quincy taken outside their precinct in New York.

'Take a seat,' he said, trying not to stare. Her movies and videos did not do her justice – this was one breath-taking woman. 'An' I hate to do this,' he added, 'only I gotta run to the john.'

'Go ahead,' she said, slightly amused.

He left her sitting there. Noticing a framed photograph on his desk, she leaned forward and took a surreptitious peek. The frame contained a photo of a pretty young girl.

She glanced around to see if she could spot a picture of his wife. *This is a twist*, she thought. *Here I am visiting an investigator about my cheating husband, and I'm checking to see if he has a picture of his wife on the desk.*

Removing her baseball cap she shook out her platinum hair and took a long deep breath. *Let's get this over with*, she thought. *I have to know.*

Michael re-entered the room, immediately noticing that with her silky hair framing her oval-shaped face she was even more stunning. 'Sorry about that,' he said briskly. 'Been out all morning, couldn't take a break.' He settled behind his desk. 'Well, uh, Miss Roman.'

'Call me Lissa,' she said, suddenly feeling unbearably tense.

He caught her vibes and sympathized. 'This is an awkward situation, huh?'

'Yes, it is,' she agreed. 'I had to get the proof, right?'

'That's the smart way of looking at it,' he said, craving a cigarette, but determined not to light up in front of her. 'Now,' he said, getting down to business, 'I'm not gonna bore you with details, so how about I play you one of the tapes?'

'What tapes?' she said quickly.

'I tapped into your husband's cellphone. It's the quickest way of catching someone. So what you're about to hear is a conversation he had yesterday.'

'I see,' she said, resigning herself to the worst.

'Want me to wait outside while you listen?'

'You've already heard it, haven't you?' she said, making an effort to stay in control. It was bad enough doing this, but she had no intention of turning into the poor little wronged woman – not her image at all.

'Uh . . . yes,' Michael said. He'd listened to all the tapes and they were pretty raunchy. The tape he was about to play for her was one of the milder ones.

'Then there's no reason we shouldn't listen together,' she said coolly. 'It'll be our entertainment for the afternoon. Big movie star listening to her husband cheat, because that's what I'm about to hear, isn't it?'

'Hey,' he shrugged. 'You wanted the information.'

'Hey,' she said, shrugging back, 'guess I've got it.'

'Don't be mad at *me*,' he said, reaching for the cassette on his desk. 'I'm the bearer, not the doer.'

'I'm not mad,' she said resignedly. 'Merely disappointed.'

'I can understand that,' he said, getting up and heading for the tape player.

'So, Michael,' she said, making conversation, 'Quincy mentioned you're from New York.'

'New York born,' he replied, 'although my grandparents were Sicilian. Moved out here six years ago, hooked up with Quincy an' never regretted it.'

'Quincy's a nice man.'

'The best.'

'Do you like living in L.A.?'

'It's different. Yeah, I like it,' he said, slipping the cassette into the machine. 'The weather. The easy lifestyle.'

'Is that your little girl?' she asked, pointing to the picture on his desk.

'Uh . . . no,' he said, hesitating for a moment, his black eyes clouding over. 'That's Bella, my niece.'

'She's a beauty.'

'*I* think so,' he said, pressing play. 'Okay, Lissa, here we go.'

She waited. And then she heard them, Gregg – putting on his so-called sexy voice – and a breathy-sounding female.

GREGG: *Hello, baby.*

GIRL: *I missed you after you left last night.* (A dirty giggle.) *You're the best sex I ever had.*

GREGG: *C'mon, you're only saying that to get me hard again. And believe me, it doesn't take much.*

GIRL: *You're the best lover in the world.* (A languid pause.) *And. . . you have the most beautiful cock.*

GREGG: *That's something my wife never tells me.*

51

GIRL: *That's 'cause she never sees it.* (This
time a knowing giggle.) *Right, honeybunch?*
GREGG: *Listen, uh . . . I'll try and get there by
eight. I'm telling Lissa I'm working late again.*
GIRL: *Does she honestly buy that tired old excuse?*
GREGG: *She buys anything I sell her.*
GIRL: *How dumb.*
GREGG: *That's my wife. She's too busy being famous to
notice anything.*

They both laughed.

'Okay, enough!' Lissa said abruptly, her cheeks flushed with
anger. 'I don't need to hear any more.' She was furious and
embarrassed. Why did this always happen to her? What had
she done to deserve it?

Michael clicked the machine off. 'Some men never
learn,' he said ruefully. 'This one must be a real loser.'

'Some women never learn either,' she said sadly.
'Gregg's my fourth husband. All four of them cheated on
me. How's that for a track record?' Now, why was she
telling a total stranger her business? God! She was pathetic.

Michael shrugged. 'It's a question of finding the right
person. When you do, you'll know.'

'How?' she asked wryly.

'The trick is never to settle for second best – or so I've
heard.'

She gazed at him intently, wondering what was going
through his head. 'Is that what you imagine *I* did?'

'I hardly know you, Lissa,' he said slowly, trying not to
stare into her diamond blue eyes, 'so I can't answer that
question.'

'How many times have *you* been married?' she asked,
certain that his track record wasn't so great either.

'Once,' he said grimly. 'That was enough.'

'Sounds ominous.'

'No reason to get married unless you want kids. You got any?'

'A daughter,' she answered restlessly. 'Had her when I was twenty – that's too young to be a mom. Makes me feel ancient now.'

'You? Ancient?' he said, raising his eyebrows in surprise. 'You're one of the most beautiful women in the world.'

Christ! he thought. *I sound like a freakin' fan. I'd better get it together here.*

'Now you're embarrassing me,' she murmured.

Their eyes met for a few seconds. It was an intimate look for two people who hardly knew each other.

Abruptly Michael broke the look and got up from behind his desk. 'Do you want copies of the tapes?' he asked. 'We usually store the originals in the safe, but I made copies in case you need them.'

'I have to figure out how to handle this,' she said, trying to sound like she knew what she was doing. 'I'd better speak to my lawyer.'

'That's a plan,' he said, handing her several cassettes.

She reached for her purse and stood up. 'Uh . . . Michael,' she said hesitantly.

'Yes?'

'Who's the woman on the tape?'

He took a moment before answering, then he said, 'A salesgirl at Barneys.'

'Oh,' she said, wishing she hadn't asked. Damn Gregg. The fact that she was Lissa Roman obviously didn't do it for him. He had to turn to a salesgirl at *Barneys* to get the sex he was denying her, because the truth was they hadn't slept together in over a month.

Well, screw him, he wasn't getting one red cent of her hard-earned money. She'd fight him all the way if he tried to overturn the pre-nuptial.

Unexpected tears filled her eyes and she hurriedly put on her shades.

'Is your husband leaving town any time soon?' Michael asked, pretending not to notice she was close to tears.

'Why?' she asked, regaining her composure.

He felt sorry for her and protective all at the same time. She might be an enormous star, but she was still a woman in pain, and he had an insane desire to put his arms around her and hold her close. 'Well,' he said, 'if he's out of town, or even gone for the day, I can arrange to have all his possessions packed up and the locks on your house changed. That way, when he comes home, there'll be a lawyer's letter waiting outside the door asking where he'd like his stuff delivered, and you don't have to see him. It's a done deal.'

'Can *you* organize it for me?' she asked hopefully.

'If you tell me when he'll be away.'

'He's supposed to be recording with a new producer all day Friday.'

'That's two days down the line. You certain you can hold it together until then?'

'I'm an actress,' she said confidently. 'Gregg will never suspect a thing.'

'I'm not so sure,' Michael said. 'Living in the same house, pretending nothing's going on, it won't be easy.'

'Don't worry about it.'

'I *am* worried,' he said, frowning. 'What if you can't hold back and get into a fight?

'I won't do that,' she promised.

'Has he ever been violent towards you?'

'No,' she lied, conveniently forgetting two extremely disturbing incidents she preferred to block out.

'If you say so,' Michael said reluctantly.

'I do.'

'Okay. I'll take care of everything.'

'Thanks,' she murmured.

'All you have to do is call me when he leaves the house on Friday.'

'That's it?'

'We'll make it smooth and easy.'

'You're very nice, Michael.'

His look was direct and disconcerting. 'That's because I'm dealing with a very nice lady.'

Chapter Six

Nicci's wedding plans were progressing well, which was good news because Evan was coming home soon, and she couldn't wait to see him.

She had finally got everything together, with a great deal of help from the woman at the venue who'd been most obliging when she'd given her Evan's mother's list. And since Saffron was in charge of the bridesmaids' dresses, all she had left to do was find a dress for herself. Lissa had suggested that she fly to New York and order something expensive from Vera Wang. Instead, she explored Robertson, discovering a shop next to the Ivy where she came across the romantic gown of her dreams. Ivory satin with floating panels of chiffon – so beautiful she was certain Evan would love it.

Today, she decided, she was going to do something she'd been putting off for weeks, and that was phone her father. She'd called Lissa and tried to talk to her about it, but all her mom had said was a noncommittal 'It's your call.'

'Do you *mind* if Antonio comes?' she'd asked.

'Why would I mind?' Lissa had answered, cool as ever.

'Are you *sure?*' she'd persisted.

'Of course I'm sure.'

She'd never got her mom to say much about Antonio,

he was more or less a closed subject, and whenever she brought him up, Lissa went onto something else. Oh, well . . . maybe one of these days she'd get her to open up about him.

She flitted around the house, making sure all was in order for Evan's return. He was extremely anal about his house. It was stark white and modern, with minimal furniture, and several highly expensive pieces of art hanging on the walls. Nicci figured that once they were married she'd change everything and make it more homey and comfortable.

Finally, with nothing left to do, she picked up the phone and called Antonio.

Fortunately he answered the phone himself, because she'd been dreading talking to her stern grandmother. 'Antonio!' she exclaimed. 'Guess who?'

There was a short silence before he spoke. 'As if I can't guess,' he said at last. 'Two years and no word, now my Nicci calls. This stubbornness you inherited from me.'

'You always like to take credit for everything,' she teased, delighted to hear his voice.

'Not always.'

'How come *you* haven't called *me?*' she demanded. 'Doesn't that make *you* the stubborn one?'

'We're *both* stubborn,' he admitted. 'However, I am pleased to speak to you, my *cariño.*'

'Really?' she asked, feeling like a little kid again.

'Of course. How are you?'

She hesitated a moment before blurting out, 'I'm . . . uh . . . getting married.'

'You are doing *what?*'

'Getting married,' she repeated, wondering what he'd say.

'You're too young,' he said sternly.

'I'm almost twenty,' she countered.

'That's too young.'

'Look at you and Mommy.'

'Yes, look at us,' he said drily.

'Anyway,' she added quickly, 'I'm marrying this like really cool guy in five weeks, and I'd love you to come to my wedding and give me away.'

There was another short silence. 'I must tell you something,' Antonio said, clearing his throat.

'What?' she asked impatiently.

'I am getting married myself.'

'Adela is letting *you* get married again?' she said disbelievingly. 'No way.'

'Adela is happy for me,' he said, quite affronted. 'And my desire is that you will be too.'

'When are you doing this?'

'Next week.'

'Oh, that's great, isn't it?' she said, trying not to sound whiny. 'At least I call and invite *you*. You weren't even going to *tell* me.'

'Eventually.'

What kind of father was he? It suddenly occurred to her that she was stuck with parents who basically didn't give a crap about anyone except themselves. 'Who are you marrying?' she demanded. At least she was entitled to know that.

'A wonderful woman,' he answered smoothly.

'Woman?' she said, needling him, because since Antonio always referred to women as girls, this one must be older. 'Hmm,' she continued. 'That sounds suspicious. Is she older than you?'

'Well . . .' he said, hesitating for a moment, '. . . just a trifle.'

Nicci jumped on that one. 'How *much* older?'

'Merely a few years.'

'How many?' Nicci persisted.

'Fifteen.'

'*Fifteen!*' she exclaimed. 'Holy shit! That means when you're fifty she'll be like *sixty-five!*' A beat, because she knew her father only too well. And then a sly – 'She must be mega rich.'

'That's not the reason we marry,' he said, offended.

Sure, Nicci thought. Then she sighed and said, 'I guess that means you can't make it to *my* wedding.'

'I will be there.'

'Promise?'

'E-mail me the details. I would not miss giving my one and only beautiful daughter away.'

She felt a sudden surge of deep affection. 'Uh . . . Antonio?' she said softly.

'Yes.'

'It'll mean a lot to me.'

'For me also, *cariño.*'

She put the phone down in a state of bemusement. Antonio was getting married again, and to a woman fifteen years his senior. The only good thing about it was that Adela must be throwing a blue fit!

And what would Lissa say?

She couldn't *wait* to find out.

'Shit!' Taylor exclaimed.

'Whassup?' Oliver muttered, rolling over on the mattress they'd been sharing for the last few hours.

'I fell asleep,' Taylor said, panicking as she consulted her watch, 'and now it's almost five and I've blown out my appointment at the beauty shop, not to mention my shrink, who's probably called the house to find out where I am. Shit! Shit! *Shit!*'

'Chill,' Oliver said unconcernedly, stretching his sinewy body.

'You fucking *chill*,' Taylor snapped, groping for her bra and panties, which were lurking somewhere under his decidedly suspect sheets. 'Larry's being honoured tonight, and we have to leave the house by six.'

'Didn't he get honoured two weeks ago?' Oliver asked, jumping off the bed, naked.

Taylor couldn't help noticing that, in spite of their earlier marathon sex session, he was hard again. Oh, the advantages of youth!

Finding her panties, she put them on. Then she continued the search for her bra, which she couldn't locate in the tangled sheets.

'Damn!' she muttered, running into the living room to recover the rest of her clothes.

Dressing quickly, she realized they hadn't even discussed her script. On her last visit she'd handed Oliver fifteen hundred dollars in cash, and for that he was supposed to read through the script and come up with some brilliant suggestions. If his ideas were any good, she was planning on hiring him at a proper fee to do a polish.

No time to get into it now. She had to get home as fast as possible and come up with a good excuse on the way.

Oliver was standing by the bedroom door watching her. He was still naked and still erect.

She had an urgent desire to stop and admire his young hard body, maybe even make love again. But she didn't dare. Larry would be beside himself wondering where she was, and there was no way he could reach her because she'd switched off her cellphone.

'I'll call you tomorrow,' she said, rushing for the door. 'We'll discuss my script then. Okay?'

'Whatever,' Oliver mumbled. And since she was already out the door, she didn't hear him add under his breath, 'It won't do any good, your script stinks.'

Quincy had asked Michael to call him as soon as Lissa Roman left the office. Instead, Michael decided to drop by and see how old Quince was doing. He felt unsettled after spending time with Lissa. She might be extremely famous, but she was also a vulnerable woman going through a tough time, and watching her face while she was listening to the tape had been quite an experience. They'd dealt with celebrity clients before and Michael had always been able to separate the job from the person. This time something was different.

Do not get personally involved. Rule one of being in the private-investigation business.

Yeah, sure, but how many times did a woman like Lissa Roman walk into the office?

He drove up to the Robbins house in the valley, Lissa still on his mind.

Amber, Quincy's pretty wife, answered the door. A plump black woman, with glowing skin and a warm smile, she gave him an all-enveloping hug, her huge bosom pressing against his chest.

'*Always* a pleasure to see you, Michael,' she said. 'Q's in front of the TV.'

'Big surprise,' he said, grinning.

'And *I* am fixing him a snack. Can I get you something? You're looking damn skinny.'

Not a visit went by unless Amber remarked that he was looking skinny. At six feet two and a hundred and eighty pounds, he didn't think so.

'No, thanks,' he said, shaking his head. Amber was a great cook, but Michael tried to avoid her food because a person could gain ten pounds just by glancing at her cakes and pies and freshly baked cornbread. Every time he ate dinner at their house he had to put in an extra two hours at the gym.

Once, long ago, when Amber was an exotic dancer, she'd weighed one hundred and fifteen pounds. Now, after three children and nine years of marriage to Quincy, she was hovering at two hundred. Standing beside her husband she still looked petite.

Michael entered the cosy family room, where his partner was happily ensconced on the couch, his cast-covered leg propped in front of him on a foot-stool.

Michael indicated the cast. 'How long?'

'How long what?' Quincy said. He was a large, over-weight black man, with surprisingly soft brown eyes, bushy hair, and extra-large hands and feet.

'How long are you shirking work and leaving everything to me?'

'*You*'re capable,' Quincy said, with a big smile, 'an' I deserve a rest.'

'You do, huh?'

'C'mon, man,' Quincy said plaintively, 'I'm gettin' up there. If I take a few weeks off, you can run things.'

'How many cases do you think I can cover by myself?'

'Shit!' Quincy complained. 'I'm an old man. At least lemme take a few days.'

'You're fifty-three, Quince. That's forty if you go by today's standards.'

'Yeah, an' you, my friend, are forty-four, so what does that make you?'

'Overworked,' Michael said. 'I expect you back behind your desk in a week.'

'Yes, *sir*!' Quincy joked. 'You got it, boss man!'

'Screw you,' Michael said good-naturedly.

They had too long a history to ever get mad at each other. They were friends first, business partners second.

'So,' Quincy said, clicking off the TV with the remote that never left his hands, 'what's goin' on that I should know about?'

'Everything seems to be under control,' Michael said. 'The personal assistant case went down this morning, there'll be a new hearing in six weeks. The gardener on the Merron estate was fired and they're not pressing charges. And, uh . . . oh, yeah . . . Lissa Roman came in. I played her one of the tapes. She wants us to take care of removing her husband from the house.'

'Ah . . . Lissa Roman . . .' Quincy sighed, a gleam in his eye. 'Some looker, huh?'

'Didn't really notice,' Michael said, keeping it casual.

'Bullshit you didn't notice!' Quincy roared. 'She's the foxiest piece of—'

Before he could finish the sentence, Amber entered the room carrying a tray loaded with goodies.

'Piece of *what*, honey?' she asked. 'Go ahead, spit it out. Don't mind me, I'm only your *wife*.'

'An' what is my lovely wife bringin' me?' Quincy said, quick to turn on the charm.

'A punch on the jaw if you don't clean up your bad-boy talk.'

'Ouch!' Quincy said. 'I was merely testin' my man here t' see if he got a hard-on in the presence of Miz Roman.'

'You're disgustin'!' Amber exclaimed affectionately. Then she turned to Michael. 'Did you?'

'Jesus Christ!' Michael said. 'The two of you are as bad as each other.'

'Did you?' they both chorused in unison.

Michael shook his head as if he couldn't believe they would ask such a thing. 'She's a lovely woman who happens to be going through a difficult time,' he said. 'The guy she's married to has to be the world's biggest moron.'

'Oh dear.' Amber sighed. 'Our Michael is definitely smitten.'

''Fraid so,' Quincy agreed. 'Shame he can't do nothin' about it.'

'Will you two quit with this shit?' Michael said abruptly. 'In case you've forgotten, I have a perfectly nice girlfriend.'

'Which one is it *this* week?' Amber asked innocently. 'Letetia? Carol?'

'Man, I can't keep up with this Casanova,' Quincy chortled. 'He's got pussy fever!'

Michael shook his head again, he was in no mood for their antics. Since breaking up with his steady girlfriend, Kennedy, three years ago, they were always on his case. The truth was that he hardly dated at all, because women somehow or other always managed to let him down. He knew women considered him exceptionally handsome, and he accepted that as a simple fact. But good looks were not what he was all about, and he resented that most women never saw beyond them. Currently he was dating Carol, a failed ex-actress, now a real estate broker. She was nice enough, but it was painfully obvious that she needed more than he was prepared to give.

He always warned them up front that there was no way he was interested in a serious relationship. They always agreed that neither were they. And then they fell in love and he was stuck. The survival instinct had taught him to get out just in time.

'I'm heading back to work,' he said. 'Glad to see you're not lacking in the smart mouth department.'

'Thanks, bro,' Quincy said, reaching for a chocolate cookie. 'I'll be walkin' before you know it.'

'Can't wait.'

Michael left their house, stopping for a hamburger on his way to the office. Lissa Roman was still on his mind. It worried him that she'd be alone in her house with a man she *knew* was cheating on her. Would she be safe? Could she handle it?

Yes. Of course she could. She was rich and famous, she could probably handle anything.

Chapter Seven

After returning the rental car to the Saks parking lot, Lissa hurried back to Barneys, entering through the front entrance and exiting through the back, where Chuck waited with her car.

As she walked through the makeup department, she couldn't help wondering if one of the girls working behind the counters was Gregg's lover. They were all attractive, young and stylish.

She glanced around, her eyes hidden beneath her dark glasses.

Which one was Gregg's choice? The Chinese girl with the glossy black hair? The pretty blonde in the unsuitable-for-work skimpy top? The languid redhead who seemed to throw her a malevolent glare?

Who knew? Who cared? Gregg Lynch was soon to be history.

Arriving home she found Gregg lying out by the pool putting in time on his year-round tan.

Gregg Lynch. Thirty years old. Handsome in an all-American, dirty-blond, football-hero way.

Songwriter – talentless, in spite of her valiant efforts to steer him in the right direction.

Lazy – she supported both of them.

Charming – when he cared to turn it on.

Sexy – sometimes.

Was that why she'd married him? Because he was good in bed?

Oh, God, she hoped not. She'd married him because he'd seemed so easy-going, was fun to be around, and quite frankly, in spite of all the glamorous trappings she'd been lonely, and after husband number three, a Washington businessman who'd refused to commute, she'd needed a man to share her life with. A man who would be there for her all the way, supporting her in everything she did.

Wrong again, dammit.

'Hi, babe,' Gregg said, sitting up and flexing his considerable muscles. 'How's my hard-working little movie star with the big tits?' Lately he'd taken to talking to her as if she was a hooker.

'Fine,' she answered coldly, wishing she could smash his lying face in. 'And how's my lazy-ass little hubby with the big cock?'

This surprised him, he was not used to Lissa tossing it back at him. 'Don't be vulgar, it doesn't suit you,' he said cuttingly.

'Oh, *sorry*,' she said, with a sarcastic edge. 'I thought cock and tits went nicely together.' And with that she marched into the house before he could come up with an answer.

Better take it easy, she warned herself. *It's not clever to signal that you know.*

She hurried upstairs to her dressing room, where she stripped down to her bra and panties. Her masseuse was due at the house soon, and she wanted nothing more than to feel a strong pair of hands releasing the built-up tension in her shoulders and neck. It was tough constantly playing the wronged woman.

Just as she was reaching for her robe, Gregg sauntered in. '*You*'re in a pissy mood today,' he remarked.

'I'm tired,' she said, turning away from him.

'Tired, huh?' he said, dodging in front of her, preventing her picking up the robe.

'Move,' she said sharply.

'Why? Can't I get an eyeful of my wife in her sexy undies?' he said nastily. 'Or is that sight reserved only for Madam's faithful fans?' And before she could stop him, his hands went for her breasts, pulling up her bra with one swift move so that they were bared yet trapped by the bra above them.

'Great tits for an old broad,' he said. 'You *sure* you never had 'em done?'

She recognized his mood. It was his 'I'll bring this bitch down to size' mood. The one where he tried to get even with her because she was successful and he wasn't.

'Stop it, Gregg,' she said, trying to stay calm.

'Stop it, Gregg!' he mimicked. 'Miss Famous Tits an' Ass wants me to stop it.' And he shoved his hand down her panties and began fingering her.

'No!' she said sharply, attempting to fight him off.

'You've been holding out on me, babe,' he said, 'and now I'm taking a piece of what belongs to me.'

She struggled, but to no avail. He was strong. Too strong. He bent her back across a stool, ripped off her panties and began thrusting himself inside her with a grunting intensity.

Lissa was so shocked that she didn't know what to do. How could she scream in her own house and accuse her husband of raping her? Because that's what the son-of-a-bitch was doing.

He finished quickly, thank God, stood up and hoisted his swimming trunks back into position.

'Not bad,' he said condescendingly. 'And I thought you were getting frigid on me. See you later, hon.'

And with that he ambled out of her dressing room as if nothing had happened.

She was stunned. What kind of a man was he anyway?

A bullying monster, that's what kind.

And the sooner she was rid of him the better.

Later in the day Saffron and Nicci sat side by side in a Korean beauty shop on Westwood Boulevard enjoying manicures and pedicures.

'I was thinking of inviting Evan's brother to dinner at the house when they get back,' Nicci said, wriggling her bare toes.

'Why?' Saffron asked. 'You told me he was a totally into getting laid jerk – and now you want to have him for dinner. What's the scam?'

'He *is* about to be my brother-in-law,' Nicci pointed out, determined not to reveal her crush, although she was dying to confide in someone, and who better than Saffron? 'So this will be my major peace move.'

'How come?' Saffron demanded, stretching out her elegant fingers as a short Korean woman applied gold polish to her long nails. 'Did you two get into a fight?'

'No. It's just that Brian's kind of cold towards me,' Nicci explained, as a second Korean woman placed her feet in a bowl of warm water. 'I know it's 'cause I'm marrying his brother and that probably doesn't *thrill* him. They may not look alike, but they *are* twins. And I've heard twins have this kind of cosmic karma – like if one gets married the other one feels deserted.'

'Twins. Very close,' the manicurist painting Saffron's nails said, in a low, sing-song voice.

'I don't get it,' Saffron said, yawning. 'You can't even cook. So what's the deal?'

'I'm planning on hiring a chef for the night.'

'Oh, wow.' Saffron giggled. 'Now you're going Hollywood on me.'

'I can't do it without you, so you'd better show up.'

'Yeah, yeah – wouldn't miss it. That's if I can find a sitter for Lulu.'

'Doesn't your mom ever sit?'

'Get real!' Saffron exclaimed, hooting with laughter. 'Can you *imagine* the great Kyndra sweeping into my tiny house and *babysitting*? Oh, when she has a free moment she takes Lulu. But you know what? That woman *never* has a free moment – exactly like Lissa.'

True, Nicci thought. *My mom always has something going on. If it's not work, it's a man.*

'Will you bring Mac?' she asked.

'I cannot *only* be seen with screaming gay men,' Saffron said. 'I might bring a studly actor I met at an audition last week.'

'Studly actor good,' the manicurist interjected, nodding knowingly.

'How come you haven't mentioned him?' Nicci asked.

''Cause you're always too busy catering to Evan.'

'I do not cater,' Nicci said crossly.

'Yes, you do.'

'I so *don't*.'

'Whatever,' Saffron said, admiring her manicure.

'Coffee? Tea?' the manicurist asked.

'No, thanks,' Nicci answered, as the other woman gently dried her feet with a towel.

'Can somebody run out and get me a Jamba Juice?' Saffron said, tossing back her long dreadlocks. 'Raspberry with all that health stuff in it. I need energy.'

'So, have you come up with any ideas for the bridesmaids' dresses?' Nicci asked.

'I was thinking short and muted purple. Something way sixties with an edge.'

'Sounds cool.'

'Maybe you should approve them?'

'When do I have time?'

'It's *me* you're talking to, Nic. You got the time to do anything you want, it's not like you have a *job*.'

'Organizing a wedding *is* a job.'

'I mean a *proper* job.'

'I've *tried* a million and one jobs. Anyway, *you* can talk, all *you* do is go on auditions and *never* get the part.'

'Thanks for reminding me,' Saffron said huffily. 'It's *so* good to have encouraging friends.'

'Sorry!' Nicci said quickly, realizing she'd stepped into a sensitive area.

'Anyway, let's get real,' Saffron said. 'We're both supported by our families.'

'True,' Nicci admitted. 'Only *I*'m marrying Evan, so no more hand-outs.'

'Then *he*'ll support you,' Saffron said. 'What's the difference?'

'There's plenty of difference,' Nicci said irritably. 'And anyway, how come that big dumb basketball player doesn't give you more money? Lulu *is* his daughter.'

''Cause I don't care to take money from him,' Saffron said, her face hardening. 'If I accept his money, then he'll think he has some big fat claim on her.'

'He should be giving you plenty,' Nicci said.

'I dunno.' Saffron sighed. 'Whatever happened to all our feminist vows growing up? We were gonna own the world. Remember?'

'Yeah, well, all *I* want to own is Evan,' Nicci said, which wasn't strictly true because she didn't want to own him, just be with him. 'Y'know,' she mused, 'it's like I've dated so many bad boys, and finally along comes a good one so I'm bagging him. Nothing wrong with that.'

'*And* let's not forget he's *mega*bucks rich,' Saffron offered.

Nicci hadn't really thought about Evan being rich. But then she realized that of course he was. *Oh my God*, she thought. *Antonio's marrying a rich woman. Am I doing the same? Copping out just so I'm comfortable for the rest of my life?*

No way. I love Evan. And if it wasn't for Brian . . .

'I mentioned the phone call I had with my dad, didn't I?' she said, trying not to think about Brian again.

Saffron nodded. 'What was Lissa's reaction?'

'Haven't told her yet.'

'C'*mon*, girl. You gotta at least *warn* her.'

'I will,' Nicci promised. 'This wedding's getting horribly close and I'm nervous. Wouldn't *you* be?'

'Don't worry about it,' Saffron said, waving her gold nails in the air. 'I'm planning an *amazing* bachelorette night for you.'

'You are?' Nicci said, perking up.

'Yeah, top secret. You, my dearest friend, are gonna *love* it!'

'Where were you?' Larry Singer asked, greeting his wife in the foyer of their Pacific Palisades mansion. He was of medium height, skinny, with a bearded, pleasant face bordering on homely, and a receding hairline. 'I've been going crazy trying to find you. I almost called the police.'

'It's a nightmare story,' Taylor said, rushing toward the stairs. 'Let me take a quick shower and get dressed. I'll tell you everything on the way to your event.'

Larry followed her up the stairs into their bedroom. 'Were you in an accident?' he asked, removing his glasses and staring at her. 'You look terrible.'

'Uh . . . sort of,' she replied, running into her bathroom and closing the door.

'What kind of accident?' he questioned, opening the door and following her in. 'Are you hurt?'

'No, sweetie, I'm fine,' she answered soothingly, 'but, please, let me get ready, then I'll tell you all about it.'

'Christ, Taylor!' he said, frowning. 'I was worried sick.'

She took a moment to placate him. 'I know, darling,' she said, patting him on the cheek. 'Everything's all right now. I promise. So go downstairs, fix yourself a drink, and I'll be right down.'

'Only if you tell me what happened to you,' Larry said stubbornly.

'I was, uh . . . mugged.'

'*What?*' he roared, enraged.

'The main thing is I'm okay,' she said. 'And I have exactly fifteen minutes to dress. So . . . in the car the full story.' And she pushed him gently out of the bathroom.

Somehow or other she managed to get herself together in record time. Black velvet Valentino strapless gown, Steiger pumps, Bulgari jewellery, hair piled on top of her head, and a regal smile. She was every inch the genius's wife. Beautiful, caring, a fine partner for such an important and respected man.

Sitting beside her husband in the back of the limo, she wove a web of lies.

I was on my way to see a writer about my script . . .

Run-down area . . .

Mugger came out of nowhere . . .

Knocked unconscious . . .

Friendly neighbours took me in . . .

Wow! She was good. By the time she'd finished her story she almost believed it herself.

Larry was very concerned, he wanted to know if she'd called the police. 'No,' she said. 'Who needs that kind of publicity? Certainly not us.'

Then he wanted to know what she'd had stolen.

'Nothing,' she answered truthfully. A pause before she came up with more lies. 'My purse was locked in the trunk, and by the time the mugger tried to pull the rings off my fingers, the neighbours came running out and scared him away.'

'Jesus Christ!' Larry exclaimed. 'Why didn't you call me immediately?'

'Because, my love,' she answered, leaning over and kissing his cheek, 'I know how you get, and I didn't want to alarm you.'

Larry shook his head in amazement. 'You,' he said, 'are my life. If anything ever happened to you . . .'

Guilt overwhelmed her.

It wasn't easy screwing around on a genius like Larry Singer.

Chapter Eight

E ric Vernon whistled tunelessly as he followed the girl in her silver BMW, watching her as she went about her business – such as it was. After weeks of trailing her, he'd soon realized that she never did much of anything. Most mornings she attended a kickboxing class, picked up a styrofoam cup of coffee from Starbucks, then sometimes she went shopping along Melrose, or met a girlfriend for lunch. Most times she headed back up to her boyfriend's house at the top of Mulholland where she lived, then spent the rest of the day lying by the pool, putting in time on her already perfect tan.

Lazy spoiled bitch. It was patently obvious she didn't have to work for a living like most people – Eric Vernon included.

He resented her lifestyle. It wasn't right that someone could go along week after week, month after month, doing exactly nothing.

Eric's mother had been a maid to a rich family in Philadelphia. She'd had no husband to support her because his dad had walked when he was only a few months old. This meant that six days a week his mom was forced to clean up after two adults and three over-privileged children, two girls and a boy. The boy was the same age as him, and sometimes his mother had dragged him along with her to help scrub the tile floors.

Help with the floors, for crissakes. He was nine years old and down on his knees, while the other boy – the sneering, spoiled prick – was playing with an expensive model train set and laughing at him behind his back. When he'd complained to his mother, she'd beaten him with a broom and told him he was useless and a burden and should learn to shut up.

It wasn't the first time she'd laid into him, and it certainly wasn't the last. Beatings were a normal part of his day.

Eric learned anger at an early age. He also learned how to hide it.

Eric smiled when the lady of the house passed on her son's hand-me-downs.

Eric smiled and pissed in their drinking water.

Eric smiled and systematically broke all of the children's toys in such a way that nobody could ever point the finger at him.

Eric smiled and spat in their food kept in plastic containers in the fridge.

Eventually his mother was fired, no reason given, simply a month's severance pay and a heartless, 'We do not require your services any more.'

She died of heart failure within months. Eric didn't particularly care. She was a mean bitch and at least he wouldn't have to endure the daily beatings she handed out.

Years later he'd run into the son of the family she'd worked for at an after-hours club. He'd recognized him immediately, the same smug features and preppy clothes. Eric had paid an acquaintance two hundred dollars to beat the crap out of him. The result – permanent eye damage – was satisfying.

After his mother's demise, Eric had been sent to live in a series of foster homes. Nobody kept him long. He was cited as being difficult, destructive and moody, not qualities anyone welcomed. He spent time with a couple of state-certified shrinks who labelled him deeply disturbed and depressed.

Depressed? Shit. Didn't the dumb bureaucrats get it? He was fucking furious.

At sixteen he was out on his own, making a living any way he could – delivering drugs, stealing cars, knocking off liquor stores. Until he got caught and suffered ten months in a correctional institution for juveniles, a place that *really* fired his anger.

As soon as he got out he was prepared for a life of crime. Realization had dawned that you sure as hell never got anything the legitimate way.

Within weeks he'd attached himself to a Puerto Rican drug dealer and his girlfriend. It didn't take long before he was cheating the man on his profits and fucking his girlfriend.

When the dealer found out, the evil bastard had hired a couple of goons to break his arms and legs. They'd left him in a downtown dumpster like a piece of useless trash.

Eric had never forgotten the pain and humiliation he'd suffered. Seven years later he'd tracked the man down and beaten him to a pulp outside a restaurant. Then he'd stood there and laughed as the man choked to death on his own vomit.

Later, the bitch girlfriend had fingered him, but with the help of a good lawyer and his entire bankroll, he got away with manslaughter.

After that, prison. Six long, grim years. Years he would never forget. Years of harsh punishment and pain.

Revenge was a good thing.

Money was even better.

At thirty-two, Eric knew it was time to make the big score.

And that score was soon to be Nicci Stone.

Chapter Nine

B y the time Lissa recovered her composure and came downstairs, she found Gregg lounging in the den watching football on the satellite TV as if nothing bad had happened.

Out of all her husbands he was definitely the worst. She'd married her first husband when she was a kid, so he didn't really count. Number two, Antonio, was a charming womanizer who simply couldn't help himself. And number three, the Washington businessman, had turned out to be more interested in business than her.

Yes, Gregg took the prize big-time. Not only was he screwing around, spending her money *and* putting her down, but he'd actually *forced* himself upon her, *raped* her, and she'd accepted it because she wanted to ease him out quietly.

She couldn't wait until Friday. Couldn't wait to never have to set eyes on him again.

'We're supposed to go over to James and Claude's tonight,' she said, forcing herself to speak in a civil fashion. 'They're running the new Mel Gibson film.'

'*You* go,' Gregg said, barely glancing at her. 'It's not my scene hanging out with a bunch of fags. Anyway, I'm working tonight.'

'Really?' She couldn't help herself. 'What are you working on now?'

'Don't you ever listen?' he fired back. 'Oh, I forgot,' he added sarcastically. 'Unless it's about *you*, Miss Famous Movie Star never hears a thing.'

'So tell me again,' she answered calmly.

'A friend of mine is interested in me scoring his movie. He's running a rough cut.'

Gregg's lies were a joke. Up until now she'd accepted them because she hadn't wanted to face up to the truth of another failed marriage.

'Would this be the same friend who tells you you're the best lover in the world and have the most beautiful cock?' she wanted to ask. But she didn't, she remained silent, remembering her promise to Michael that she wouldn't initiate a fight. 'Okay,' she said, keeping it light. 'I'll see you later.'

She didn't feel like going to James and Claude's by herself, and she certainly had no desire to sit through a movie. But it sure beat the alternative, which would be watching Gregg get ready for a rendezvous with his latest girlfriend. And that, she knew, she couldn't stand.

'You're distracted,' Carol said, busily loading the dishwasher. 'What's up?'

'Huh?' Michael answered. They had recently finished an early steak dinner, which she'd cooked, and now they were contemplating catching a movie.

'Distracted,' Carol repeated. 'Not here with me.'

Michael had a strong suspicion it was time for the speech. *You're too good for me. I'm not ready for a relationship. I don't want to hurt you. You'll find someone better than me.* Sooner than anticipated, but he had a feeling that if he allowed Carol to get any closer, she'd be hard to shake.

Not that there was anything wrong with her. She was thirty-two, an attractive redhead with a pleasing personality and a good body. She was successful at her real estate job, not too bitter about failing as an actress, an excellent cook, and very fond of him.

Too fond. He knew that any second she was about to come out with the L word, and he had to avoid that at all costs. *No thankyouverymuch.* The L word smacked of commitment, and Michael Scorsinni was a loner. That's the way he liked it, and that's the way it had to stay. 'I'm not distracted,' he said vaguely. 'Just thinking.'

'About what?' Carol asked, as she finished loading the dishwasher.

'About what movie we should see,' he replied, annoyed that she was attempting to invade his private thoughts.

'Oh,' she said mockingly. '*Such* concentration.'

He couldn't stand it when she tried to be cute. Carol was definitely beginning to grate.

'I wouldn't mind seeing the new Mel Gibson movie,' he said, wondering why he always allowed himself to get caught in a trap.

'It doesn't open until Friday,' she said, taking off her apron.

'Clint Eastwood's got a new one,' he suggested.

'Too violent for me.'

'Hey, *you* choose,' he said, thinking that's what she was doing anyway.

'Julia Roberts, of course,' she said with an irritating smile. 'The critics claim her latest is a woman's film, but you can sleep if you get bored.'

He shot her a look. 'Big of you.'

'I'll call the theatre, see what time it starts,' she said, leaving the room.

Why did she have to call? Why couldn't she look up the time in the paper like everyone else?

All night long he'd been thinking about Lissa Roman, wondering what was going on at her house. Was she doing okay? Should he phone and check?

No. That wouldn't be cool. What if the husband answered? He had a bad feeling about Gregg Lynch. The guy was a jerk. How could any sane man cheat on Lissa? She was so talented and beautiful, and on top of that she seemed genuinely nice. A rare combination. Michael had come across a few movie stars in his line of work, and as far as he could tell, they were all neurotic wrecks who looked better on the screen than off.

Carol came back in, a sweater knotted loosely across her shoulders. 'We'd better get a move on,' she said briskly. 'It starts in ten minutes.'

So now he had to sit through a woman's movie. Great. But it was probably easier than giving Carol the break-up speech. He had to prepare himself for that. It took time and courage, and he wasn't quite ready.

Claude St Lucia's mansion in Hancock Park was lavish in the old Hollywood style. There was an enormous entry hall, an old-fashioned sweeping limestone staircase and several entertaining rooms all filled with an over-abundance of French Baroque furniture.

Dinner at James and Claude's always included a mix of interesting and gifted people, most of whom were regulars. They dropped by once a week to have dinner and see the latest movie before it hit the theatres.

Lissa knew almost everyone. She circulated, trying her best to look as if she was having an enjoyable time. Mel Gibson's agent, the always charming Ed Limato, was there. Lissa often wished he was *her* agent because he was the best, but so far she'd remained loyal to Craig Lloyd, the agent who'd negotiated her first big deal. She also spotted Anne and Arnold Kopelson, the superstar producing team. And across the room was the statuesque actress Anjelica Huston, one of Hollywood's finest, with her imposing husband, the famed sculptor, Robert Graham.

James was the only one who sensed she wasn't her usual self. 'Something wrong?' he asked, putting his arm around her shoulders.

Now was not the time to tell him, he'd find out soon enough. 'Everything's fine, James,' she said lightly. 'Why wouldn't it be?'

'Where's Gregg?' he asked, peering at her knowingly.

Out fucking his new girlfriend.

'Uh . . . collaborating on the score for a movie.'

'Isn't *that* good news? Makes a pleasant change to hear he's working.'

'Don't be bitchy.'

'Why not?' James said archly. 'Surely you know it's my thing.'

'And he's proud of it too,' said Charlie Dollar, joining in. Charlie was a permanently stoned, award-winning movie star, with droopy eyelids and a lopsided grin. Charlie had been hitting on Lissa for years, but so far she'd resisted his fifty-something charms.

'I got a movie for you an' me t' do together, kiddo,' Charlie said with a sly wink. 'An updated version of *Last Tango*. You an' me, babe, add a pound or two of butter, an' it's got mega-hit written all over it.'

'Think I'll pass, Charlie.'

Another sly wink. 'You're makin' a big mistake.'

'I don't think so,' James said, hustling her away from Charlie's lecherous leer.

Somehow she got through the evening, and when she arrived home she was relieved to find that Gregg was still out.

Only one more day and night, she thought. *I can do it. And I will.*

Early Thursday, Nicci sped out to the airport in her BMW to meet Evan. She was excited about seeing him. Even more excited about seeing Brian – although her attraction to him was her deep dark secret, a secret she wouldn't admit to anyone.

She watched the private jet land, and when the brothers alighted, trailed by Teena, she raced across the tarmac, arms outstretched.

Evan grabbed her in a bear hug and twirled her around. He genuinely loved her, she knew *that*. At least she was sure of *something*.

Brian, walking behind, nodded in her direction. 'Hey,' he said abruptly.

'Hey, Brian,' she said, matching his mood. 'Need a ride?'

'Nope, I got one,' he said, striding ahead of them, allowing her an excellent view of his tight butt in faded Levi's.

She observed that his ride was a short-haired blonde in a convertible Mustang. 'Hmm . . .' she said to Evan, as they got in her car. '*Where* does he find them? I've like *never* seen him with the same one twice.'

'Who cares?' Evan said, throwing his carry-on bag onto the back seat. 'As long as he doesn't get them from the set.'

'I'm *so* totally psyched you're back!' she exclaimed, trying to forget about Brian, although every time she was in his company he got her adrenaline pumping in a most unsettling way. 'I hate it when you're away.'

'You should've come with me,' he said, cracking his knuckles.

'Not when you're working.'

'Why's that?'

'Brian wouldn't like it,' she said, brushing her long bangs out of her eyes.

He threw her a quizzical look. 'Since when do we care what Brian likes?'

I care, she thought, *because even though I love you, I've got this stupid little crush on your brother, and there's nothing I can do about it. Sorry, Evan, I'll get over it.*

Eventually.

Lying in bed in her Pacific Palisades fifteen-million-dollar mansion, Taylor was in a reflective mood. Being Mrs Lawrence Singer was an easy job on account of everyone kissed her ass big-time.

Taylor knew why, and she also knew what would happen if she stopped being Mrs Singer. She would be out with a capital O. *Persona non grata.* Hollywood ranks would close, and that would be that.

There is nothing colder than the ex-Hollywood wife of a famous, powerful man. Unless that ex-wife creates her own particular brand of heat, she is useless to all her former best friends.

Oh, yes, Taylor knew there would be exceptions. Lissa for one. Lissa had known her when she was a working actress, before she hooked up with Larry, and in spite of her own enormous fame, Lissa had always been a loyal friend.

Stella, of course, would take off like a getaway car racing away from a heist. No way would Stella hang with someone who wasn't in the upper echelons of the Hollywood hierarchy.

James would be ambiguous. He wouldn't go out of his way to see her, and yet if they bumped into each other, he wouldn't ignore her.

Kyndra could go either way. There was no anticipating anything Kyndra did.

Not that Taylor was thinking of ending her marriage. On the contrary, her marriage was the only secure thing she had. Plain fact of life – Larry adored her and would do anything she asked.

Well . . . almost anything. He wouldn't put her in one

of his movies – claimed it would smack of nepotism. He wouldn't offer to direct *her* movie. He wouldn't even executive produce. When it came to all things career-wise, Larry stood firm.

Damn him for that. All she needed was a little help.

Okay, so he'd got her a deal at Orpheus pending script approval, but he could've done more. He *should*'ve done more.

That's why I'm having an affair, she rationalized. *To punish him for* not *doing more.*

Last night she'd watched him being honoured again. She'd watched them all bow and scrape and hang onto his every word.

In the limo, on the way home, she'd closed the smoked-glass partition, shutting off their regular driver, and given Larry the blow job of his life.

Nobody gave a better blow job than Taylor. If they were giving out master's degrees for blow jobs, she'd be top of the class.

She'd reduced Lawrence Singer – man of the moment – to a quivering wreck as her tongue and mouth teased him into an earth-shattering orgasm, made all the more exciting because they were in the car and the driver probably suspected what was going on.

When it came to sex, Taylor was in control. She had all the power in that department, and Larry was her willing slave.

Her thoughts turned to Oliver Rock. Falling asleep at his place yesterday had been quite dangerous. And the annoying thing was that they hadn't even got around to discussing her script, which was supposed to be the reason she was there.

Today would be different. Work first, play second. And to make sure she didn't fall asleep, she'd take her small Cartier alarm clock with her.

Oliver Rock.

She couldn't get enough.

Sometimes Nicci wondered if Brian even knew she existed. His attitude at the airport had been typical, a cool 'Hi' and that was it. He *never* said more than a few words to her.

Was *that* the attraction? Could it be that he piqued her interest because he *was* so cool?

Usually men came on to her big-time. But not Brian. Oh, no. He acted as if she didn't exist. And it was really weird because he obviously loved women since he was always with a different one.

So what the hell was wrong with *her?*

'Brian doesn't like me,' she announced in the car on their drive back to the house.

'Why would you say that?' Evan asked, popping a breath mint.

'He never *says* anything to me,' she complained.

'He never says anything to me either.'

'That's nuts,' she said, shuddering the BMW to a sudden halt at a stop sign. 'You two work together.'

'Yeah, talk about a laugh a minute,' Evan said caustically. 'All Brian does is bitch, get stoned and complain about everything.'

'Then maybe you *shouldn't* be working together.'

'We've had this discussion, Nicci,' Evan said, tightening his seat-belt as she gunned the accelerator and took off again. 'Whatever it is we have, it works. Can't argue with *that.*'

She was silent for a moment, thinking about the fact that they *were* brothers, twins, and it would be impossible to separate them unless that's what they both wanted.

'Was this trip difficult?' she asked.

'It's always difficult,' he said. 'Brian and I fight about everything.'

'You do?'

'Yeah, but what comes out on the screen is special, and believe me, that's the bottom line.'

'Hmm . . .' she said, overtaking a Mercedes on the turn into the freeway. 'Maybe we should invite him over to the house for dinner with one of his many girlfriends.'

'Why would you want to do that?'

Yes, why would I want to do that? ''Cause he's about to be my brother-in-law *and* your best man,' she said, hitting the freeway at full speed.

'I was forced into that by my mother,' Evan grumbled. 'When Mom wants something . . .'

'Oh, right, your mother,' Nicci said, sliding over to the fast lane. 'She'll be pleased to hear that I've got everything organized for our wedding.'

'That's great,' Evan said, looking genuinely pleased. 'I knew you could do it.'

'The woman at the venue is getting it all together for me. She's like totally into details.'

'Mom'll be very happy. Did I tell you she'll be here soon?'

'She's not staying with us, is she?' Nicci questioned, so alarmed that she almost veered out of her lane in front of a fast-moving Cadillac.

'She *always* stays with me when she comes to L.A.,' Evan said patiently. 'There's no way I'd allow her to check into a hotel.'

The thought of having Evan's overbearing mother staying in the house with them was quite terrifying.

'Now that I'm living with you, won't it be awkward?' she said, thinking, *Oh, God! How will I deal with this?*

'What's awkward about it?' Evan said casually. 'Mom loves you.'

No, she doesn't. She's putting up with me because I'm marrying one of her precious sons. And you don't get it, 'cause when it comes to your mom, you think the sun shines out her big, interfering ass.

'By the way,' Evan added. 'She's looking forward to meeting Lissa, so set something up.'

Crap! Nicci thought. *Lissa and the mother-in-law from hell. That's gonna be a laugh a minute.* 'Anyway,' she said, quickly reverting to her dinner-party idea, 'I think I'll ask Brian over tomorrow night.'

'Why?' Evan said, frowning. 'He'll probably turn up with some brain-dead bimbo.'

'Who cares?' Nicci said, crossing lanes, barely glancing in her rear-view mirror. 'It'll give me a chance to get to know him.'

'If you're serious, put together a group. There's no way I can take Brian on his own.'

'Like who did you have in mind?'

'Is Saffron seeing anyone?'

'Well . . . she's met some new stud, and there's a gay guy she hangs with. Maybe I'll tell her to bring him.'

'That'll go down well with Brian,' Evan said with a short, brittle laugh. 'He's homophobic, you know.'

'*Brian*'s homophobic?' she said, totally startled by this new information. 'In *this* town? In *his* business?'

'You got it.'

'How do you know?' she said, cutting off a truck as she exited the freeway.

'I'm his brother, remember?'

'Oh, yeah,' she said, almost rear-ending a small van.

'Jesus, Nicci,' Evan said, clutching onto the dashboard, 'has anyone ever told you that you drive like a maniac?'

'All the time,' she said, with a quick smile.

'Maniac or not, I missed you,' he said, patting her on the knee. 'And I love you.'

'You too,' she responded automatically.

How nice it was to find a man who could actually

express his emotions. She couldn't imagine Brian being able to do that.

'I know, I'm irresistible, aren't I?' Evan said, with a big, goofy grin.

'Let's not get carried away,' she answered, grinning back. 'There's love and then there's irresistible. *You* come somewhere in the middle.'

Evan laughed. 'It's good to be home,' he said.

And Nicci sped off along Sunset, still thinking about Brian.

Chapter Ten

The first thing Lissa did when she opened her eyes on Thursday was check to see if Gregg was home.

Yes, he was there, asleep on the far side of their California King custom-made bed.

She gazed across at him for a moment, remembering how in the early days of their romance she'd loved watching him sleep. He always slept naked, but now she couldn't stomach the sight of his hairy balls and limp cock.

She experienced a brief Lorena Bobbitt moment before throwing a sheet over him. Then she hurried into her bathroom and put on her yoga clothes. Her private instructor was arriving soon, and after an hour of uplifting yoga, she planned on spending the rest of the day rehearsing for her upcoming Vegas show.

Last night she'd realized it was about time she started concentrating on work again. Gregg had been slowing her down, filling her with self-doubt. Now she had to get herself together, remember who she was and what she'd achieved.

Over the last six months Gregg had taken great pleasure in constantly calling her stupid and dumb, while picking on everything from her clothes to her choice of scripts and songs.

Too bad for him she was so resilient, a true survivor.

When Gregg was history there'd be no more men coming into her life, spending her hard-earned money and telling her what to do. She wanted to enjoy more time with her friends and Nicci. Lately she'd been lamenting that they weren't as close as they should be. Nicci was getting married soon, and it certainly wasn't too late to become more involved.

Once Gregg was gone, she had big plans.

Somehow or other Carol ended up spending the night. Michael hadn't intended for her to stay, but one thing led to another and before he could think about it she was in his bed.

He made love to her automatically. As far as he was concerned there was no passion left in their relationship, the sex was a series of going-through-the-motions moves, and he was pissed at himself for not ending it sooner.

The sad truth was that if he finished with Carol, he'd be alone again, and sometimes spending time with the wrong person was better than being alone. He also realized that if they broke up, he'd probably start with somebody new, leading to the same old dance.

Rita, his deceased wife, had ruined his trust in women. Rita had lied to him from day one, going so far as to pretend that the baby she was pregnant with when they got married was his. For five years he'd thought he had a daughter, until one day he'd found out the real truth. Bella was not his daughter, Bella was the child of his low-life brother, Sal. And when Rita moved to L.A. she'd decided to send Bella back to New York to live with Sal and his wife. Only nobody had told him. He'd found out by accident – well, more like he'd paid for the information from a stripper pal of Rita's who'd been desperate for money. As soon as he'd found out, he'd flown straight to his brother's house in New York where he'd beaten the crap out of Sal and had the story confirmed. It had been the worst day of his life.

'I wish I didn't have to work today,' Carol said wistfully, as she stood in his small kitchen cooking bacon, eggs and sausage for breakfast. 'Maybe on Saturday we can drive to Santa Barbara for lunch. Can we, Michael?'

'I'll be working this weekend,' he answered, wishing she wasn't so needy.

'All weekend?' she said, making a disappointed face.

'Looks like it.'

'How come?'

'High-profile client. Needs plenty of attention.'

'Who?'

'You know our policy, Carol. No names.'

'Oh, come *on*, you can tell me.'

''Fraid not.'

She was about to say something, thought better of it, and went back to pouring him more coffee.

Smart girl, Carol. Knew when *not* to push it.

By the time Taylor arrived at Oliver's it was past noon. She'd planned on a morning visit, but it was not to be, too much stuff going on that she had to deal with. She was on the board of several charities and – because of her position – they were always asking her to do something. 'Can you get us Ricky Martin to perform at an upcoming event honouring Tom Hanks?' 'How about a signed script from Steven Spielberg for our auction?' 'Would Larry be willing to donate a walk-on role in his next movie?' Stupid requests. But she was who she was, and occasionally she was able to oblige.

Sometimes in the morning she joined Lissa and her private yoga instructor. Today she didn't have time because a facial, manicure and pedicure were definitely more important. Not to mention a Brazilian bikini wax.

When she finally arrived at Oliver's, he was on his

cellphone pacing up and down in front of his beach-view window, speaking animatedly. He waved her away when she attempted to hug him, which kind of pissed her off. He should be kissing her ass, because not only did they have great sex, but she was paying him to work on her script.

It looked like he'd been entertaining, there were empty bottles of beer everywhere, several overflowing ashtrays, and empty pizza boxes piled high.

She watched him as he talked on the cellphone. He was clad in a torn USC T-shirt and dirty khaki shorts. His outfit didn't matter, he still looked hot.

Idly she wondered how risky it would be to check into Shutters At The Beach and spend some quality time together. Not to mention clean sheets and a working shower.

Too risky. Much too risky.

This morning, before leaving for the studio, Larry had asked what her plans were for the day.

She'd answered him vaguely.

'No more visiting writers in bad neighbourhoods,' he'd admonished sternly. 'In future have them come to the house. You can use my office.'

'Thanks, sweetie,' she'd said, imagining herself naked in her loving husband's office, making crazed, passionate love to a horny, out-of-work screenwriter.

Now here she was at Oliver's, impatiently waiting for him to get off the phone.

'It's, uh . . . like friggin' unreal,' Oliver said into the phone. 'I'll be there pronto.'

'Be where?' Taylor asked, as soon as he clicked off.

'You're not gonna friggin' *believe* this,' he said excitedly.

'What?'

'My agent sold my spec road-trip script for a million friggin' bucks!'

* * *

Concentration was everything. At least her parents had taught her *one* useful lesson. *Work hard and don't expect thanks.* Well, yes, she worked hard all right, but she got *plenty* of thanks. Her fans loved her. They adored her. They *never* let her down. Unlike her parents, who had no idea of the success she'd achieved.

Or maybe they did, and had no desire to contact her. It made her angry and sad when she thought about them, so she tried not to do so.

Lissa easily outpaced her dancers at rehearsal: she had enough stamina to keep going all day without a break.

'You're the bomb, honey,' her sleek black female choreographer informed her admiringly. 'Dunno how you do it.'

Hard work. That's all it takes.

She kept going until six, then lingered at the rehearsal studio going over stuff with her publicist. Max had all kinds of television and magazine interviews lined up for her. She said yes to some, nixed others.

She knew she should inform Max about her impending break-up, but somehow she couldn't bring herself to mention it. Another divorce made her feel like such a loser, and yet she knew that wasn't true. Gregg was the loser, not her.

When she finally arrived home, there was a message from Gregg saying he'd be working late again. She was relieved. If only she'd known, she could have arranged to have him thrown out sooner.

Tomorrow was the big day, and with any luck she'd never have to see him again.

Taylor was in a dazed state of confusion. She was in her car, driving home, trying to figure out what the hell had just happened. Oliver, *her* writer, *her* lover, was about to get paid one million dollars for a spec script. While she, Taylor Singer, married to *the* Lawrence Singer, was still struggling after two years to get her lousy movie made.

And she wasn't too happy about Oliver's attitude either. He'd hustled her out of his house as if she had the goddamn clap!

'What about *my* script?' she'd asked, as he'd shoved her towards the door. 'Have you even looked at it?'

'We'll talk tomorrow,' he'd said. 'I gotta get over to my agent's.'

Graciously she hadn't pursued it. Not that he'd given her much choice.

A fuck would've been nice. A celebratory fuck.

Maybe tomorrow.

She phoned Larry from the car.

'Where are you?' he asked.

'Shopping,' she replied.

'I'm putting Edie on – give her the name and address of those people who helped you yesterday.'

'What people?' she asked, totally blanking on her lies.

'The neighbours.'

'Oh, yes,' she said quickly. 'The neighbours . . . I uh . . . didn't get their exact address. And you know – I'm not sure of their name.' A pause. 'Why do you need to know anyway?'

'Because I thought we should send them a gift basket, or champagne. Something to let them know we appreciate what they did.'

'Absolutely,' she said. 'I'll find out and let Edie know.'

'Speak to her now, give her the name of the writer you were on your way to see. She'll get the information.'

'I'll deal with it myself,' Taylor said quickly. 'I'd like it to seem more personal.'

'Don't forget.'

'I won't.'

She clicked off the phone. Larry was always so worried about other people. He had his precious personal assistant, Edie, who'd been with him forever, do everything. Send flowers. Write notes. Buy gifts. God forbid someone didn't get a proper thank-you.

Taylor drove her car directly to Neiman's and indulged herself with two hours of ferocious shopping to calm herself down. Everyone was getting what they wanted.

When was it *her* turn?

Deidra Baker was fed up with working for a living. She had a plan, and that plan was to snag herself a rich man. She didn't care what he looked like or how old he was: as long as he had big bucks he would do.

Deidra was twenty-five, not a beauty, but an attractive, if somewhat short, brunette, with long hair and a compact body. Her best asset, unfortunately for her, had to be kept under wraps. Deidra had quite phenomenal nipples. They were huge and dark brown, and when aroused, startlingly erect. Men flipped over her nipples, but she had yet to find the man who'd flip out enough to pay her rent so she could give up her job and start enjoying herself like the affluent women she waited on at Barneys, where she was a salesgirl. It was better than her previous job, which was working at a children's clothing store in the valley.

Crossing over the hill had been the best move she'd ever made. At least she got to meet people now. Rich people. Rich *men*.

At night she hung out at the latest clubs, always on the look-out for a man who could take her places. Sitting at the bar she made connections, although never the right ones, merely guys who were looking to get laid and nothing else.

Then one day along came Gregg Lynch. Deidra recognized him immediately when he wandered into the store to check out cashmere sweaters. Mr Lissa Roman. Husband of the superstar.

Deidra was smart, she didn't let on she knew who he

was. After some banter back and forth, he came on to her. She responded. Why not?

He took her out for coffee a couple of times, and before long they were sleeping together.

Gregg discovered her nipples with a vengeance, toying with them for hours on end. He truly got off on them – most men did.

Deidra didn't mind, for she was under the impression that she'd finally found her ticket to the big time.

Only one problem. He *was* married.

It took him weeks before he told her who he was. When he did, she acted all surprised, especially when he revealed the identity of his wife.

Because she didn't throw a fit, he started to feel very comfortable with her, and soon he was complaining about his famous wife non-stop. According to him, Lissa Roman was a cold, unloving bitch with the biggest ego in the world, and his most fervent complaint was that she refused to help him with his career.

Deidra had listened to a few of his songs, immediately understanding why Lissa couldn't help him. The man had no talent except in bed.

Of course she didn't tell him that. She told him he was the most gifted, fabulous, hot, sexy man she'd ever slept with. And he had the biggest, most admirable cock she'd ever seen. And his wife was an idiot because she did not appreciate him.

Gregg believed every word – he was a man, wasn't he?

After a while it occurred to Deidra she was not getting anything out of the affair except a litany of complaints about Lissa Roman. Gregg was not offering to pay her rent. Gregg was not buying her presents. Gregg was not mentioning that he would divorce his wife – thereby ending up with big alimony. He wasn't even taking her out to dinner, claiming it was too risky for them to be seen together in public.

All they were doing was hanging out in her tiny apartment indulging in endless sex. Which wasn't a bad thing because Gregg *was* quite a cocksman. On the other hand, Deidra had to think about her future, and if Gregg wasn't prepared to come up with a plan that suited both of them *and* some big bucks, she'd better start looking elsewhere. After all, she wasn't getting any younger, and Hollywood was chock-a-block with beautiful babes, a new batch arriving every day.

Deidra decided she'd better make a stand, so when Gregg arrived at her apartment on Thursday night, she was ready.

He entered, complaining. Nothing new about *that*.

Deidra listened for a while, stifling a yawn because it had been a long day – even though she'd had the pleasure of admiring Brad Pitt from afar when he'd come into the store with his wife, Jennifer Aniston. How lucky could one girl get? A hit TV series *and* Brad Pitt. It didn't seem fair.

Gregg fixed himself a Scotch. *Her* liquor, he didn't even spring for *that*.

He sat down on the couch, still complaining about Lissa, then said something that *really* got her angry. 'Take off your bra, babe. Shake those titties an' gimme an eyeful.'

Who did he think he was talking to? A hooker? A stripper? A lap dancer?

She was suddenly livid. 'Gregg,' she began, in an uptight tone, 'I've been thinking . . .'

'You have?' he said, interrupting her. 'Clever girl.'

'Don't talk down to me,' she snapped.

He was surprised: it was the first time Deidra had raised her voice to him. 'What's up?' he said.

'First you ask me to take my bra off, then you treat me like I'm some kind of bimbo,' she said, steaming. 'I am *not* a bimbo, I'm your . . . your lover. And I've been thinking.'

'Don't give me shit, Deidra,' he said, starting to frown.

'What makes you think it's shit?' she said, still simmering.

''Cause you've got that face on.'

'*What* face?'

'The face women get when they're gonna say something that's gonna bug the crap outta me.'

'You come here, we make love, you go home,' she nagged. 'What's in this for me, Gregg? Are you planning to divorce your wife or what?'

'Jesus Christ!' he said, standing up. 'Who mentioned divorce?'

'*I* did,' she said defiantly.

'Hold on a minute,' he said, his expression tight and nasty. 'We've only been seeing each other a few weeks.'

'It's not a few weeks, Gregg. You've been coming over here most nights for the last two months.'

'What're you doin', counting?'

Her voice rose to a high pitch. 'And *I*'m not getting anything out of it.'

What the fuck? Why couldn't women keep their pissy little complaints to themselves? 'Didn't realize you were looking to get something out of it,' he said with a sneer.

'I can't waste my time if this isn't going anywhere,' she said, now in full nag and unable to stop. 'You talk about Lissa as if she's the worst thing that ever happened to you. If you divorced her, we could be together and start living normally, instead of sneaking around. I want to live some-where nice, move up in the world. I want to be with you.'

'This is *all* I fucking need,' Gregg groaned.

'*What*'s all you fucking need?' she said, her patience snapping. 'Me to take off my bra and parade around so that you can stare at my tits?'

He slammed his drink down on the table. 'Why else d'you think I'm here, baby? For your intelligent conversation?'

'What did you say?' she asked, her lower lip trembling with indignation.

'I get enough shit at home,' he growled. 'I'm not listening to it here. So if you don't like our arrangement, screw you!'

He started towards the door.

She went after him. 'Where are you going?' she demanded, nervous because this scene was not playing out the way she'd imagined.

'Wherever the fuck I want,' he snarled.

She grabbed his arm.

He lashed out, knocking her to the ground.

'You bastard!' she cried.

He looked down at her with contempt. 'Like I'd divorce Lissa for a pitiful tramp like you,' he spat. 'Don't you get it? Lissa's somebody. Who're you? Just a nobody with sideshow nipples. S' long, Dcidra. Thanks for the ride.'

And then he was gone.

Chapter Eleven

T hursday night Michael and Carol were invited to dinner at the Robbins house. Since Quincy was laid up, Michael decided it might be a good time to fill him in on office business.

The first thing Quincy wanted to hear about was Lissa Roman's situation.

'I told you,' Michael explained. 'She's waiting until tomorrow. I'm expecting a call from her first thing, then I'll go right over and deal with it.'

'Lissa's a nice lady,' Quincy said. 'You gotta make sure she's taken care of.'

'I will,' Michael said.

'And that's *all* you gotta do,' Quincy added warningly.

'What're you getting at?'

'*Mister* Casanova.'

'Bullshit, Q.'

Carol was in the kitchen with Amber, the hum of their conversation drifting into the living room as the two women chatted about their daily lives. The children were upstairs in bed.

'My wife's cookin' you *my* favourite meatloaf,' Quincy announced, 'along with sweet potatoes, collard greens an' black-eyed peas. You're a lucky man to be invited to sample her fine cookin'.'

'And *you*'re a lucky man to have married a woman who'll put up with you.'

'Put up with me!' Quincy roared. 'I treat her like a queen. An' while we're on the subject of women, how come *you*'re not thinkin' 'bout settlin' down? Carol seems real nice.'

Michael rubbed his chin, stood up and began pacing. 'I'm not looking to get involved after Kennedy,' he said.

'Kennedy was several years ago,' Quincy pointed out. 'Never did understand why you two split.'

'She was no more into a relationship than I was,' Michael said restlessly, remembering his feisty ex-girlfriend with a touch of nostalgia. 'We had a great couple of years together, then we *both* decided it was time to move on.'

'Y'know what *your* problem is?' Quincy said, swigging beer from the bottle.

'What?' Michael said, hardly interested in Quincy's take on his problems.

'It's all about that crap with Rita and the kid. You gotta let it go.'

'Don't call Bella the kid,' Michael said sharply.

'Face it, you're her *uncle*, not her daddy,' Quincy continued, 'an' that's not such a bad thing.'

'I'd like to see what *you*'d do if the same thing had happened to you.'

'Hey, *I*'d friggin' kill,' Quincy said, swigging more beer. 'But you gotta leave it behind. You dealt with gettin' shot, you can deal with the Bella thing. Carol can help, it's obvious the woman cares for you. How about makin' this one a keeper?'

'How about butting out?'

Dinner was so good that Michael ate himself to a standstill, then he immediately wished he hadn't. No wonder Quincy was so out of shape, Amber's cooking was a heart-attack on a plate.

'Y'see?' Quincy said, leaning back and patting his stomach happily. '*This* is marriage.'

Amber giggled, 'Throw in some shoppin' an' you got it, honey.'

'Now we'll watch the game on TV an' sample my wife's sweet pumpkin pie,' Quincy said, winking at Michael. 'With a lotta sex later.'

Amber rolled her eyes.

'That's what I'm always telling Michael,' Carol said, joining in enthusiastically. 'A good relationship only takes two people.'

'Keep *on* tellin' him,' Quincy said. 'He'll get it one of these days.'

Carol laughed. '*My* turn to cook next. Shall we fix a night now?'

'No,' Michael said quickly. 'Next week is out. This case I'm working on is taking up a lot of time.'

'Work, work, work,' Quincy said, patting Amber's fine behind.

'*You* can talk,' Michael said. 'Considering you dumped everything on me this week.'

'Hey—' Quincy began.

'Now, now,' Amber interrupted. 'No fighting amongst the boys.' She smiled at Carol in a conspiratorial way. 'These two are like a couple of bad-assed brothers. You should've *seen* 'em in the old days. I had to *pry* 'em apart.'

'Yeah, sure,' Michael said. 'It was you an' Quince that *I* had to separate. And it looks like you're still at it.'

'Ain't nothin' wrong with *that*,' Quincy joked.

It seemed only natural when they left the Robbins house that Carol came home with him.

Michael had his speech ready. He'd give it to her when the time was right. So what was wrong with waiting a few more weeks?

Who knew? Maybe Quincy was onto something, maybe she *was* a keeper.

Prowling the bars, an angry gleam in his eyes, Gregg Lynch was furious that a nothing piece of ass like Deidra had spoken to him the way she had. How dare she think that a girl who worked in a department store could tell *him* how to run his life? He was married to Lissa Roman, for crissakes. Did she honestly believe that he'd divorce his wife for her? What kind of a dumb cunt was she?

Women were all the same. Rich, famous and beautiful, or passably attractive with a great pair of tits, they were all the same. Mangy, nagging cunts. He didn't like any of them. They were there for the fucking, that's all they were good for.

And paying the bills, he thought. Although lately, Miss Moneybags, Lissa Roman, was getting a little tight around the edges. The last time he'd asked for a hundred thousand to put into the market, she'd demurred, saying that her business manager had invested all her available cash, and that he'd have to wait. That *really* pissed him off. He didn't believe her. He was her husband, she should give him whatever he wanted, no questions asked.

He was especially annoyed at Deidra because tomorrow was a big day for him. He was working with a new producer, a young up-and-coming guy he was paying to record a couple of his songs. Tonight he'd wanted to relax, get it on with Deidra, go home, have a good night's sleep, and be out of the house early. Now he was screwing himself over by prowling bars and getting wasted. And it was all Deidra's fault.

By midnight he was sitting in a strip club on Sunset Boulevard, flicking twenty-dollar bills at an energetic girl with silicone boobs and sinewy thighs. She rode the shiny pole like it was her long-lost lover, and after a while, Gregg decided he wanted to fuck her.

That is, until the manager sidled over and said, 'Mr Roman, it's a pleasure to welcome you to our club. Come in any time – the check's on us.'

He was furious that he'd been recognized. Even more furious that the prick had called him Mr Roman. Wouldn't do to get caught by the tabloids, Lissa would be pissed. She had a bug up her ass about her precious reputation. 'Name's Lynch,' he growled. 'Gregg fucking Lynch. Got it, asshole?'

The manager did not appreciate being called an asshole. 'Sorry, Mr *Lynch*,' he said tightly. 'I know you as Mr Roman.'

'Whaddaya mean, you know me as Mr Roman?' Gregg said, scowling. 'My *wife* is Roman, I'm *Lynch*.'

'Maybe you should cool it with the drinking,' the manager suggested. 'Are you driving?'

'What the fuck does it matter to you?'

'State law. We can be held responsible if you have an accident. I'll arrange a taxi to take you home.'

'Fuck you,' Gregg said. And he stumbled out of the club muttering to himself.

By the time he arrived home he was in a state. He staggered into the master bedroom, and there she was – queen of videos, princess of movies, little Miss Sex Bomb – asleep in their bed, looking more beautiful than ever.

Most broads when they removed their makeup looked like death took a holiday. Not Lissa Roman. No. She was *always* fucking gorgeous. A prime piece of ass, and she was all his.

He was so drunk that he wasn't aware of what he was doing as in a fit of spite he dragged her out of bed by her hair.

She awoke, screaming.

''S your husband,' he slurred. 'Remember me?'

'My God, Gregg,' she exclaimed, cringing away from him. 'You scared me.'

'Did I now?'

She could smell the booze wafting off him. 'You're drunk,' she said accusingly.

'That okay with you?' he said sarcastically. 'I got the Queen's permission?'

She stared at him for a moment, wondering what to do.

Tomorrow's Friday. Tomorrow he'll be out of my life forever. Tonight's the last time I have to face him.

'Why don't I go downstairs and make you some coffee?' she said soothingly.

'*You* wanna make *me* coffee?' he sneered. 'Why doncha *call* somebody t' do it? 'Cause *you* sure as shit never lift a finger.'

'Gregg, I've been rehearsing all day, I'm exhausted,' she said quickly. 'Perhaps it's a good idea if I sleep in the guest room.'

'Perhaps it's a good idea if I sleep in the guest room,' he said, mimicking her voice. 'Fuck *you!* I'll tell you where you're gonna sleep – right here next to your husband.' And he started unzipping his pants.

She had no intention of enduring another rape. Oh, no! Enough was enough. She glanced at the phone. One buzz and Chuck would come bounding upstairs.

She reached for it.

'No fuckin' way!' Gregg said, wrestling the phone out of her hand.

'I'm calling Chuck,' she said, speaking fast. 'He'll make you coffee. You're recording tomorrow. Surely you want to be in good shape for that?'

'Whadda *you* care?' he said belligerently. 'I'm fucking bored with you. Bored living in this house, I hate it. I hate you.'

'You're drunk. Sleep it off.'

'Don' wanna do that,' he said stubbornly. 'Wanna fuck my wife.'

And he began pawing her.

'Don't touch me,' she warned, backing away.

'Don' touch you?' he repeated, and grabbing hold of her, he ripped the front of her nightgown, exposing her breasts. 'How's that for not touching you?' he said, with a maniacal laugh. 'How's that, *bitch*?'

She continued to back away. He came after her. He was easier to avoid than last time because he was so drunk and unsteady on his feet. As he tried to grab her again, she kneed him hard in the balls. He staggered a bit, but kept on coming. Then, just as she was about to run from the room, he grabbed her leg, toppling her to the floor.

'How does it feel?' he crowed, standing over her and unzipping his fly. 'How does it feel t' be down, bitch?'

She managed to get to her feet and once more tried to make it to the door.

He came after her again.

'Leave me alone,' she yelled. 'Don't *ever* touch me again.'

'You're *my* fuckin' property,' he shouted. 'I'll touch you whenever I goddamn want to.'

And then he lifted his arm and hit her across the cheek.

Somehow she managed to flee from the room, her heart thumping. She made it into the guest bedroom, slamming and locking the door behind her.

He was too drunk and confused to follow. With a loud guttural groan, he fell across the bed, still clothed, and passed out.

Friday morning, Nicci awoke early. She lay in bed for a moment staring at the stark white ceiling, thinking about everything. Saffron was right, her wedding was creeping closer every day, so the sooner she filled Lissa in about Antonio coming to L.A. the better. No good putting it off any longer.

Propping herself up on one elbow, she watched Evan sleeping beside her. Yes, she decided, he'd make a great husband. He was smart and interesting and crazy about her. They'd even discussed having kids. What more could she ask for?

You're only nineteen, her inner voice whispered. *And you're marrying a man who wants a wife, kids, and a settled life. He'll be having an amazing time making his movies on location, while you'll be stuck at home taking care of a bunch of screaming brats.*

No way, she told herself sternly. *I love him. Marriage to Evan will be cool. If there's one thing I need it's some stability in my life – considering I've never had any.*

The previous night they'd celebrated his home-coming by making love. Evan was not as experimental as she would have liked, he was more into pleasing her, which was nice, but did not exactly lead to wild, uninhibited sex.

I'm nineteen, she thought. *I want wild uninhibited sex.* Not that she hadn't experienced it already, but it hadn't been with Evan.

Surely the fun and excitement and getting crazy wasn't all over?

She slid out of bed without disturbing him and hurried into the all limestone and chrome bathroom. Stripping off her T-shirt, she stood under the shower and decided that she'd skip her kickboxing class and visit her mom instead.

Saffron was right, the least she could do was warn her about Antonio's impending visit. It was only fair.

Lissa slept fitfully. By six a.m. she was up. She took one look in the bathroom mirror and realized she was in trouble. Her left eye was swollen and bruised. The bastard had given her a black eye.

She had no intention of leaving the safety of the guest room until he'd left, so she listened at the door until she heard him go down the stairs. Once she was sure he'd gone, she unlocked the door and hurried into her bedroom, immediately calling Michael.

'He's on his way out,' she whispered into the phone. 'Can you get here as soon as possible?'

'I'll be right over,' Michael said.

'Please. It's important that he never comes back.'

'I get it, Lissa.'

Gregg was on his way out as Nicci drove up to the house. She realized for the hundredth time that she couldn't stand him. He had cowlick hair, a permanent tan and big muscles. Why did her mom always go for looks? Didn't personality count too?

'Hi, Gregg,' she said, jumping out of her car, hoping that he wouldn't try to make *conversation*. He had an 'I'm stripping you naked' way of looking at her that was not at all welcome. 'Is Mom up?'

He cast an appraising eye over her. 'Lookin' foxy, Nicci,' he said, licking his dry lips. 'Shouldn't walk around like that. One of these days somebody's gonna take advantage of you.'

'And it sure as hell ain't gonna be my stepdad, is it?' she said sharply, wishing she'd worn something more substantial than low-rider shorts and a stomach-baring tank.

Christ! He had a hangover from hell, and now he had to listen to this little cunt's smart mouth. Things were going to have to change around here. He deserved some respect, and Lissa better make sure he got it. 'Your loss, baby,' he said, getting into his Ferrari, a wedding gift from Lissa.

Turning her back, Nicci entered the house, encountering Nellie, Lissa's long-time housekeeper. Nellie, a stout, capable woman who originally came from Germany, lived to take care of her famous boss.

'Mom around?' Nicci asked.

'In her bedroom,' Nellie replied, adding a stern, 'Knock before you enter.'

Nicci headed for the master suite and barged right in.

Lissa was sitting in the darkness on the side of the bed speaking on the phone. The drapes were drawn tightly shut and she was still in her robe. As soon as she saw Nicci, she covered the mouthpiece with her hand. 'What are *you* doing here?' she asked.

'Nice greeting,' Nicci remarked, plucking a handful of grapes from a dish on the bedside table. 'Your own daughter, and that's all I get?'

'I didn't mean it that way,' Lissa said, slightly flustered. 'Usually you call when you're coming over.'

'I've got something to tell you,' Nicci said, perching on the end of the bed. 'Didn't want to get into it over the phone.'

'Right now?'

'I thought this would be a good time.'

'Well, it's not,' Lissa said, thinking that her daughter's timing couldn't be worse. 'You'll have to wait outside while I finish this call.'

'Whatever,' Nicci said, getting up and slouching out of the room. She always slouched when in the company of her mother. Lissa was so freaking amazing, that she made Nicci feel totally insignificant in the looks department.

Shutting the door behind her, she stood outside and attempted to listen. *Hmm . . . very interesting*, she thought. *Gregg's on his way out, and Mom's on the phone. Maybe she's getting it on with another guy.* Damn those big heavy doors! She couldn't hear a word.

Wandering into the kitchen, she opened the fridge, removed a carton of orange juice, and swigged from the carton.

'Your mommy wouldn't like that,' Nellie scolded, busily polishing the granite counter.

'I'm not Mommy's little girl anymore,' Nicci reminded her.

'No, but you certainly act like it,' Nellie muttered disapprovingly. 'And you're too damn skinny. You need to put some flesh on those bones.'

'God! Why do I feel like I'm still living at home?' Nicci complained, pushing back her long bangs. 'Now I know why I left.'

'It wouldn't hurt you to drop by for a decent meal once in a while,' Nellie nagged.

'I eat like a pig,' Nicci said. 'Can't help it if my metabolism keeps me this way. Anyway, Nellie, only *you* think I'm too thin.'

After a few minutes Lissa emerged from her bedroom. She was now dressed in a white silk shirt, casual pants and Nikes, her platinum hair piled on top of her head, opaque black wraparound sunglasses covering her eyes.

'Whassup?' Nicci demanded. 'You're like so *mysterious* this morning. And how come you're wearing shades in the house?'

'Let's go sit in the den,' Lissa said, her face serious.

Nicci followed her mother into the den and flopped into a chair.

Lissa shut the door. 'Here's the situation,' she said tensely. 'And this information is for you only.'

'I thought *I* was the one who came here to tell *you* something,' Nicci said, wondering what was up.

'I'm throwing Gregg out,' Lissa said, sighing deeply.

'*Nooo?*'

'The locks are being changed, his things will be packed up. By the time he gets back this evening, everything will be taken care of.'

'No shit!' Nicci exclaimed. 'You only married him two years ago. What's the deal?'

'As we both know,' Lissa said, brushing back a loose

strand of platinum hair, 'my history with men is not exactly stellar. Unfortunately, once again I found out things I refuse to put up with. I can't take another confrontation, so this is the clean and easy way of getting rid of him.'

'I never liked him,' Nicci remarked. 'Thought he was a lech.'

'Nor did any of my friends,' Lissa admitted.

'Well, gee, this *is* a surprise,' Nicci said. 'And now I've got another one to lay on you.'

'You're pregnant,' Lissa said quickly, the thought flying into her head.

'No way,' Nicci said, annoyed that her mother would think she was stupid enough to get knocked up. 'Antonio's coming to town. He's giving me away at the wedding.'

'I guess it's better than being pregnant,' Lissa said, relieved that she was not about to become a grandma. Lissa Roman. Movie star. Sexy singing superstar. Four-time divorcee. And . . . *grandma*. What an image-breaker *that* would be.

'And,' Nicci added, glad that Lissa was taking it so calmly, 'he'll probably be with his new wife.'

'*What* new wife?'

'Antonio's getting married again.'

'When?'

'He's doing it this week.'

Lissa couldn't help feeling a tiny frisson of jealousy. Antonio was about to get married, and she was about to get divorced. Again. What a failure she was at marriage, she simply couldn't get it right. 'Who's he marrying?' she asked.

'Dunno,' Nicci said casually. 'Some older *rich* woman. Adela will like totally *freak*!'

'How do *you* know all this?'

''Cause I called and invited him to my wedding.'

'You did?'

'Hey, *somebody* has to walk me down the aisle, and it sure as hell wasn't gonna be Gregg. And in view of the circumstances, I'm *sooo* glad I called Antonio.'

'He can't stay here,' Lissa said hurriedly.

'She's rich, Mom, they'll probably take a bungalow at the Beverly Hills Hotel.'

'Good,' Lissa said, wondering what it would be like to see Antonio again – another cheating son-of-a-bitch.

'Hey, Mom, you okay?'

'Well . . . this *is* kind of upsetting,' Lissa admitted. 'I suspected Gregg was seeing someone for months. Hiring a private investigator was merely confirmation.'

'A PI!' Nicci exclaimed, wrinkling her nose. 'Gross!'

'Anyway,' Lissa said sadly. 'The PI found out everything.'

'Like *what?*' Nicci demanded, dying to hear the whole sordid story.

'For God's sake,' Lissa said snapped. 'Don't expect me to go into details. It's bad enough that this will eventually become tabloid fodder.'

'Great.' Nicci groaned. 'Once again I get to read all about my mom in the supermarket.'

'Maybe not,' Lissa said, wishing that her daughter would show a little more sympathy.

'You *know* they're gonna nail you.'

'Perhaps,' Lissa said vaguely, her mind on other things. 'Anyway, it's good to see you, Nicci. Is everything on track for the wedding?'

'Zoomin' along.'

'I wish I could help more.'

'No, you don't,' Nicci said matter-of-factly. 'You're hopeless with arrangements.'

'I'm glad you understand. You know I'll pay for everything. Have all the bills sent to my business manager.'

'Thanks.' Nicci hesitated a moment before continuing. 'Uh . . . I know you think I don't appreciate all the stuff you've done for me, but, uh . . . I do.' A beat. 'And I'm sorry about Gregg. So . . . if you need anything, call me.'

At last some compassion. 'Thanks, sweetheart,' Lissa said. 'I appreciate that.'

'I'll get out of your way now,' Nicci said. Stopping at the door she added an impulsive – 'We're having a dinner party tonight. You're welcome to come.'

'*You*'re throwing a dinner party?' Lissa said, surprised. 'You're not actually *cooking*?'

'Who, me?' Nicci said, grinning. 'Like no way. I've hired a chef.'

'Sounds like fun.'

'It's only like, y'know, a few people. Saffy's showing up with her new boyfriend.'

'Saffron has a new boyfriend? Has Kyndra met him?'

'Kyndra's exactly like you, Mom,' Nicci said patiently. 'She doesn't give a rat's ass.'

'That's not a very nice thing to say,' Lissa said, frowning. 'Of course I care. I'm just not your average mother.'

Hmm, Nicci thought. *That's the understatement of the year.* 'Yeah, yeah,' she said. 'I'm sure you care in your own way, but let's not get into it now.'

'Get into what?' Lissa said tightly.

'Nothing,' Nicci said quickly. 'So . . .' she added. 'Maybe I'll see you later?'

Lissa nodded. The prospect of being alone tonight was not an appealing one. Perhaps she *would* go to Nicci's dinner party – it might make a welcome change. Anything to block out the nightmare of the last few days.

Chapter Twelve

Several weeks previously Eric Vernon had quit his job so he could concentrate fully on the task at hand. Shortly after that, he'd driven to San Diego and held up a bank – enabling him to fully finance his project. The pickings were good. Not good enough. Eric was on track for the big score, and he knew that to achieve his objective, everything had to work perfectly. There could be no screw-ups. Kidnapping Nicci Stone was his one chance at the big time, and he'd kill anyone who blew it.

Arliss was on board. Eric had picked him because of the huge deserted building he looked after. It was the perfect place to stash the girl until the ransom was paid. Eric had given him enough money to set up a soundproof and secure room. A room with no windows and no way out.

When he'd told Arliss what the job was, the skinny man had blanched. 'Kidnapping,' he'd whined. 'That's a federal offence.'

'Not unless you transport the victim to a different state,' Eric had said, reassuring him. 'We'll hold the victim no more than twenty-four hours – less if the ransom's paid fast enough. Before we make a move, every detail has to be in place.'

'What kinda ransom you askin'?' Arliss had inquired, a greedy expression distorting his thin face.

'That's for *me* to know,' Eric had answered. 'Your cut'll be twenty-five grand. If we bring the other guys in, they'll each get ten grand.'

'Cash?'

'Cash,' Eric agreed.

'Do we get the money up-front?' Arliss had wanted to know, licking his cracked lips in anticipation.

'No. You'll have to trust me.'

'The others'll never go for it.'

Eric had given him a long, cold stare. 'If they want in, that's the way it has to be.'

Eric continued to track Nicci on a daily basis, noting her every move. There was a place in the steep brush outside the back of her boyfriend's house where he could watch everything she did. With no shades on the large glass windows he got an unobstructed view as he crouched in the bushes for hours on end. He even bought night-vision goggles to observe her more intimate moments, such as when she was taking a bath or preparing for bed.

Nicci Stone was a sexy young piece, and sometimes Eric found her getting to him – even though he'd sworn off women.

Damn her! Experiencing sexual feelings put him out of control, and above all else, Eric knew he had to stay in control. No weaknesses. Weaknesses led to mistakes. And Eric could not afford to make any mistakes.

He kept in touch with Danny, leading him on with a story he'd concocted about a mystery boyfriend with whom he was involved. Danny was a sympathetic listener, especially when Eric was buying the drinks.

Danny was also a talker, and Eric heard all about how Lissa was planning on dumping her current husband, preparing for her Vegas show, and attempting to get closer to her daughter. The more information he could find out the better.

The next step was recruiting Arliss's three friends, which he did not consider a difficult task. Offer enough money, and people were inclined to say yes to anything.

It was only human nature after all.

Chapter Thirteen

Lissa was a wreck watching Michael Scorsinni and Danny methodically packing up Gregg's clothes and other personal possessions. In spite of the fact that her soon-to-be ex had turned out to be a cheating, violent son-of-a-bitch, it all seemed so final. And when he was gone, once more she'd be alone. Although she'd already decided that being alone was certainly better than spending one more moment in Gregg's company.

She remembered their first meeting at a friend's house in Malibu. Gregg had seemed so easy-going, warm and sexy. He hadn't been in awe of her, like most men, and in spite of the ten-year age gap, they'd fallen into a fast and exciting relationship. She'd thought that this was it. True love at last. And yet, after a while, he'd turned out to be like all the rest. Worse than the rest, because he was also an abusive bully, and now she could add rapist to his list of credits.

'You shouldn't be here,' Michael finally said, noticing how agitated she was getting. 'I suggest you check into a hotel for the weekend, or go stay with a friend. By Monday Gregg Lynch'll be history, and you can come safely home.'

'You don't know Gregg, he won't give up easily,' she said, thinking that when Gregg realized what she'd done, he'd go berserk.

'Here's another suggestion,' Michael said. 'How about next week I move into your guest room, make *sure* he doesn't give you any trouble?'

'You'd do that?' she asked, quite liking the thought of having Michael Scorsinni permanently on the premises. He made her feel secure and safe.

'You're paying me, Lissa, I'll do whatever you want.'

'Really?' she said in a sexy voice, teasing him.

'Within reason,' he countered.

'Oh, nuts!' she joked, laughing. 'And I thought I could have my way with you.'

Michael didn't smile: he was too angry. He had a strong urge to get hold of Gregg Lynch and beat the crap out of him. Men who hit women were the lowest, and although Lissa refused to reveal anything, the black eye she was featuring told its own story.

'Did that son-of-a-bitch hit you?' he'd demanded, as soon as he'd walked in.

'I ran into a door,' she'd replied, too embarrassed to tell the truth.

He'd stifled a desire to reach out and hold her close. But of course he couldn't do that – as he kept on reminding himself – this was business, personal feelings were not allowed.

Why not? his inner voice demanded.

Because she's a client, and she's also a movie star. And movie stars are different.

By late afternoon, Danny had booked her into the Peninsula under an assumed name. A short drive later she was ensconced.

'Maybe I'd better stay here for a while,' Danny said, quite concerned as he fussed around the suite making sure there were flowers and wine and a large fruit basket.

'That's okay,' she said, dismissing him. 'Have Michael call me later.'

Reluctantly Danny left.

Filled with mixed feelings, Lissa wandered around the luxurious suite, pacing from the living room to the bedroom, feeling like a caged tiger.

It was so strange being in a hotel in her own town. So strange and lonely. And yet she knew this was what she had to do, because after Gregg's behaviour last night there was no going back. Her husband had turned into a frightening stranger – she was lucky to have got away with only a black eye.

'Did you send those people a gift?' Larry inquired, standing over Taylor.

She was sitting at her desk, trying to sort through the stack of invitations that arrived daily. She glanced up at her husband. Here was this man, this Oscar-winning *genius*, and all he cared about was whether she'd sent the fictitious neighbours something. Go figure.

'Yes,' she said shortly. 'I took care of it.'

'It's good karma to give back,' Larry remarked.

He was home early because his best friend from college, Isaac, was celebrating his birthday, and Isaac's wife, Jenny, was throwing him a party. And even though Isaac, whom Taylor had only met on a few occasions, lived in the wilds of Calabasas, Larry had insisted they go.

Taylor had tried to get out of it – in vain. 'They don't want to see *me*,' she'd said modestly. 'It's *you* everyone's interested in.'

'Taylor,' Larry had assured her, 'I wouldn't *dream* of going anywhere without you. *You* are my reason for getting up every day. I love you so much. You do know that, don't you?'

Like she didn't feel guilty enough. If Larry ever found out she was screwing around it would destroy him. Earlier today she'd driven over to Oliver's, only to find no one home. She'd hung around for a while, hoping he'd put in an appearance, and when he didn't appear, she'd driven home in a sulk.

Since that time, she'd called him several times. Receiving no answer had put her in even more of a sulk.

'Shouldn't you be getting dressed?' Larry asked.

'What *is* the dress code for Calabasas?' she drawled sarcastically.

Larry didn't appear to notice her sarcasm. 'It says California casual on the invite, so wear that white outfit I like.'

Sure, Taylor thought. *There's no way I'm wasting Valentino on a trip to the boondocks.*

Larry went upstairs. Taylor reached for the phone and tried Oliver one last time.

If he didn't pick up soon, she was asking for her money back.

The chef Nicci had hired – sight unseen – arrived late. He was a gaunt, scruffy-looking man, with dyed black hair greased into submission, an off-white chef's jacket worn with stained white bell-bottoms, and orange hiking boots.

At least he's here, Nicci thought, *although he's not exactly what I had in mind.*

She was upset, because the flowers she'd ordered had not arrived, and, according to Evan, the wine she'd purchased at the market was cheap crap. If this is what entertaining was all about, she would not be doing it again any time soon.

'*You* should've picked up the wine,' she informed Evan, who for the first time in their short relationship was starting to bug her. 'Men are supposed to take care of things like that.'

'Dinner parties are *your* job,' he answered, between phone calls. 'Besides, you're the one who wanted to do this.'

Earlier he'd told her that their director was having a nervous shit-fit, and he'd been on the phone most of the day trying to deal with it.

'My *job*,' she retorted, outraged. 'My fucking *job*! I don't work for you, in case you haven't noticed.'

'Don't start, Nicci,' he said, shooting her a filthy look.

Christ! He sounded like her *mother*. Tight-lipped, she left the room before she told him to shove it up his ass with bells on.

The chef was in the kitchen unpacking supermarket bags, a cigarette dangling loosely from the corner of his slack lips.

'I thought we'd sit down to dinner around nine,' she said, trying to sound as if she'd done this before.

'You got it, sweetbuns,' he answered, with a jaunty wink.

Sweetbuns! What was *that* all about? 'You're serving steak and salad, right?' she said, deciding it was best to ignore his overly familiar attitude.

Another wink. 'You're gonna *love* my meat, *sweetbuns*,' he said, cigarette ash falling on the counter top.

She hurriedly left the kitchen and retired to the privacy of their bedroom, where she lit up a joint, even though Evan – who didn't do drugs of any kind – had asked her not to smoke in there.

Too bad. She was giving this lousy dinner party to make *him* happy, and he had the temerity to criticize her!

She stalked into her closet and picked out the one dress she owned. A short, backless, red Azzedine Alaïa. Very sexy. Especially when she added Jimmy Choo heels, making her six feet tall. Evan would not appreciate her towering over him – he claimed it made him feel inadequate.

That was his problem. Tonight she was doing whatever she felt like.

* * *

Around six Michael phoned the hotel, using Lissa's alias to get through to her. 'Everything's in place,' he said. 'His stuff's outside, the locks are changed, I've sent your housekeeper to stay with relatives for the weekend, and your security guard knows Mr Lynch no longer has access to the premises.'

'Are you *sure* I can do this?' she asked nervously.

'You checked with your lawyer, didn't you?'

'Yes.'

'Then you know it's okay.'

'I suppose so,' she said listlessly.

'It's your house, Lissa, not his,' Michael said, his voice low and reassuring.

'I realize that.'

'Then what's the problem?'

'No problem,' she answered quickly.

'So, what are you up to in your luxury suite?' he asked, attempting to lighten the situation.

'Becoming a television junkie,' she said, switching channels as she spoke, keeping the volume on mute.

'Sounds like fun.'

'If you like TV.'

'Do you?'

'No.'

'Hey, don't go getting depressed on me,' he said cheerfully.

'I'm not.'

'You're sure?'

'Positive.'

'And you're okay being in a hotel by yourself?'

'Of course I am,' she lied.

'Then there's nothing else I can do for you tonight?'

'Nothing.'

'I'll give you my cellphone number in case you need me.'

'I won't,' she sighed, 'but give it to me anyway.'

'You want me to drop by?' he asked, sensing she was depressed.

'Not necessary,' she said, although his company would've been most welcome.

'Just remember,' he said sternly, 'do *not* go home.'

'I have no intention of doing so.'

She put down the phone, then picked it up again and ordered dinner from room service, instructing the waiter to leave the trolley outside the door. She didn't want anyone knowing she was there, let alone a room-service waiter who probably had a hot line to the *Enquirer*.

When the food arrived it did not tempt her. She hated being in this situation, and the prospect of sitting alone in a hotel room all night was a grim one, especially as she felt so vulnerable. She called James. His service informed her he was in New York for the weekend.

Next she tried Kyndra, whose assistant told her that her boss was shut up in the recording studio, and had left instructions not be disturbed unless there was a major earthquake.

Nice. Just when she needed them, her two best friends were unavailable.

She considered phoning Stella or Taylor, then decided against it. Stella was too abrasive, and would lecture her on her bad choice of men, and Taylor was so completely caught up in her movie project that lately she seemed to care about nothing else.

By eight Lissa was completely on edge. She'd watched TV, attempted to read, found she couldn't concentrate on either, and didn't know what to do next.

I can't just sit here, she thought. *It's driving me crazy.*

Then she remembered that Nicci was having a dinner party.

Maybe I'll go, she thought.

Maybe I won't.

And once more she tried to settle down and watch TV.

* * *

The drive to Calabasas was long and boring. Especially as Larry insisted on driving them himself in his new SUV.

'Can't we take the Mercedes or my Jaguar?' Taylor had asked.

'I think this vehicle suits the occasion better,' Larry had said.

He was *always* concerned about other people's feelings, and since his friend, Isaac, was not exactly in the big leagues, it was obvious he didn't want to arrive in an expensive car, even though it was no secret that he was one of the most successful men in Hollywood.

As she sat in the passenger seat, Taylor steeled herself for the evening ahead. She wasn't exactly a snob, but on the other hand, she'd worked hard to gain her position among the Hollywood élite, and mingling with Larry's not quite so successful friends did not interest her.

'No valet parking?' she remarked, as they finally drove up to the modest home.

'Come on, Taylor,' Larry chided, 'you're not in Beverly Hills now.'

'I was merely thinking that if they're expecting a lot of people . . .' She trailed off, Larry wasn't buying it.

'This is a quiet street in a family neighbourhood,' he pointed out. 'I'm sure we can find a parking spot.'

'Maybe we'll get mugged walking from our car.'

'No, honey,' he admonished. 'That's what happens in town, not here – remember?'

Isaac Griffith was a tall, good-looking black actor, who had appeared in quite a few movies, only never in the leading role. Larry made sure there was always something for him in every one of his films, another thing that pissed Taylor off. If he could find roles for his friends, why couldn't he find one for her? She was, after all, an established actress with a long list of credits. They might not be the best credits in the world, but that was only because of circumstances.

Isaac and Larry hugged each other like long-lost friends, which of course they were.

'This means so much to me, you two coming out here,' Isaac said, including Taylor in his greeting.

'You think I'd miss *your* fiftieth birthday?' Larry said happily. 'You are now an official member of the old farts club!'

'Thanks,' Isaac responded, laughing. 'I'll tell Jenny, it's her turn next year.'

Both men laughed.

Jenny, Isaac's wife, was small, thin and white. She resembled an anorexic ghost with her long, blonde hair and exceptionally pale complexion. She and Isaac had met when they'd both done a stint in an off-Broadway production. They'd fallen in love and she'd moved back to California with him. That had been twenty years previously, and they'd been happily married ever since. They had two children and three dogs.

Taylor was aware that Jenny had been a good friend of Larry's first wife, which did not exactly thrill her. They exchanged cordial greetings, although neither of them was particularly fond of the other.

Once they entered the house, Larry was swamped by a sea of old friends and acquaintances.

Alone, Taylor walked around the large comfortable house, wondering how long Larry would want to stay. Kids and animals seemed to be everywhere. This was not the sort of party she was used to. This was her past, and that's where she wanted it to remain.

She glanced over at Larry. He seemed quite at ease, talking to people as if they were his equals. He simply didn't realize how important and famous he was.

Round tables were set out in the garden, and there was

125

a long buffet trestle, stacks of plastic plates, knives and forks, and a pile of paper napkins. Isaac and some of his friends had begun working the barbecue.

'Why don't you sit down?' Taylor said, finding Larry. 'And I'll fetch you a plate.'

'Don't be silly,' he replied. 'We'll all pitch in.'

He stood in line beside his wife, grinning broadly, waiting for his hamburger and hot dog like everyone else.

'*We* should entertain like this,' he said. 'Our dinners are getting too fancy.'

'You think so?' she said, recalling their last dinner, which had been impeccably catered by Spago. Nothing wrong with *that*.

Larry nodded. 'This is more down-home and friendly,' he said. 'I'm talking to a lot of people I haven't seen in years, and I like it.'

'Whatever you want, darling,' Taylor murmured. She wasn't about to argue with him here.

Isaac came over, dragging another couple. The man was in his fifties, nice-looking with a vaguely familiar air about him. His wife was a short, plump woman with a big gummy smile.

'Say hello to my friends, the Rocks,' Isaac said, flashing his 'I could've been a big star' smile. 'Their son, Oliver, recently sold a spec script for a million bucks. How do you like *that*?'

Taylor was quite speechless. She didn't like it at all.

Chapter Fourteen

By the time their first guests arrived, Nicci was happily stoned, the chef was busy doing his thing in the kitchen, the flowers had arrived and were safely on the table, and Evan was still on the phone.

'Honey,' she called sweetly, buzzing him in his office at the back of the house, 'people are arriving. Can you get off the phone, please?'

'Not now,' he snapped. 'How many times do I have to tell you I'm in the middle of an emergency?'

If it's such a freaking emergency, she thought, *how come Brian isn't by your side helping?*

Actually, she was well aware that Evan was the one who took care of all the business details, while Brian handled the artistic side. Although surely an insane director fell more into the category of artists than business?

She took a quick peek in the kitchen. The annoying chef was balanced on a stool reading her latest copy of *Talk* magazine; an empty bottle of beer stood on the counter in front of him. No food in sight.

'Everything under control?' she asked, trying to sound like an experienced hostess used to dealing with staff.

'Nine o'clock,' he said, winking.

'Shouldn't you be . . . doing something?'

127

'Nine o'clock, sweetbuns,' he repeated, barely glancing at her.

She backed out of the kitchen with a horrible gut feeling that he was a total fuck-up.

Saffron was the first to arrive, dragging her date behind her. He was not exactly what Nicci had expected. Rather than a studly young actor, he was a forty-something, surly, long-haired Latino, in a scuffed brown leather jacket, red Tee, and tight jeans that showed off all his best assets.

Hmm . . . Nicci thought. *Maybe that's the attraction. There has to be* some *reason why Saffron's always attracted to older guys.*

'Meet Ramone,' Saffron said, exotic in a flowing antique coat over cobalt blue satin pants and a sequined tube top, her dark skin gleaming. 'My new best friend.'

'Hi, new best friend,' Nicci said, trying not to stare at his crotch.

His answer was a nod. A man of few words.

'The bar's over there, go fix yourself a drink,' Nicci said, pointing him in the right direction. She turned to Saffron. 'Evan'll be out in a minute – he's on the phone.'

'Place is lookin' good, girl,' Saffron proclaimed, checking everything out. 'How many people you got coming?'

'Brian and whatever date he drags with him. A couple of friends of Evan's, and uh . . . I guess that's it.'

'Quite a stud, huh?' Saffron said, indicating Ramone at the bar.

'If you say so,' Nicci answered evenly. There was no arguing with Saffron when she thought a guy was hot. 'Trust me, he's a stud,' Saffron said, all pleased with herself. 'I'm sure you eyeballed the package?'

'Couldn't miss it.'

Saffron chuckled and hitched up her top. 'I may be getting veree, *veree* lucky later.'

'Oh, and I forgot – my mom might drop by,' Nicci said. 'But that's highly unlikely.'

'Lissa?'

'No,' Nicci said caustically. 'I have another mom I keep in a closet somewhere. *Of course* it's Lissa, you retard.'

'Why would *she* come *here?*' Saffron said, not looking happy.

'Because I invited her.'

'*You* invited your mom?'

'Anything wrong with that?'

Saffron rolled her eyes. 'Can you *imagine* if I had Kyndra to one of *my* dinner parties?'

'You don't *have* dinner parties.'

'No, but I might.'

'And if you did, what would be wrong with Kyndra showing up?'

'For God's sake, get it together, girl. There's *no way* you can cut loose with a *mother* around.'

'Sure you can if your mom is Kyndra or Lissa. They're both way cool.'

'Don't you get it?' Saffron said irritably. 'All the attention gets focused on *them. They* become the dinner party, and *we* become invisible.'

'Oops! Hadn't thought of that.'

'You see my date over there, the one fixing himself half a bottle of Scotch at the bar? You think *he*'ll pay attention to *me* if Lissa Roman walks in? Forget about it.'

'Sorry, I didn't think.'

'No, you didn't,' Saffron said bad-temperedly.

'The thing is,' Nicci explained, lowering her voice, 'Lissa's having a hard time.'

'Yeah,' Saffron drawled sarcastically. 'It must be *real* hard being such an *enormous* movie star, with your CDs selling up the kazoo, and millions of people worshipping your fine ass. Man, I should have it so tough.'

'You don't understand,' Nicci said patiently. 'She's going through a personal crisis.'

'Another one!' Saffron exclaimed. 'Jesus, Lissa and her marital shit suck.'

'I didn't *say* it was marital shit,' Nicci responded, annoyed that Saffron was getting into something that wasn't her business. 'And keep it down, I'm not supposed to tell anyone.'

'Whatever.' Saffron sighed. 'Maybe she won't show.'

Nicci resented Saffron not wanting Lissa there, although she understood her attitude only too well. Having a famous mother was definitely no walk in the park.

Fact of life. Most people were star fucks.

Fact of life. Most people would kick you out of the way to cosy up to a star.

Before she could give it any further thought, Brian strolled in with a zaftig redhead clinging to his arm. Nicci checked her out, she looked as if she'd recently strayed from the grotto at the *Playboy* mansion with her huge fake boobs, cut-out white dress, which could easily double as a swimsuit, and vacant expression.

'Hey, Nic,' Brian said, noncommittal as usual. 'Meet Luba.'

'Hi, Luba,' Nicci said, trying to muster some enthusiasm, although she disliked the girl on sight.

'Luba's Russian,' Brian offered. 'Doesn't speak English, so don't bother.'

What was it about Brian Richter that got her adrenaline pumping? Was it his mussed-up hair? Bedroom eyes? Hard body? No. It was the whole damn package.

'Then how do *you* communicate?' she asked politely.

'How do you *think?*' he replied, squeezing Luba's tiny waist. 'Where's Evan?'

'On the phone, where he's been all day dealing with some kind of director thing.'

'Yeah, that's right,' Brian said disinterestedly. 'Our director, it turns out, is a major fuckhead. I warned Evan about him. As usual he refused to listen.'

'I thought you were partners,' Nicci said. 'Shouldn't you be *helping* Evan deal with it? It's quite obviously some kind of crisis.'

'I let him handle the difficult shit.'

'Big of you,' she said sarcastically.

'It's his deal,' he said, raking her up and down with his sleepy eyes. '*Sexy* dress, Nic. Didn't realize you had a body as well as a mouth.'

'You're so rude,' she said, frowning, although she got off on the compliment.

'Never seen you in a dress before,' he remarked.

'You'll be seeing me in my wedding dress soon enough,' she said crisply.

He leaned towards her. 'Do I smell the faint aroma of my favourite smoke?'

'You do.'

'Hmm . . . you mean Evan allows you to smoke pot? He's always bitching when *I* do it.'

'That's the difference between us,' Nicci said defiantly. 'Evan doesn't tell me what to do about anything.'

'*That*'ll all change when you're married to old Uptight. All you gotta do is wait.'

She tried not to gaze into his bedroom eyes. *This is silly*, she thought, *a schoolgirl crush. It's Evan I love.* 'How come you two don't get along, and yet you still work together?' she asked.

'Get off my case, Nic,' he snapped. 'If you've got a joint stashed somewhere, let's go smoke it. If not, I'm into the vodka.'

'What about Luba?' Nicci asked, indicating his date. 'Is she coming too?'

'I can't take her *everywhere* I go,' he said, straight-faced.

'Then let's dump her,' Nicci said, feeling a tad mean, but so what?

They deposited Luba with Saffron and Ramone at the bar.

'Where you goin'?' Saffron asked.

'We'll be right back,' Nicci promised.

Brian followed her into the bedroom. She opened her bedside drawer, reached in the back and handed him a rolled joint.

'You're more down than I thought,' he said, lighting up.

'What *did* you think – that I was uptight?' she countered.

'Not uptight,' he answered casually. 'Just a kid.'

'Thanks!'

He took a long slow drag, inhaling deeply. 'How come you *wanna* get married? Especially to Evan.'

'I love him,' she answered simply. 'Is that a good enough reason?'

'Nope,' he said, passing her the joint and squinting slightly. 'You need more than that.'

She took a hit. 'Why are you saying this to me?' she asked, determined to find out why he didn't seem to like her.

''Cause I know my brother, and you two are *not* a fit.'

'I'm glad to hear your opinion, Brian,' she said, taking a second hit and almost choking. 'It's very special to me. But we *are* getting married, whether *you* approve or not.'

'Hey, no skin off mine,' he said, as she handed him back the joint. 'Here's to wedded bliss,' he said, once more inhaling deeply. 'Now I'd better return to my scintillating date. She's probably pining for me.'

'Is that what they do, Brian?'

He grinned and shrugged. 'Not my fault they fall all over me.'

Jesus, he was conceited!

'Anyway, thanks for your good wishes,' Nicci said stiffly, adding under her breath as he left the room, 'and fuck you too.'

As soon as he'd gone, she hurried into the bathroom, brushed her teeth, then went into Evan's office, where he was just putting down the phone.

'Everyone's here,' she said, hoping he wouldn't notice she was stoned. 'Well, almost everyone, 'cause that other couple you invited hasn't arrived yet, and since I don't know them anyway, you'd better come out.'

'Jeez!' Evan said, running a hand through his spiky hair. 'Dealing with directors is getting to be worse than dealing with actors.'

'Did you solve everything?' she asked, playing Miss Considerate Wife-to-be to the hilt.

'I hope so,' he said, getting up.

'It's like the United Nations out in the living room,' she said, speaking too fast, but unable to stop herself. 'Brian's with a Russian hooker who doesn't understand English. Saffy's dragged along some old Puerto Rican actor stud, and *I*'m playing perfect hostess trying to make everyone happy.'

Evan gave her a long, appraising stare. 'Have I seen that dress before?' he asked.

'I don't get to wear it much. It was a present from my mom.'

'It's pretty sexy. Are you sure this motley group deserve it?'

'I didn't wear it for *them*. I wore it for you.'

'She *always* knows what to say.'

'Exactly like you.'

'About those shoes,' he said. 'You know I hate it when you're taller than me.'

'Live with it for once,' she purred, snaking her arms around his waist. 'And later, if you're *very, very* good, I'll wear the shoes and nothing else.'

* * *

Dinner was a total disaster. Obviously drunk, the so-called chef served an almost inedible limp Caesar salad, followed by steak so tough a dog would have a hard time eating it.

Evan had marched into the kitchen, paid him off and thrown him out. Then they'd sent out for pizza.

Now Eminem blared on the stereo, his misogynist lyrics and mesmerizing beat assaulting the room.

'What's that music?' Evan asked, not happy with Nicci's choice.

'You don't like it?' she asked.

'It's crap.'

'Everything's crap to you tonight,' she responded. 'The wine's crap, the dinner's crap. It's not *my* fault the chef turned out to be a falling-down drunk.'

'Who recommended him anyway?'

She shrugged. 'Somebody at my kickboxing class.'

'Somebody who's not your friend.'

Fortunately she was too stoned to care that Evan was criticizing her and that their first dinner party was a dud.

Talk about a mismatched group! Ramone was a surly loser, barely speaking to anyone – including Saffron; Luba sat stiffly next to Brian, silent and sulky, huge tits dominating the table. And the other couple Evan invited had failed to turn up. They were the fortunate ones.

'How about putting on some blues or soul?' Saffron suggested, biting into a slice of mushroom and tomato pizza. 'I'm not into this rap deal.'

'Thank you,' Evan said pompously, 'At least *someone*'s got ears.'

Nicci and Brian exchanged a look. He mouthed, 'I like it.'

She grinned and mouthed back, 'So do I!'

And then, with perfect timing as usual, Lissa arrived.

Ramone almost fell off his chair when he saw who it was. Evan immediately jumped up and fussed around her as if she was the President. Saffron scowled.

Nothing like a star to get the evening going.

'We've almost finished dinner,' Nicci said.

'Don't worry, I've already eaten,' Lissa replied graciously, sexy and sleek in black silk pants and a halter top, her platinum hair loose around her shoulders. 'Thought I'd drop by and say hello.'

'And we're very pleased you did,' Evan said, offering her his chair. 'It's always a pleasure to welcome my future mother-in-law.'

'Don't call me that,' Lissa said coolly. 'It sounds so comedic.'

Saffron grimaced at Nicci behind her back. 'Told you so,' she muttered.

'Lissa Roman,' Ramone said reverently, addressing her directly as if they were old friends. 'Your fine videos – they kick ass like a mule.'

Nicci and Brian exchanged another look. 'Who *is* this moron?' he mouthed incredulously.

She shook her head, desperately trying to control a sudden fit of the giggles.

'Glad you like them,' Lissa responded politely.

'The one with the crucifix, the black dude an' the three white chicks,' Ramone continued, eyes on fire, 'that, if I may say so, is one steamin' video.'

'And *you* are?'

'Ramone Lopez,' he announced, flaring his nostrils. 'I should *be* in one of your videos.'

'I'm glad you're so sure,' Lissa murmured.

'Course I'm sure,' Ramone said confidently. 'I'm an actor, an' I dance too. Maybe you saw me on *Law and Order*? I played Rezio – the king-pin drug dealer. Man, I was kickin' it big-time.'

'Missed that, I'm afraid.'

'I can do anythin',' Ramone boasted, shooting her a meaningful look. 'An' I do mean *anythin'*.'

'This is *not* a freakin' audition,' a furious Saffron hissed in his ear. 'For God's sake, cool it.'

He ignored her. Ramone Lopez – no relation to the exquisite Jennifer – was sitting in a room with Lissa Roman, and he was seizing the opportunity.

'So, whaddaya think, Lissa?' he said, preening. 'I gotta give you my number, yes?'

'Well . . .' Lissa said vaguely, then turning to Nicci, she swiftly changed the subject. '*Pizza?* What kind of chef did you hire?'

'Don't ask,' Nicci said, grimacing.

'The chef was a mistake,' Evan said.

'Some *big* mistake,' Brian agreed.

'Have you met Brian, Evan's brother?' Nicci said. 'He's the polite one with the great attitude.'

'Hi, Brian,' Lissa said. She could smell the pot wafting off him. She turned to Saffron. 'Your mom's locked in the recording studio. Even *I* can't get through.'

'What does *your* mom do?' Ramone asked Saffron, quick to sniff out another likely opportunity.

'She's a cleaner,' Saffron snapped, glaring at him.

'Then what's she doin' in a studio?'

How dumb could one guy get? 'Cleaning, of course,' Saffron said, giving him an if-looks-could-kill glare.

'Oh,' Ramone said, focusing back on Lissa. 'I sing, too,' he said, leering in what he considered a sexy fashion. 'An' play the saxophone.' A long, meaningful pause. 'I use my mouth.' He gazed into her eyes. 'A man needs plenty control to play such a . . . sensual instrument. Y'know what I'm sayin'?'

'Christ!' Saffron exclaimed in disgust, jumping up from the table.

Nicci excused herself and followed Saffron out to the patio. 'Sorry,' she said frantically. 'You're like *so* right. I admit – it doesn't work.'

'Can you *believe* that loser?' Saffron said, eyes flashing. 'He's freakin' *auditioning*. On *my* time.'

'Look, it's not Lissa's fault,' Nicci pointed out. 'Ramone's all over *her*.'

'It's not *my* mom's fault either when every guy I ever brought home kissed her ass and ignored me.'

'Some night!' Nicci said, wrinkling her nose.

'Yeah,' Saffron agreed, and then she started to giggle. 'Why am I getting mad anyway? The dude's not worth it. He's just another stud with a big dick and no brains.'

'Dime a dozen,' Nicci said, suddenly giggling too.

'You got it, girl,' Saffron agreed.

And then they both broke up laughing.

Carol was learning new tricks. Either that or she'd decided that hooking Michael sexually was the way to go.

'Oh, my *God*, I'm *so* wet,' she moaned, as they made love balanced on the edge of the bed. 'You make me so very hot, Mikey. I *love* the way you fuck me.'

He did not appreciate her sudden vocal abilities. Nor her calling him Mikey, an abbreviation of his name he'd never liked. Sex to Michael was not a lot of explicit talk, it was more touching and feeling and being together as one. Carol's dialogue reminded him of his ex-wife, and that wasn't a good thing.

'*Please* – I want you to put your cock in my mouth,' Carol crooned. 'I want you to come all over my—'

'Be quiet,' he said abruptly, interrupting her.

'What?' she said, startled.

'Don't speak like that.'

'But I thought—'

'It's not for me, Carol,' he said. What he *really* wanted

to say was 'It makes you sound like a cheap hooker – exactly the way my wife turned out to be.'

Carol was crushed and humiliated. Amber had assured her that after cooking, the second best way to a man's heart was a little sexy talk in bed. 'Low down an' dirty does it every time,' Amber had confided, with a wicked chuckle. And Carol had listened.

'Sorry,' she muttered, highly embarrassed.

But it was too late, he'd already withdrawn.

Chapter Fifteen

After half an hour of being hit on by Saffron's boyfriend, tempered by a few surly remarks from Evan's stoned brother, Lissa realized she had made a big mistake. Excusing herself, she hurried into the bedroom and called Michael from her cellphone. 'Sorry about this,' she whispered. 'I know I'm probably interrupting you in the middle of dinner or something.'

'It's ten o'clock,' he said, keeping an eye on Carol as she scurried into the bathroom, obviously upset. 'I'm not in the middle of anything. Why are you whispering?'

'I did something stupid.'

'You didn't go home I hope.'

'No, I, uh . . . took a cab up to my daughter's fiancé's house for dinner. *Not* a good idea. I am now trapped.'

'In other words,' he said, ridiculously pleased to hear from her, 'you need rescuing?'

'I hope you're in the rescuing business.'

'Give me the address,' he said, reaching for a pad and pencil. 'Rescuing is my specialty.'

'Please get here fast, Michael. I'll wait outside.'

'You're *that* desperate?'

'Believe me.'

She gave him the address, clicked off her cellphone and returned to the living room.

'You're not leaving?' Nicci said, coming in from the patio.

''Fraid so.'

'Everything all right?' Evan asked.

'Uh . . . yes. It's just that I have an early rehearsal for my Vegas show, so I should get going. My back-up dancers are all twelve,' she joked. 'Gotta keep up.'

'I'll walk you to the door,' he offered.

'No need,' she said quickly. 'My driver's right outside.'

Ramone was on his feet in a second. 'Better give you my number,' he said, frantically groping in the pocket of his tight pants for a piece of paper.

'Give it to Nicci,' Lissa said. 'I'll be sure to pass it onto my agent.'

'I'm makin' you a promise,' he said, honouring her with another long, smouldering stare. 'I *am* the man for your next video.'

'I'll keep that in mind, Ramone.'

'See you at the wedding, Mother-in-law,' Brian said, with a lazy grin.

Little stoned shit, she thought. *He knows I don't like the title. Thank God Nicci chose the other brother.*

Once outside she took a long, deep breath. *What a bad move that was*, she thought. *Nicci and her friends – no thank you.*

'I gotta go out,' Michael said, as Carol emerged from the bathroom.

She knew immediately it was because of what she'd said, the dirty words which were so foreign to her. She was mad at herself. Why the heck had she listened to Amber? 'Michael,' she said, wrapped in his white toweling robe. 'I have to explain. You see, it—'

'No need to explain anything,' he said, anxious to get going. 'I really *do* have to go out.'

'Oh,' she said, deflated.

'There's a client who's in trouble,' he explained, trying to let her down easily because she looked so crestfallen. 'An important client.'

'Can I help?' she asked hopefully.

'No.'

'Then I'll wait up for you,' she said, clutching his robe tightly across her body.

'Uh . . . Carol, I think it's better if you go home tonight,' he said, pulling on his pants.

'Why?'

''Cause I'll probably get back late,' he said, reaching for his favourite sweatshirt. 'And I wouldn't want to wake you. It'll suit me better if you go home.'

'It'll suit *you* better,' she repeated, a touch tight-lipped.

He could smell a fight a mile away, and now was definitely not showdown time. 'For me, honey,' he said, giving her a quick kiss to soften the blow. 'Sometimes I need to be alone. You can understand that, can't you?'

She nodded miserably. He wasn't giving her much choice.

Michael arrived in record time. Lissa hurriedly climbed into his jeep before he had a chance to get out. 'Thanks for coming,' she said breathlessly.

'No problem,' he said, shooting her a quick look.

'The hotel was closing in on me,' she explained, noting how good he looked in Levi's and an old sweatshirt. 'I had to get out.'

'No explanations,' he said, starting to drive.

'I wish I could go to my own home now,' she said wistfully, as they headed down the hill.

'And what'll you do if Gregg turns up at four in the morning ready for a fight?'

'You think he might?'

'Pissed-off husbands are capable of anything,' he said, shooting her another quick look. 'You're not gonna like me asking this – but does he have a gun?'

'Aren't you being overly dramatic?' she replied, drumming her fingers on the dashboard.

'Does he?' Michael persisted.

'Not that I'm aware of.'

'Maybe he keeps one on him.'

'Now you're making me nervous.'

'Didn't mean to do that.'

'Are you suggesting that if he *did* have a gun he might use it?'

'You never know with people,' Michael said, his handsome face serious. 'I've seen things you wouldn't believe.'

'Really?'

'Yes, really, Lissa.'

She was silent for a moment. Why had she phoned Michael to come and get her? She could've called for a cab, summoned Chuck, contacted Danny.

But no, she'd called Michael Scorsinni. Why?

Because you like him.

No. I don't. Well, yes, maybe I do, but not in a romantic way.

Sure.

'I hope I didn't drag you out of bed with your girlfriend,' she said, fishing for information.

'*What* girlfriend?' he responded with a half-smile.

'There must be *someone* special.'

A beat while he didn't answer. Then – 'Do you fancy stopping for ice cream?'

'Ice cream?' she said, laughing softly. 'What are we – back in high school?'

'I'm having a sugar-attack,' he explained, which was a lie: he simply wanted to spend more time with her.

'Ice cream – no,' she said slowly. 'But I wouldn't mind a drink.'

'I don't drink,' he said, staring straight ahead.

'How come?' she asked, studying his almost perfect profile.

He took a long slow beat. 'Lissa, I'm a recovering alcoholic,' he said at last, wondering why the hell he was revealing such a personal piece of information to a woman he barely knew.

'Oh,' she said, suddenly uncomfortable. 'Sorry.'

'Hey,' he said easily, 'there's nothing to be sorry about. I've been sober ten years, it's no big deal.'

'Then why do you call yourself an alcoholic?' she asked curiously.

'Because that's what I am,' he stated flatly, 'and that's what I'll always be.'

There, he'd told her. He usually waited a while before telling people. But he kind of liked the idea of being totally up-front with this woman. Not that they were headed towards anything other than a business relationship.

'Do you go to AA?' she inquired.

'I try to make it to a weekly meeting.'

'Even though you don't drink any more?'

'It keeps me sane.'

'Well, then,' she said lightly, 'I wouldn't want to tempt you by luring you into a bar.'

'Nothing tempts me, Lissa,' he said, rubbing his chin with his index finger. 'I got will-power of steel.'

'Lucky you,' she murmured. 'I wish I did.'

'So,' he said, 'we'd better come up with a place where you won't be recognized.'

'How about my hotel room?' she suggested, realizing that it probably wasn't appropriate, but it was the only private place she could think of.

'No,' he said, shaking his head.

'I promise I won't jump you,' she responded, amused.

He ignored her stab at humour. 'It's not a clever idea for me to be seen going into your room,' he said. 'If Gregg got to hear about it . . .'

'I'll give you the key,' she said, strangely reluctant to say good night. 'Wait five minutes, *then* come up.'

He glanced across at her. 'You're serious?'

'Why do I have to explain myself?' she said, a tad irritated. 'I'm not tired and I feel like talking. Is that okay with you?'

'*You*'re the client, Lissa,' he said evenly. And then he smiled. 'Although you gotta realize I'll have to charge you overtime.'

'You drive a hard bargain, Mr Scorsinni,' she said, smiling also.

'Yeah.' Another long beat. 'I know.'

'You're very quiet,' Larry said, on the drive home. 'I had a good time. How about you?'

Taylor adjusted her seat-belt. She didn't know *what* to think. She'd just spent an evening with Oliver Rock's parents, his proud *parents*, for crissakes, and Larry wanted to know if she'd had a good time.

'It was enjoyable,' she managed.

'Yes,' Larry said firmly. 'It was. I'd like to see more of Isaac and Jenny.'

'We will,' she murmured.

'*You*'re our social director,' Larry said. 'Make it happen.'

Was he giving her an order? She wasn't one of his minions he could boss around.

Maybe she should give him a blow job just to prove who the *real* boss was. Then again, maybe not. She was tired and hardly in a terrific mood.

'The Rocks were nice, too,' Larry said. 'We should invite them over with Isaac and Jenny. Make a date for next week. Okay?'

'No, it's not okay,' she wanted to say. 'They're my lover's parents, for God's sake. It's not okay at all.'

But, of course, Larry didn't know that. And she had no intention of him ever finding out.

'Thank *God* Lissa's gone!' Saffron exclaimed, jumping up and cornering Nicci. 'I'm dumping Ramone big-time,' she confided. 'Have you ever *seen* such a suck-up loser?'

Nicci wasn't listening, she had one eye on Brian, who was also on his feet.

'Thanks for dinner, Nic,' he said, heading for the door. 'Now I gotta split.'

'It was horrible, wasn't it?' she responded, half hoping he'd disagree.

'Pretty bad,' he said, with a jaunty wink.

'We can always do it again,' she said, observing that Miss Russia was already standing by the door – no doubt anxious to get him to herself so she could ravish his sexy body.

'Gonna pass on that.'

'Maybe at *your* house next time?' she suggested, imagining him and the Russian indulging in wild sex.

'Don't have a house. Got an apartment, an' it's a pit.'

'Why am I *so* not surprised?'

He gave her a long, stoned look. 'Don't ever use that chef again.'

She stared right back at him. 'Don't ever bring Miss Russia here again.'

A slight grin. 'Oh, so now you're a girlfriend critic?'

She moved a little closer to him. 'Can I ask you something, Brian?'

'Ask away.'

'How come you're with someone who doesn't even speak English?'

'Who needs conversation?'

'Is sex the only thing on your mind?'

'You've been spending too much time with my brother, Nic. Better get yourself a life.'

And so the evening ended. Nicci was crushed. It had not turned out exactly as expected.

'That was a shitty night,' Evan grumbled, after everyone had finally left.

He was right, it couldn't have been any worse.

'*Now* can you turn that crap music off?' he said, busily emptying ashtrays. 'It's giving me a headache.'

She did as he asked and waited for him to say something nice. He didn't.

For once they went to bed without making love.

Their first dinner party.

Their first fight.

If this is what marriage to Evan was going to be like, then maybe she was about to make the biggest mistake of her life.

Lissa called room service, ordered a selection of ice creams with hot chocolate sauce, and instructed the operator to have the waiter leave the cart outside the door. Then she raided the mini bar and poured herself a brandy.

As soon as room service delivered, Michael stepped outside and brought the cart in.

'This is crazy.' Lissa sighed, settling on the couch and kicking off her shoes.

'Crazy how?' Michael replied.

'Me, in a hotel room,' she said restlessly. 'Do you realize how much *work* I've got coming up? There's my Vegas show, a book I'm supposed to be collaborating on, a new CD to plan. I don't have time to sit around in a hotel doing nothing.'

'Hey, listen,' he said, trying not to stare, because in spite of the black eye well-disguised with makeup, she truly was *the* most breathtaking woman he'd ever seen. 'You wanted your husband out, right?'

'Yes.'

'Then that's what you got.'

'Fine, but please can I go home in the morning?'

'You can,' he said, dipping into the ice cream. 'And if it's okay with you, I'd like to put on extra security for a week or two.'

'You don't think he'll do anything crazy, do you?' she asked anxiously.

'He'll probably use the media to get to you. He can hide behind 'em.'

'You don't even know Gregg, yet you imagine the worst of him.'

'I've dealt with this kind of case before – you're not my first famous client.'

'I'm not, huh?' she said, mildly flirting because she couldn't help herself. 'And I was under the impression I was special.'

'You *are* special.' A long beat. 'All of our clients are special.'

She did not appreciate being lumped together with the entire roster of Robbins-Scorsinni's clients. 'How's the ice cream?' she asked, finishing her brandy.

'Pretty damn good.'

She got up and helped herself to another small bottle of brandy from the mini bar. 'I used to make ice cream from scratch when I was a kid,' she said, remembering one of her few happy childhood memories.

'Hidden talents, huh?'

'You could say that,' she replied, settling back on the couch.

He felt tense and yet comfortable in her presence. There was something about her that kept drawing him closer.

'Tell me about your ex-wife,' she said, slowly sipping her brandy.

'There's not much to tell.'

'There must be *something*,' she insisted, fixing him with an intent look. 'When did you get divorced?'

'I guess you could say that technically we never did. She ran off to L.A. while I was still living in New York.' He was silent for a moment before adding, 'Later she was found . . . murdered.'

Lissa sat up straight. 'Are you *serious?*'

'She got involved with the wrong people. Rita had a way of doing that.'

'Michael . . . I'm so sorry.'

He shrugged. 'It was a difficult time.'

'I *bet* it was.'

Christ! If he kept this up, she'd think he was the world's worst loser. First the alcoholic thing, and then the murdered wife. 'Uh . . . listen,' he said, 'if you don't mind, I'd sooner not discuss it.'

Hmm, Lissa thought, *a man who doesn't want to talk about himself. How unusual.*

'Tell me about you instead,' he said, determined to change tracks.

'I'm sure you've read all about me.'

'I'm probably one of the few who hasn't,' he replied, 'and I'd like to know.'

'Why?'

'Do I have to come up with a reason?'

'Well . . .' she said slowly. 'How about I give you the condensed version?'

'Go ahead.'

She started the recital, a tale she'd told hundreds of times – usually to journalists. 'I ran away from home at sixteen. Went to New York to be a dancer, married a boy my age, moved to L.A. where we lived in one room with three other people for a year.' She grimaced at the memory. 'Naturally he cheated on me, so we got divorced. Then a few years later I was discovered.'

'Discovered?'

'Oh, you know, "I'm gonna make you a star" kind of discovered. There was a producer who liked me – he put me in a movie, and after that my career kind of took off.'

'Sounds like you made all the right moves.'

'Not really,' she said wryly. 'I met Antonio, husband number two, when I was nineteen, and before I could even think about it we were on a plane to Vegas where we got married. Nine months later I had a baby girl.'

'Makes you a young mother.'

'Raising a child is such a big responsibility.' She sighed. 'I know I haven't devoted enough time to Nicci. She spent most of her teenage years with her father in Europe.' Another long sigh. 'We're not as close as we should be.'

'It's never too late to do something about that,' he said, finishing his ice cream and taking a quick peek at his watch. 'Gotta go,' he said, standing up. 'You get some sleep. I'll be back in the morning to drive you home.'

'I don't want to be alone, Michael,' she said, suddenly panicking. 'Not in a hotel. Not tonight. Can't you stay?'

He wasn't quite sure if she was coming on to him or not. But he reasoned that even if she was, he had to keep this on a business level. Quincy would kill him if he got involved with a client.

And yet . . . he wasn't made of stone, and Lissa Roman was an incredibly vibrant and sexy woman. Although, at this particular moment in time, she was also a very vulnerable woman, and the worst thing he could do would be to take advantage of the situation.

'Y'know, Lissa,' he said slowly, 'I'm not good at sleeping on couches. I'll come back tomorrow.'

She gave him a long, lingering look. 'And I'm not good at taking no for an answer.'

'I can believe that,' he said, as he headed briskly for the door. 'Eight o'clock too early?'

'You're a hard man,' she murmured softly, liking him even more because he didn't jump, and most men usually did.

'I have to be in my profession,' he said.

And then he was gone. Leaving her thinking that he was probably the most interesting man she'd come across in a long time.

Chapter Sixteen

When Nicci's boyfriend arrived back in town, it put Eric in a foul mood. The things they got up to were making him ill. They were disgusting, perverted sexual sickos. It was all he could do to force himself to watch.

And watch he did. Day and night.

He watched them bouncing around like a couple of acrobats doing things he'd imagined only took place in porno movies. He was outraged. Nicci was a slut and a whore – like her mother. She deserved everything she was about to get.

In his mind he knew Nicci better than she knew herself. He knew her favourite clothes, what she liked to eat, her reckless driving, how she hardly ever saw her famous mother. He even went through her trash on a daily basis.

He also knew that even though they weren't close, once he had her precious daughter, Lissa Roman would pay. Oh, yes. Because if she didn't . . .

That night, crouched in the bushes with his usual view of the house, he was surprised to observe that Nicci and her boyfriend were entertaining. He could see everything – he even spotted the chef pissing in their salad dressing. He almost laughed aloud at *that* little scenario. It reminded him of the times *he'd* pissed in other people's food.

The kick was seeing their dinner guests sitting around

the dining table, thinking they were being grandly entertained, while the chef was in the kitchen pissing in their
salad! The things you saw when people lived in glass houses.

When Lissa herself arrived, he was surprised.

Lissa Roman. Money-cow. Slut. Whore.

The following afternoon he went with Arliss to the
building where he worked as caretaker. The skinny man had
done an excellent job of setting up an escape-proof room in
a gloomy, windowless basement buried at the bottom of the
building. Arliss was quite proud of himself. 'See? I put an
old cot bed in the corner,' he boasted. 'An' a bucket for
pissin'. An' over there's an orange crate for puttin' food
on.'

He'd also affixed two heavy-duty locks and a padlock to
the door, plus he'd fashioned a crude peephole, which
pleased Eric. It meant he could watch her at close quarters
whenever he felt like it.

'Good work,' Eric said.

Not used to praise, Arliss preened.

This is going to be easy, Eric thought. *Why didn't I come
up with this idea years ago?*

Tonight they were recruiting the others. Arliss had set
up a meeting, warning everyone beforehand that something
was about to go down that could make them big bucks. By
the time Eric arrived at the bar that night, Arliss had Little
Joe, Davey and Big Mark all settled in a booth.

'Hiya, big boy,' Pattie said, accosting him on his way in.

Why don't you put on some clothes? he wanted to say. *What
kind of a job has you standing around with your tits hanging
out?* Instead he nodded curtly and headed for the booth.

Arliss jumped up as he approached. 'You know everyone,' he said, chewing on a strand of straggly hair.

'I certainly do,' Eric replied, his flat, cold eyes carefully
checking them out. 'How about I buy you boys a round of
drinks?'

'Sounds good to me,' Davey 'The Animal' said. He'd got the nickname 'The Animal' because he resembled a ferret, and whenever he spoke he made disgusting snorting noises in the back of his throat.

'Me, too,' said Little Joe, a rotund, short man, with pop eyes and a moth-eaten moustache.

Eric knew everything about both of them. Little Joe worked as a male orderly in a mental home, and Davey toiled in a wrecking yard. Two useful jobs for what Eric had in mind.

He clicked his fingers for Pattie.

'Yes, hon?' she called, hurrying to the booth, pleased that he'd summoned her. Eric was about the only gentleman she'd ever encountered, so she paid him extra attention. The trouble was, he never seemed to notice she existed, a sad fact she planned on doing something about.

'Drinks for everyone,' Eric said magnanimously. 'Give 'em anything they want.'

'Oooh, *you*'re a big spender tonight,' Pattie said archly, sticking her droopy tits in his direction.

Eric ignored her.

Big Mark shifted in his chair. 'When we gonna find out what's on yer mind?' he said, reaching down to scratch his balls with an over-large, hairy hand.

'Any minute now,' Eric said smoothly, thinking that if anyone was going to give him grief, it would be this huge hulk of a man. '*If* I bring you in, I expect loyalty all the way. We'll work as a team, which means anyone who doesn't care to be involved, should get up and leave now.'

Big Mark looked like he might do just that. But then he changed his mind and stayed put.

It was at that moment that Eric knew he had them exactly where he wanted them.

Greed had drawn them in.

And very soon it would be time to put his plan into motion.

Chapter Seventeen

Lissa's dumping of her fourth husband hit the airwaves with a vengeance. And Gregg Lynch was not about to depart quietly. Angry and out for revenge, he'd decided to be more than vocal, trying to sell his story to every magazine and television programme that would pay him. According to him, Lissa Roman was a selfish, obsessed, career-crazy bitch, with absolutely no concern for anyone except herself.

To Lissa's great relief, he'd not shown up at the house except the first night when he'd arrived to find the locks changed and his possessions stacked up outside. Fortunately, thanks to Michael, she'd not been there to witness his fury.

Exactly as Michael had predicted, Gregg had gone straight to the media. What a publicity whore *he*'d turned out to be. She hated the fact that she'd actually *married* the asshole. Another big mistake. When was she going to learn?

She instructed her lawyer to arrange the quickest divorce on record.

Michael had put on extra security in case of trouble. Two ex-cops who worked part-time for the agency patrolled the grounds of her house, making sure she was not bothered by the hordes of paparazzi and TV crews who'd taken up residence outside her gates – all thanks to Gregg, who kept on promising them a public showdown.

A public showdown. Who the *hell* did he think he was?

She knew exactly who he was. A dead-beat songwriter, with no money, a vicious temper and a big dick. Like *he* could create a public showdown.

Unfortunately, she was well aware that if he wanted to, he could. She vaguely remembered an Oscar-nominated English actress whose long-time husband had created a horrible scene outside the Oscar ceremony because he wasn't invited. The press had gone berserk, writing about the event as if it was headline news. Lissa dreaded that kind of publicity. She didn't mind promoting her movies and music, but when it came to anything personal, she cringed.

Her friends rallied as soon as they found out. James came to the house and spent hours counselling her on how she'd done the right thing. He claimed he knew Gregg had been screwing around for months.

'Then why didn't you tell me?' she'd wanted to ask. But she didn't, because what good would it do to get on James's case?

Stella dropped by and talked incessantly about the impending birth of her twins, the perils of using a surrogate, and the movie she was in pre-production on. 'I hope he signed a pre-nup,' were Stella's final words before departing.

'Of course,' Lissa said, silently thanking her lawyer for insisting that Gregg sign.

'He'll try to break it,' Stella warned. 'They always do.'

Kyndra phoned. So did Taylor. They both promised to visit soon. Danny, Chuck and Nellie were great – her faithful home team – anticipating anything she wanted and protecting her in every way. She was lucky to have them.

A huge number of acquaintances tried to reach her, but she refused to take any calls, realizing that all they were after was juicy gossip they could pass around.

She threw herself into rehearsals for her Vegas show, and attempted to ignore the publicity blitz.

Max was beside himself. 'Why didn't you warn me?' he complained, almost jumping up and down in frustration. 'I need an immediate statement from you, *something*. Your soon-to-be ex is shooting his mouth off everywhere.'

'I can't help that,' Lissa answered, feeling surprisingly calm. 'In a few weeks this'll all go away.'

'Bullshit,' Max grumbled. 'Gregg is money-hungry and vindictive, a bad combination. He's out to destroy you, Lissa, and *you* don't get it.'

'Do you really think he can, Max?'

'No. However, I'd sooner you gave me a statement showing him up for the liar he is. The press loves you, but you gotta give 'em *something*.'

'I have no intention of indulging in a public show-down,' she said coolly. 'You know that's not my style.'

'A brief statement does not make it a showdown,' Max spluttered. 'Say nothing, an' the press'll *never* leave you alone.'

'Okay,' she said reluctantly. 'I'll come up with a statement.'

'Soon,' Max warned. 'We'd better get some kind of lid on this before your Vegas appearance.'

'I understand, Max. I'll get something over to you today.'

The reporter was small, blonde and compact, with an ageless, well-preserved air about her. Her name was Belinda Barrow, she'd been on television for quite a number of years, and considered herself equally as important as the stars she interviewed. Currently she was the on-camera talent for a weekly half-entertainment, half-reality show called *The Real News*.

Gregg looked her over and decided she was easy pickings. He needed a score and she could be it.

They made polite conversation before the cameras started to roll, he gave her the sincere act, and she seemed to go for it.

As soon as the red light came on, Belinda switched into interviewer mode. 'So tell me, Gregg,' she said, an eager, almost hungry look in her guileless hazel eyes, 'you were married to Lissa Roman for almost two years. If she was as difficult as you *say*, then how come you stayed married for as long as you did?'

'Lissa is a very insidious woman,' Gregg said, playing to the camera. 'She gets off on drama. Whenever I attempted to leave, she always managed to pull me back in.'

'How so?'

'Well . . . she kinda threatened suicide, told me she couldn't live without me, that sorta thing.'

'How soon after you were married did you try to leave?'

'It must've been on our honeymoon. I immediately realized she was unstable. I stayed because I felt sorry for her. And naturally, I loved her.'

'I see,' Belinda said. 'So you stayed with her because you felt sorry for her?'

'Yeah, that's right.'

'Do you realize how many men watching this programme will be pulling their hair out to hear you say that? After all, Lissa Roman is one of the most beautiful and talented women in movies today.'

'Beauty's only skin deep, Belinda,' Gregg said, liking the sound of his own cliché. 'It's what's within that matters. And within Lissa Roman there lurks a black soul.'

'Isn't that rather harsh?' Belinda asked, playing up the sympathy angle.

'She threw me out on the street in the middle of the night with no warning, nothing,' Gregg complained. 'Now I'm virtually penniless. Not only did I give up my career to help her, I also spent all my own money on her.'

'That's too bad, Gregg,' Belinda murmured.

'None of this seems to bother Lissa Roman,' Gregg continued angrily, 'although I hope it bothers her fans. I hope that when they realize the kind of woman she is, they'll stop buying her music and watching her movies.'

'That's not a very charitable thing to say, Gregg,' Belinda said, not wishing to come across as a bitch.

'*You* didn't have to live with her for two years,' Gregg snapped.

And so the interview continued in the same vein.

When they were finished, Gregg leaned across to Belinda, feeling quite pumped up with his own importance. 'When does this air?' he asked.

'Next week,' she said, shuffling her notes. 'I'll edit later.'

'You'll leave in the plug for the CD I'm about to record?' he asked eagerly.

'Well . . .'

He decided she needed some extra attention. 'Can I buy you a drink, Belinda?'

'Sure,' she said, slightly flustered. 'I guess that's possible.'

'Anything's *possible*, right?'

And she nodded her neat blonde head.

A week after their disastrous dinner party, Evan left for another location. Fortunately his bad mood had not lasted past that one evening. Since then he'd returned to his normal self – he'd even bought Nicci a present from Tiffany's, an exquisite diamond butterfly pin with emerald wings. She already had a diamond engagement ring (six carats), which, much to Evan's annoyance, she wore on a black ribbon hanging around her neck, claiming that wearing it on her engagement finger was too traditional.

'What's this for?' she'd asked suspiciously, when he'd given her the pin.

'For promising to marry me,' he'd said.

How could she have ever experienced any doubts? He was amazing. They were destined to be deliriously happy. One wedding coming up.

Antonio had sent her an e-mail informing her of his arrival. It so happened that on the day he was flying in, Lissa was leaving for Vegas.

Gregg was behaving as badly as everyone had expected, literally hogging the headlines. He'd even managed to drag Nicci into some of his stories, calling her the poor little neglected daughter.

Poor little neglected daughter indeed! How *dare* the creep involve her? She was beyond furious. Gregg Lynch was an untalented piece of crap. Why did her mom have such bad taste in men?

And yet Lissa had taught her well. *Ignore the tabloids. Do not answer back. Keep a dignified silence.* Which is exactly what she did, failing to return the many calls she received from the press.

Saffron dropped by, waving a copy of *Truth & Fact*, a particularly scurrilous rag. 'Get an eyeful of *this!*' she announced, thrusting the magazine at Nicci.

On the front page there was a picture of Ramone Lopez in a shirt opened to the waist, multiple gold chains and tight black jeans. He was leaning against a wall, leering at the camera. The headline read: *My Night of Bliss With Lissa Roman.*

'Oh . . . my . . . God!' Nicci gasped, horrified. 'I don't believe it!'

'*You* don't believe it,' Saffron snorted, tossing back her

dreadlocks. 'How do you think *I* feel? *I'm* the sucker who brought him into your house.'

'This is unreal!' Nicci said, starting to read the story aloud. ' "Our eyes met and I knew there was something between us that could never be forgotten. Lissa looked at me and said, 'You are the man I've been searching for.' " Like what planet is this asshole from?'

'Wait till you read the rest of it,' Saffron said, opening the fridge and helping herself to a Sprite. 'According to Ramone, they've formed a bond for the rest of their lives, and she's starring him in her next video.'

Nicci threw the magazine down in disgust. 'I'm sure Mom's lawyer will have a major party when he sees this crap.'

'And speaking of parties . . .'

'Don't tell me *you*'re entertaining?'

'Better than that,' Saffron said, with a secretive smile. 'Very shortly *you* are being kidnapped.'

'Huh?'

'Kidnapped, babe,' Saffron crowed. 'One spectacular bachelorette night coming up, so be prepared. You'll be blindfolded, taken out of your house, and you'll have no *idea* what is gonna happen. Cool?'

'Wow!' Nicci said, thinking it sounded like a blast. 'What'll I wear?'

'Anything you like. You may not be keeping it on all night.'

'Will I be leaving the state?'

'Maybe,' Saffron said mysteriously.

'You gotta tell me more than that.'

'I don't gotta do anything,' Saffron said, laughing. 'It's all one big surprise.'

'Fine.'

'How's Lissa doin' with all this bad publicity?'

'She's cool.'

'You goin' to Vegas to see her show?'

'She doesn't think it's a good idea.'

'How come?'

''Cause of all the press,' Nicci explained. 'Lissa has always tried to keep me out of the papers.'

'That's 'cause having a nineteen-year-old daughter makes her feel old.'

'Lissa, *old?*' Nicci burst out laughing. She's only forty, Saff, an' looks unbelievable.'

'I'm tellin' you – having a grown kid makes 'em nutto,' Saffron insisted. 'Kyndra's the same way, she'd *love* to keep me under wraps – it pisses her off when I'm in *People* an' shit. But I'm an actress, so I need all the publicity I can get.'

'Okay, so back to my special night,' Nicci said, decidedly psyched at the thought of a wild night on the town. 'Tell me when, and gimme the guest list.'

'It's a kidnap, babe,' Saffron said succinctly, revealing nothing. 'Everything that happens is a *big* mystery.'

'As long as you don't have Ramone strip for me.'

'Girl, *believe* me, *that*'s a promise.'

Gregg knew there was one place he was in complete control, and that was in bed. Nobody had ever accused him of being a dud between the sheets. He'd always been lucky in that respect, and women were so stupid that they always fell for his boyish charm and bullshit lines. All he had to do was turn it on.

Gregg was well aware that he'd better get himself into a new relationship fast, because since Lissa had thrown him out, he'd been forced to move into a crummy hotel due to lack of funds. Lissa had controlled the money. Miss Moneybags's business manager had doled him out an allowance, which came to an abrupt halt the minute his luggage was shoved out the door. All he had going for him was his Ferrari.

Man, would he like to show the cunt a thing or two. But

what he needed now was somewhere to stay, and money, so he could hire himself a sharp lawyer and start figuring out what to do next. Belinda seemed a likely prospect.

'Where do you live?' he asked, as they entered the Polo Lounge.

'I have a house in the Hollywood Hills,' she said.

Sounds promising, he thought.

They sat in the Polo Lounge drinking martinis, and he listened as she poured out her woes. Naturally she had many, considering she was a woman of a certain age who lived and worked in Hollywood. He reckoned that although she looked pretty good – probably on account of major plastic surgery – she had to be at least fifty-two or -three.

They talked for two hours. Or, rather, he allowed her to ramble on. She let it all out, telling him how she'd been married three times and how her last husband, a sometime actor, had run off with the pool man. Then she revealed that her station manager didn't like her, and she'd had to leave her last job because her co-presenter would not quit coming on to her. And finally she complained about what a struggle it was to stay young and fresh-looking – a prerequisite for any woman on TV.

He managed to look interested. He managed to throw in a compliment here and there, so that when it came time to leave, she was not averse to him stopping by her house for a drink. And everyone knew what *that* led to.

By the time he got into her bed she was frantic – it had obviously been a while. She was a screamer, too, and he worked diligently, making her very happy indeed, tending to all her needs, including going down on her for a full twenty minutes, which left a sour taste in his mouth. It didn't matter. Gregg knew what worked when he was out to achieve something in a hurry, so he held nothing back.

Apart from his prowess in bed, there was also the added attraction that he was Lissa Roman's husband. He was sure that Belinda wouldn't mind boasting that she'd entertained *him* in her bed and that *she* was the replacement for one of the most famous women in the world.

Yes, Gregg wanted more than one night, and he certainly knew how to go about getting it.

Chapter Eighteen

'Brian's flying into L.A. for a day,' Evan said over the phone from Utah, their current location.

'So?' Nicci replied. She was in her car on the way to a final fitting for her wedding dress, and she didn't want to hear about Brian. She had him tucked firmly to the back of her mind.

'He'll drop by the house to pick up some papers. They're in the bottom left-hand drawer of my desk.'

'How come Brian's coming back and you're not?'

'It's crazy here, Nic. This movie is the most difficult I've ever worked on.'

'I thought that when it came to work you and Brian did everything together.'

'We do, but he's got to take care of a couple of things in L.A. He'll only be there one night, so he'll phone you. Where are you now?'

'In the car.'

'Call me from my desk when you get home, and I'll tell you exactly what to put in the envelope. Don't let Brian anywhere near my desk. Hand him the envelope and get him out of there.'

'Yes, *sir*!'

What was this? A test? Was God testing her to see if she could be a good girl in Brian's presence? Not that he'd ever

164

indicated he liked her, but they'd shared a joint and a couple of moments across the room at that unmemorable dinner party.

So why was her heart beating so rapidly? And why had she lost all interest in a fitting for her wedding dress?

'I hate dresses,' she muttered to herself. 'Dunno why we're having such a big wedding anyway.'

Because Evan's mother wants it, that's why. And what Evan's mother wants, apparently Evan's mother gets.

Larry was driving Taylor insane. So was Oliver. It was almost as if they'd formed a conspiracy designed to make her crazy. First of all, Larry was insistent that the very next week they invite Isaac and Jenny for dinner along with the Rocks.

'Why would you want that other couple?' Taylor complained. 'We have nothing in common with them.'

'It's not necessary to have things in common to spend an enjoyable evening,' Larry explained. 'Stan Rock seems like an intelligent man. Anyway, I promised I'd have them over, so that's what we're doing. He wants to talk to me about his son – thinks this huge sale on the boy's script might go to his head. After all, the kid's recently scored himself a million bucks, so Stan has asked me to give him some pointers on how to handle himself.'

'Give *who* pointers?' Taylor asked, alarmed.

'His son,' Larry said patiently.

'His son,' Taylor repeated dully. '*You*'re going to meet with his son?'

How had this happened? How had she fallen into such an impossible situation?

The day after Isaac's party, she called Oliver. He sounded out of it, but at least he picked up his phone.

'Where were you yesterday?' she demanded.

'Uh . . . Jeez!' Oliver mumbled. 'Guess I was out gettin' stoned. Sorry – did we have a meeting?'

'I told you I was coming by to discuss my script.'

'Yeah, well, this has all been kinda like one big surprise.'

'It's a surprise to me, too,' she said frostily. 'And I had an even bigger surprise last night. We went to a friend of Larry's for dinner, and guess who I met?'

'Who?'

'I'm sure they'll call you with the news any minute.' A dramatic pause. 'I met your parents.'

There was a dead silence.

'Your parents, Oliver,' she repeated, waiting for his reaction.

'Jesus Christ!' He began laughing hysterically. 'You met Molly and Stanley? The original Mr and Mrs Suburbia? How the fuck didja meet *them?*'

'It's a long story,' she said grimly. 'I'm coming over now.'

'Okay, but I got a lunch.'

Her surprise was evident. '*You*'ve got a lunch?'

'My agent's fixed it for me to meet some of the other agency dudes. Everyone's kinda blown away by what's happenin'. I'm like in shock myself.'

'I'm sure you are, only let's not forget that you and I have a business deal.'

'No contract, right?'

His words infuriated her. Had he been getting legal advice on the side? 'I paid you, Oliver,' she said coldly. 'You promised to read my script, make comments, help me with it. *Now* what are you saying?'

'Like I didn't realize I'd be selling my screenplay, did I?'

'Obviously not.'

'Don't sweat it, Tay, I got comments for you.'

'How comforting.'

'An' if you're not happy, I'll give you back your money. Course,' he added jauntily, 'I gotta get it first, 'cause I spent what you gave me. But now I got big bucks comin' in – eventually.'

'I sincerely hope you haven't been wasting my time, Oliver.'

'Neither of us was exactly wasting time,' he said with a lewd chuckle. 'We were both gettin' something we wanted.'

'I'm on my way,' she said, irritated by his cocky attitude. 'We'll talk then.'

She'd driven over to his place and things weren't the same. Neither of them initiated sex. The million dollars – not to mention his parents – had come between them with a vengeance.

Oliver informed her that the dialogue in her script was tired and old-fashioned.

She informed him that he was an arrogant little prick and she wanted her money back.

They parted bad friends.

Several days later Larry walked into the house accompanied by Oliver. She could not believe her eyes, her stomach did a double flip.

'Hi, sweetheart,' Larry said, pushing his glasses up on his nose. 'Decided to come home for lunch. This is Stan Rock's kid, Oliver, the million-dollar wonder.'

Oliver had the temerity to look her straight in the eye, extend his hand and say, 'Pleasure to meet you, Mrs Singer.'

It was a good job she was an actress, because how she managed to keep an impassive expression was a miracle when all she really wanted to do was run screaming from the house.

'We'll be in my office,' Larry said. 'I read Oliver's script and it's quite something. Can you be a sweetheart and have Edna fix us a sandwich?'

Taylor nodded numbly, thinking all the while, *This isn't happening to me, this isn't happening to me . . .*

So now it was obvious that Larry was planning to help Oliver with his script – not that Oliver needed any help: he'd sold his damn script for a shitload of money.

When it came to *her* script, Larry had no time. But for Oliver Rock, a total stranger, he had plenty of time. This was a ludicrous situation.

She yelled for the housekeeper and told her to see what Mr Singer and his guest wanted for lunch. Then she marched into her dressing room, picked up the phone and called Dennis Mann, her agent. 'Remember that cable offer you came to me with a couple of weeks ago?' she said briskly.

'The one Larry made you turn down?' Dennis said.

'He didn't *make* me,' she said irritably. 'He simply didn't think playing a lesbian was good for my image.'

'Or *his*,' Dennis interjected.

'I've decided to accept it,' she said, not interested in Dennis's comments.

'You have?'

'Definitely.'

'I thought you were working on your script.'

'My damn script is taking too long to come together. I need to do something creative. I've been out of action long enough.'

'Didn't Larry get you a deal at Orpheus?'

'Pending script approval. Only I can't seem to find a writer who's worth a damn.'

'I recommended Oliver Rock, didn't I?'

Her eyes narrowed. 'You certainly did.'

'Well . . . he just sold an original screenplay for a million big ones. Not bad for a novice.'

'I found him to be useless,' she said coldly.

'Sorry you feel that way.'

'Get me that part, Dennis. Messenger me the contract. I'll sign today.'

'Good. Because as far as I know they start shooting almost immediately.'

She slammed the phone down. She was mad at Larry.

Even more so at Oliver – although he was too stupid to realize who he was screwing with.

Well, let's see how Larry liked it when she hooked up with some delectable young actress on the screen. Let's see his reaction when she was actually kissing a woman in front of the world.

She'd show Larry Singer. And how.

Lissa was lonely. With Gregg gone she noticed a big void. Although the last six months had been hell, it was still strange adjusting to not having him around.

The days were taken care of with a vigorous rehearsal schedule and various meetings on new projects. The problem was that at night, unless she made arrangements to see friends, she was by herself in a house large enough for a family of ten. Of course Chuck had a room over the garage, Nellie lived in the maid's quarters, Danny usually stayed late, and the guards were outside, but it wasn't as if she was hanging with the help.

A few months ago she would've been into her computer, visiting chat rooms and various sites – but that was when Gregg was around, and on good days they'd had a laugh doing it together. Now the thrill was gone. She had no desire to converse with strangers in cyber-space. Too weird.

James tried to persuade her to get back on the party circuit. She refused: she'd never enjoyed lavish Hollywood parties and events at the best of times, and now – with Gregg and his big mouth – going out in public would be an ordeal.

As soon as the news was out that she was available, the herd of perennial Hollywood bachelors – a motley crew of ageing playboys, upstart agents, big-time actors and all-out rich jerks – sprang into action, calling non-stop. Lissa couldn't have been less interested.

Nicci dropped by a couple of times and commiserated about what a piece of crap Gregg was. Lissa was pleased that her daughter had taken the time to be supportive, especially since Nicci was busy organizing her wedding.

Lissa decided that once Vegas was behind her, she would spend more time helping Nicci. It was not too late to have a really good mother-daughter relationship, although the truth was they were more like sisters.

Quincy came to see her. He hobbled in on crutches, a big fat smile on his face. 'So, did I leave you in good hands or what?' he demanded.

'You certainly did,' she answered, adding an offhand, 'Where *is* Michael?'

'Around. Anythin' you need, all you gotta do is call.'

'Just like the song, huh?'

'And the two new guards, they're okay?'

'I hardly see them – they're busy patrolling the grounds – but Chuck's pleased to have the extra help. Three photographers tried to jump the wall yesterday. They soon put a stop to that.'

'Yeah, they're good guys. Ex-cops are always the best.'

'So . . . will Michael be dropping by any time soon?' she asked casually.

'Do you need him?'

'I *should* talk to him, shouldn't I?'

'I'll have him call you.'

'How's your leg doing?'

'I'm gettin' around.'

'That's good, isn't it?'

He pulled a face. 'My old lady's drivin' me. Man,' he complained, 'Amber's the worst damn driver to ever hit the road.'

Lissa laughed softly. 'Where is she now?'

'Outside in the car. Waitin' to torture me some more on the drive home.'

'Why don't you bring her in?'

'Got a rule,' he said. 'Never mix things up.'

'In that case, I'm coming out to meet her.'

'Aw, Jeez,' Quincy exclaimed. 'She'll have a heart-attack. Thinks you're the bomb.'

'Then let's go,' Lissa said, smiling.

She strolled outside the house with Quincy, surprising Amber, who was sitting behind the wheel of their car reading *People* magazine.

'Hi,' Lissa said, leaning in through the window. 'I wanted to meet the woman who snagged the great Quincy.'

'Oh, my *God*!' Amber exclaimed, completely flustered.

'You have a great husband,' Lissa continued. 'He's done a lot of good work for me.'

'*I* like him,' Amber said, beaming proudly.

'Thanks for lending him to me,' Lissa said. 'I'm giving him back to you in one piece.'

'Did you sign his cast?' Amber asked.

'Was I supposed to?'

'Yes, you were supposed to,' Amber said, glaring accusingly at her husband. 'I *told* the fool to get your signature.'

Lissa grinned, she immediately liked Quincy's feisty wife. 'Not too late,' she said.

Danny, hovering behind her, produced a pen. Lissa bent down and put her signature on Quincy's cast.

'They're *never* gonna believe this at the hospital,' Quincy crowed. 'When they take this motha off, they're gonna havta frame it.'

Everyone laughed.

'Nice meetin' you, Miz Roman,' Amber said, still slightly in awe.

'Next time we'll do lunch,' Lissa said. 'And you can tell me all of Quincy's deep dark secrets.'

'Ha!' Amber snorted. 'Like *he* has secrets!'

'Come on, baby,' Quincy said, manoeuvring himself into the passenger seat. 'Be nice.'

'You're prettier than you are in the movies,' Amber said to Lissa admiringly. 'Is it okay if I tell you that?'

'Of course.'

'Let's go,' Quincy said, anxious to leave before Amber embarrassed him.

''Bye,' Lissa called, waving, as their car took off down the long, winding driveway.

She waited until they were out of sight, then walked back into the house. Her thoughts turned to Michael Scorsinni, and she wondered why he hadn't come with his partner. Was he working on a new case? Following some other cheating husband?

She was entitled to know, wasn't she? After all, she *was* a client so, therefore, he should have come too.

And then she realized, with a shiver of surprise, that she actually missed him. A man she hardly knew. A man it would certainly be folly to get involved with.

She shook her head. Silly thoughts.

Or were they?

Chapter Nineteen

'You're making a mistake,' Taylor said, as she and Larry sat at the breakfast table on their patio, where they had a magnificent view of the Santa Monica mountains and the ocean.

'What kind of a mistake would that be?' Larry answered, eating his oatmeal.

'This Oliver Rock person, *why* are you taking such an interest in him? It's not like he's a relative or anything.'

'That's true,' Larry said, taking a sip of hot water and lemon, his preferred morning beverage.

'Anyway,' Taylor continued, 'I thought you never read other people's material. You get sent scripts all the time and you always have Edie send them back unread. I've seen you do it a hundred times.'

'Isaac has known Oliver's parents forever,' Larry explained, 'and the kid needs guidance.'

'He doesn't look like he needs any guidance to me,' Taylor snapped. 'He looks like a real smartass. And he's *not* a kid, he's a grown man.'

'You're always so critical of people,' Larry remarked, moving onto a plate of sliced papaya, apple and banana.

Taylor stared at her genius husband. He ate exactly the same breakfast every day – it drove her a little bit nuts. Why did he always have to be so precise? 'I'm merely being honest,' she said sharply.

'That's your prerogative,' he responded.

'Anyway,' she said, deciding to upset him, 'I've got my own news.'

'You have?'

She picked up her glass of freshly squeezed orange juice and took a sip. 'Remember that movie I discussed with you a few weeks ago, the one for cable?'

'Yes.'

'I've decided to do it.'

That stopped him half way to a slice of papaya. 'You *what?*'

'I'm taking the part, Larry. It doesn't suit me sitting around doing nothing.'

'You're not doing nothing. You're still developing your script.'

'Yes, but it's not right yet, and I have to keep myself busy until it is. I need my creative urges fulfilled.'

'But, darling—'

'You go to the studio every day,' she said, interrupting him. 'It's fine for you, you're a very busy man. I'm an actress, and I want to work.'

'Where is all this coming from?' Larry said, frowning. 'I thought you were perfectly happy.'

'I find it extremely frustrating not being creatively involved,' she said restlessly, 'so I've accepted the role. We start filming immediately.'

He took off his glasses and placed them on the table next to his neatly folded copies of the *New York Times, USA Today,* the *Wall Street Journal,* and the trades. 'Shouldn't I read the script?' he said.

'No, Larry,' she said, shaking her head. 'It's not written by some young writer who's craving your advice.'

He began tapping his fingers on the table, a sure sign that he was disturbed. 'Can I ask who the director is?'

'A woman.'

'I suppose that's understandable,' he said peevishly. 'After all, it *is* a gay movie.'

'Now, now, Larry,' she chided, quite enjoying her moment of triumph, 'that's not a very politically correct thing to say, is it? And for your information, it's not a gay movie, it's a touching love story between two women.'

'I'm surprised you made this decision without consulting me first.'

'Why would I bother you?' she said guilelessly. 'You're busy with your movie.' A heartfelt sigh. 'It's such a shame there isn't a role for *me* in *your* film, although I'm sure you'll find something for Isaac as usual.'

Larry was silent for a moment. 'Is everything all right between us, Taylor?' he asked tentatively.

'Of course.'

'You're *sure?*'

'Why wouldn't it be?' she countered.

'I know you're angry that I haven't done more to get your movie made, but sweetheart, you have no idea what a cut-throat business this is.'

'Larry,' she said impatiently, 'I've been a working actress in this town for years. I've made ten movies and countless TV shows. You might not remember most of them, but before you, I *never* stopped working.'

'I know,' he said. 'However, we're talking about a production where real money is involved. Yes, I admit that I have been dragging my feet when it comes to your project, and that's only because it would hurt me to see you fail.'

'Why would you think I'd fail?' she asked coldly.

'Anyway,' he said, quick to move on, 'I did set something up at Orpheus. Now all you have to do is deliver a script they like.'

'I've submitted three scripts to them, Larry,' she said

caustically, 'and what do you know? They don't like any of them.'

'I can understand your frustration.'

'Can you?' she said, her eyes flashing. 'Can you really?'

'Yes, sweetheart.'

Then give me a role in your fucking movie.

But he didn't say a word.

When she'd finished ruining Larry's day, she decided to deal with Oliver. Unannounced, she drove over to his beach-front apartment.

He was home, Kid Rock blaring on the stereo, the smell of pot in the air.

Oliver was dancing around the place shirtless, wearing only a gold stud earring and a pair of torn Hawaiian shorts, a residue of white powder decorating his nostrils.

The bedroom door was open, and Taylor glimpsed a naked girl lying on the mattress, gazing blankly at the ceiling. 'Sorry,' Taylor said coldly, directing her words at Oliver. 'Didn't realize you were entertaining.'

'Hey – shit, whasshappenin', man?' he said, blinking rapidly.

He was stoned. Taylor wished *she* was stoned – not that she was into drugs any more, she'd only indulged in the old days when she was young and foolish. Now she was the wife of an upstanding member of the community, and couldn't do that sort of thing.

'I came for my money,' she said. 'I'm sure you don't want a bad reputation in this town now that you're mixing in the big leagues, so I figured it would be in your best interest to pay me back.'

'Jeez,' he mumbled, 'you're a hard one.'

'A hard one, huh?' She lowered her voice so the girl couldn't possibly hear. 'You come walking into *my* house with *my* husband. What kind of respect does that show for my feelings?'

'*He* called *me*,' Oliver said indignantly. 'What am I gonna do – turn down a meeting with Larry Singer?'

'He's my *husband*, Oliver,' she said furiously. 'Don't you get it? You're *fucking* his wife.'

'You're not gonna tell him, are you?' he whined. 'That'd ruin everything.'

'You know what?' she said disgustedly. 'You really are a pathetic little prick. I can't imagine what I ever saw in you. Write me a cheque and I'll get out of this dump you call home.'

'You *sure* you want your money back?'

'Since you couldn't do anything with my *tired, old-fashioned* script, I'd definitely like my money back, and I'd like it now. Otherwise, I *will* tell Larry about you and me, and we'll see how helpful he is to you then.'

'Shit, Tay,' he mumbled, rubbing the tip of his nose.

'Knowing Larry,' she continued, quite enjoying herself, 'he'd put a stop to your career altogether. And Larry can do that, he's an extremely powerful man.'

'Okay, okay,' Oliver muttered, scratching his head. He grabbed his chequebook and scribbled her a cheque. She plucked it from his hand.

'Ollie – you comin' back to bed?' the girl called from the other room.

'Yeah, babe, hang on a minute.'

'How old is she? Fourteen?' Taylor asked icily.

'No.' Oliver gave a twisted smile. 'Fifteen. Cute, isn't she?'

'Fuck you!'

And with that, Taylor stormed out of his apartment.

After spending another lonely night, and thinking things over, Lissa called Michael on his cellphone. Even though Quincy had been to see her the day before, she still had this nagging feeling that she should talk to him – after all, *he* was the one who'd been dealing with her case.

He answered immediately.

'Hi,' she said, friendly yet cool. 'This is Lissa Roman.'

'Hey,' he said, sounding pleased. 'How're you doing?'

'Okay. And you?'

'The same.' A beat. 'Any problems, Lissa?'

'No. Gregg's gone, I'm here, the guards are outside. Everything's under control.'

'That's good,' he said warmly.

'I was, uh . . . thinking that we should discuss a couple of things.'

'Go ahead.'

'Remember you asked me if Gregg had a gun? Well, now that I've had time to think about it, I seem to remember he has.'

'That's *not* good.'

'He told me he didn't have a permit, so I kind of forgot.'

'You know, Lissa, maybe we shouldn't talk about this on the phone.'

'You're right,' she said quickly.

'I could drop by.'

'I'm about to leave for another rehearsal, but I'll be home tonight. Is that any good for you?'

'Yeah, I think it is.'

'Should I have Nellie fix you something to eat? Do you like pasta?'

'I'm Italian, what do *you* think?'

'Nellie's German, but I'm sure she can handle pasta.'

'What time?'

'Seven thirty?'

'See you then.'

She put down the phone, a smile on her face. It seemed so stupid because she hardly knew him, yet she'd actually *missed* seeing him.

It's only business, she told herself sternly. *I need to make sure he realizes I still need protection.*

A few minutes before she left the house, James called. 'I refuse to take no for an answer,' he said firmly. 'We're going to the Davis's tonight, whether you like it or not.'

'I already told you, James, I'm not in the mood to socialize.'

'I know, but I spoke to Barbara D and she's such a darling, and she *insists* that you come.'

'I already have . . . other arrangements.'

'You do? What?'

'I'm seeing Nicci,' she lied.

'That's nice.' He hesitated for a moment. 'I should warn you, there's a show on TV tonight, and my contacts tell me it's not very flattering. Perhaps your lawyer should tape it.'

'What show is that?'

'A piece of garbage called *The Real News*.'

'Never heard of it.'

'You could say it's *Hard Copy* on speed.'

She sighed. 'I suppose Gregg's on it.'

'You know Gregg – any chance to shine.'

'Why can't he go away quietly?'

'Because, my sweets, he always prayed for stardom, and now he's got his five minutes.'

'What does he say?'

'Talks about you, of course. Why else would anyone put him on TV?'

'I'll watch it.'

'Not by yourself, princess. View it with Nicci.'

'Thanks, James, I'll do that. And if I don't speak to you later, I'll call you in the morning.'

Nicci and Saffron cruised into Fred Segal on Melrose, their favourite shopping spot. As they walked around inspecting all the new clothes, Nicci kept checking her cellphone messages.

'*Why* do you keep on doing that?' Saffron asked. 'I

mean, you *speak* to Evan like *seven* times a day. So what's the deal, girl?'

'I *am* getting married, you know,' Nicci reminded her.

'I *know*,' Saffron replied, tossing back her dreadlocks. 'Only it's not *him* you're checking on.'

'What *do* you mean?' Nicci said innocently, pulling a pair of studded leather pants off the rack.

'C'mon, you *know* you can't keep secrets.'

'No secrets,' Nicci said, holding the pants up for further inspection.

'Yeah?' Saffron said, giving her a knowing look.

Nicci was dying to confide in someone – but if she did, wouldn't that be incredibly disloyal to Evan?

'It's nothing,' she said vaguely. 'Evan's brother is flying in from the location, and I'm supposed to give him some papers. If I miss him, it'll piss Evan off.'

'Hmm . . .' Saffron said with a wicked grin. 'The *babe* brother?'

Nicci shot her a surprised look. 'You think Brian's a babe?'

'Oh, yeah, the dude is smokin'. Didja get an eyeful of that ass? Man! Gives "tight" a whole new meaning.'

'Brian's a major player,' Nicci said, startled that Saffron had noticed. 'He sleeps with anyone.'

'Somethin' wrong with that?' Saffron joked. 'Maybe *I* should date him.'

'Let's *not* keep it in the family,' Nicci said pointedly, throwing the leather pants down and walking off.

'Jealous?' Saffron said, right behind her.

'Are you *losing* it? Jealous – of *Brian*? He's a sleaze-bag, the kind of guy you go out of your way to avoid.'

'Uh-huh,' Saffron said knowingly. 'The girl is jealous all right.'

'I am *so not*,' Nicci said indignantly, snatching up a red T-shirt with BAD GIRL emblazoned in sequins across the front.

'What's the deal, Nic?' Saffron persisted. 'Don't tell me you like Brian too?'

Nicci shook her head vigorously. 'I *so* do *not* appreciate this conversation.'

'Check your messages again,' Saffron teased. 'Maybe he's called. And, girl, that T-shirt is *not* for you. You gotta have no boobs to carry it off.'

'Anyone ever told you you're a twenty-carat bitch?' Nicci demanded, well aware she'd been busted.

Saffron grinned and twirled her gold nose-ring. 'All the time, girl. All the time!'

Michael and Quincy were in the car on their way to meet a new client, a real estate developer who suspected his business partner was ripping him off.

'I dropped by to see Lissa Roman yesterday,' Quincy said, as Michael drove them over the canyon. 'She seems happy enough.'

'I doubt she's happy,' Michael answered carefully. 'She's all over the tabloids.'

'We didn't get into *that*,' Quincy said, flipping open a stick of gum. 'All she did was keep asking about you.'

'Oh,' Michael said, his expression blank.

'Yeah,' Quincy continued. 'She seemed quite interested in what you were doin'.'

'I'm sure it's business only.'

'I'm sure it's not,' Quincy responded, throwing Michael a sideways look. 'Did anythin' go on between you an' her?'

'No,' Michael said, concentrating on his driving.

'Ha!' Quincy said disbelievingly.

'What's with the *ha*?'

'Nothin'.'

They drove in silence for a few minutes, then Quincy said, 'You'd better give her a call.'

'Why?'

''Cause we're workin' her case, an' you should check she's feelin' good about everything.'

'I thought *you* saw her yesterday.'

'I did, but it's you she wants.' Quincy chuckled. 'Mister Casanova scores again.'

'That's a dumb thing to say, Q.'

'Yeah? I can tell when a babe is interested in makin' it somethin' more.'

'First of all, she's no babe, she's a client. So, I'm wondering why you would even be encouraging this. And secondly, I *am* seeing her. Tonight. She wants to . . . go over some things.'

'I knew it!' Quincy crowed. 'Go over what things?'

'Whether the ex has a gun or not, 'cause if he *does* carry an unregistered weapon, I'm thinking I should arrange to have him pulled over, get him thrown in jail for a couple of nights.'

'Yeah, an' what else does she wanna go over?'

'I dunno,' Michael said, anxious to get off the subject. 'She wants to see me, that's all.'

'Didn't *I* just say that?'

'It's not what you think.'

'An' what *do* I think?'

'You think she wants to get it on with me, right?'

'She's a woman, an' she takes one look at you, an' she's gotta say to herself, "Here's a *real* guy, not one of them fancy actor dudes."'

'Jesus, Q, you should be writing soap operas. There's no way she's interested in me.'

'Wanna place a bet, my man?'

'No, thanks,' Michael said evenly. 'In case you've forgotten, I am *not* a gambling man.'

'Yeah, you're a lover, right?

'Get off it, asshole. You're starting to piss me off.'

Chapter Twenty

Eric Vernon did not consider himself a dreamer, he considered himself a realist. Lately he'd been dreaming a lot. When he closed his eyes at night he saw money, piles and piles of money, raining down on him. Sometimes in those moments between sleeping and waking, he'd imagine he was lying on a bed made of crisp new hundred-dollar bills. Then he'd open his eyes and reality would hit him in the face.

Saturday morning he set off to meet Arliss and his cronies again. The first meeting had gone well. Once he'd convinced them that kidnapping wasn't the heinous crime it used to be, he'd arranged another meeting to discuss exactly how the job would go down. Now he was on his way.

'Who're we goin' t' snatch?' Arliss immediately wanted to know.

Eric regarded the skinny man with cold eyes, he was sick of Arliss asking the same old question. 'That's something I can't tell you right now.'

'When *do* we get t' know?' Big Mark demanded belligerently.

'On the day of the job.'

'Is it someone famous?' Joe asked, his pop eyes bulging in anticipation.

'This is not *Twenty Questions*,' Eric snapped.

Pattie appeared at the table, sad tits drooping as usual. 'What can I get you, gentlemen?' she asked.

'Anything they want,' Eric said, barely glancing in her direction.

As soon as she walked off, he laid out his plan. Davey would be in charge of transport: he'd pick a car from the wrecking yard, and that would be the vehicle they'd use. 'When the job's done, you'll take the car back to the yard and make sure it gets junked immediately.'

Davey nodded eagerly. He could do that.

'Joe's job is to get the chloroform to put her out while we transport her to the location.'

'So it's a woman,' Big Mark crowed triumphantly.

'Women are easier to handle,' Eric answered, not giving away any more than he had to.

'Is she famous?' Joe said, repeating himself.

'I told you, I have no intention of revealing her identity until the time is right.'

'Why?' Arliss asked, his thin face twitching uncontrollably.

'It's not important. What *is* important is keeping this to ourselves and working as a team.'

'How much ransom you gonna ask?' Arliss said.

'That's nobody's business,' Eric replied sharply. 'You're all getting well paid.'

'That's for *you* to say,' Big Mark said loudly.

Eric turned on him. 'This is *my* scam, do you understand?' he said harshly. 'You'll get your share once the money is paid. If that's not good enough, you'd better walk now.'

'Nobody's walkin',' Arliss said, still twitching.

'Glad to hear it.' Eric stared at Big Mark. 'Your job is handling the physical part. Once she's unconscious, you'll get her to the car and put her in the trunk. When we reach

184

the building, you'll carry her to the room Arliss has prepped. Can you handle that?'

'I can carry *two* women,' Big Mark boasted, 'an' don't think I ain't done it.'

'We probably won't have to keep her longer than twenty-four to forty-eight hours before the ransom is settled.'

'When's this goin' down?' Arliss asked.

'Next Saturday,' Eric said, 'so keep yourselves available. By Monday or Tuesday it should all be over. You'll get your cash, and you'll keep your mouths closed. Because if you don't, I can assure you there will be very bad consequences.'

'Sounds easy,' Arliss said.

'Not easy, foolproof,' Eric replied. 'Unless one of you screws up.'

'Nobody's screwin' up,' Big Mark growled.

'Good,' Eric said. He still had a gut feeling that Big Mark could turn out to be bad news. He resolved to watch him closely at all times.

Now all he had to do was decide exactly what time to snatch Nicci. Late afternoon would be good. The maid always left by noon, and when Nicci came home after her lunches or shopping or kickboxing classes, she was alone in the house, and didn't usually go out again until nine or ten at night, when she drove herself to meet friends at a restaurant or club. He'd noticed that she was not at all security-conscious – he'd seen her open the door to anyone.

The following Saturday worked well, because that weekend Lissa Roman would be getting her big pay-day in Vegas, so it should be no problem for her to come up with the cash. Danny had already informed him that they were all off to Vegas on Thursday and that Nicci never accompanied her mother to public events.

'Lissa likes to keep her out of the spotlight,' he'd confided. 'She says it's for her own safety, but *I* think it's 'cause having a nineteen-year-old kid might make her seem *old*. Although, of course, my princess could *never* seem old. She's ageless.'

Danny adored his boss. Eric had learned to pretend that he adored her too. He elicited more information that way.

Nicci, he thought. *You are my ticket to ride. You are my one-way flight to the Bahamas, where I am planning to live happily ever after.*

And if his team of losers didn't fuck up, he would be gone before anyone realized it. Gone with all the money, for he had no intention of paying one dime to this loser group of misfits.

And what the hell could they do about it?

Nothing.

Because by the time he got the money, Eric Vernon would have ceased to exist.

Chapter Twenty-one

Michael was in the middle of a shower when Carol called. He ran out of the bathroom, almost slipping and breaking his neck on the wet tiled floor. He grabbed the phone, thinking it might be Lissa cancelling their date – not that it was a date – but, anyway, he didn't want to miss her if it was her.

When Carol said hello, his stomach dropped. He'd forgotten about her. He'd also conveniently forgotten about the dinner she was cooking at her apartment the following night for Amber, Quincy and him.

'All I need to know is if you're allergic to anything,' she said, sounding surprisingly cheerful considering he hadn't called her since the night he'd left to rescue Lissa.

She knew he wasn't allergic – they'd had that discussion the first week they'd gone out, so she was obviously checking to make sure he remembered her dinner.

'Seven thirty,' she said crisply. 'I'm entering into competition with Amber.'

'Huh?'

A light laugh. 'I'm cooking enough for ten people, so bring your appetite.'

He felt obliged to make excuses for not calling.

She seemed unfazed. 'Don't worry,' she said. 'Amber told me how busy you and Quincy have been.'

He clicked off the phone and stood there for a moment. He was stark naked, dripping wet, and looking forward to seeing Lissa Roman – a woman who could do nothing for him except complicate his life. He hated himself for stringing Carol along, it was only fair that he cut her loose. The main reason he'd kept on seeing her was because he knew he was going to break it off one day, therefore removing all the commitment pressure. How selfish was *that*?

Tomorrow night, after dinner, he'd give her the speech. And it wasn't a line, she *did* deserve better than he was capable of giving.

He was well aware that he'd closed down emotionally when his daughter was taken away from him. It was only by the grace of God that he hadn't started drinking again. Christ, what a nightmare *that* would've been.

Whenever he thought about his drinking years he was filled with dread. He *never* intended to go down that rocky road again. He'd been drunk when he'd married Rita. If he'd been sober, he might have seen her for the damaged woman she was and not been caught in her devious trap.

The phone rang again. This time he knew it would be Lissa, cancelling. But no, it was Amber.

'Michael,' Amber said, cutting straight to the chase like it was any of her business, 'I love you as if you was Quincy's brother, which is why I'm gonna tell you that you're makin' a mistake goin' over to Lissa Roman's house tonight. An' don't get me wrong, she's a lovely lady I'm sure, but, honey, you're *way* out of your league, and Quince an' I do not want t' see you gettin' hurt, so I thought I'd have my say.'

What *was* it with Quincy? Couldn't he keep *anything* to himself? Now Amber would go running to Carol with her information.

'It's not a date, for crissakes,' he snapped. 'And I do not appreciate you telling me what I should do.'

'That's what friends are for, Michael,' Amber said, all holier-than-thou. 'Lissa Roman is a movie star. She'll break your heart an' scatter the pieces wherever the fancy takes her.'

'Do me a big one, Amber. Keep your opinions to yourself. The agency is doing *work* for Lissa Roman, and that's all it is. *Work*.'

He clicked off before she could say another word, suddenly realizing that the two girls who lived in the apartment across the street were standing at their window enjoying the free show.

He stomped back into the bathroom. Talk about raining on a parade. And it wasn't even a date.

It's not a date, Lissa thought, as she rummaged through her closet frantically searching for the right outfit. *It's a meeting to—*

The phone. Dammit. She was sure it was Michael calling to tell her he couldn't make it.

She picked up without waiting for Danny to get it.

Bad move.

Gregg's voice.

Unmistakable.

Filled with hate.

Drunk.

'You fucking dumb-ass cocksucking *bitch*. I'm gonna—'

She slammed the phone down before he could tell her *what* he was going to do.

It rang again immediately.

This time she didn't pick up. She was shaking. Now she had a legitimate reason to talk to Michael. She waited a few minutes, then buzzed Danny. 'Who was that?' she asked.

'A hang-up,' he responded.

'Tomorrow I'd like you to change all our numbers.'

'Including your cell?'

'Everything.'

'If you're sure.'

'Yes, I'm sure, Danny. Please do it.'

'Brian hasn't called,' Nicci said over the phone.

'Shit!' Evan said. 'He was supposed to pick up those papers and fly right back. I can't trust him to do a goddamn thing.'

'Well . . .' Nicci ventured. 'Could be he had other stuff to take care of first.'

'Are you making excuses for him?' Evan said irritably, daring her to do so.

'No, but—'

'Oh, for Crissake, Nicci,' Evan exploded. 'When are you going to realize that my brother is a total fuck-up?'

Was this becoming a habit, Evan screaming at her?

She hoped not, because she didn't like it one little bit.

'I'm sorry, Evan,' she said, keeping her aggravation level under control because, after all, he *was* the man she was planning to marry. 'It's not my fault he hasn't called.'

'Yeah, yeah, I know,' Evan said, calming down. 'Try him on this number and tell him to get over there and pick up the papers. I should've had you Fed-Ex them, it would've been faster.'

'I can still do that.'

'No, that's okay. By the way, my mother's flying out to L.A. earlier than expected.'

'She is?' Nicci said, alarmed. 'Like *when*?'

'Wednesday or Thursday. She hasn't decided. I'll let you know.'

'Evan, you won't be back until next week,' she pointed out.

'That's okay, she's very independent.'

Crap! Nicci thought. *Don't tell me I'm going to be stuck with the intimidating Lynda all by myself. This is a nightmare!*

Evan gave her Brian's number and hung up.

Naturally, when she called, a girl answered.

'Is Brian there?' she asked.

'He might be,' the girl said, sounding sulky. 'Who wants him?'

'His sister-in-law,' Nicci said.

'Didn't know he *had* a sister-in-law,' the girl muttered.

'I'm sure there's a lot about Brian you don't know.'

'What?' the girl said, sounding stupid.

Obviously Brian's type, Nicci thought.

'Tell him he's supposed to pick up some papers from his brother's house. It's important, dear.'

'If I see him, I'll tell him,' the girl said, in an uptight voice.

Nicci hung up. What was it with Brian? Did he need a new girl every week? Why couldn't he have kept Miss Russia around for a while?

How come this jerk keeps on getting to me? she thought.

She had no answer to that. He just did.

Shortly before Michael arrived, Kyndra called Lissa. 'I'm feelin' guilty, hon',' she confessed, in her low-down smoky voice. 'I've been locked in the studio, so I haven't been following what's been going on. I know I should've come to see you before, I'm on my way over now.'

'Bad timing,' Lissa said, coming up with a quick excuse. 'You've caught me in the middle of a meeting.'

'How long will it go for?' Kyndra asked.

'I'm not sure,' Lissa replied offhandedly. 'Tomorrow's good. I'm rehearsing in the morning, free in the afternoon. We could have lunch.'

'Tomorrow's the day before my wedding anniversary,' Kyndra reminded her. 'Our big party is coming up on Wednesday. And you *know* we expect to see you, so you'd better not let us down.'

'I'm not feeling very social right now,' Lissa explained, hoping Kyndra would understand. 'Everywhere I go the paparazzi follow, and according to James, there's a show on TV tonight featuring my soon-to-be ex.'

'Yeah, that *would* be his style,' Kyndra drawled. 'Major exposure for loser of the year.'

'How's the album going?' Lissa asked.

'Sweet an' soulful,' Kyndra said. 'Exactly the way we like it.'

'I'm looking forward to hearing some tracks. I'll be in the studio myself soon.'

'You writing?'

'I'll probably jot down a couple of heartbreak songs. Although, I have to say my heart is not broken. Saying goodbye to Gregg was a big relief.'

'We all warned you.'

'Don't remind me,' Lissa said tersely. 'In future I'll learn to listen.'

'Okay, hon, I'll see you at our party. Oh, an' Saffron's bringing some friends, including Nicci.'

'They're not sitting with us, are they?'

'Don't sweat it, they'll be at the kiddies' table. Neither of us will have to put up with their juvenile delinquent behaviour.'

'Nicci's no longer a juvenile delinquent,' Lissa said. 'Ever since she got engaged she's a changed girl. Did you know that she actually threw a dinner party the other night?'

'No shit?'

'Yes. Saffron was there with some desperate Mexican guy who was of the opinion he should star in my next video. Where *does* she find them?'

'Unfortunately, desperate guys are Saffron's specialty,' Kyndra said with a throaty laugh. 'I gave up trying to control that child ever since she had a baby with the deadbeat football player. Right now she's goin' through a crisis – can't seem to make up her mind whether she wants to be a singer, an actress, a movie star, or a mom. I've tried telling her that she can't do all of them at the same time.'

'*Some* people manage it.'

'Yeah, honey – only *you*.'

'Thanks for calling, Kyndra. I promise I'll try to make it to your party.'

'You'd better, or you'll have Norio to answer to. You know he adores you.'

'It's mutual,' Lissa said, thinking how much she loved both of them. She'd met Kyndra and Norio when she first came to L.A. Kyndra was already a singing star, and Norio had scored Lissa a gig singing back-up on one of Kyndra's recordings. They'd both been really good to her before she was anyone, and the three of them had remained friends ever since.

As soon as she put down the phone, she buzzed Chuck at the front gate. 'Are the paparazzi still out there?' she asked.

'There's a few scattered around,' Chuck replied.

'I'm expecting Mr Scorsinni for a meeting. When he arrives, make sure he's not bothered.'

'You got it, Miz Roman.'

'Thanks, Chuck.' She glanced at her watch. 'He'll be arriving soon.'

She wandered into the kitchen, where Nellie was busy preparing a large dish of lasagna.

'So you *can* cook Italian?' she said affectionately. 'I'm impressed.'

'I can cook anything,' Nellie boasted, wiping her hands on her apron.

'I never doubted it.'

'Miz Lissa looks very pretty tonight,' Nellie said knowingly. 'Someone nice coming over?'

193

'It's only a business meeting,' Lissa said quickly.

'Shall I serve dinner at the dining table?'

'No, let's keep it low-key. Trays in the den, and put some of those small votive candles on the trays, they always look pretty.'

She left the kitchen and went into the den, thinking about what music he might like. He was Italian, so maybe he'd go for the old-fashioned sounds of Frank Sinatra and Tony Bennett, or would he be into something more classical, such as Bocelli? She decided to play it neutral and put on a selection of Sting, Van Morrison, and the Gypsy Kings.

Michael arrived on time. She heard the buzzer ring and shivered slightly. This was silly. Why was she so excited about seeing him? Could it be because he was good-looking?

No. Absolutely not. There were hundreds of handsome men in Hollywood, and most of them usually turned out to be boringly self-obsessed, or actors.

There was something special about Michael – he didn't treat her like a star, he treated her like a real person. It had been a long time since anybody had done that.

On the drive over to Lissa's house, Michael experienced a crazy urge to bring her flowers. He passed a man selling roses at the side of the street, and stopped himself from pulling over and buying some.

Sanity prevailed. How stupid would he look arriving with a bunch of roses, when she probably had flowers coming out her ears? She was Lissa Roman, for crissakes. In her world he was a nobody, so why was he building this up into something it wasn't? Although, deep down, he knew that if he wanted it to be something, it could, because Michael had always experienced great success with women.

He had no intention of getting involved with someone

who was capable of breaking his balls. Lissa Roman couldn't help it, she was a star, and stars broke a man's balls just by looking at them.

He began laughing to himself. That didn't sound right. No way would Lissa Roman be looking at his balls tonight.

He'd worn black – black pants, a black turtleneck, black leather jacket, he'd even put on shades. *It's my Hollywood look*, he told himself.

Yeah, right, Mr Hollywood, I don't think.

He waved at Chuck, who opened the big gates for him. A couple of paparazzi sprang forward and tried to take his picture, but he was up the driveway before they could.

He was still annoyed about Amber calling him. Screw Quincy for telling her what he was doing. It was nobody's business except his. Quincy had a big mouth, and it was about time they had a serious talk.

Meanwhile, he was visiting Lissa Roman, and he felt pretty high. Even Amber's lecture over the phone couldn't spoil it for him.

Just remember, he told himself sternly, *this is purely business. Lissa Roman is a client. Nothing more, nothing less.*

Chapter Twenty-two

Nicci made up her mind to stay at home for a change. After all, she was getting married soon and she had much to do. She decided it would be nice to wander around the house by herself before Evan's mother arrived and ruined everything. Hopefully, Evan would be back from location soon after Lynda Richter presented herself, although his movie seemed to be running way over schedule.

She'd bought a new mudpack facial treatment at Fred Segal, and after taking a leisurely swim, she put on an old In Sync T-shirt, and applied the messy pack to her face.

Man, do I look like a clown? she thought, mugging at herself in the mirror. *Thank goodness Evan's away. If he saw me like this . . .*

She'd asked Saffron if she wanted to come over, but Saffron had a date with another hot stud. Obviously Ramone hadn't been enough of a deterrent.

Alone in the house, she was intent on enjoying herself. She put on a Limp Bizkit CD and danced crazily around the living room.

When the doorbell rang she didn't think much of it. 'Who's there?' she called out.

'Delivery,' a male voice said. 'Need a signature.'

'Okay,' she said, throwing open the door. Standing there was Brian.

'Jesus!' he exclaimed. 'Didn't realize it was Halloween!'

'I'm auditioning for a role in the next *Survivor*,' she said, hardly taking a beat, although inside she was totally humiliated that he'd caught her in such a state. 'Uh . . . how come you didn't call?'

'My brother wants his papers, so here I am. Gotta fly back early tomorrow.'

'You were supposed to be here yesterday.'

'What did you say to my girlfriend?' he asked, entering the house. 'You pissed her off.'

'You don't *have* a girlfriend,' she retorted.

'Let's put it this way,' he said, heading for the bar, 'I *did* have one this morning, now I don't.'

'She must have been a temp, 'cause every time *I* see you, you're with a different girl.'

'Hey,' he said, grinning, 'variety's the spice of my libido.'

'Help yourself to a drink,' she said sarcastically, as he picked up a bottle of vodka. 'I'll be right back.'

She raced into the bathroom and hurriedly rinsed her face, wiping off the dried mud with a towel.

I look like a freak, she thought miserably. *This is* so *dense. How could I have gotten caught like this?*

Brian was drinking straight from the vodka bottle when she returned.

'We *do* have glasses,' she said caustically.

'How about grass?' he asked.

'Why?' she said.

'Why?' he repeated. ''Cause I thought I'd call the cops an' have the place raided. Whaddaya think?'

'I think you're like *nuts*.'

'Gimme a joint, for crissakes. Thanks to you, I had a drag-out fight with my girlfriend.'

'I keep reminding you, Brian, you don't *have* a girlfriend.'

'Yeah, yeah,' he said, taking another swig of vodka.

197

'Well, let me tell you, this one was Miss January last year, and believe me, you don't want Miss January walking out when you're feeling horny. And I *am* feeling horny, 'cause I can't get anywhere near our star on the movie. *Somebody's* banging her, and it sure as hell ain't me.'

'Sorry to hear about your sexual problems,' Nicci said sarcastically.

'I'm sure, 'cause you and my bro never have any, right?'

'Evan's very romantic,' she said, jumping to his defence.

'No shit?' Brian said disbelievingly. 'That's not what his last fiancée said.'

'Evan's never been engaged before me.'

'Apparently big bro doesn't tell you everything.'

'What're you talking about?' she asked, frowning.

'Let's go get somethin' to eat, an' I'll fill you in.'

'*Now?*' she said, pushing back her long bangs.

'You're hungry, aren't you?' he said. ''Cause *I'm* freakin' starving.'

'Well . . .' She wasn't sure whether to accept his half-hearted invitation or not. 'Okay,' she said at last. 'I suppose I could eat something.'

'How about a joint before we go?'

'Isn't the vodka enough?'

'Jesus Christ! You sound like my freakin' *brother.*'

She went into the bedroom, got a joint from her bedside drawer, lit up, inhaled deeply, re-entered the living room and handed it to him.

'You'll have to wait while I go get dressed.'

'No!' he said in mock dismay. 'And I thought I was taking you like that. It'd be like dragging around a scraggly little sister.'

'You're such an asshole, Brian,' she said crossly. 'I don't think I *want* to go to dinner with you.'

'Yes, you do,' he said, grinning again. 'I'm the irresistible brother. Remember?'

Oh, God, and he had a giant ego too!

'I'll be back in a minute,' she said, deciding that this was an opportunity she couldn't turn down. Now she'd be able to see for herself what a pain in the butt he really was, and then she could stop fantasizing about him once and for all.

She hurried into her closet, grabbed her Dolce & Gabbana jeans, cowboy boots, a red tank and her motorcycle jacket. She dressed quickly, then brushed her hair and applied a fast makeup.

Brian was standing out on the patio gazing at the view when she returned. He still had the bottle of vodka in one hand, and the joint in the other.

'You certainly get off on enjoying yourself, don't you?' she said.

'Hey, what else is important?' he replied, taking a deep drag.

They walked outside.

'Whose car shall we take?' she asked.

'Yours,' Brian said, walking around to the driver's seat of her BMW.

'If we're taking mine, *I'm* driving,' she said.

'Oh, no, baby,' he answered, shaking his head. 'You're not with Evan now. When you're with me, *I'm* the one in the driver's seat.'

'You look good,' Lissa said, answering the door herself.

'Hey,' Michael said, smiling, 'compliments from the boss. I'm flattered.'

'I'm not your boss,' she said, smiling back, 'simply one of your many clients, right?'

'Our most important client.'

'Really?'

'Would I lie?'

'Maybe.'

'Not me,' he said, following her into the den.

'So here we are,' she said, thinking how nice it was to see him.

'You're looking good yourself, Lissa,' he said, wishing he *had* bought her flowers. It would've been a friendly gesture – nothing to be misconstrued.

'Now that my black eye has kind of faded,' she murmured.

'I can see that.'

She walked towards the bar. 'Can I offer you a – no, I can't, can I?'

'I *do* drink,' he said, impressed that she'd remembered. 'Water, orange juice, soda, or maybe you've got a non-alcohol beer?'

'I doubt it,' she said, opening the small fridge behind the bar. 'I could send Chuck out to get some.'

'Don't bother. I gotta stop drinking it anyway – don't want to end up with a big beer gut.'

'Oh, yes,' she teased. 'I can just imagine you with a big beer gut. Sort of like a white Quincy!'

'Ouch! That's mean.'

'Don't take it the wrong way,' she said quickly. 'I love Quincy, he's like a big, cuddly bear.'

'Q's the best guy I know. A true stand-up.'

'How's orange juice?'

'Healthy.'

She smiled, poured him a glass and handed it to him.

'Thanks,' he said, watching her as she opened a bottle of Evian for herself.

'By the way,' she said, 'there's a TV programme on tonight I should see. Something called *The Real News*. Have you heard of it?'

'Yeah, crap TV at its worst,' he said, leaning on the bar. 'Why do you have to watch it?'

'Apparently Gregg's making an appearance.'

'He is?'

'I've alerted my lawyer. Anything he says about me can be held against him, and I assure you, I am *not* anxious to pay him alimony.'

'Didn't he sign one of those pre-nuptial deals?'

'Fortunately he did, only because my lawyer insisted.'

'You must have a smart lawyer.'

'I do,' she said, thinking how good he looked all in black. 'Only can you imagine how difficult it is when you're just about to get married to suddenly have to say, "Oh, by the way, can you please sign this pre-nup?" *Not* exactly the most romantic words in the world.'

'How'd he take it?' Michael asked.

'Badly. Got very uptight. Then, when he saw that my business people meant it, he backed off and finally signed.'

'Here's *my* take,' Michael said thoughtfully. 'If two people are getting married, why would one of them object to signing something that only comes into being if they get divorced? Hey, I'd sign a piece of paper saying I didn't want anything from anybody, but that's just me.'

'You're an original, Michael,' she said, smiling warmly. 'Especially in this town.'

'Right,' he said ruefully. 'I'm the one with the murdered wife, and the alcoholic past. Oh, yeah, and I haven't told you about how I got shot when I was a cop in New York. You've got that sorry story to come.'

'Quincy already told me about that. Besides, I like your stories,' she said quietly.

'I'm glad somebody does,' he said, with a wry grin.

'I thought we'd eat in here,' she said. 'After all, this *is* a casual business meeting, right?'

'Nothing else,' he said, clearing his throat.

'Well,' she said, walking out from behind the bar, 'let's go in the kitchen and I'll introduce you to my cook, Nellie. She's making lasagna. Whatever it's like, please smile and say it's great. Nellie's very sensitive to criticism.'

'I can understand that.'

'And . . . if you're *very* good, maybe she'll fix you a milkshake before dinner.'

'Lasagna and a milkshake,' he said, shaking his head. 'How lucky can one guy get?'

Belinda Barrow was starting to think that she might have made a mistake. Moving Gregg Lynch in had seemed like a good idea at the time. After all, he'd been married to Lissa Roman, he was a singer-songwriter, not bad-looking, and could be potential husband material – especially if he scored plenty of alimony from his famous wife.

Now she was discovering that he might be nothing more than an angry drunk, although she had to admit he was an energetic performer in bed.

As usual, she discovered him in the bar. 'Y'know, you'll ruin your looks if you keep on drinking the way you do,' she remarked.

'Are you talking to me?' Gregg said, looking at her like he couldn't believe what he was hearing.

'Yes, I am,' Belinda said. 'It's for your own good.'

'It is, huh?' he said, pouring himself a shot of vodka.

'You want to be a star, Gregg, and over the next few weeks you'll probably get a lot more exposure, so I suggest you control your drinking for a while.'

'What is it with you women?' he said belligerently. 'If you want me to stay here, you'd better cool it with the nagging.'

She bit back a sharp retort. She'd been around too long to take abuse from a man. On the other hand, there were not a lot of available men in Hollywood. The single ones were either burned-out perverts or totally gay. She decided she'd give Gregg a chance. After all, they'd only been together a short while.

'Just a suggestion,' she said, keeping it light. 'Doesn't

make any difference to me. I'll make sure the bar is stocked up and you can go ahead and lose your looks. Only when you do, that's the time I'll say goodbye.'

'You *bitch!*' he said disbelievingly.

'No name-calling,' she said curtly. 'You may have gotten away with it with your wife, but you can't move into *my* house and call *me* names. Now, do we have something going here, Gregg? Or are you intent on playing the bitter, disillusioned husband?'

He realized the alternative. Another hotel. Another set of bills to pay with money he didn't have. 'Sorry,' he muttered. 'Dunno what comes over me. I'm so bummed out by this whole thing.'

'I can imagine.'

'I don't think so.'

'I've asked a few people over tonight to watch the programme,' Belinda said. 'A captive audience.'

'Who?' Gregg asked suspiciously. He wasn't in the mood to socialize.

'Friends of mine, including a journalist who might be willing to buy your story. He writes for *Truth and Fact.* We go way back, he used to be my boyfriend, until we had a major split. He's a good writer, and if you can come up with something new, I'm sure he can get the paper to pay you plenty of money.'

'I like the sound of *that*,' Gregg said.

She nodded. 'So do I.'

'Y'know, Lissa, you're not like I thought you'd be,' Michael said. He was settled on the comfortable couch in her den feeling very much at home.

'How *did* you think I'd be?' she asked, amused.

'The same as all the rest.'

'All the rest of what?'

'Celebrities,' he said. 'Most of them have that whole

203

entourage thing going – y'know, a bunch of hangers-on who treat 'em like they walk on water.'

She knew exactly what he was talking about, she'd worked with enough of them.

'They're not into being real,' he continued, leaning towards her. 'You're real, Lissa.'

'The only reason you're saying that is because I fed you ice cream,' she said, smiling. 'You like me because I encourage your bad habits.'

'And . . . apart from anything else, you have a beautiful smile,' he said, unable to stop himself from coming out with what sounded like a corny line. 'But then,' he added, 'how many times a day do you get told that?'

'Let me see . . . hmm . . .'

He stifled an overwhelming urge to reach out and touch her. 'I'm happy you're doing okay,' he said. 'Even happier you haven't heard from Gregg.'

'Actually, I have,' she said, her mood changing to sombre. 'He called today. Unfortunately, *I* answered the phone.'

'You shouldn't be speaking to him.'

'Tell me about it.' She sighed. 'He spewed a bunch of four-letter words at me, so I hung up. It didn't bother me, because after that I didn't pick up again. Silly me for doing it in the first place. I've told Danny to change all my numbers.'

'I asked you to do that the first day I came over.'

'Please don't say you told me so.'

'Well, I did.'

'Michael—' she said warningly.

He grimaced. 'Okay, okay. But I want you to know that if Gregg ever touches you again, he'll have *me* to contend with. I should've dealt with him the last time.'

'I like to think he's being punished enough.'

'And she's kind-hearted too.'

'Don't get carried away,' she said, taking a sip of Evian. 'I can be a bitch on wheels.'

'Not you.'

'Oh, yes, me.'

'I don't believe it.'

She smiled. 'So . . . Michael, did you have to cancel something to be here tonight?'

'No. Why?'

'It's just that I have this feeling you've probably got women crawling all over you.'

'Hey,' he said, feigning a quick look around, 'I don't see any women all over me. Do you?'

'You're a good-looking guy, and straight—'

'I am?' he joked.

'So I, uh . . . wondered if you're seeing anyone special?'

'I date around,' he said carefully. 'Why?'

'Anything serious?' she asked, hoping it didn't sound as if she was giving him the third-degree.

'You know what it's like, Lissa,' he said casually. 'Sometimes the other person thinks it's more serious than it is. In fact, right now I'm about to say goodbye to someone who feels that way.'

'Hmm,' Lissa said. 'What're you going to do? Give her the old break-up speech?'

He raised an eyebrow. 'You *know* that speech?'

'I've used it a few times myself,' she said, smiling.

'Yeah.' He nodded. 'I *bet* you have.'

Their eyes met. They both realized they were flirting, but neither of them could help it. The chemistry between them was on fire.

'Come on,' Lissa said breathlessly, realizing she was falling into something she wasn't sure she was ready to handle. 'Let's go in the kitchen and see how Nellie's doing with the lasagna.'

* * *

Brian took Nicci to dinner at Matsuhisa and proceeded to tell her all about Evan's previous fiancée.

She listened in stunned silence. 'I had no idea he was engaged before me,' she said, shaking her head.

'You mean he never told you?' Brian said, knocking back his third glass of sake.

'No, he didn't,' she said, wondering if Brian was telling the truth.

'And you never asked?'

'It's not the kind of thing you ask – I like naturally assumed he wasn't. Anyway,' she said, determined to hear everything. 'What happened? Why *didn't* they get married?'

''Cause my mother put the kibosh on it.'

'She did?'

'I'm sure you must've realized by this time that Evan's her favourite.'

'I kind of guessed,' she said thoughtfully. 'They speak on the phone a lot. And apparently, when she comes to L.A., she always stays with him.'

'He wouldn't have it any other way.'

'How come *you* never get lucky?'

'*I* refuse to put up with her shit,' Brian said.

'What kind of shit is that?' Nicci asked curiously.

'You've met her, haven't you?'

'Is she *that* bad?'

'She's a witch, babe. Sucks the blood out of everyone.' He narrowed his eyes. 'You ever spent any time with her and Evan?'

'Not really.'

'Just you wait,' he said, laughing bitterly. 'You're in for a trip.'

'Evan informed me she's arriving here any day now,' Nicci said, 'so I guess I'll have to put up with her on my own.'

'At least she *likes* you,' Brian offered. ''Cause if she didn't, she'd manage to break you and bro up in a flash.'

'I don't think so,' Nicci said, quite insulted that he thought she'd be that easy to get rid of. Evan genuinely loved her, and if it came down to a choice between her and his mother, she was sure he'd choose her.

'How long have you and Ev been together?' Brian asked.

'Almost six months.'

'Well, babe, *she's* had him for thirty years. If there's a contest, guess who wins?' He handed her a glass of sake. 'Drink up,' he said. 'You're gonna need it.'

She didn't know what to think. Evan not telling her that he'd been engaged before was a major gap in communication. She drank the sake and picked up a piece of sushi with her chopsticks.

'Who was Evan engaged to?' she asked, deciding that she may as well find out everything.

'A script girl on one of our movies,' Brian answered, waving at a slinky blonde.

'And?' Nicci persisted. 'What happened?'

'Mommy didn't think the girl was good enough for her precious little Evan.'

'Why not?'

''Cause she didn't come from a famous family like you, and she had no money of her own. Lynda convinced Evan she was only chasing his big bucks and he should dump her. So he did.'

'Oh,' Nicci said flatly. 'How long ago was this?'

'About a year.'

'A year?' she said, confused and upset that this information had not come from Evan himself. 'That's only a few months before he met me.'

'Right,' Brian agreed, drinking more sake.

'What was her name?'

'It's not important, Nic,' Brian said, yawning. 'She's out of the running, an' believe me, she'll never come back. By the time my mother's finished with someone, they're gone.'

'I can't believe he never mentioned it to me.'

'There're probably a lot of things he hasn't mentioned to you. I'm telling you, Nic, he's not the man you think he is. Oh, yeah, he's my brother an' we work together, only you got no clue what you're getting yourself into. Haven't you noticed that he's a screamer? Moody? An asshole?'

'Everyone has their bad moods,' she said quickly.

Brian stared at her intently. 'Jesus Christ, you take some convincing, don't you? How old are you anyway?'

'Nineteen,' she said, wishing he'd drop the subject.

'Too young to screw up your future. Take my advice and hit the road while you can.'

'Evan calls you a total fuck-up,' she blurted.

'I bet he does. He's been trained by the best.'

'Anyway,' she said defensively, 'how do I know you're telling me the truth?'

'All you gotta do is ask Lynda. She'll be happy to fill you in.'

'There must be a reason he hasn't told me,' Nicci said weakly.

'Evan's secretive. Always has been.' He gave her a sleepy bedroom-eyed stare. 'Drink up, we're goin' to a rave.'

'We are?'

'Yeah. Nic, I've decided it's about time you got back into livin' again.'

Chapter Twenty-three

Over dinner Michael revealed more than he was planning to. It seemed Lissa had a way of getting him to talk about things that were intensely personal. He found himself telling her about his estrangement from his family because of Bella, and the difficulties he'd had being raised by a violent stepfather after his real dad had left home when he was ten. 'Eddie used to beat the crap outta me,' he confessed. 'Until one night, when I was sixteen, I took off for eighteen months, and didn't come back until I was sure I was stronger than him.'

'How did you support yourself?' she asked, her blue eyes wide with interest.

'Lied about my age an' got a job as a bartender,' he said ruefully. '*Real* smart for a budding alcoholic.'

'What happened then?'

'I finally went home, decided I wanted to be a cop, and made it into the Police Academy. That *really* pissed the family off, considering my brother, Sal, *and* my stepfather regarded all cops as the lowest form of life.' He laughed at the memory. 'Too bad. It gave me a feeling of strength and purpose, and I kinda moved through the ranks fast. Then, much to Eddie and Sal's disgust, I got promoted to detective.'

'Good for you.'

'By the way,' he said, eating heartily, 'this lasagna is delicious.'

'Tell Nellie.'

'I will.'

'Only please,' she added, with a slight smile, 'try to look businesslike when you do it. I'm sure she thinks there's something going on between us.'

'Now why would she think that?'

Lissa shrugged. 'Who knows?'

Their eyes met for a long, intimate look.

'Hey, I guess I've been talking too much,' he said, breaking the contact.

'Not at all,' she said. 'Your stories are so interesting, especially after I bored you with *my* life story the other day.'

'You told me nothing,' he said, trying not to stare at her lips. 'What you gave me was a press release.'

'No, I didn't,' she objected.

'That's exactly what you did,' he said, cleaning his plate. 'Any chance of hearing the real truth? Like why you left home so young? Sounds as if you might've been stuck with violent parents too.'

'No,' she said, vigorously shaking her head. 'They were merely emotionally bankrupt.'

He gave a hollow laugh. 'I know *that* feeling.'

'My shrink informed me that emotional neglect is equally as damaging as violence, and I think she's right. After I left, they never tried to find me.'

'You haven't seen them since?'

'No,' she said, as if it didn't matter, although deep down it still hurt when she dredged up the painful memories.

'Sounds to me like you should call them, Lissa.'

'Why?' she said defensively. 'They mean nothing to me. If they'd wanted contact, they would've come looking. Believe me, Michael, I'm glad they didn't.'

'You don't *know* that they didn't,' he said, pushing his plate away.

'I also don't know that they did.'

'I think you *should* call.'

'Do you?'

'Yeah, why not?'

'Have you called *your* family lately?' she asked sharply.

'Hey, I *told* you what my brother did. He stole my daughter and claimed she was his.'

'You also told me she *was* his.'

'Yeah,' he said, his stomach churning every time he thought about it. 'When she was five years old he kidnaps her, and I'm the last to find out. My mom didn't even tell me.'

'I'll make a deal with you,' Lissa said, thinking he looked even more handsome when he was angry. 'When *you* talk to *your* dysfunctional family, *I'll* talk to mine.'

Nellie knocked and entered the room. 'It's five minutes before nine, Miss Lissa,' she said. 'You asked me to remind you to switch on the TV.'

'Thanks, Nellie,' Lissa said. 'You can take the trays, we're finished.'

'And, wow, was it good!' Michael said, flashing a killer smile in Nellie's direction. 'You can cook for me any time.'

Nellie beamed and removed the trays, first placing the small votive candles on the coffee table.

'She likes you,' Lissa said, when Nellie left the room.

'I meant every word. I ate like food was going out of style!'

'I'll have to invite you again,' she said, with a good-natured grin. 'I appreciate a grateful guest.'

'Name the day. If Nellie's cooking, I'm here!'

Lissa picked up the remote and clicked on the TV.

'Have we *really* gotta watch this?' Michael groaned. 'You know he'll have nothing nice to say.'

'I think I should stay informed.'

'Why? It'll only piss you off.'

'No, it won't,' she said firmly.

'Here's an idea,' Michael said. 'You go put on a movie in the other room, and I'll monitor the show for you. How's that?'

'I *want* to see what he has to say. I want to hate him even more.'

'Hate's not good, Lissa.'

'Then why are *you* so full of it?' she questioned.

'I've got a legitimate reason to be mad at my family. My scumbag brother *stole* my daughter.'

'It must have been very tough,' she said sympathetically.

'You have no idea,' he said, shaking his head at the memories. 'I loved that kid.'

'I'm sure,' she murmured.

The Real News started, and they settled down to watch.

Belinda Barrow appeared on the screen, blonde and brittle. She favoured the camera with a superior smile. 'Good evening. I'm Belinda Barrow bringing you the real news.'

'Isn't she a little tight around the eyes?' Michael observed.

'This is Nip and Tuck City,' Lissa said. 'One has to stay looking good.'

'I don't get it – what's the point of looking thirty if you're fifty?'

'Who says she's fifty?'

'I can tell.'

'Oh,' Lissa said, amused. 'So you're an expert on women, huh?'

'Didn't say that.'

'How old am *I*?'

'Pushing seventy,' he joked. 'But I gotta say – you look great!'

She burst out laughing. 'Forty,' she said. 'I'm forty.'

'I know,' he said, laughing too.

'And you?'

'Gettin' up there,' he said ruefully. 'Forty-four.'

'You look good.'

'You should see the picture I got hangin' in the attic.'

'You're funny when you let yourself go,' she said, smiling.

They exchanged another long look.

'Here we go,' Lissa said, turning up the volume on the TV.

'Tonight we'll be talking to up-and-coming singer-songwriter, Gregory Lynch,' Belinda said, reading the teleprompter with assured professionalism, her eyes barely moving as they scanned the words. 'Gregory's been in the headlines lately because of his separation from superstar, Lissa Roman, and later on we'll be bringing you *his* side of the story. Our interview with Gregory Lynch makes particularly fascinating viewing, so don't go away, because we'll be right back after the break.'

'Oh, God,' Lissa groaned, running a hand through her platinum hair. 'This is making me nervous. Why would he want to get on TV and talk about me?'

'For money.'

'You should've heard what he said on the phone earlier.'

'What?'

'I can't tell you,' she said, hesitating for a moment. 'It'll only make you mad.'

'Did he threaten you, Lissa?' Michael asked, angry at the thought. ''Cause if he did, I'll pay him a visit.'

'I hung up before he had a chance.'

'Do me a favour, don't answer your phone again. By tomorrow you'll have all new numbers.'

'It won't be too difficult for him to get them.'

'What does your lawyer say?'

'He informed me that I'll have to agree to a settlement since we were married for two years.'

'Doesn't your pre-nuptial cover that?'

'I'm supposed to pay him two hundred thousand dollars a year for every year we were married. My lawyer says I'm getting off cheaply.'

'That's cheap?' Michael said, raising an eyebrow.

'According to him it is.'

'Jesus!'

'So I'll pay, and hopefully he'll go away. Wouldn't *that* be nice?'

'You'd better remind your lawyer to have Gregg sign a confidentiality agreement. Something that'll stop him going public.'

'I'd like nothing better than to shut him up,' she said, adding a venomous – 'Permanently if I could.'

'We should be discussing whether he has a gun,' Michael said. 'That's why I'm here, isn't it?'

'So *that*'s why you're here,' she said, powerless to stop herself flirting.

'Can't think of any other reason,' he said, trying not to react.

'No?' she said, still flirting.

'No,' he said, meeting her gaze.

The sexual tension between them was mounting.

'Maybe I saw him with a gun once,' Lissa said. 'I'm not sure.'

He gave her a sceptical look. 'You're not sure?'

'I can't remember.'

The commercials finished and the show started. Belinda Barrow teased the Gregg Lynch interview again, then proceeded to introduce a segment about cloning.

'Gregg must love this.' Lissa sighed. 'He was so

desperate to be a star. When we'd arrive at premières and everyone would yell *my* name, he hated it because *he* wanted the attention. Sometimes I think he simply grew out of love with me because I'm famous and he isn't.'

'Hey,' Michael said, staring at her intently, 'nobody in their right mind could grow out of love with you.'

'Why are you so nice to me, Michael?' she said softly.

'Because I can see it's time somebody was.'

Taylor loved the excitement of being back on a movie set. It made her feel unbelievably comfortable, surrounded by a crew who almost always became like one big family. Since marrying Larry she hadn't worked at all, and she'd genuinely missed it. She was enamoured with everything about film-making – even the long hours between takes.

She especially enjoyed being treated like a star. Larry was the star in their household and she was his wife – a role she'd never coveted. She'd always had a burning desire to be equally important, and now she planned on achieving her objective one way or the other.

The director of the movie was Montana Gray, an interesting and smart woman who'd been around Hollywood for quite some time. Montana wrote and directed all her own projects, preferring to maintain control, which was one of the reasons she worked mostly for cable where she found she could get the freedom she desired. Succeeding as a female director was not easy. If a male director made a film that flopped at the box office, he soon got another deal. If a female director did the same thing, her career was almost over. Montana had done the unusual – she'd managed to survive in what was basically a male arena.

Montana had been married to Neil Gray, the famous English director. Neil had expired of a massive heart-attack fifteen years ago. The rumour was that, at the time, he'd been in bed on top of Gina Germaine, a luscious blonde screen siren.

Apart from being a talented writer-director, Montana had a reputation for being a wild woman. Once, when a certain producer had pissed her off, she'd delivered an enormous gift-wrapped package of bullshit to his office. He'd discovered it on his pristine desk early one morning and gone totally berserk.

The story had sent shock waves of laughter around Hollywood. And the message was clear – Montana Gray was *not* a woman to be messed with.

When Montana strode onto the set, everyone took notice. She was, at five feet ten inches, a lean, striking-looking woman in her mid-forties, with waist-length black hair worn in a braid down her back, and direct, gold-flecked tiger eyes usually hidden beneath tinted shades.

Taylor and she hit it off immediately. Taylor was secretly thrilled that Montana had requested her for the part. No interviews, no auditions, she was the actress of choice, and that boosted her confidence.

'What did you see in me that made you request me?' she'd asked Montana, during the lunch break on her first day of shooting.

'Well,' Montana had answered thoughtfully, 'I remembered your work, and when you married Larry Singer, I noticed you at various events. It struck me that, even though I was sure you had a strong marriage, there was a vulnerability about you, a need within you that works perfectly for this part.'

'Oh,' Taylor had said, somewhat taken aback that Montana was so intuitive. 'Yes, I do have a strong marriage.'

'Good. That's the way it should be.'

'That's the way it is,' Taylor had assured her.

'I like Larry,' Montana had said. 'We've known each other a long while.'

'You've never worked together, have you?'

'Neil and Larry worked on a movie once. It was not a happy experience.'

'What film was that?'

'Nothing anyone remembers,' Montana had said lightly. 'And I have a suspicion Larry would prefer to forget it, too.'

On the second day of shooting they worked late. Taylor phoned their housekeeper to make sure Larry got his dinner on time. The moment he arrived home he called her. 'You didn't warn me this was a night shoot,' he said, obviously put out.

'It happens in the movie business,' she replied. 'How many times have *you* called *me* from the studio to say you won't be home until midnight?'

'That's true, Taylor. However, I'm not happy about you being out by yourself. Have they got a car and driver for you?'

'Of course, Larry,' she said, savouring the words. 'I'm the *star* of this movie.'

'Hmm . . .' he said. 'I'm still uncertain about you accepting the role.'

'Why?'

'You have a reputation to maintain.'

'*What* reputation?' she said scornfully. 'I'm married to *you*, so anything I do should be acceptable.'

'Would you like me to visit the set one day?'

He was backing down, which pleased her. 'Do you have time?' she said.

'I'll make time.'

'Now don't forget, tomorrow night is Norio and Kyndra's anniversary party, so in case I'm working late, be *sure* to have your secretary remind you. I'll join you at their house as soon as I can.'

'Does this mean you'll be working late *every* night?' he asked, not sounding at all happy.

'No, darling,' she said smoothly. 'However, you know I can't leave whenever I feel like it. I have to be responsible.'

'I understand that, Taylor, and I've been thinking.'

'About what?'

'When you get home tonight we should talk about your project. I might have come up with an answer for you.'

'What kind of answer?'

'How about *I* find you a writer to work on the script?'

'You mean you'd get involved?'

'It's what you've always wanted me to do, isn't it?'

'Yes, Larry, that's exactly right.' Taylor clicked off her phone, a triumphant smile playing across her lips. At *last* Larry was getting involved.

And about time too.

Nicci hadn't been to a rave in a long time. It occurred to her that since she'd been engaged to Evan, she hadn't done much of anything except cater to her future husband.

What happened to me? she thought, as she danced and jumped and yelled like a crazy person, sweat pouring off her body as she totally gave herself up to the blaring sounds – all inhibitions out the window. *I used to be a free spirit who did whatever I wanted whenever I felt like it. Then I got engaged, and suddenly I turned into a mini Hollywood wife. Holy shit!*

She was stoned. What with the grass at home, the sake in the restaurant, vodka in the car on the way to the rave, and Ecstasy when she'd got there, she was very, very wasted. It didn't matter. She *wanted* to be stoned. She didn't care to think about Evan and his duplicity.

All she wanted was to hang loose, get wild, zone out. And she was doing that with Brian, who was way more fun than she'd ever imagined. He was manic and out there. He was interesting and funny and great. He was . . . *Jesus!* She almost fell as the room began spinning around and around, and she knew she'd better lie down or she'd throw up.

She was giddy and disoriented until Brian grabbed her, and then she started laughing uncontrollably.

'You've . . . got . . . great . . . teeth,' she managed. 'I get off on your teeth. Cool teeth!'

He was laughing too as he pulled her over to the side. They were both laughing hysterically and she didn't feel sick any more, and then the room was taking off again, and the music was louder than ever, and Brian suddenly pinned her against the wall and began kissing her, his insistent tongue pushing into her mouth.

She could not remember kissing Evan like this. Brian's kisses were better than sex. It was like *so* hot that she almost came.

She closed her eyes. Somewhere in the back of her head she knew she shouldn't be doing this. It didn't matter, nothing mattered. There *was* no tomorrow. *Today is tomorrow. Tomorrow is today.*

What the fuck! She didn't have a care in sight.

Monday was an exceptionally long day, they didn't finish until ten. When Montana invited her for a drink, Taylor decided she had no reason to rush home. Larry was probably in bed watching all the political programmes he enjoyed, while her adrenaline was in overdrive. There was no way she could sleep.

'Where did you have in mind?' she asked.

'We usually hang out at my favourite Mexican bar,' Montana replied. 'Sonja's coming. I think it would be helpful for you and she to get together before tomorrow when we shoot the love scene. Sorry about getting to the love scene so early, although sometimes it works out better that way.'

'I made a movie with Charlie Dollar once,' Taylor reminisced. 'I only had a small role, but the first time I met him I was naked in bed – watched over by a crew of seventy. I was mortified!'

'I presume that was before Larry,' Montana said drily.

'Way before,' Taylor said, laughing at the memory.

'How does Larry feel about you doing *my* movie?' Montana asked curiously.

'I make my own decisions.'

'Glad to hear it,' Montana said. 'Nothing worse than a man telling you what to do. I've had a few of those in my time. Believe me, they don't last long around me.'

'I can imagine,' Taylor murmured, thinking that she wasn't calling Larry to tell him she was going for a drink. Even though he'd said he was prepared to talk about her project, it could wait.

This way he might sweat a little, wonder what she was up to. He was way too secure in their relationship.

'I could kill him,' Lissa said, tight-lipped.

'Calm down,' Michael said, although he could understand how she felt.

'*You* calm down,' she responded, getting up and pacing around the room. 'I'd like to kill the son-of-a-bitch! How *dare* he get on television and say all those terrible things about me?' She turned to him with an appealing expression. 'You *know* they're not true – don't you, Michael?'

'Of course I do,' he said, wanting nothing more than to hold her in his arms and comfort her.

'Yes,' she worried, 'but the public are likely to believe him, and then the tabloids will pick it up. Oh, God! I'll be vilified everywhere.'

'I'm telling you, Lissa,' he said, trying to placate her, 'this'll go away. *You*'re the famous one in the family, he's just the jerk who wants to get his face on TV. You gotta let it go.'

'I'm calling my lawyer immediately,' she said, a determined jut to her chin.

'There's nothing you can do now.'

'Yes, there is, there has to be.'

Michael couldn't take his eyes off her, she was so goddamn beautiful and womanly. He knew that if he stayed he was going to find himself in deep trouble. He *wanted* to stay and comfort her, and yet he knew the smart thing was to get out while he could. Becoming involved with Lissa Roman would be a bad move. She'd use him and discard him. She was a movie star, she wouldn't even realize she was doing it.

'I gotta be going,' he said, getting up.

She turned on him, blue eyes flashing. 'Why are you always taking off on me?' she demanded. 'Do *you* think I'm a self-obsessed bitch like Gregg says?'

'Don't be crazy.'

'I'm not being crazy, Michael, but all you seem to do is run.'

'Hey, listen,' he said, 'I'm trying to keep this on some kind of level here.'

'What does *that* mean?'

'You and I are messing with each other's minds, Lissa,' he said, staring at her with an intense expression.

She narrowed her eyes. 'What the *hell* are you talking about?'

'I'm not a good candidate for Rebound Man,' he muttered.

'Is *that* what you think?' she said angrily. 'That I'm so mad at my soon-to-be ex that I'm looking for a *Rebound* Man? Don't flatter yourself, I'm not looking for anything – *especially* not a man.'

'Let's not get into this, Lissa. We live in two different

worlds, and I'm not the kinda guy who'd fit into yours.'

'Are you saying that because I'm famous we can't hang out?'

'No, I'm saying that if I stayed, it could be dangerous for both of us.'

She gave him a long, steady look. 'Dangerous, Michael?'

'You know what I mean,' he said, realizing that he wanted to kiss her more than he'd ever wanted to do anything else. She was standing there before him, vulnerable, angry, gorgeous. And yet . . . something held him back.

Get out, his inner voice warned. *You're not boyfriend-of-the-star material. Get the fuck out while you still can.*

'You should phone your lawyer and decide what to do tomorrow,' he said gruffly. 'I'll call you in the morning.'

She stared at him for a moment, her diamond blue eyes turning into ice cold chips. 'Fine,' she said coolly. Lissa was not used to being rejected, and that's exactly what she felt he was doing.

'Thanks for dinner,' he said. 'The lasagna was sensational.'

'My pleasure,' she said, her voice an icy blast. 'Oh,' she added, 'and by the way, don't forget to send a bill.'

'A bill?' he said, frowning, because he knew she was now trying to piss him off.

'For your services.'

'You have us on retainer, Lissa.'

'Sorry, I forgot. It's all inclusive, isn't it?'

'Don't take your shitty husband's remarks out on me,' he said, still frowning.

'We'll talk about it some other time, Michael,' she said brusquely. 'I'm tired. See yourself out,' and she marched out of the room.

He walked outside, got in his car and drove off.

The moment he hit the street he was angry at himself.

What the hell was wrong with him? Why hadn't he stayed around when she obviously needed a friend?

Because she'll hurt me. Because that's what women I care about always do.

And Michael was through with being hurt. He'd suffered enough betrayals to last a lifetime.

Taylor soon found out that drinking with the girls was a revelation. Sonja Lucerne was a fine actress who had once played leading-lady roles until she'd got too old for the Hollywood they-gotta-be-in-their-twenties scene. Like Meryl Streep and Glenn Close before her, she'd kept her dignity, was incredibly talented, and still looked wonderful.

'It's such a pleasure to meet you,' Taylor said, finding herself somewhat in awe. 'I've always admired your work.'

'So *you*'re my little tootsie in this film, huh?' Sonja drawled in a deep husky voice. She was a pointy-faced woman with a mass of red hair, piercing eyes and high cheekbones.

'*Nobody*'s a tootsie in one of my films,' Montana said, ordering a tequila straight up.

'It's a fine script,' Sonja said, playing with one of her many gold bangles. 'You'll love working with Montana.'

'I know I will,' Taylor said enthusiastically.

'Montana knows how to treat women,' Sonja offered. 'Male directors simply don't understand us, hard as they try.'

'I'm into that,' Taylor agreed. 'Although, of course, my husband—'

'He doesn't get it either, darling,' Sonja interrupted, waving a dismissive hand. 'I saw his last film. His leading man was sixty-something, while his leading lady was a twenty-something twinkie. You should talk to him. He seems smart, and he's certainly talented enough.'

Taylor had never thought about it before, but Sonja

223

was right – Larry did the conventional thing and usually cast an older male star with a much younger actress. It was time he changed that. 'Listen,' she said ruefully, 'he won't even cast *me* in one of his movies, that's how much influence I have.'

Sonja gave her a penetrating stare. 'You'd be surprised what kind of influence women have over the men they live with. The trick is to exert that power. If you play the woman you *think* they want you to be, nothing ever changes. If you become strong, you'll make *him* stronger because of it. *That*'s when things change.'

'Hmm . . .' Taylor said.

'It always amazes me how accepting women are at being treated badly,' Montana said, joining in. 'Especially in this town. How many couples do you see where the husband is some old goat, and his wife is a two or three decades younger beauty?'

'Everywhere I go,' Taylor said.

'And yet,' Montana continued, 'they play the charade that it's true love and everything is perfect. And because the husbands get away with it, *that*'s what they end up putting on the screen – old men, young women.'

'Exactly!' Sonja said.

'But what they're really doing is reflecting their own lives,' Montana said, downing her tequila in one fast gulp. 'Then, of course, when they see an older *woman* with a younger *man*, it's "Oh dear, isn't that shocking!"'

'You're so right,' Taylor agreed.

'Of course I'm right,' Montana said forcefully. 'That's why I make cable movies and not theatrical blockbusters, because the men in this town are frightened of my ideas, which is okay with me because I get to do exactly what I want. For instance, this film we're making now is about two women in a meaningful relationship – nothing wrong with that, only you won't see it on the big screen. Too threatening for the Hollywood boys. The only time *they* want to see two women together is when they're making out in a soft-porno flick.'

Taylor nodded, her eyes gleaming. This was not the kind of conversation she was used to and she loved it. Female power – both women exuded it. She felt privileged to be in their company.

Chapter Twenty-four

On Tuesday morning Nicci couldn't open her eyes. She could barely breathe, let alone anything else. Gradually, she surfaced, only to find that she was surfacing in an unfamiliar bed.

With a supreme effort she forced herself to wake up. *Oh, God!* she thought in a panic. *I am naked, I am in a strange bed, and there is a man sleeping next to me.*

Her head hurt so much she didn't even dare to look to see who it was. But then she recognized the shaggy beach-blond hair, and knew it was Brian.

What the hell had she done?

She rolled out of bed, realizing that this must be his apartment. It was spacious and untidy, with a panoramic view of the city.

She searched around for her clothes, and spotted them scattered all over the floor.

Grabbing her jeans, she wriggled into them. Then she found her top and put it on.

Memories began flooding back, including Brian's revelations about Evan and his fiancée.

Oh, great! Evan had a former fiancée, and that information had made her jump into bed with his brother. What kind of girl *was* she?

So Evan had kept something from her. It wasn't *that*

bad, it wasn't like he'd *murdered* someone. Brian was much worse, he'd got her drunk and stoned, then taken advantage of her.

God, how she hated him! He'd done it to get back at his brother. What a scumbag.

She stared at the object of her fury, still asleep, or passed out, one or the other. Goddamn it, he'd ruined her life. Now she'd have to look at him forever and remember that she'd slept with him.

Or had she? She couldn't remember. Although her clothes, strewn all over the floor, should give her a clue.

She shoved his shoulder. 'Brian,' she said excitedly, 'wake up!'

'What?' he mumbled, flinging his arms out, almost hitting her in the face.

'Don't you have a plane to catch?' she said.

'*Fuck!*' he muttered, reaching for his watch on the bedside table. 'Guess I blew that.' Bleary-eyed, he focused on her. 'Christ, Nic, what're *you* doing here?'

'That's what *I*'d like to know,' she said grimly. '*How* did we get here? And *why* did I wake up in your bed?'

'You woke up in my bed?' he said, struggling to sit up. 'Jeez!' A big grin spread across his face. 'I must be more irresistible than I thought.'

'Brian, that's not funny,' she said, standing beside the bed, glaring at him accusingly. 'I don't remember anything. What did you do? Slip something in my drink?'

'Yeah, like I'd do that,' he said, pushing his long, shaggy hair out of his eyes. 'Jesus, Nic, I don't remember anything either.'

'Did we, uh . . . do anything or didn't we?' she demanded.

'How would *I* know?' he said, yawning.

Dilemma. Neither of them could remember.

'Well,' she said matter-of-factly, 'I don't think we did. In fact, I'm *sure* we didn't.'

''S long as you're sure,' he mumbled.

'Yes,' she said firmly. 'I'm sure. We simply got carried away at the rave, came back here and passed out.' She shot him another accusing look. 'I don't know why you took me there in the first place.'

'To have a blast,' he said, yawning again.

'It might've been a blast last night, but I feel like total crap, and I wanna go home. Is my car downstairs?'

'How would I know?'

'This *is* your apartment.'

'True.'

'You're not being very helpful. And you haven't even picked up Evan's papers,' she said, beginning to panic again. 'For God's sake, Brian, you'd better get it together. I've got a wedding to plan, your mom's arriving any minute, Evan's been lying to me, and now this.'

'Keep it down, you're hurting my head,' he muttered, stumbling out of bed. 'Let's figure this out. Your car must be downstairs, 'cause that's what we were in.'

'Exactly.'

'Okay, I'll throw on some clothes, we'll go back to your place, pick up Evan's papers, then I'll get the next plane outta here. After that we'll forget this ever happened.'

'Right,' she agreed, unable to take her eyes off his rather impressive naked body. 'And perhaps you can put your pants on.'

He ignored her request and padded into the bathroom.

'You'd better not tell Evan I filled you in on him being engaged before,' he yelled out, ''cause he'll be major pissed, an' *I*'ve gotta work with the asshole.'

'I *have* to mention it,' she shouted back. 'Why should I keep it a secret?'

'Then get Lynda to tell you. Mommy Dearest has the biggest mouth going.'

'How do I achieve *that*?'

'Say somebody told you, *not* me,' he said, emerging from the bathroom in a pair of striped underwear. 'She'll tell you, an' *then* y' can take it up with him.'

'Any other secrets you'd like to share with me about my future husband?' she said, wishing this would all turn out to be nothing more than a bad dream.

'You'll find out,' he said, pulling on a pair of crumpled pants.

And then she remembered kissing him, and how good it had been.

Maybe they *had* taken it to the next level. After all, they'd both woken up naked . . .

She didn't want to think about it.

'C'mon,' she said impatiently. 'Let's do this. I have a wedding to organize.'

'Well?' Quincy asked, the moment Michael walked into the office.

'Well, what?' Michael responded bad-temperedly. He was in no mood to be questioned.

'What went on last night?'

'Nothing,' Michael said, sipping from a mug of hot, strong coffee.

'Nothin', huh?' Quincy said disbelievingly. 'You had a meetin' with Lissa Roman, an' nothin' went on.'

'Oh, yeah, that,' Michael said casually. 'It went well.'

'*What* went well?' Quincy said, exasperated.

'The meeting.'

'You gonna tell me what happened or not?' Quincy demanded.

'Nothing happened, Q,' Michael said, like it was no big deal. 'I met with the woman, we discussed what to do about her husband's gun, and, uh . . . that was that.'

'That was that, huh?' Quincy said, not believing him for a moment.

'Yeah.'

'You're *sure* nothin' happened I should know about?'

'Talking about things you should know about,' Michael said, placing his coffee mug on Quincy's desk, 'your wife called me last night.'

'*Amber* called you? About what?'

'About me *not* getting involved with Lissa Roman.'

'Aw, Jeez,' Quincy groaned. 'There she goes again.'

'What's with this shit, Q? I never said I had anything going with the woman, an' now I've got your wife on my case. I don't fucking appreciate it.'

'Sorry about that,' Quincy said abashedly. 'You *know* Amber, she gets carried away.'

'Goddamn it, Q—'

'She *likes* Carol,' Quincy interrupted. 'Thinks the two of you make a perfect couple.'

'Oh, good,' Michael said sarcastically. 'I got your wife's approval. Maybe *she*'d like to spend more time with Carol.'

'She is. We're havin' dinner there tonight. I've been reminded twenty times, so you'd better not forget.'

'Why would I forget?' Michael said.

Quincy shrugged. 'Amber said I should remind you.'

'For crissakes, I'll be there. Okay?' he said, reaching for a cigarette, indulging himself in a habit he was trying to break.

'What's happenin' with you an' her anyway?' Quincy persisted.

'I dunno,' Michael said, inhaling deeply. 'I'm not looking for anything permanent. Carol's nice enough, and that's about it.'

'She looks sexy to me.'

'The *cleaning* lady looks sexy to you.'

'Amber would *love* to hear that,' Quincy said, roaring with laughter. 'She's got a real bad jealous streak.'

'If she keeps up the shit she's giving me, maybe I'll tell her what a pussy-chaser you *really* are.'

'No, man,' Quincy begged. 'You do that an' my sorry ass won't be worth shit.'

'So get her to stay the fuck outta my business. Okay, Q?'

'I'll try, but nobody ever said bein' married is easy.'

'I want to sue him,' Lissa said calmly, sitting in her lawyer's Century City office, quite composed.

'Sue him for what?' her lawyer replied.

'Defamation of character. I want to sue him, the television station, and that blonde who introduces the show.'

'Lissa, I thought you wanted Gregg to go away quietly. Isn't that our objective?'

'No,' she said sharply. 'I'm fed up with being maligned. It's time to get in his face, like he did mine. How *dare* he say those things about me? I have a daughter to think about, a reputation, *and* I have my fans. I will not allow him to get away with saying those things about me.'

'You're serious about suing?'

'Yes.'

'I've never seen you so determined.'

'You probably haven't, but I'm not all sweetness and light. I can be a bitch too.'

'I noticed.'

'So find out where he is and sue the son-of-a-bitch. Okay?'

After she was finished with her lawyer, she dropped by her dress designer's showroom and had the final fittings for her Vegas clothes. The Desert Millennium Princess Hotel was sending a plane for her on Thursday, two days before her appearance. That way she could rehearse with the band and her dancers, and get acclimatized. Since they were paying her so much money, her one-night show was a very big deal, and she wanted to be totally prepared.

Claude was flying everyone in on Saturday on his plane.

So far the group included James, Larry and Taylor, Kyndra and Norio, and Stella and Seth. All her best friends.

In one way she was nervous about her upcoming performance, and in another she was looking forward to it. Performing on stage was where she felt most at home, more so than being in front of a movie camera or in the recording studio. She got the greatest thrill from the surge of adoration the audience gave her. Live applause *wrapped* her in love.

Since Kyndra couldn't make lunch, she called James and he happily agreed to meet her at Le Dôme. They sat at a corner table studying menus.

'Did you see it?' James said, as soon as they'd ordered.

'Yes, I saw it,' she replied evenly. 'And I'm suing him. I've already met with my lawyer.'

'On what grounds can you sue?'

'Defamation of character. Seems like a pretty good lawsuit to me.'

The waiter brought James a Martini, and Evian for her. 'You're taking it well,' James remarked.

'I'm angry, not upset. If Gregg thinks I'm about to fade away and play the hard-done-by little superstar who doesn't care to ruin her public image, he's very much mistaken.'

'Good for you,' James said, sipping his Martini.

'I'm *trying* to handle everything,' she explained, 'and I can, as long as I get Gregg out of my life forever.'

'Nobody can blame you for that.'

'And remind me *never* to get involved with another man ever again,' she added forcefully, thinking of the strong attraction she felt for Michael. 'You're all as bad as each other.'

'Kindly do not put *me* in that category,' James said tartly. 'I'm gay, remember?'

'Gay guys have their trip too.'

'As if *you* would know.'

'I'm your best friend, aren't I? How many times have you shared outrageous stories about you and Claude?'

'Too many,' James said regretfully. 'And do not forget your promise to *never* repeat them.'

'I'm perfectly *happy* on my own,' Lissa said. 'No more involvements. No more falling in love with a handsome face and a hard body.'

'*And* let us not forget a delicious dick,' James murmured reverently.

'You always go for the dick, don't you?' she said, with the trace of a smile.

'I thought that was *you*, dear,' James observed. 'Surely I'm not mistaken?'

'*Very* amusing.'

'Do I sense that you're interested in someone?' he ventured. 'The moment you say that you're not is the moment I know that you are.'

She managed to look suitably surprised. 'What *are* you talking about?'

'I know you so well, Lissa,' he said fondly. 'Are you *sure* there's not a little something you'd like to reveal to me?'

'Absolutely not.'

'Shame!'

'Your imagination is far too active, James. You need to get a hobby.'

'Ah . . .' he crowed triumphantly. 'So there *is* someone?'

'Will you *quit*?'

The waiter brought their order. Grilled swordfish for James and a chopped salad for Lissa.

'Who is he?' James persisted, picking up his fork. 'Anyone I know?'

She thought about Michael for a moment. He'd run out on her again, that's twice he'd done that. Maybe she *was* nothing more than business to him. How sad.

It wasn't good for her ego. She was Lissa Roman,

superstar. She could probably have any man she wanted. Except the one she did want, which was Michael.

So, you do want him?

No, I don't.

Yes, you do.

After lunch, Chuck drove her home. The usual paparazzi were milling around outside the gates of her house. TV cameras were also present, a result of Gregg's new surge of publicity.

'Miz Roman, do you have any comments on your husband's interview last night?' yelled one of the TV reporters, running up to her car.

She ignored him, staring stoically ahead as Chuck drove through the heavy iron gates.

Nellie greeted her with a cup of green tea, while Danny bounced forward with a long list of phone messages.

She checked the list, searching for Michael's name. It wasn't there.

She took her tea and went upstairs to her bedroom. On the centre of her bed was an envelope with her name on it. The name was not written – it was made up of individual letters cut from a magazine. *LiSsA*. She opened it. The message was clear. *You will Die In VeGas bitch.*

It was not the first time she had received a threatening letter, although usually they didn't reach her bedroom. She called down to Nellie on the intercom. 'There's a letter on my bed. Can you find out how it got there?'

Nellie called back five minutes later. 'Sorry, Miz Lissa, the new maid found it out by the front gate this morning and thought it was important. I've told her that in future she should give everything to Danny, and not bother you.'

At least the maniac hadn't got into the house. Maybe it was Gregg trying to scare her. This was exactly the kind of stupid stunt he'd pull.

She immediately called the Robbins-Scorsinni office and

asked for Michael. He was out, so she spoke to Quincy. 'I received a death-threat letter,' she said, remaining surprisingly calm, 'so I need one of you to come to Vegas with me. Of course I have Chuck, and there'll be plenty of security at the hotel, however, I'll feel better if you or Michael are with me.'

'What kind of letter?' Quincy asked.

'It's probably a hoax, or Gregg playing games. I'll messenger it over so you can take a look.'

'Lissa,' Quincy said apologetically, 'you know I got this broken leg thing goin' on, otherwise I'd be there.'

'Oh, yes. I forgot.' A beat. 'Michael will do, send him. We leave Thursday morning. If he comes to my house promptly at ten, he can drive to the airport with us.'

'It's done, Lissa, he'll be there.'

To Nicci's horror, when they got downstairs, she discovered a huge dent in the front of her BMW. 'How did *this* happen?' she wailed, circling her car.

'Who the fuck knows?' Brian mumbled, groping for his sunglasses.

'Were we *so* out of it that we had an accident and didn't realize?' she demanded, turning on him. 'We could've *killed* someone.'

'*You* were driving,' he said accusingly.

'No, I wasn't,' she argued. 'You insisted, remember?'

'C'mon, Nic, get in the car and let's get this over with. I gotta get back to the location before my brother drives everyone insane with his nagging.'

She slid into the driver's seat. He didn't argue – he was too hung-over. So was she, although it hardly seemed to matter.

They drove to Evan's house slumped in their individual hangovers. As soon as they got there, Nicci ran inside and fetched the envelope containing Evan's papers. By the time she got back, Brian was sitting in his Porsche, which had been parked outside the house all night.

She handed him the envelope. 'There you go,' she said. 'Remember, not a word to Evan about any of this.'

'Maybe there's nothing to tell,' Brian said, peering over the top of his sunglasses. 'The way *I* see it, we got back to my place an' passed out. I think if we'd *had* sex, one of us would remember. I've never had a girl say she *doesn't*.'

'You certainly have a high opinion of yourself, don't you?' she said, wishing he wasn't so damn attractive.

'Somebody's got to,' he said, grinning.

'Oh suck it up, Brian. You're a total flake.'

He started his car, revving the engine. 'I'll give your love to Evan.'

'Don't bother,' she said, going back into the house.

As soon as she was sure he'd gone, she took a shower, standing there for fifteen minutes, letting the cold water rain down on her body. When she got out, she wrapped herself in Evan's big towelling bathrobe, took two aspirins, drank a bottle of water, and collapsed onto the bed. Then she called Saffron.

'Where've you *been*, girl?' Saffron asked. 'I get withdrawals when you vanish outta sight.'

'Don't ask.' Nicci sighed. 'I need to see you. Got stuff to talk about.'

'Like what?'

'Like can you come by later?'

'If I get a babysitter.'

'Bring Lulu, I never see enough of her. You can both stay the night.'

'Lemme call you back.'

'I need you to be my shrink,' Nicci said. 'I've got a bad feeling I might've made a *major* mistake.'

'Forget about it. There's no way I'm going to Vegas just 'cause she received some crank's letter,' Michael said

236

stubbornly. He'd just got back to the office after meeting with a husband who suspected his wife was a cocaine addict. Now Quincy was immediately on his case.

'You *gotta* go,' Quincy retorted, trying to persuade him. 'Lissa Roman's one of our most important clients. We have a contract to take care of all her security needs.'

'I'm *not* a freaking bodyguard,' Michael said grimly.

'Nobody said you were. You'll be goin' there as a representative of our office, makin' sure everything's okay. Anyway, what the fuck's *with* you an' Lissa? *Why* doncha wanna go?'

'Cause I'm not about to be summoned like some flunkey. What am I supposed to do? Hold her hand?'

'Hey, man, that's up to you.'

'Quit with that shit, Q. I've had it.'

'Okay, okay, we'll talk about it later.'

Saffron turned up at the house with her three-year-old daughter, Lulu, whom Nicci adored.

Lulu threw herself into Nicci's arms, smothering her with hugs and kisses.

'Why don't I see more of my baby?' Nicci demanded, swinging her godchild around in circles. 'I *am* her godmother.'

'It's *your* fault,' Saffron said as Lulu yelled excitedly. 'You're always busy doing nothing. Anyway, wait until you see Lulu's dress. She'll be *the* most beautiful flower-girl ever. Won't you, baby?' she said, grabbing her daughter.

'Not a baby,' Lulu said sternly. 'Me big girl.'

'Sure you are,' Nicci agreed.

'Anyway . . . guess what?' Saffron said.

'What?' Nicci said.

'Prepare yourself, babe,' Saffron said, with a secret smile. ''Cause this Saturday is kidnap night.'

'It is?' Nicci said excitedly.

'You bet your fine ass. Saturday's the night we take off on our magical mystery tour. So from five in the afternoon you'd better be ready for anything. And don't even bother askin' me questions 'cause, girl, I am not tellin' you a damn *thing*.'

'I'm totally psyched,' Nicci said, momentarily forgetting about her massive hangover. 'I've always wanted a wild bachelorette night – which I hope includes male strippers with huge—'

'Shush!' Saffron interrupted, indicating Lulu.

'Sorry.'

'Hungry! Hungry! Hungry!' Lulu yelled, jumping up and down.

'We'd better order food,' Saffron said. 'She's like me, wants what she wants as soon as she wants it!'

'How about burgers?' Nicci suggested. 'Isn't that what small people eat?'

'It's what this kid eats,' Saffron said.

'Lulu, sugar-pie,' Nicci asked, 'what d'you want for dinner?'

'Burger an' french flies,' Lulu said, all huge eyes and baby dreadlocks, a small version of her mommy.

'Fries,' Saffron corrected.

'Flies.' Lulu giggled.

'I'll call Johnny Rocket's, they deliver,' Nicci said. 'Do you think burgers are good for a hangover?'

'No.'

'Then what is?'

'A drink.'

'Like that's *such* a fine idea. Let's get Lulu settled, then I'll open the wine and tell you everything.'

Quincy was still arguing with Michael about accompanying Lissa to Vegas, but now it was four hours later and they were sitting in Carol's apartment, which she'd decorated with scented candles and vases of fresh flowers. She was busy in the kitchen with Amber.

Michael was pissed that Quincy was telling him he had to go to Vegas when he was trying his best to stay away from Lissa. He knew that somehow it was inevitable they'd eventually be together, and yet he was making a conscious effort to avoid it, because his gut instinct kept on warning him it would lead to nothing but trouble.

'C'mon, man,' Quincy persisted, 'stop givin' me grief on this. The woman needs protection.'

'*You* go.'

'I would if I could.'

'Oh, yeah, your leg – very convenient.'

'I'm tellin' you, it'll be good for the agency,' Quincy urged. 'She'll recommend us to people, so make sure you take plenty of cards with you.'

'What am I? A salesman for the Quincy Roadshow?'

'It's not the Quincy Roadshow. It's the Robbins-Scorsinni Roadshow.'

'Shit,' Michael muttered.

'What's your fuckin' problem?' Quincy bellowed, finally getting angry.

'Okay, okay,' Michael said. 'Don't get your balls in a sweat. I'll go.'

'Go where?' Amber asked, entering the room.

'Nowhere,' Michael said.

Carol came in from the kitchen, holding aloft a tray of canapés. 'You'll love these,' she said, with a bright smile. 'I splurged – baby baked potatoes with sour cream and caviar. What do you think, Michael?'

'Who cares what *he* thinks?' Quincy boomed. 'Bring 'em over here!'

Later, Michael had made up his mind to give her the speech. He wasn't looking forward to it, and wished he could do it over the phone. Only that would be the coward's way out, and if there was one thing Michael wasn't, it was a coward.

'What're you cooking?' he asked.

'Roast beef, English Yorkshire pudding, and three different vegetables,' she announced proudly.

'Sounds good,' he said, remembering how comfortable he'd felt sitting with Lissa in her den eating lasagna on trays and getting to know her.

Carol ruffled his hair affectionately. 'And later, after dinner, I have a surprise for you.'

'You do?'

'Something special.'

Yeah, he thought, *and I have one for you, too.*

He couldn't wait for the evening to end.

While Michael was at Carol's, Lissa was on her way to Kyndra and Norio's anniversary party with James and Claude. She wore a white Armani suit, Harry Winston diamonds, and an upswept hairstyle. It was her first social outing since the news of her split with Gregg, and she was determined to hold her head high. She preferred not to think about how many people might have seen the TV programme the night before. If it hadn't been Kyndra and Norio's party, there was no way she would have gone. But since they were such long-time friends, she couldn't let them down. So here she was, sitting in the back of Claude's black Rolls with James, while Claude sat up front next to his chauffeur. At sixty-three, Claude was a man used to immediate service. A record and media tycoon, he'd made his first million by the time he was twenty. Now a billionaire, he'd enjoyed a ten-year live-in relationship with James. They were complete opposites. James, so tall and elegant and English. Claude, a small nut of a black man, with energy to spare and a hearty enthusiasm for all the best things in life.

'Don't worry, darling,' James said, reaching for her hand. 'We will not leave your side.'

'It's good you're coming out now,' Claude agreed.

'Yes,' James said. 'After all, your show is on Saturday, and everybody will see you there.'

'That's different. My show is a public event. I can handle those kind of appearances. It's this private stuff I hate. All those Hollywood wives . . .'

'Ah, the bitch brigade,' James drawled. 'And every one of their sweet honey tongues will be sharpened to kill.'

'Thanks, James,' she said. 'You've made me feel *so* much better.'

'*Crap!*' Saffron exclaimed, leaping up half-way through her burger.

'*Crap!*' Lulu repeated, giggling with delight. '*Crap! Crap! Crap!*'

'What's up?' Nicci asked, staring at Saffron who was looking a little wild-eyed.

'Tonight's their anniversary,' Saffron wailed. 'And I forgot!'

'*Whose* anniversary?' Nicci asked patiently.

'My parents! And we're all supposed to be there, Lulu, too.'

'Wanna go t' Grandma's,' Lulu chanted. 'Wanna go! Wanna go!'

'Don't call her that,' Saffron said. 'You know she hates it. Call her Kinny.'

'Wanna go t' Kinny's.' Lulu giggled. '*Now! Now! Now!*'

'Guess you blew it,' Nicci said, picking up a french fry and popping it in her mouth. 'It's too late now.'

'Too late?' Saffron exclaimed. 'It's my parents' twenty-fifth anniversary, for God's sake. *Of course* I gotta go. And so do you.'

'Leave me out.' Nicci groaned, warding her off with a dismissive hand. 'I'm totally finished.'

'Then you'd better get it together, girl,' Saffron said firmly, ''cause Kyndra's expecting *all* of us. C'mon, let's check out your closet and find something to wear.'

'Please,' Nicci said, clutching her head with a dramatic expression, 'I'm sick. I can't do this.'

'Sometimes we gotta do things we don't want to,' Saffron said. '*I* took care of the bridesmaids' dresses, so now it's your turn t' do something for me. Move it, Nic. This is pay-back time.'

'Crap, Saff,' Nicci complained. 'You're giving me no choice.'

'Right,' Saffron said, pulling her up. 'So let's go do the closet thing.'

Chapter Twenty-five

T he time for action was drawing close, and Eric liked to think that he had everything under control. Every day he followed Nicci as she went about her usual routine of doing nothing much at all, although the previous night she'd shocked him by changing her pattern and spending the night with her boyfriend's brother. Oh, yes, Eric knew all the players. He'd tracked the brother through the licence plate on his car, which he'd left parked outside Nicci's house all night.

The girl was obviously a whore – exactly like her mother. Eric wasn't surprised. Most women were whores one way or the other. He'd never met one he could trust.

He was in daily touch with Arliss, who was supposed to make sure everyone took care of what they were instructed to do.

On Tuesday night he met with Danny in the same gay bar they always went to.

As far as Danny was concerned they had become friends. Nobody listened to him the way Eric Vernon did, or bought rounds of drinks with such a generous spirit. He found himself telling Eric everything – including the troubles he was experiencing with his much older boyfriend.

Eric always listened sympathetically, and told Danny of

his problems with *his* partner. Danny had this tingling feeling that when they were both free, they would finally get together in a sexual way.

'We're off to Vegas on Thursday,' Danny confided, taking small sips of an apple Martini – his new favourite drink. 'On a private plane no less. The hotel is sending it for us.'

'Sounds exciting,' Eric said. 'Does she always travel by private plane?'

'Whenever she can,' Danny replied, toying with his new gold stud earring. He felt it gave him a jaunty, macho look.

'It's just you and her, then?'

'And her makeup and hair people, and security, of course.'

'No daughter?'

'She never has Nicci to public events.'

'Do *you* go with her all the time?'

'Whenever I can,' Danny said. 'Which is one of the main problems between me and George.' He lowered his voice. 'George is *jealous* of her,' he whispered as if it was a state secret. 'The nerve! Jealous of *my* princess.'

'I read in the papers that she's getting three million dollars for one night's work. Is that true?'

'Of course,' Danny said crisply. 'And she deserves every cent. My princess works so hard, and has such dreadful luck with men. The last one was very bad.' Again with the lowered voice. 'I think he used to *hit* her.'

Eric made appropriate noises of horror. If he was the bitch's husband he would've beaten her non-stop.

'Oooh, look,' Danny said, pursing his lips. 'Isn't that *delicious*?'

Eric glanced up as a steroid-enhanced, muscle-bound giant in tight shorts passed by their table.

'Not my type,' he said.

'What *is* your type?' Danny asked, getting slightly misty-eyed at the thought that *he* might be.

Eric shrugged, for once at a loss.

'Do you know,' Danny said, in a confidential tone, 'when we first met I had *no* hint that you were a friend of Dorothy's?'

'Three million bucks,' Eric said, swiftly changing the subject. 'That's a lot of money. What do they do? Give her a cheque?'

'*I* don't know,' Danny said, clamming up.

Yes, you do, you dumb-ass faggot, Eric thought. 'Well,' he said, digging in his pocket. 'Here's a twenty. Put it on number thirty-five for me. And stay out of trouble.'

'I'll try,' Danny said, with a high-pitched giggle. 'Can't promise!'

'If I should want to call you, is there a special number?'

'We'll only be there four days.'

'In case I feel lucky and want to make another bet.'

Danny wrote down the private number and handed it to him. 'This number goes straight to the suite,' he said. 'Only use it if you're desperate to speak to me. I'm not supposed to give it out.'

'Sure,' Eric said. 'And when you get back—'

'Yes?' Danny interrupted, an eager-puppy look on his cheerful face.

'We should talk about *us*.'

'Oooh, yes,' Danny cooed. 'We definitely should.'

Later, Eric met with Arliss, who assured him everything was set. Davey had his eye on exactly the right vehicle. Little Joe had already stolen the chloroform and a stash of sleeping pills to keep their victim sedated. And Big Mark was set for action.

'Good,' Eric said. 'We'll do it on Saturday. Be ready. I'll let you know where we meet before then. Keep yourself available, and not a word to anyone. Got it?'

Arliss nodded his greasy head. He was as ready as he'd ever be.

Chapter Twenty-six

The party was in full swing when Claude's Rolls drove up to Kyndra and Norio Domingo's palatial estate in Bel Air. Set in over thirty acres, the Domingos had lived there for over twenty years.

The Rolls was soon stuck in a line of limos and cars.

'For God's sake, how many people have they invited?' Claude grumbled.

'Too many,' James answered.

'Are you *sure* I should be doing this?' Lissa said, worrying, because she didn't know how she'd handle it if any rude comments came her way.

'Of course, my angel,' James assured her. 'You'll be the star of the party. And if anyone says anything untoward to you, they'll have *me* to deal with.'

'You're sweet.' She sighed.

'Yes, I'm so sweet that you reveal *nothing* to me. Claude,' he said, leaning forward and tapping his partner on the shoulder, 'are you aware that Madam has a new love?'

'I do *not*,' she objected, furious that James was so intuitive.

'You cannot fool me,' James said with confidence. 'It's written all over your pretty face.'

'I've just gotten rid of one,' she answered guardedly. 'Why would I even *think* about a new one?'

246

'I suppose when you're a stunning superstar, men simply fall into your lap. They can't help themselves.'

'Bullshit, James.'

'I can see it, darling. You're glowing.'

'I am *not* glowing.'

'How long do we have to sit here?' Claude complained, a man not used to waiting. 'This is a joke.'

'Sorry, Mr St Lucia,' his driver said, apologizing as if it was his fault.

'I wish they'd learn to stagger the guests,' James said. 'That would be the civilized way of doing it.'

'I can just see them staggering the guests,' Lissa said. 'What did you have in mind, James? The A group first, and the C group later?'

'There *is* no C group at the Domingos',' James said imperiously. 'Everyone's a star. And if they're not, they're married to one.'

Lissa adjusted her diamond earrings. She was getting more and more nervous about facing everyone. Would they think she was a failure? No. They would simply feed on her fame, because that's all that really mattered in Hollywood.

She wondered what Michael was doing. He'd said he was getting ready to give someone the let's-break-up speech. Hmm . . . who was that someone? A long-term affair? A casual three-weeker?

The Rolls was almost at the entrance to the house.

'We don't have to stay long, do we?' Lissa asked, taking a deep breath.

'Just as long as it takes for you to dazzle and shine,' James said. 'Then, I promise, we'll have you home by midnight, exactly like Cinderella.'

Kyndra greeted her guests resplendent in a full-length gold, strapless gown, her ebony skin gleaming with gold flecks, a diamond choker, long diamond and ruby earrings, and her jet hair piled high on her head in an Erykah Badu do. She looked amazing, like an exotic African queen.

Norio, standing beside her, was a tall, distinguished-looking Colombian man, with hypnotic eyes, a bald head and a sly way of flirting that made every woman feel special.

Their marriage had endured through several affairs on both sides, and now they'd settled into an easy togetherness.

'Where *is* that child of ours?' Kyndra murmured to her husband. 'She promised to be here early.'

'When did you speak to her?' Norio asked, adjusting his onyx and diamond cufflinks, an anniversary gift from his wife.

'A few days ago.'

'Knowing Saffron, she's probably forgotten.'

'And she's supposed to be bringing Lulu.'

'Good. We don't see enough of our grandchild.'

'Now, Norio, please remember – no pictures of me with Lulu. I have a certain image to preserve.'

'Of course, darling,' he said, smiling. He knew his wife, and as much as she adored Lulu, she had a thing about *not* being labelled Grandma – even though she was in excellent company – including grandparents Mick Jagger, Whoopi Goldberg and Jack Nicholson.

Larry Singer walked in alone.

Kyndra greeted him with a kiss on both cheeks. 'Where's Taylor?' she asked.

'Working,' he replied, feeling quite lost without his wife beside him.

'Oh, yes,' Kyndra said. 'I heard she's shooting a movie with Montana Gray.'

'I didn't know it was Montana's film,' Larry said, surprised that Taylor hadn't mentioned the name of her director.

'You'd better watch out,' Kyndra said, with a wily smile. 'You know what a feminist Montana is. Before you know it, Taylor will be runnin' your ass!'

'Not even remotely funny, Kyndra,' he said stiffly.

'Happy anniversary, Larry.'

'It's not *my* anniversary.'

'Sure it is,' she teased. 'It's the anniversary of your wife becoming a major feminist!'

Larry was unamused. He didn't enjoy attending these big social events at the best of times. And he certainly didn't need Kyndra making cracks at his expense.

As soon as they realized he was present, people began coming over to him. He felt vulnerable and trapped, and there was nothing he could do about it because he had no Taylor by his side to protect him from the onslaught of would-be deal-makers who all wanted something from Larry Singer.

Slowly he managed to edge his way into a corner, finally spotting Lissa Roman, whom he quickly waved over. Lissa was his favourite of all Taylor's friends. Not only was she beautiful and talented, she had a certain sweetness about her, in spite of her sometimes raunchy public image.

'You look lovely,' he said.

'Thanks, Larry,' she replied, glancing around. 'Where's Taylor?'

'Haven't you spoken to her?'

'We've been missing each other.'

'She's shooting a movie.'

'Your movie?' Lissa asked.

'No, a cable film.'

'I was hoping you'd say that she'd finally gotten *her* movie off the ground.'

'It hasn't happened yet,' Larry said.

'That's a pity, I know how much it means to her.'

Larry was silent for a moment. The previous evening he'd been asleep when Taylor had finally come home. When he'd awoken in the morning, she'd already left for the studio. He'd wanted to tell her that he'd hired a new writer for her project, and that if she wanted him to, he'd put his name on as executive producer. Better she should be starring in her own film rather than making a lesbian-themed cable movie. And now that he'd heard Montana Gray was the director, he was less than pleased.

'Are you okay, Larry?' Lissa asked.

'Yes, why?'

'You seem a little lost in thought.'

'More important, how are *you*?' he asked. 'I was sorry to hear about you and Gregg. Are you coping okay?'

'You know what it's like when you're tabloid headlines,' she said ruefully.

'Yes, I'm afraid I do,' he replied, remembering his very public divorce from his first wife.

'It's so embarrassing to have one's soon-to-be ex mouthing off all over TV and the tabloids,' Lissa confided.

'Everyone says they don't read those papers,' Larry remarked.

'I know,' Lissa agreed. 'They *claim* they glance at them while they're standing in line at the supermarket.'

'As if any of these women stand in line at a supermarket,' Larry said.

Stella and Seth joined them, both balancing Martinis.

'My God!' Stella exclaimed, pert and pretty in a red Valentino dress. 'We were sitting in our car for twenty minutes.'

'So were we,' Lissa said.

'Who's we?' Stella asked, curious as usual.

'I came with James and Claude.'

'Good move,' Stella said, adding an irreverent – 'Safety in fags.'

'Don't be rude. You know James *hates* that word.'

'I tell it like it is,' Stella said, surveying the room. 'Can you *believe* this turn-out? I've already bumped into Luther

Vandross, Stevie Wonder *and* Gladys Knight – this is like an old-time soul reunion.'

'Norio *has* been a successful producer in the music business for years,' Larry pointed out.

'Yes, and Kyndra *is* a major diva,' Lissa added.

'I always get a kick out of the music-business crowd,' Stella said. 'I'm thinking of using a B. B. King track on our next project. Soundtracks are so important today. Did you know that you can launch a movie with the soundtrack alone? That's if you do the right marketing on the Internet.'

'You can't possibly believe that,' said Seth, a wiry-haired man with cordial features and ruddy cheeks.

'Yes, I can.'

'You and your ideas,' he said. 'There was a time when we made movies and the story alone brought people into the theatre. Right, Larry?'

'Don't be so old-fashioned, darling,' Stella chided. 'Listen to me, you *know* I'm always right.'

'The women are taking over, Larry,' Seth said warningly. 'We'd better watch out.'

Larry nodded in agreement.

A silicone blonde walked by, her large boobs barely covered by a few strategically placed stuck-on sequins.

'I do so *love* rock 'n' roll parties,' Stella said, staring at the girl. 'And judging by the way your eyes are bulging out of your heads, you guys love it, too.'

'What?' Larry said. He honestly hadn't noticed the girl.

Seth nudged him. 'She's referring to the almost naked blonde.'

'Who?' Larry said, wondering when his wife would arrive.

Seth burst out laughing. 'Larry,' he said. 'You're truly an original!'

* * *

'Cool,' Saffron said, parading in front of the mirror. She'd raided Nicci's closet and come up with a black leather jumpsuit which fitted her perfectly. Fortunately, they were more or less the same size.

'Mommy pretty,' Lulu said, tilting her head to one side and inspecting her mother.

'You're *always* pretty, angel peaches,' Saffron said, scooping her daughter up and giving her a big kiss. 'Now it's Mommy's turn.'

Nicci had decided to wear her red Azzedine Alaïa dress again, and her Jimmy Choo heels. Her power outfit. Not that it had done her much good at their ill-fated dinner party.

'Hot look, babe,' Saffron said admiringly.

'Yeah, hot and hung-over,' Nicci answered wryly.

'Pretty, pretty,' Lulu repeated, jumping up and down. 'Everybum pretty!'

'Will you be quiet?' Saffron scolded. 'You're startin' to sound like a parrot.'

'Mommy's a parrot, Mommy's a parrot,' Lulu chanted.

'Shush,' Saffron said. 'Nicci's got a big bad headache. We mustn't make it worse.'

'*Baaad!*' Lulu giggled.

'Come on,' Saffron said, picking the little girl up and taking her into the bedroom. 'I'm putting you in front of the TV until we go.'

'You know,' Nicci said, when Saffron returned, 'I'm a *very* a good friend.'

'You are?' Saffron said, clipping on large gold hoop earrings.

'Yes, 'cause I'm going with you tonight, when I'd *so* prefer to lie down and quietly die.'

'Aren't *we* the dramatic one?' Saffron said, admiring herself in the mirror again. 'Where *did* you go last night that you've got this amazing hangover?'

'To a rave.'

'A rave?' Saffron shrieked. 'Girl, you haven't done that since you an' Evan got together. Who'd you go with?'

'The bad-boy brother.'

'Oh, wow!' Saffron exclaimed. 'Didja get it on?'

'That's just it,' Nicci said glumly. 'I feel like one of those Doris Day movies you see on late-night TV. Did we or didn't we? I have no freakin' clue. I only know I woke up in his bed this morning totally bare-assed.'

'No *shit?*'

'It's true.'

'You gotta *know* if you screwed him.'

'*He* can't remember either. We were so wasted – what with the booze and drugs and God knows what else.'

'I'm proud of you, girl!' Saffron said, with a wide grin. 'The old spirit lives! An' I thought I'd lost you.'

'I'm engaged, Saff,' Nicci said unhappily. 'Don't you get it?'

'Yeah, I get it,' Saffron said. 'You're engaged, not *dead.*'

'Evan's a great guy, except . . . there's one small problem.'

'And what would that be?'

'According to Brian, Evan was engaged to someone else before me.'

'How's *that* a problem?'

''Cause it is,' Nicci said. 'When you're *engaged* to someone, they're supposed to share that kind of information with you. That's the stuff you have to talk about.'

'Get real, Nic. You didn't think he was a virgin, did you?'

'Getting laid and getting engaged are two different things. *I* told him everything about *me.*'

'You did?' Saffron teased. 'And he still wants to marry you?'

253

Nicci couldn't help giggling. 'Well . . . not *quite* everything.'

'Hey – maybe it's cool.'

'What's cool?'

'Hangin' with the brother,' Saffron said. 'You're gettin' *married*, girl. You gotta let it loose before you do it.'

'This is a lot more than getting loose, Saff,' Nicci said miserably. 'I might've *slept* with his brother.'

'Oh, yeah, I can see where that would be kinda upsetting.'

'*Kind of* upsetting?'

'Let's go party. An' I promise, when we get back I'll stay up with you all night talking. Deal?'

'Anyone for second helpings?' Carol asked. There was an anxious air about her, as if she was frightened everyone would get up and leave before she had time to offer them dessert.

'Give me more food an' I'll bust right outta my clothes,' Amber said, smoothing down her skirt.

'Nothing like a satisfied customer,' Carol said, with a grateful smile. 'How about you, Michael? Interested in seconds?'

'No, thanks, Carol,' he said, feeling uncomfortably full. 'It was good, you're quite a cook.'

'Thanks,' she said, glancing around at her guests. 'What did I do to deserve all this praise?'

'*Everything*, honey,' Amber said warmly. 'If I was a guy, I'd think you were the perfect woman.' She threw Michael a penetrating look. 'Right, Michael?'

He wanted to take a piece of adhesive tape and stick it right across her mouth. Amber was getting on his nerves big-time.

'What's for dessert?' Quincy asked, patting his extended stomach.

'Everyone's favourite,' Carol announced. 'Peach cobbler with vanilla ice cream, nuts and caramel sauce.'

'You're *my* kinda woman.' Quincy sighed. 'Michael, you're a lucky man.'

Michael had a strong feeling he was being set up and he didn't like it.

He wondered what Lissa was doing. Was she thinking about him? Because he sure as hell couldn't stop thinking about her. The way she looked. The way she smiled. Her blue eyes. Her luscious lips.

Carol went back into the kitchen, closely followed by Amber.

'Will you stop setting me up?' Michael hissed, glaring at Quincy. 'For your information I'm giving her the speech tonight.'

'Oh, fuck!' Quincy said. 'After she's cooked you this meal, you're givin' her the speech?'

'She's taking things too seriously.'

'You can't do it tonight, man.'

'Why not?'

''Cause you gotta give it to her right after you've taken her out for a fine dinner, *not* when she's been slavin' away in the kitchen all day. Doncha know *anythin'* about women?'

'I have to do it,' Michael insisted. 'It's only fair to both of us.'

'Not *tonight*,' Quincy repeated. 'Be a gentleman about this. I'm tellin' you, take her out to dinner, an' let her down easily.'

'Jeez!' Michael complained. 'I never thought the day would come when I'd be getting lessons on how to handle a woman from *you*.'

'I'm married,' Quincy said, with a self-satisfied smirk. 'I *know* what I'm talkin' about.'

'Like hell you do.'

And then it occurred to Michael that Quincy was right. How *could* he eat her food, accept her hospitality and then dump her?

No, he couldn't do it tonight. It would have to wait until he got back from Vegas.

Chapter Twenty-seven

Lissa managed to look like she was having a good time, although she was quite sure everyone was talking about her behind her back.

'You're paranoid,' James said.

'I'm not,' she retorted.

'Surely you understand that all the women here would give their fake boobs to be you?' James informed her.

'Not *this* week,' she said ruefully.

'Do not underestimate yourself,' James said sternly. 'Your talent overcomes everything. Now that you're rid of Gregg, your full potential will come to the fore.'

'I thought my full potential already did,' she said, with a wry grin. 'I'm forty years old, James. I've probably had my best years.'

'*Pu-lease*,' James said scornfully. 'Look at Madonna, she's still dancing around the stage like a teenager, and she's *older* than you. Did you see her at the Grammys? The woman's amazing, and so are you.'

'She doesn't have a nineteen-year-old daughter and four ex-husbands. She has a talented, *smart* English guy, who makes stylish, entertaining movies, and two adorable little kids.'

'What has that got to do with anything?' James said. 'I'm so tired of you denigrating yourself. Now stop it, or I'll

257

get cross. Come, it's time for dinner, and I do believe we're at the head table.'

Saffron entered the party with Lulu balanced on one hip, and Nicci by her side. She headed straight for her father.

'How's my two favourite girls?' Norio exclaimed, grabbing Lulu, throwing her up in the air and catching her with a big hug. 'We thought you'd gotten lost.'

'Hi, Daddy,' Saffron said, kissing him on both cheeks as Lulu screamed with delight. 'We almost did.'

'And hello there, Nicci,' Norio said. 'How's my favourite *other* daughter?'

'Cool, thanks,' she said, adding a mischievous – 'Did you and Lissa ever have an affair?'

'Your mother never gave me a second glance,' Norio said regretfully. 'Although I always harboured a secret passion for her.'

'Daddy!' Saffron exclaimed. 'If Kyndra ever heard you say that, she'd have your balls for breakfast.'

Norio rolled his expressive, heavy-lidded eyes. 'My daughter, the mouth.'

'Oh, *c'mon*, you're in the music business, you've heard it all before.'

He laughed heartily. 'Go have a good time, girls. I'll keep Lulu – it'll give me an opportunity to play the proud grandfather.'

'Let's go get a drink,' Saffron said, grabbing Nicci's hand. 'It's what we both need desperately.'

Taylor was still in a state of excitement. Working with Montana Gray was indeed an experience. And performing a love scene with Sonja Lucerne even more so. She was in awe of both women: they were mistresses of their craft.

The crew were great, too, because Taylor had to admit that the thought of taking her clothes off in front of a full crew had been terrifying. Sure, she'd done it when she was younger, but that was before she was Mrs Larry Singer. Now everyone would be looking at her in a different way.

However, the scene had taken place without incident. And in a way Taylor found that being in bed with a woman was easier than making love to a man in front of the camera.

She'd never experienced a lesbian lover, so at first she'd not known how she'd handle the difficult scene. But Sonja was so gentle and firm, so loving and tender, that suddenly Taylor had found herself wondering what it *would* be like to have an affair with a woman.

She'd smiled to herself. If Larry only knew what she was thinking.

At the end of the day's shoot, Montana knocked at the door and entered her trailer. 'You were excellent, Taylor,' she said enthusiastically. 'You gave of yourself one hundred percent, became your character all the way. I knew you could do it, although I wasn't absolutely sure. Now I'm so happy I made the right decision.'

'Thank you, Montana. That means so much to me,' Taylor said, thrilled at the lavish praise.

'Perhaps you can explain to me why Larry has kept you under wraps,' Montana said. 'How come you're not working in *his* movies?'

'That's what *I'*d like to know,' Taylor said, liking Montana more and more.

'Hmm . . .' Montana mused. 'I remember Larry as being somewhat insecure and possessive. When Neil worked with him, he was still with his first wife. She used to complain about him constantly.'

'She did?' Taylor said, surprised.

'Yes. She used to bitch that he couldn't get it up, and was extraordinarily needy. I'm sure I'm not repeating anything you don't already know.'

'His ex and I weren't exactly friends,' Taylor explained,

remembering how much Susan had hated her. 'After all, I *was* the cause of his divorce.'

'I see,' Montana said. 'Well, it's a noon call tomorrow, so I'm glad I didn't work you too late.'

'So am I,' Taylor said. 'I'm on my way to meet Larry. I've barely seen him in two days.'

'Going anywhere exciting?'

'The Domingos' anniversary party.'

'That's exactly where I'm headed,' Montana said. 'Why don't I get someone to dismiss your driver, and we'll ride together? You'll *love* my new Ferrari.'

It occurred to Taylor that she had not mentioned to Larry that Montana Gray was directing her movie. Montana had a reputation in town, and Taylor was sure Larry might have objected. Like most men in Hollywood, he was threatened by strong women.

What the hell? He hadn't asked, so she hadn't mentioned it.

'Great,' she said. 'All I have to do is change clothes.'

Montana nodded. 'And I'll dazzle 'em with lip gloss, remove my glasses, let down my hair, and be ready in five minutes.'

'Wow! I'm impressed. It takes most women three hours.'

'Hollywood wives,' Montana said, with a slow smile. 'I know most of them. I think Neil fucked a few, not only the lovely Gina.'

Taylor couldn't help herself, she had to ask the burning question. 'Is it true,' she said, 'that Neil expired on top of Gina Germaine while they were making love?'

'Not exactly,' Montana answered matter-of-factly. 'Gina merely precipitated his decline. Neil actually expired in the parking lot of a Santa Monica drinking establishment after an excess of Scotch.'

'So the story about him and Gina isn't the way it happened?'

'He *did* suffer a heart-attack while they were having sex, and some physical thing caused them to be joined together. So, yes, they *were* hauled off to the hospital – much to the delight of the tabloids. It was not a happy time for anyone. Although I have to say, Neil did have his moments.' She smiled at the memories. 'He was quite an unusual and brilliant man.'

'You seem so calm about it.'

'You have to remember it was fifteen years ago,' Montana said. 'A lot has happened in fifteen years.'

'I know – but, still, it *is* a famous story.'

'Well, now you've heard the correct version,' Montana said briskly. 'It certainly doesn't bother me. I've managed to have a pretty nice career.'

'Is there a man in your life now?'

'Man? Woman?' Montana said casually. 'I travel both roads.'

'Oh?' Taylor said, slightly shocked. 'I didn't know.'

'It makes life *so* much less complicated,' Montana said with a slight smile. 'Still want to go to the party with me?'

'Can't wait,' Taylor said.

Saffron and Nicci cruised the party.

'I feel like a snake died in my stomach.' Nicci groaned. 'And you know what? I haven't spoken to Evan since yesterday.'

'You mean a whole day has gone by and you haven't called him?' Saffron said. 'Now *that*'ll make him *major* suspicious.'

'What do I say to him?' Nicci wailed. 'I'm like *so* not a good liar.'

'Tell him you've been having an awesome time without him,' Saffron suggested. 'Oh, yeah, *then* tell him you screwed his brother.'

'Shut *up*,' Nicci said crossly. 'I'm upset enough.'

'No, you're not,' Saffron argued. 'You're hung-over. Hey – what's a fuck between friends?'

'We're *not* friends, and I keep on reminding you, I'm *marrying* Brian's brother. Anyway – nothing happened.'

'Was nothing good?' Saffron asked slyly.

'For God's sake, Saff,' Nicci said, taking out her cellphone. 'I'd better call him now. He's left me six messages.'

'Isn't that like *obsessive*?'

'No. When he's in L.A. he speaks to his mother all the time.'

'So now you're mommy number two, is that it?'

'He likes to keep in touch.'

'Doncha mean keep tabs on you?' Saffron said.

'It's not that way.'

'I'll tell you somethin', Nic. From what I've seen of him, Evan seems kinda uptight.'

'What do you mean?' she asked, staring at her friend.

'C'mon, you *know* what I mean. The dude's only thirty, an' acts like he's sixty!'

'No, he doesn't,' she said, defending the man she planned to marry.

'Yeah, he *does*,' Saffron insisted. 'He never wants to hit the clubs, or hang with our friends. I'm always inviting you, and you always say, "Evan's not up to it. Evan doesn't feel like it. Evan's busy working." I mean, what *is* that? Are you gonna shut yourself away when you're married to him? You're nineteen, not some old lady.'

'It's 'cause our relationship is new,' Nicci explained. 'Evan prefers to spend time with me alone.'

'Yeah,' Saffron said disbelievingly. 'Keep on foolin' yourself, girl.'

Nicci found a quiet corner and made the call.

Evan answered his cellphone on the second ring. 'Where the *hell* have you been?' he demanded.

'I was busy,' she said, feeling incredibly guilty. 'Uh . . . y'know, like with wedding arrangements and stuff.'

'And you couldn't keep your phone on?'

'Didn't realize it was off.'

'I tried you all night, and God knows how many times today. You've ruined my day, you know that?'

'Sorry.'

'Why didn't you call me when you got up this morning?'

'I was going to, then I figured you were busy on the set.'

'I don't appreciate this behaviour, Nicci,' he said sternly. 'I don't like it at all.'

'Sorry,' she repeated sulkily. He might not like her behaviour, but she was getting real pissed at the way he was speaking to her.

'Is that all you've got to say for yourself?' he demanded.

'You're not my freakin' *father*, Evan!' she said, suddenly losing it. 'And while we're questioning each other, I heard a rumour you were engaged before me, is that true?'

'Who told you *that?*'

'I'm asking you if it's true.'

'It wasn't really an engagement.'

'Did you give her a ring?'

'Yes,' he answered reluctantly.

'Then you *were* engaged?'

'I didn't marry her, did I?' he said belligerently.

'No, and you also didn't tell me about it, did you?' she responded. 'When I asked you if there had been anyone serious before me, you told me, "Absolutely not."'

'This is not something to be discussed over the phone,' he said.

'No, it's not,' she said. 'And I don't like being spoken to as if I'm a fucking *child*.' She punched the off button.

Now he was going to think that Brian had told her. She'd better warn him. She quickly punched out his number. Thank God for cellphones!

Brian's voice. 'Yeah?'

'It's me.'

'Hello, me.'

'You back at the location?'

'Yup.'

'Did you give Evan the envelope?'

'Yup.'

'You're gonna hate me.'

'What have you done now?'

'I think I blew it.'

'How?'

'Evan and I had a fight on the phone, and I told him I knew he'd been engaged before.'

'*Shit*, Nic.'

'I didn't say it was *you* who told me. Only in case he accuses you, deny it. What d'you think?'

'I think you're a crazy girl who I never should have gotten involved with.'

'I'm *not* a *girl*,' she said furiously. 'I'm *not* crazy, and we're certainly *not* involved.'

'What are you – a boy?' he teased.

'Suck it up, Brian. I've taken enough crap for one night.'

'How d'you feel?'

'Lousy. And you?'

'Worse.'

'Good.'

'"Good," she says. Thanks.'

'I just wanted to warn you.'

'I'm duly warned.' And he clicked off.

Quite frankly, if she never spoke to either of the Richter brothers again, she'd be a happy person.

It was eleven o'clock and the Domingos' party was still going strong, which was unusual for Hollywood, as most people scampered home at ten, claiming they had to be up early, even if they didn't. In L.A. the impression of being incredibly busy was most important, and there were certain rules to adhere to.

Lissa wanted to go home, she'd had enough. She'd sat through dinner making polite conversation, but now Vegas was on her mind and she knew she should get an early night. When Nicci came over, she was delighted to see her.

'How're you doin', Mom?' Nicci asked.

'Surprisingly well,' Lissa replied, thinking how pretty her daughter looked. 'Off to Vegas on Thursday.'

'I know.'

'Sorry you're not coming with me, but you know how I feel about exposing you to the whole publicity circus, and no doubt they'll be out in force.'

'Saff's arranged my bachelorette party on Saturday, so I couldn't've come anyway,' Nicci said.

'I'm sorry I'll miss that.'

'C'mon, Mom,' Nicci said, grinning. 'You wouldn't've been invited anyway.'

'Thanks.'

'Like I hardly think naked male strippers and macho studs dangling it in front of your nose would be your scene.'

'That might be exactly what I need right now,' Lissa said, laughing ruefully.

'No way,' Nicci said. 'Oh, yeah, and like before I forget, Evan's mom is flying in. She wants to meet you.'

'Arrange something for when I get back. How soon is the wedding now?'

'Two weeks,' Nicci said, trying not to mind that her mother had forgotten the date of her only daughter's wedding. 'And I'm nervous.'

'It'll be wonderful,' Lissa assured her, determined to be more involved. 'Can I come and see your dress next week?'

'If you want to.'

'Of *course* I want to.'

They kissed and hugged. Nicci wished her luck with her show, and Lissa said she hoped the bachelorette night was a blast.

'I'll call you Sunday morning, find out all about the dangling macho studs,' Lissa said, with a smile.

'Thanks, Mom,' Nicci said, grinning. 'I'll be sure to take notes especially for you!'

By the time Lissa tracked James down, he was ready to go, although Claude seemed to be having an excellent time catching up with all his pals in the music business, listening to the Latino band, and admiring the two gorgeous Latino singers, male *and* female.

'I'm gonna stay a while,' Claude announced. 'You an' Lissa take the car an' send it back for me.'

'Very well,' James replied, somewhat tight-lipped. 'Come, Lissa.'

'You're an amazing couple,' Lissa remarked, as they stood outside the front door waiting for the Rolls.

'What do you mean?' James said.

'The two of you are complete opposites. You're so English and proper. Well,' she said, laughing lightly, 'not exactly *proper*, but you know what I mean. And Claude is Mister Music Biz.'

'Sometimes those are the relationships that work the best,' James said mysteriously. 'Although I'm not at all thrilled about Claude wanting to stay. He has eyes for the sleazy singer in the tight pants, the one with the eyebrows and the attitude. The poor dear is experiencing a slut night!'

'Are you faithful to each other?' Lissa asked curiously.

'If you're inquiring as to whether we're always true to each other, the answer is . . . sometimes.'

'Sometimes?'

'Yes, dear. Do not question me further. It's a gay thing.'

Montana drove her sleek black Ferrari extremely fast. She roared up to the front of the Domingo estate, pulling up just as Lissa and James were about to get into Claude's Rolls.

'Lissa!' Taylor said, frantically waving. 'My best friend! How *are* you?' She jumped out of the Ferrari, ran over to Lissa and gave her a big hug. 'I know you must think I'm the disloyal friend of all time, but I'm working. Isn't *that* something?'

'Larry told me.'

'Lissa, do you know Montana Gray?' Taylor asked as Montana walked over.

Lissa turned and extended her hand to the tall, striking-looking woman. 'It's a pleasure to meet you,' she said. 'I've heard many good things about you.'

'Thanks,' Montana replied, smiling. 'The admiration's mutual.'

'I hope *we* get to work together one day.'

'Talk to your agent, I'm available,' Montana said.

'Right now she's mine!' Taylor interrupted. 'And I'm having the *best* time.'

'See you inside,' Montana said, still smiling. 'Nice meeting you, Lissa.'

'Can you believe I'm working with her?' Taylor said excitedly, as Montana entered the house.

'She seems great,' Lissa remarked.

'Not great – amazing!' Taylor enthused. 'It's only a cable movie, but it's *such* a moving script. Today we shot my love scene with – guess who?'

'Can't wait to hear.'

'Sonja Lucerne.'

'Really?'

'The movie's about two women in love. And it's powerful – especially the love scenes. Oh, God, Lissa, I am *so* happy to be back in action. Why did I ever stop?'

'You *stopped* to be there for Larry,' Lissa reminded her.

'And, speaking of Larry,' James said, joining in, 'he's inside, and extremely pissed you're not here.'

'Oh dear. I suppose I should've called.'

'That would've been a good idea,' James said.

'I'd better go see him. Is it a good party?'

'If you're into the music scene you'll be here all night,' Lissa said. 'They've got a sensational Latino band.'

'Not *that* good.' James sniffed.

'The actors are fleeing now,' Lissa said, 'getting ready for their early calls.'

'Sure,' Taylor said, laughing. 'Like some of them haven't had an early call in years, right?'

Everyone laughed.

'As soon as I'm through with this movie, I'll come over and you can fill me in on everything,' Taylor said, hugging Lissa. 'Of course, you *do* know that I never liked Gregg.'

'Who did?' James said, *sotto voce*.

'How come everyone's telling me now?' Lissa said irritably. 'I can't understand why nobody mentioned it *before* I married him.'

'We did, only you weren't listening.'

James nodded. 'Blinded by love, dear.'

'And probably incredible sex,' Taylor added.

Lissa shook her head. 'See you in Vegas,' she said. 'And for your information, the sex was *not* that incredible.'

'Maybe I'll ask Montana if she wants to come to Vegas,' Taylor said.

'I'm sure Larry will be ecstatic,' James drawled. 'You know how he *adores* sharing your company.'

'He'll have to get used to it,' Taylor said crisply. 'I've decided to change my lifestyle.'

'That'll be amusing to watch,' James said, getting in the car with Lissa. 'You mark my words,' he said, wagging a long, thin index finger. 'There'll be nothing but trouble in the Oscar winner's paradise. Those two are on a collision course, and it won't be pretty.'

By the time Amber and Quincy left Carol's apartment, it was past ten. Michael stretched and yawned, he was dying to leave too. 'I got a real busy day tomorrow,' he said to Carol, who didn't seem to be listening.

'I was thinking,' she said, picking a rose out of a vase and sniffing it.

'About what?'

'I was thinking that you might want to stay over tonight,' she said, handing him the rose.

'Y'know, I'd love to,' he said, already on his feet. 'Only I've got one of those days tomorrow, an' Q's kinda putting in half-days. So, you know what it's like, everything's left to me.'

She put her arms around him, running her fingers through the hair at the back of his neck. 'Michael, Michael,' she murmured dreamily, 'I'm falling more in love with you every day. You do know that, don't you?'

Oh, Jesus! She'd just come out with the L word. Why hadn't he given her the speech? Screw Quincy and his ideas. This was getting too hot to handle.

'Uh, listen,' he said, wondering how he could make a fast escape without hurting her feelings, 'you're a terrific woman, Carol, but I've told you before, I'm not ready to be involved in a serious relationship.'

'I'm not asking you to,' she answered smoothly. 'However, I do have to talk to you about something important.'

'You do, huh?' he said, inwardly groaning.

'Will you sit down and have a brandy with me?'

'You know I don't drink,' he said, irritated that she didn't remember.

'Sorry, I forgot. Do you mind if *I* have one?'

Oh Christ! What was she going to say? More declarations of love?

'Go ahead, I'll have water.'

'I've got that non-alcohol beer you like.'

'No, that's okay,' he said, immediately thinking about Lissa and her joke about the beer gut.

Yeah, Lissa. What was she doing? She'd probably hooked up with some handsome stud by now and forgotten all about him.

Carol poured herself a brandy, passed him a bottle of Evian, and sat down on the couch, patting the space beside her. Reluctantly, he joined her.

'I'm glad you enjoyed dinner,' she said.

'You're an excellent cook.'

'Thanks. My mother taught me,' she said, edging closer.

'Yeah?' he said, wondering how soon he could back off without it appearing obvious.

'Although Amber couldn't help giving me a few helpful hints.'

'Amber's really something.'

'Yes, she is,' Carol agreed. And then all of a sudden she moved in and began kissing him.

Michael found it most off-putting when a woman initiated kissing. It meant you couldn't stop, you had to go forward, even if you didn't want to.

He kissed her back, he had no choice.

She had an annoying habit of running her tongue over his teeth, and as she did that, he realized there was absolutely nothing left between them. He couldn't have got a hard-on under any circumstances. The thrill was long gone.

I've gotta get out of here, he thought. *I've gotta get out of here right now.*

'Uh . . . what did you want to talk about, Carol?' he asked, finally extracting himself.

'Before I tell you what it is,' she said, sitting up very straight, 'I want you to know that I'm not asking you for a thing.'

'Huh?' he said, wondering what the hell she was coming up with.

'I *want* to do this,' she said earnestly. 'I'm doing it for me. So . . . you can be as involved as you want, or not involved at all. Whatever you decide, I promise I'll understand. And I'll *never* ask anything from you financially.'

He felt a bad feeling enveloping him. 'What?' he managed.

'I'm pregnant,' she said.

Chapter Twenty-eight

Larry was anxious to leave the party as soon as Taylor showed up. 'I've been here for hours,' he complained, tapping his watch, 'and I'm very tired.'

She was having none of it. 'Well, I'm *not*,' she said, quite exhilarated.

'Aren't you working tomorrow?'

'Late call,' she said, waving at Stella and Seth across the room.

'We have important things to discuss regarding your project,' Larry said, hoping to lure her home that way.

'Do you mind if we sit down first, so I can at least get something to eat?' she said, pulling him out to the tented patio.

'I've already eaten,' he said. 'It would be better if we talked at home. This band is too noisy for conversation.'

'You're such a grouch,' Taylor said, obviously on a high. 'Please *don't* spoil my great day.'

'I have things to tell you, Taylor. Things that will please you.'

'So tell me at the table, darling,' she said, holding onto his arm. 'Come on, I want you to meet Montana.'

'I already know Montana,' he said, in a surly voice. 'I worked with her husband once.'

'She mentioned it. You were married to Susan at the time.'

272

'What has that got to do with anything?'

'Nothing.'

'Then why bring it up?'

'I'm having the *best* time with Montana,' Taylor said, refusing to let him ruin her night.

'I'm sure you are,' Larry said, getting more uptight by the minute.

'She's an amazing director, *so* in touch with her actors.'

'That's nice,' Larry said.

'Of course, *you*'re always in touch with your actors, aren't you?' she said, grabbing a glass of champagne from a passing waiter.

'I try to be,' Larry said, sensing it was going to be a long night. 'Taylor,' he said seriously, 'I've been giving a lot of thought to your project, and you're right, you *should* be in control, not working for other people.'

'What if the other person was you, Larry?'

'Meaning?'

'There's a wonderful female role in your next movie,' she said, seizing the opportunity. 'Why can't *I* play it?'

It was the first time she'd asked if she could be in one of his films, and she felt particularly bold doing so. But what the hell? She was an actress, for crissakes, and he was her husband. Why *couldn't* he give her the part?

'I . . . I hadn't thought about it,' he said hesitantly. 'The studio—'

'Oh, please!' she interrupted. '*You* tell the studio what *you* want. Everyone knows you make all the creative decisions.'

'I wasn't aware that you had any desire to be in my movie.'

'Why wouldn't I? You're an incredible director. Most actors would kill to work with you.' She took a gulp of champagne. 'Montana said I was brilliant today, absolutely brilliant.'

'What did you do?'

'Shot a love scene between me and Sonja Lucerne, who, I must say, is extremely charming, and totally professional.'

'I'm glad you're enjoying yourself,' he said, not liking the thought of *his* wife indulging in a love scene with another woman. Quite frankly, it disgusted him.

'Anyway, darling,' Taylor said, 'if *you* want to go home, I'll understand. And I'm sure you won't mind if I stay and wind down. You know what it's like when the old adrenaline is pumping. I won't be able to sleep for hours.'

'I'll stay with you,' he said stiffly. 'And then you can hear what I've arranged.'

'What?' she said, her eyes darting around the room to see if she could spot Montana.

'I gave your script to a new writer,' Larry said, stroking his beard. 'I think he can do something special with it, something the studio will approve of. So I've gone ahead and arranged a meeting with him and a couple of Orpheus executives. Naturally you'll be there. And if you want, I'll come too.'

'Larry,' she said happily, 'this is fantastic news. Who's the writer?'

'Now don't get excited, because the studio has already approved him.'

'They have?'

'You have to trust me on this, because if there's one thing I know, it's talent.'

'*Who*, Larry?'

'Oliver Rock.'

There were more messages from Evan when Nicci got home. Saffron had not come with her, she'd decided it was better for Lulu to sleep in her own bed.

Nicci played the messages over several times. Saffron

was right, he *did* sound uptight, especially when he called her unreliable.

Ha! She might be unreliable – although she didn't think she was. But *he* was a liar – he should've told her about a former fiancée, it was unsettling that he hadn't.

She switched all the phones off, including her cell, and went to bed. Tomorrow she'd get into it. Tonight she was still too hung-over.

And as she drifted off to sleep her last thought was of Brian with his sleepy bedroom eyes and crooked grin.

Brian, Brian, Brian . . .

Did we? Or didn't we?

The workforce were out in droves, running in and out of Lissa's house as if it was a 7-Eleven. Fabio was all over the place.

'My darling, I want you to try out these extensions,' he said, holding up swatches of blonde hair. 'They'll be absolutely divine!'

'I'm not sure I want extensions, Fabio. Too much hair when I'm dancing gets in my way.'

'Darling, they'll look amazing! And I've been dreaming of gold makeup. You have to be a *golden* beauty. Lissa Roman, you will *own* the stage.'

'Maybe,' she said unsurely.

'Shall we test it today, my sweets?'

'No, we'll do it in Vegas. I'm not in the mood today.'

Her clothes designer and his three assistants were dashing in and out of the house, ferrying back and forth several outfits, all of which she had to try on. Her favourite jeweller, Neil Lane, was busy tempting her with fabulous pieces of art-deco jewellery, and she was trying to decide what to borrow to wear in her show. She finally decided on an amazing emerald and diamond necklace from the twenties, and two magnificent Cartier diamond cuffs from the thirties. She toyed with some earrings from the Mae West estate, then decided they were too flamboyant.

Max was running around, attempting to persuade her to grant an interview to the *L.A. Times*.

She demurred. 'It's too soon,' she said. 'They'll want to talk about Gregg.'

'They have strict orders not to,' he assured her.

'You know how it happens, Max. Whether I talk about him or not, they're bound to mention him in the piece.'

'The journalist is a personal friend of mine,' Max said. 'We can trust him.'

'Fine.' She sighed, realizing that Max was not about to let up. 'When would you like me to do it?'

'Lunch at the Beverly Hills Hotel?'

'I wasn't planning on leaving the house today.'

'Then should I have Nellie organize a light lunch here?'

'You know I don't allow journalists into my home.'

'Make up your mind, Lissa,' Max said, getting quite testy. 'What *do* you want to do?'

'All right,' she said reluctantly. 'Lunch at the Beverly Hills Hotel.' She buzzed Danny. 'Is everything set for tomorrow?'

'All organized, Miz Roman,' Danny said.

'Add Mr Scorsinni to the list. He's coming with us on the plane.'

'Certainly,' Danny said, quite pleased at the prospect of seeing the extraordinarily handsome private investigator again.

Lissa wondered if she should call Quincy and double-check that Michael was indeed coming. Then she decided no, it wouldn't do to look too anxious. If Michael *wasn't* coming, Quincy would have let her know.

Why did she want him there anyway?

She couldn't answer that. He made her feel safe. Yes,

that was it – safe and secure, protected from anything Gregg might do.

She called Kyndra to thank her for the party. Kyndra was still asleep, even though it was past noon.

James phoned and launched into a litany of bitter complaints about Claude, who apparently had not come home at all. 'He *said* he went to the beach house and slept *there*,' James said. '*Of course* he did, and he probably took that Latin slut with him. Men!'

'What are you planning to do about it?' Lissa asked.

'Nothing,' James said sullenly. 'I *will* get my revenge – just you wait until Vegas.'

That's all she needed, James in his drama-queen mood prancing around Vegas, trying to get back at Claude.

Across town Gregg Lynch sat with Patrick, the Australian journalist friend of Belinda's, in a café on Larchmont Avenue, drinking black coffee while trying to dredge up any new information about Lissa Roman he could think of.

'The bitch won't even take my calls,' he complained. 'She's a first-class cunt.'

'They all are,' Patrick said sympathetically. 'I've dealt with enough movie stars to know what a bunch of useless wankers they are.'

'Right,' Gregg agreed.

'You gotta understand,' Patrick said, a heavy-set man with greased-back dyed black hair. 'Anything you come up with is worth money. What about her childhood? Nothing's ever been written about that. You got any dirt?'

'Nothing,' Gregg said. 'She told me she left home and ran off to New York when she was sixteen, hasn't seen her parents since.'

'Bingo!' Patrick crowed, waving his pen in the air. 'That's good enough.'

'It is?' Gregg said blankly.

'There's your story – dumped her family. Never seen them since.'

'I'm not sure,' Gregg said hesitantly. 'She never talked about them, always said they never came looking for her, so she never went looking for them.'

'This is juicy stuff,' Patrick said, scribbling down a few notes in a tattered notebook. 'Now all you gotta do is tell me what town she came from. Maybe you've got an address or something? I can take it from there.'

'How'm I supposed to know that?' Gregg said.

'Christ, you were *married* to the skirt. You gonna tell me you don't know where she's from?'

'We weren't exactly investigating her history,' Gregg said. 'We were too busy fucking.'

'Yeah, yeah,' Patrick said. 'We'll play up the nympho angle. But I gotta have more. Did she keep a journal, shit like that?'

'As a matter of fact,' Gregg said, 'she did have a bunch of old journals from when she was a kid.'

'Where'd she keep 'em?'

'In a big storage room behind her pool house. That's where she stores all her old junk.'

'Can you get into it?'

'How? She's got guards crawling all over the property. I can't get into a fucking thing. They packed up my stuff and dumped it outside the front door. What a *bitch!*'

'You must have *some* connections. A maid, one of the guards, the friggin' gardener, for crissakes?'

'She has a gay assistant, Danny,' Gregg said. 'He kind of had eyes for me.'

'How about calling him?'

'I could do that.'

'Go for it,' Patrick said, waving at the waitress to bring him more coffee. 'If you want big bucks for your story, we gotta dig deep. The diaries could be the stuff we need. I can see the headline now.'

'Maybe I can get in the house when she's in Vegas,' Gregg said, thinking it might be possible. 'She's opening the Desert Millennium Princess Hotel on Saturday night with her show.'

'Legally you're still her husband,' Patrick said, encouraging him. 'You have rights. I don't see how they can keep you out. And the security won't be so intense if she's not home.'

'That's true,' Gregg said. 'I'll call Danny, see what I can find out.'

'You do that, mate. Big score – here we come!'

'What the *fuck* is the matter with you today?' Quincy said, staring at his partner as they sat in his office.

Michael had spent the day wandering around in a daze. He was so shocked by Carol's news that he didn't know what to do next. The first thing he'd wanted to ask her was if she'd slept with anyone else, only that would have been insulting. And, anyway, he knew she hadn't, because when they'd first started sleeping together she'd promptly informed him she was planning on being monogamous, and she hoped he was too. That had been months ago.

'I don't feel so good,' he said, rubbing his chin.

'You don't look so good either,' Quincy observed. 'You're still goin' to Vegas tomorrow, right? You know I'd go if I could, but look at me – I'm on crutches, for crissakes.'

'Yeah, yeah, I'm goin',' Michael said, lighting a cigarette. 'I'll be glad to get out of town.'

'Somethin' happen after we left last night?' Quincy asked curiously. 'You didn't give her the speech, did you?'

Michael wanted to tell him the truth, only then Q

would go running back to Amber, she'd open her big mouth to the world, and who needed that?

On the other hand, if he *didn't* tell Quincy, what was he going to do? Keep it to himself?

He got up and closed the door. 'Here's the deal, Q. I'll tell you what went on, but you have to give me your word not to run back to your wife, who probably knows anyway. This is strictly between us, okay?'

'What the fuck you talkin' about?' Quincy asked.

'Carol's pregnant.'

'She's *what?*'

'Pregnant, knocked up – a bun in the oven.'

'Yours?'

'According to her,' Michael said, exhaling a stream of smoke. 'I could get her to take a test, but I know it's mine.'

'Aw, jeez, there goes your let's-say-goodbye speech.'

'You can say that again.'

'What're you gonna do?'

'What *can* I do? I don't believe in abortion, and even if I did, she wouldn't do it. She says she's having the kid and doesn't want anything from me.'

'Shit!' Quincy said. 'I'm sorry, man.'

'You think I want another child coming into the world that's not really mine?' Michael said.

'You just said it's yours,' Quincy reminded him.

'Don't you get it, Q? I can't do this,' he said, getting up and pacing around the room. 'I don't want to be with Carol, I don't want to marry her. I don't even want to spend any time with her. Now she's having *my* kid. Damn! I've already lost one, and I'm not saying that this could turn out to be anything like that, but Jesus Christ, I'm fucking *trapped.*'

'You should've used a rubber,' Quincy said.

'It was one of those nights. She told me she was on the pill and I believed her. *Fuck!* I don't know what to do.'

'Nothing you *can* do,' Quincy said. 'You gotta eat it.'

'Is that what I gotta do, Q?' he said, staring at his partner. 'Is that what I gotta do really? 'Cause I don't think I can do that.'

'You got no choice.'

'No,' he said glumly. 'I guess I don't.'

The first thing Taylor thought about when she awoke on Wednesday was Oliver Rock. How could Larry have done this to her? How could he have hired Oliver without consulting her first?

They'd argued all night. 'I don't *want* a new writer,' she'd said.

'Yes, you do,' he'd said. 'Oliver recently sold a script for a million bucks. He's hot right now. He's exactly who you need.'

'How do we know he's any good?'

'I'm *telling* you he's good. I read his script, it's got heat. If you want me involved, you have to accept what I say.'

When it came to the movie business, Larry was in charge. There was no arguing with him. He thought he was giving her what she wanted, and in a way he was.

The good news was that, with Larry involved, her project would finally take flight, especially as he'd offered to put his name on as executive producer. Suddenly she'd started thinking about how exciting it would be to actually star in and direct her own movie. So what if Oliver Rock rewrote the script? As long as the movie got made, that was the main thing.

But she was still angry. How dare Larry go behind her back? And how dare Oliver accept the assignment?

When she got downstairs in the morning, Larry was settled on the patio eating his usual breakfast and reading the *New York Times*.

'I'm off to work,' she said. 'I'll see you later.'

'I thought you had a late call,' he said, putting down the newspaper.

'I want to get to the studio early to go over my lines.'

'Are we in agreement on your project?' he asked. 'Can I confirm the meeting and go forward?'

She bent down and kissed him on the cheek. It wasn't smart to be *too* independent. 'Okay, go ahead. I do appreciate your help. It's just that I was shocked you chose someone so inexperienced.'

'Trust me, Taylor,' Larry said, in his most annoying 'I'm always right' voice. 'When it comes to talent, I know what I'm doing.'

'I understand, darling. I'll see you later.'

'Another late night?'

'No, it's a short day, I'll be home before seven.'

'Good.' He hesitated a moment. 'Maybe we can spend some private time together for a change.'

She knew what he meant by that. They hadn't had sex in a while, and he was getting anxious. 'Of course, sweetie,' she said, lightly kissing him on the forehead. 'And while you're at work today, think about what I said.'

'And that is?'

'The role in your movie. I'd be perfect.'

Lynda Richter flew into town like a hot-air balloon – big, blustery, and full of energy.

Letting herself in with a key, she marched into the bedroom and stood over the bed where Nicci was still sleeping.

'Surprise, surprise!' she said in a loud voice. 'And I've caught the bride-to-be sleeping. Wakey, wakey, dear, you must have tons of things to organize.'

Nicci looked up at her, bleary-eyed. 'Mrs Richter,' she mumbled, 'I wasn't expecting you until Friday.'

'Decided to come early,' Lynda said briskly. 'Didn't Evan mention it?'

'He must've forgotten.'

'Bad boy. He'll be home on Sunday, so I thought I'd make everything cosy and comfy for him by the time he gets here. I'm sure you've got too much on your mind to think about poor little Evan at a time like this.'

'He's not poor little Evan,' Nicci said irritably, wishing that she was up and dressed so that she could properly confront this intrusive woman. 'He's working hard on his movie, and he's a big boy now. I can look after him.'

'I'm sure you can, dear, although I'm certain you'll need help with the wedding,' Lynda said, pausing to swoop up a couple of dirty Kleenex and a half-empty mug of cold coffee from the bedside table. 'This place is a *mess*. What time does the maid get here?'

'Soon,' Nicci said.

'I can see I'd better have a word with her,' Lynda said, running her finger along a shelf and inspecting the dust. 'Dear me. Maids never do a damn thing unless you're on their tail day and night. Of course, Evan's a man, so they never listen to *him*, but shouldn't *you* have talked to her by this time?'

'About *what?*' Nicci said defiantly.

'About cleaning the house so that it's spotless,' Lynda said. 'That's what we pay them for, dear.'

'Excuse me,' Nicci said, jumping out of bed. 'I'm taking a shower and getting dressed.'

'Late night?' Lynda said, raising an eyebrow.

'A party with a friend,' Nicci replied.

'A party?' Lynda said disapprovingly. 'Surely you shouldn't be running around to parties when you're about to get married?'

'It was my best friend's parents' anniversary,' Nicci said, wondering why she was bothering to explain to this bossy, overbearing woman. 'My mother was there.'

'Oh, your mother,' Lynda said. 'I'm looking forward to meeting her.'

'It'll have to be next week,' Nicci said. 'She's off to Vegas for her show.'

'What show is that, dear?'

'She's opening the Desert Millennium Princess Hotel with a one-night show.'

'Are we going?' Lynda asked.

'*I'm* not,' Nicci said.

'Well, *I'd* like to,' Lynda said. 'Can it be arranged?'

'Evan never told me you wanted to go.'

'I didn't know such a show was taking place,' Lynda said. 'The three of us should go to offer respect to your mother.'

'My mother doesn't like me to see her perform publicly,' Nicci said. 'It makes her uncomfortable, and she protects me from the media.'

'I've never *heard* such nonsense,' Lynda said vigorously. 'Before you, dear, I used to accompany Evan to all of his premières. The cameras *loved* me. I was on *E.T.*, *Access Hollywood* and—'

'What about Brian?' Nicci interrupted. 'Did you accompany him too?'

'Brian can look after himself,' Lynda said dismissively. 'He always has.'

'Well,' Nicci said, 'I'm sure you know where the guest room is.'

'Of course I do, dear, *I* decorated it,' Lynda said. 'In fact, I decorated this entire house. Now, where's that damn maid of yours? I'd better make sure she's spring-cleaned my room before I unpack. And then I want to go see your dress, and hear all about the wedding arrangements.'

Nicci hurried into the bathroom and shut the door. *This* was going to be a nightmare.

* * *

'You little *shit*!' Taylor said, sweeping into Oliver's seedy apartment.

'What now?' he said, reminding himself to lock his door in future.

'How dare you?' she said, steaming.

He was sitting at his computer, bare-chested, wearing cut-off jeans and a Lakers baseball cap. She was dressed for work in sweats and sunglasses – the transformation would take place when she reached the studio. On the way, she'd stopped by Oliver's to tell him exactly what she thought of him.

'What kind of balls do you *have* accepting an assignment to work on *my* script from *my* husband?' she demanded.

'Brass ones,' he said, with a ribald snigger.

'What's *wrong* with you?' she said coldly. 'If Larry ever found out about us, the consequences would be disastrous for *both* of us. Don't you *understand* that?'

'Cool it, Tay,' he said casually. 'I thought you'd be pleased.'

'*Pleased?* Why would I be pleased?'

''Cause it means we can see each other again,' he said, standing up, all skinny, rippling *young* muscles. 'Gotta say I've missed you.'

This caught her completely off-guard. As far as she was concerned her affair with Oliver Rock was over. Except . . . he did look exceptionally appealing today. He wasn't stoned . . . and . . . he'd missed her.

She glanced down. He had a hard-on, and it was fast coming towards her.

'Didja miss *me?*' he asked, putting his arms around her waist and pulling her close.

This was the moment she was supposed to say, 'No, I didn't. And get your juvenile hands off me.'

However, it was too late for that, because his juvenile

hands were all over her, and it was as if he'd pressed a trigger, because once she felt his touch she was powerless to push him away.

'Oliver,' she managed, 'we shouldn't—'

His lips shut her up as they descended on hers, biting and sucking, while his fingers sneaked under her sweatshirt, lightly stroking her nipples, causing her to gasp with excitement.

He took her hand and placed it on his impressive erection. She unzipped his pants, releasing him.

'Eat it,' he commanded.

'I don't have much time—'

'Eat it,' he repeated.

There was something about Oliver Rock. The arrogance of youth. The confidence that she would do exactly as he asked.

She got on her knees and opened her mouth to oblige him.

He put his hands on top of her head and pushed down. She took as much as she could, deep-throating him with a great deal of expertise.

He groaned and came fast. She swallowed. Taylor knew how to please a man.

He was ready to go again immediately – one thing about Oliver, he was not selfish. He pulled down her tracksuit pants, tore off her highly expensive black lace thong, and bent her back across the table next to his computer.

She shuddered with excitement as he thrust himself inside her. Knew she should tell him to wear a condom.

Too late. She was past the moment of no return.

Her climax was so powerful that she screamed out his name. Then, while she was still coming, he withdrew, quickly buried his face between her legs, and began sucking and licking – prolonging her orgasm until she cried out for him to stop.

'Oh, God,' she moaned, feeling quite weak. 'That was amazing.'

''S nice t' be back in business together,' he said, with a cocky grin. 'I think it's all gonna work out pretty good, don't you?'

Chapter Twenty-nine

The streets on the drive downtown were congested with traffic. Eric found himself quite bad-tempered by the time he reached his destination. It was only after he received the goods he'd ordered that his mood turned pleasant.

After the balance of the money he owed changed hands, he found himself in possession of a passport, driver's licence, and social-security card. All the documents were impeccable. Nobody could possibly tell they were fakes.

He studied them for a minute as he sat in his car. Norman Browning. By next week he would be Norman Browning, and Eric Vernon would have ceased to exist. He liked his new name, it had a certain quality, almost a literary bent.

He put the documents in his jacket pocket. First-class work. It had cost him, but it was worth every cent.

Next he stopped by another connection and picked up a gun. Not that he was planning on using it, but it would certainly keep Arliss and friends in line if need be.

Eric felt confident about the kidnapping. Grab Nicci, demand money, pick up the ransom, get on the next plane to the Bahamas, and goodbye, Eric Vernon.

He drove back to his apartment in the valley feeling very satisfied.

When he opened his front door he was surprised to see

an envelope slipped underneath. Eric didn't get mail, nobody knew his address, he had no friends, so why would anyone write him?

He picked up the pink envelope with his name scrawled across the front. 'Eric Vernnon' – The Vernnon was misspelled with two Ns. It alarmed him. Who was sending him mail? Was it that moron, Arliss? Had he gone out of his way to find out where he lived?

He tore open the envelope. Inside was a piece of pink notepaper decorated with flowers and stinking of some vile perfume. Scrawly handwriting covered the page.

> *Dear Eric:*
> *I know you must think I'm forward.*
> *Sorry. I've been watching you, and I like you,*
> *and I think you like me. I am writing this*
> *note 'cause I know we're both shy. So, please*
> *can we go for a nice dinner one night?*
> *Your friend, Pattie (the bar)*
> *PS My night off is Monday.*

Eric stared at the piece of paper in horror. Pattie, the barmaid. How the hell had she found out where he lived? Nobody knew. Nobody was supposed to know.

He simmered with fury, then grabbing his jacket, he set out for the bar to find out.

Sam's Place was more or less empty. The regulars didn't congregate until five or six, and there was no Pattie either. Sam, the owner of the place, sat on a high stool behind the scuffed bar, studying the sports page of the paper. Down the other end of the bar was a hunched-over drunk.

'Early for you, isn't it?' Sam said, glancing up from his newspaper.

'What time does Pattie get here?' Eric asked.

'Five,' Sam replied.

'Where does she live?'

'Can't give out that information,' Sam said.

'I'm sure you can,' Eric said, slipping him a ten.

Sam glanced at the ten, shoved it in his pocket and said, 'Around the corner to the left. The brown building, you can't miss it.'

'If you see her,' Eric said, 'don't tell her I was looking. I want to surprise her.'

'She's a slag, you know,' Sam remarked.

'What?' Eric said.

'She's a slag.'

'What's a slag?'

'English for hooker. Get it?'

'I'm not trying to sleep with her,' Eric said, offended. 'I owe her money.'

'You're a strange one,' Sam said, squinting his small, piggy eyes. 'You've never said two words to me before today.'

'Didn't know you were looking for conversation,' Eric said.

'You hang out with the guys enough. Anythin' goin' on I should know about?'

'Nothing,' Eric said. 'Why?'

'I got a feeling somethin's goin' down. An' if it is, I wouldn't mind bein' included.'

'Keep your feelings to yourself,' Eric wanted to say. But he stayed silent, loathing the fat man.

This was a joke: some skank got hold of his address and now everyone was into his business.

He left the bar, muttering under his breath, thinking about his options. He could wait and see Pattie when she came in to work that night. Or he could pay her a visit now and find out exactly how she'd discovered his address.

Damn her! He'd suspected she liked him, but it had never occurred to him that she'd try to find him.

Since he didn't want everybody in the bar knowing his business, he finally decided to go to her apartment.

He drove around the corner, looking for the apartment building. It was a four-storey structure, seedy and rundown. He parked on the street, got out of his truck, and pressed the buzzer.

'Yes?' a woman's voice said.

'Pattie?'

'Wrong apartment,' the woman said.

He tried the second bell. No answer.

The third. A barking dog and nothing else.

Then the fourth. 'Is Pattie there?'

'Who wants her?'

'Eric.'

'Eric? Is that really you?'

'Yes.'

'Oh,' she said, sounding flustered. 'What're you doing here?'

'Can I come up?'

'I'll buzz you in.'

She pressed the buzzer and the downstairs door swung open.

Eric entered the building. He didn't know what he was going to do. He only knew that he had to find out why she'd been tracking him.

And when he did . . .

Chapter Thirty

Abbey Christian was young, gorgeous, famous and a pain in the ass. She gave new meaning to the word 'vacuous'.

Brian Richter had thought when they'd hired her to star in *Space Blonde* that he'd definitely fuck her – not that he found her so irresistible, it was simply that she was there, on location, and so was he, and Brian could usually score with any woman he chose. However, Abbey was not responding in the usual way to his considerable charm, so he'd come to the conclusion that someone else on the shoot was nailing her.

He considered the various contenders and narrowed them down to Harry Bello, her much older co-star, Chris Fortune, their boy-wonder director, or Andy Moon, their Rod Stewart lookalike camera operator.

He watched Abbey and Harry's interaction on the set. It was painfully obvious they loathed each other. He observed her behaviour with Chris Fortune. She treated him like dog shit – one of the reasons the poor guy was close to a nervous breakdown. And Andy, well, Andy was busy banging the script girl.

Which left . . . who?

Brian went to the source of all gossip – Billie, their Bronx-born hairdresser on the shoot. He sat in her chair while she trimmed his hair, staring at an assortment of

Polaroids of various stars taped to her mirror and asked the question. 'Who's slipping it to our leading lady?'

Billie gave him a sceptical look. 'You mean *you* don't know?'

'I just got back from L.A.,' he said. 'I'm not up on what's goin' on.'

'You're always up on everything,' Billie said, waving her scissors. 'And since *you*'re not slipping it to her, guess who is? It should be easy enough for you to figure out.'

'Who?' he said.

She leaned close to his ear and whispered, 'Evan.'

'*What?*' He began to laugh. 'You *gotta* be kidding.'

'Everyone knows. Andy caught him creeping out of her room at six a.m. the other morning. He didn't see Andy, thinks it's a deep, dark secret.'

'*Evan* is screwing Abbey? My *brother*, Evan?'

'Do we have *another* Evan on this movie?' Billie said, snipping away with her scissors.

'Jesus Christ! He's *engaged*.'

'Like *that* ever made any difference. Must run in the family, right, Brian?'

He shook his head. He was in shock. Evan *never* fooled around with the hired help. No wonder his brother had warned him to stay away from Abbey.

And what about Nicci? There she was in L.A., preparing to marry the guy. And she was a nice kid, *really* nice.

'It's a hoot, doncha think?' Billie said.

'No, it's sad,' Brian replied. 'Listen, honey, *I* screw around, but not if I'm in a committed relationship.'

'You wouldn't know what commitment meant if it bit you on the ass,' Billie said scornfully. 'You're a hound dog, man.'

'Yeah, well, if I *was* committed, I wouldn't fuck around. And Evan's getting married to someone special.' Now that he'd said it aloud, he realized that Nicci *was* special.

'When's this supposed to be happening?' Billie asked.

'In two weeks.'

'*Ooh*, now *that*'s naughty.'

'Yeah, it is,' Brian agreed.

As soon as Billie finished trimming his hair, he headed straight to the set, not quite sure what he would do.

Evan wasn't around. Abbey was sitting in her director's chair sucking on a lollipop. She wore short shorts and a tiny tank, every curve on view – not to mention extremely erect nipples. She loved turning the crew on, it gave her a big kick.

'Hey, Abbey,' he said, wandering over to her.

'Brian – when did *you* get back?'

'Yesterday. I was on the set, didn't you see me?'

'I was too busy working my cute little ass off,' she said modestly.

'Yes, you were,' he agreed.

'How was L.A.?' she asked, sucking away. 'I miss it.'

Yeah, he thought. *What you miss is your dealer.*

Abbey was a total coke-head, another thing that shocked him, because Evan was so anti-drugs.

'Seen my bro today?' he asked.

'Evan's around somewhere,' she said vaguely.

'I hung out with his fiancée in L.A.,' Brian said. 'Terrific girl. Pretty, smart – they make a great couple.'

He watched Abbey's face change. She was not the best actress in the world. Lucky for her career she had an irresistible smile, which lit up the screen.

'Evan's got a fiancée?' she said, no smile in sight.

'Yeah – Nicci. What a girl!'

'I didn't know Evan was engaged,' she said, thunderclouds forming.

'That's my brother for you. Secretive to the end. See you, darlin'.'

And, job done, he left her stewing.

* * *

Lissa lunched with the reporter from the *L.A. Times*, delicately dodging all the questions she didn't care to answer. The man gazed at her adoringly, and she knew it would be a puff piece – which was all right with her, because after Gregg's character assassination she could do with some positive publicity.

Later she informed Max that she was not prepared to do any more sit-down interviews for at least a few months.

'Your choice, babe,' Max said. 'The *Times* was important. And you'll do the electronic media in Vegas.'

'If I have to,' she said reluctantly.

While Lissa was at lunch with the reporter, Danny received a phone call from Gregg Lynch. He was most surprised.

'Danny,' Gregg said, sounding overly friendly, 'how've you been?'

'Fine, thank you,' Danny replied in his best guarded voice, quite perturbed at having to speak to the bad husband, although he'd always harboured a secret crush on Gregg, and had been quite dismayed by the break-up and subsequent betrayals.

'Listen, Danny,' Gregg said, 'you and I always got along well, didn't we?'

'Uh . . . I . . . I suppose so,' Danny stammered, not quite sure where this was leading.

'I wasn't even given a chance to say goodbye to anyone,' Gregg complained. 'And you were always nice to me, Danny. I never had any complaints – although Lissa did her share of bitching about you.'

'*Excuse* me?' Danny said, his face reddening at the thought of his princess saying anything negative about him.

'So I was thinking,' Gregg continued, 'there's no reason why I can't come to the house to collect some of my things that were left behind in the rush to throw me out.'

'There's security at the house, Mr Lynch,' Danny said quickly. 'I'm afraid you're not allowed here.'

'Isn't that unreasonable? And probably not legal. I *am* still her husband.'

'I only work here, Mr Lynch,' Danny said. 'I don't make the decisions.'

'And I wouldn't think of making it uncomfortable for you, Danny.'

'What is it that you wanted to get?' Danny sighed, feeling sorry for him.

'I don't need to go in the main house,' Gregg said. 'There's a box in the pool storage room that contains some of my possessions. Letters from my mother, personal things like that. You can understand why I'd like to retrieve them, can't you?'

'I suppose so,' Danny said unsurely. 'What are you asking me to do? Get you the box?'

'No, there's a lot of junk in that room. I need to look for it myself.'

'Well . . .' Danny said, thinking that there couldn't possibly be any harm in Gregg collecting his personal letters, especially since they were from his mom, and probably had sentimental value. 'We're leaving tomorrow at ten. I'm sure if you came when the pool man is here, nobody would object to you taking your box of personal letters. As long as you don't go anywhere near the house.'

'What time does he come?'

'About noon.'

'Thanks, Danny, you've been a big help. I always knew you were a good guy, in spite of Lissa's comments.'

'That's very nice of you, Mr Lynch,' Danny said, wondering exactly what Lissa's comments were.

'And remember,' Gregg added.

'Yes?'

'There's always two sides to every story.'

Danny hung up the phone full of mixed feelings. He knew he was supposed to hate Gregg Lynch, only he couldn't. And what possible harm could there be in the poor man claiming some of his personal stuff?

By the time Lissa arrived home, Danny had conveniently put the phone call out of his mind. Not that he would have told her. She would be livid if she knew he'd spoken to Gregg.

Some things were better left unmentioned.

When Taylor arrived at the studio she felt fucked, literally. Montana sensed it immediately: she had an uncanny knack of psyching into people's private secrets.

'Hmm . . . Larry must be performing better than he was when he was married to Susan,' Montana remarked.

'What do you mean?' Taylor answered, sitting down in the makeup chair.

'It's written all over your face. *Somebody* had great sex this morning, and it wasn't me.'

'I never discuss my sex life,' Taylor said primly. 'I've always found that people who do are usually not getting it.'

Montana laughed. 'You're so right.'

'How late did you stay at the party last night?' Taylor asked.

'Long after you,' Montana said. 'I'm directing Kyndra's next video as a favour to Norio. We go back years, he's a very interesting man.'

'I've always liked him,' Taylor said.

'Where do you know them from?' Montana asked.

'There's a group of us who get together for lunch whenever we can. Lissa put everyone together. When she was first starting out she sang back-up for Kyndra.'

'And how did *you* meet Lissa?'

'I had a small role in one of her movies and we bonded. She's the best. Never changes.'

297

'Yes, she does have a dynamic presence,' Montana said thoughtfully. 'I'd love to work with her.'

'Then you should,' Taylor said. 'Anything's possible, right?'

'It certainly is.'

'And speaking of anything being possible,' Taylor added, 'guess what I did last night.'

'I'm not into guessing games.'

'I actually asked Larry why he didn't put me in one of his movies.'

'Good for you,' Montana said. 'It's about time you did that.'

'I mean, here I am, an actress, married to one of the most powerful men in town, and he's never even suggested that I appear in one of his films.'

'What was his reaction?' Montana inquired.

'He got very edgy and changed the subject, started talking about *my* project, which he's *finally* decided to help me with.'

'What's your project?'

'I developed a script I've been trying to get off the ground for two years. One of the reasons I haven't been able to is because Larry would never put his weight behind it. Now that I'm acting again, it's making him nervous. So he's hired a young writer to do another rewrite, and he's also promised to attach himself as executive producer. It'll make a big difference.'

'I'm sure it will,' Montana murmured. 'Who's the writer?'

'Oliver Rock,' Taylor answered casually.

'Don't think I know him.'

'He's a young guy who just sold a spec script for a lot of money. Larry seems to think he has plenty of talent.'

'Never heard of him,' Montana said, 'but that means nothing 'cause I don't read the trades. Gave them up a long time ago when I realized they were full of deals that never materialized.'

* * *

By the end of the day on Wednesday Michael knew he couldn't avoid it any longer. He had to call Carol.

She was still at her office. 'I might've sold a two-million-dollar house today,' she said cheerfully, as if nothing else was going on in their lives.

'That's good,' he said.

'Good!' she exclaimed. 'Don't you mean great?'

'Yeah, uh, that's great, honey,' he said, wishing he never had to see her again. 'And thanks for dinner last night.'

'I knew I could snare you with my cooking,' she joked.

He laughed nervously. 'Uh . . . Carol, I'm off to Vegas tomorrow. It's work, and I won't be back until Monday. So Monday night you and I should sit down and talk.'

'Yes, Michael. My place or yours?'

'I'll come to you.'

'Around seven?'

'See you then.'

He didn't know what he was going to say to her, he only knew that something had to be worked out. He'd already decided he would support the child financially; it was the least he could do.

Memories of Bella kept drifting back to haunt him – the little girl he'd thought was his. He remembered the day she was born, her first steps, the way she'd called him Daddy. He tried to put her out of his mind. It was impossible.

Quincy put his head round the door and asked if he wanted to drop by the house for dinner.

'Does Amber know about Carol?' Michael asked.

'*I* didn't tell her, man,' Quincy assured him. 'Not me.'

'So you're saying she *does* know?' Michael said, lighting up a cigarette.

'Carol talked to her,' Quincy admitted.

'*Shit*!'

'She's cookin' her famous fried chicken.'

299

'I'll pass.'

'You're not pissed at *me*, are you?'

'No, Q. I'll be better off alone tonight.'

'If you change your mind—'

'Thanks. I gotta pack, get ready for tomorrow.'

He stayed late at the office, and by the time he got home he was too tired to think. He switched on the TV, watched ten minutes of *The Sopranos*, and fell into a deep sleep.

Nicci was frantic. Evan's mother was impossible, sticking her nose into everything as if she had a right. During the course of the day, the maid almost quit, and the gardener mumbled a few Spanish insults in Lynda's direction after she'd nagged him about the state of the grass, the hedge and the flowers. Unfortunately, Lynda understood Spanish, so then she was hot to fire the gardener.

Nicci called Evan. 'Your mom is driving me totally nuts!' she complained. 'Why didn't you tell me she was arriving today?'

'I would've if you'd called me,' he said, still in an uptight mood.

'When will you be home? I can't take her on my own. She's impossible.'

'I don't believe you said that.'

'What?'

'You're talking about my *mother*, Nicci. She's only trying to help.'

'How do *you* know?'

'Because I've already spoken to her, and she's told me the maid and the gardener are both useless.'

'Oh, *really*? So what do *you* suggest we do? Dump them right before our wedding?'

'My mother can handle it, she'll find us new people, she's an expert at that.'

'No!' Nicci said sharply.

'No, what?'

'No, I'm not allowing her to walk in and upset everything.'

'Don't be childish, Nicci.'

'Did you call me childish?'

'Why don't we discuss this when I get back.'

'Why don't *you* go to hell?'

She slammed down the phone and marched into the kitchen where Lynda was busily reorganizing the canned-goods cupboard. 'What are you doing?' she demanded.

'Some of these cans are out of date,' Lynda said disapprovingly. 'Serve them, and you could be serving pure poison.'

'I don't think so,' Nicci said, very close to losing it.

'Yes, dear,' Lynda assured her. 'A friend of mine had to be rushed to the emergency room after eating a can of soup three months after the date.'

'That's a *sell-by* date,' Nicci pointed out, grabbing a can of tomato soup earmarked by Lynda to be thrown away.

The phone rang. *Saved by the bell*, Nicci thought.

'Hello,' she said bad-temperedly, thinking it was Evan.

'*Cariño!* This is your father.'

'Antonio?'

'You have another father?'

'How *are* you?'

'We are here, at the Peninsula Hotel.'

'You are?'

'We come early because Bianca wishes to do the shopping on Rodeo.'

'Bianca?'

'Contessa Bianca de Morago. My wife.'

Chapter Thirty-one

By the time Michael arrived at the house on Thursday morning, Lissa was in the front hall, all packed and waiting to leave.

'I'm not late, am I?' he said, quickly checking his watch.

She gave him a cool smile. 'I said ten o'clock, it's five minutes before, you're perfectly on time.'

'That's what I thought.'

'Why don't you wait in one of the limos? I have a couple of last-minute things to take care of.'

He walked outside. She was being off with him, and he didn't blame her.

'Good *morning*,' Fabio said, emerging from the house. 'And you are?'

'Michael Scorsinni.'

'I am Fabio. Lissa's hair and makeup artist,' Fabio said, tossing back his mane of hair.

'Nice meeting you, Fabio.'

'The pleasure is all mine,' Fabio said, looking Michael up and down and licking his lips.

There were two limos parked in the driveway. Michael wasn't sure which one he was supposed to get in. He walked over to Chuck, who was talking to one of the drivers. 'Morning, Chuck,' he said. 'Which car d'you think she wants me in?'

'Ride follow-up,' Chuck said. 'I'll go with her.'

'Sure,' he said, taking out his dark glasses and putting them on, because even though it was early, the sun was quite bright. He remembered when he'd first moved to L.A. and partnered with Quincy. It was the weather that had lured him, followed by the laid-back lifestyle.

Danny emerged and started speaking with Fabio.

'How's everything?' Michael said, going over to him.

'Couldn't be better,' Danny said, ready for his Vegas adventure, all dressed up in a pale yellow leisure suit.

'Who's going to be on the plane?' Michael asked.

Danny produced a list. 'Let me see, there's *me* and Fabio, Chuck, and Madam, of course, and *you*. Everyone else is flying commercial.'

'So we're on a private plane?'

'Yes, the hotel is sending it,' Danny said. 'It's the *only* way to travel.'

Michael got in the limo, followed by Danny and Fabio.

They sat there for ten minutes until Lissa finally appeared. She stopped and talked to Chuck for a minute.

Chuck came back to the second limo. 'Miz Roman wants you to ride with her,' he said to Michael, his face expressionless. 'I'll go in this car.'

Fabio and Danny exchanged knowing looks as Michael got out of the limo and headed to the front one, where Lissa was already sitting.

He climbed in and took off his dark glasses.

'How are you, Michael?' she asked.

'Fine,' he replied, copying her cool tone. 'And everything's good with you?'

'Seems to be,' she said, putting on a pair of Gucci sunglasses with pink-tinted lenses.

'Heard any more from Gregg?'

'No,' she said, shaking her head. 'I guess he's gotten bored and gone away.'

'Let's hope.'

'I *am* suing him,' she said. 'I mentioned that, didn't I?'

'You told me you were seeing your lawyer.'

'He seems to think I have a case. Then again,' she mused, 'do I really need the publicity?'

'No,' Michael said. 'You should do what I advised and get him to sign a confidentiality agreement – one that'll shut him up for good.'

'I told my lawyer that.' A long beat while she thought it over. 'Maybe I'll drop the case. I don't need to put myself back in the headlines.'

'You look beautiful, Lissa,' he said, unable to stop himself – the words just came pouring out.

'Don't tell me that,' she said brusquely.

'Why?'

'Because we don't have a *personal* relationship, Michael. You made it very clear that you're not interested. So please save the compliments for your girlfriend or girlfriends, whatever you've got going.'

'I'm not allowed to say you look beautiful?' he asked, wondering if she was planning to shut him out the entire trip.

'I'd prefer that you didn't.'

'Okay,' he said, deciding to go along with whatever she wanted to do. 'We'll keep it all business. You're right, Lissa, that's the way it *should* be.' He was furious with himself for weakening, but it seemed that the moment he was around her, he couldn't help himself.

They rode in silence to the airport.

Michael wondered why she'd wanted him in the car with her if she didn't have anything to say to him. Then his thoughts moved on to Carol and the baby she was carrying – *his* baby. By the time they reached the airport, he'd slumped into a deep depression.

The Desert Millennium Princess had sent a sleek Gulfstream IV plane to fetch Lissa and her entourage. Two extremely attractive hostesses in short, white and gold, form-fitting uniforms, were waiting to greet her as she got out of the limo and started up the steps to the plane. The two pilots stood on the top step, eager to say hello.

Lissa was gracious to everyone, smiling and shaking hands.

As soon as he was aboard, Michael walked around the interior of the plane, checking it out. There was a small luxurious bedroom with its own private marble bathroom, a spacious living-room area, and a rear cabin, where Fabio and Danny settled. Lissa sat in the living-room area, which featured a round dining table and several comfortable seats, plus a bar and large-screen television.

'Michael, you sit in here with me,' she commanded.

For someone who wanted a business relationship, she was certainly giving him preferential treatment. Chuck threw him a look and went into the rear cabin with Fabio and Danny.

'You look tired,' she remarked, fastening her seat-belt.

'I've had a rough couple of days,' he said, sitting in the seat next to her and buckling up.

'Chasing more cheating husbands?'

'Everything's fallen on my shoulders since Quincy can't do too much on account of his leg. Apart from that, I've, uh . . . got kind of a personal problem.'

'Join the club,' she said, as one of the stewardesses approached, a tall, leggy blonde.

'Can I get you anything, Miz Roman?' the girl asked.

'Evian, please.'

'Certainly, Miz Roman,' the stewardess said. She then turned to Michael, giving him a long, flirtatious look. 'Mr Scorsinni? How about you?'

'I'll have Evian too.'

'We'll be taking off in approximately five minutes,' the stewardess said, giving him another flirtatious look. 'I'm Cindy. Anything you need, feel free to buzz me.'

Lissa leaned back and closed her eyes.

Michael wondered why he'd told her that he had a personal problem. He wasn't about to reveal what it was, so why even mention it?

He couldn't help staring at her. She was so beautiful and yet even looking at her was dangerous.

Stay away, a little voice screamed in his head. But he knew that staying away was getting more and more difficult each time he saw her.

'Hi.'

'Who's this?' Nicci asked suspiciously.

'Who do you *think* it is? Your partner in crime.'

'Brian?' she said tentatively.

'Yeah.'

'Why are you calling me?'

'To advise you that Evan didn't say zip about the fiancée thing.'

'We had a raging fight on the phone,' she said, keeping her voice low because Lynda was lurking somewhere. 'Your mom's here, and she's every bit as bad as you warned me she was.'

Brian began to laugh. 'Hate to say I told you so.'

'Why are you laughing?' Nicci said indignantly. 'It's not even remotely funny. She's been here twenty-four hours and she's already driving me insane, and Evan won't be back until Sunday. Oh, yeah, and apparently she's like *talking* to him on the phone all the time, *mostly* to complain about me.'

'That figures.'

'What can I do?'

'Tough it out, babe.'

'You don't understand. She's impossible, Brian.'

'I *do* understand. She's my mother.'

'She talks about Evan endlessly. Sometimes, to piss her

off, I bring *your* name up, and she like doesn't even *give* a rat's ass. Says you can look after yourself.'

'That's 'cause she knows I won't put up with her shit, so she's let go of me. The bad news is she's still got Evan jumping hoops.'

'What can I do about it?'

'Marry the guy, then the three of you can live happily ever after. Isn't that what you want?'

'Screw you, Brian.'

'When?'

'Ha ha. Not funny.'

'So what else is up?'

'I'm beginning to have doubts.'

'Yeah?'

'Right now, things seem so kind of like *strange*. And every time I speak to Evan, we get into a major fight. I suppose when he gets back on Sunday, everything will be all right.' A beat. 'It's nice of you to call, Brian.'

'I gotta make a confession.'

'Yes?'

'You an' I – we didn't do anything.'

'About what?'

'We didn't have sex, Nic.'

'You're kidding?'

'I might've been wasted, but here's the thing – I can take all the shit going an' it doesn't affect me. So, uh . . . apart from the fact that I dented your car, and I *do* remember that, we didn't do anything.'

'Then how come we ended up in your bed with no clothes on?'

'We were just about to get down to it when you passed out on me. So, good guy that I am – or stupid, whichever way you wanna look at it – I carried you into bed, crawled in beside you, and fell asleep.'

'Oh, my God! Why didn't you tell me before?'

'I'm telling you now, aren't I?'

'I can't decide whether I'm relieved or not.'

'Huh?'

'I didn't mean that,' she said quickly. 'I'm confused.'

'Sounds like it,' he said.

She attempted to gather her thoughts. This was a good thing . . . wasn't it? No sex with Brian. No guilty feelings. Yes, it was a good thing.

'Uh, Brian,' she ventured.

'Yes.'

'When you get back, can we sit down and talk? I think I need help.'

'I told you before, Nic, you're nineteen, if you're not sure about the marriage thing, don't do it.'

'How can I back out now? The wedding plans are all in place, your mother's here, my father just flew in, and Saturday night Saffron's throwing me a bachelorette night. Wild times, here I come!'

'Then you'd better make sure you enjoy it, babe, 'cause come Sunday, your wild times are *way* over.'

Gregg parked his car a block from his former residence, and waited. When he saw the pool man's truck driving up the winding street, he got out of his car and waved for him to stop. 'Hey, Lou,' he yelled. 'Pull over.'

The pool man, a tall, blondish ex-surfer gone to seed, stopped his truck and squinted. 'Mr Roman?' he said.

It had always infuriated Gregg that the idiot called him Mr Roman, but he wasn't about to get into that now. 'Yeah, yeah – how're you doing?'

'Can't complain, Mr Roman.'

'I'm taking a ride with you up to the house,' Gregg said. 'Picking up some of my stuff from the storage room.'

'You don't wanna drive your car?'

The man was a moron who'd obviously burned his

brains out while doing all that surfing in his youth. Which was good, because he obviously didn't read the papers or watch TV.

'Naw, it's easier to put it in your truck and bring it back to my car,' he said, jumping into the truck.

Now all he had to do was get through the front gate. With any luck, Chuck would have gone to Vegas with Lissa, and there'd be a new guard at the gate who wouldn't know him.

The truck drove through with no trouble. Lou circumvented the house and parked in the back by the pool. Gregg jumped out and headed for the storage room, which was not within sight of the house, another plus.

The room was unlocked. Things were definitely going his way today.

He entered the overcrowded storage room, which smelled musty and damp. There were old suitcases, miscellaneous junk, boxes and boxes of stuff piled high. He remembered saying to Lissa once, 'Why the hell do you keep all this crap?' That had been in the early days when they'd been making love out by the pool, and she'd gone into the storage room to see if she could find an old Polaroid camera. They'd thought it would be fun to take some pictures.

He'd followed her into the stuffy little room, and that's when he'd asked her what she kept in there.

'My life,' she'd said, turning to him, 'from when I was ten years old.'

'That's a lot of boxes, babe.'

'Yes,' she'd agreed. 'One day I'll go through them.'

Each box had a date scrawled on it in heavy felt pen. Gregg tried to count back in his head. Lissa was forty, which meant that when she ran away from home at sixteen, it would've been around 1977. He decided to play it safe and took the boxes marked '74, '75, and '76.

He carried them to Lou's truck, and loaded them in the back. Then he waited for the pool man to finish.

It was easy. And nobody said a word when they drove out.

'I set up a dinner with Oliver Rock,' Larry said. 'I thought it would be a good idea for us all to get together before the meeting at the studio.'

'You could have checked with me,' Taylor said, feeling incredibly guilty, because it was one thing having Oliver work on her script, and quite another sitting down to dinner with him and her husband.

'I tried, but you were working and your phone was off.'

'Where are we going?'

'Spago at seven thirty. Can you be ready?'

'I'll go get dressed,' she said, hurrying upstairs, still feeling guilty. This was a dangerous road she was travelling, and she knew it. Sleeping with Oliver Rock was *not* a good idea. As enjoyable as it was, it had to stop, because she knew without a doubt that if she continued doing so, it would lead to big trouble.

She'd experienced another great day at the studio. Recently she'd begun to realize that the one big mistake she'd made in her marriage to Larry was giving up her career. Now that she was acting again, she felt so much more fulfilled. And if her project came off, everything would be perfect.

The only bad thing was her affair with Oliver Rock. And how bad could that be? Larry would *never* find out. *She* wasn't about to tell him, and Oliver certainly wouldn't.

By seven fifteen, they were on their way to the restaurant. Larry was driving and full of conversation. 'I read through the script myself today,' he said, 'and I have a few suggestions for Oliver. You and I should definitely sit down and discuss it this weekend. You're not working, are you?'

'No,' she said. 'I only have another few days on the film, then it's over.'

'You're enjoying it, aren't you?' he ventured.

'I should have never given up my career, Larry,' she said fervently. 'I *love* acting.'

'I can tell.'

'Going to lunches, and working on all those charity events with a bunch of women who have nothing else to do except bitch about each other doesn't do it for me. All that is *so* boring.'

'It's my fault,' he said, nodding to himself. 'I should have realized you needed more.'

'Well, as I suggested,' she said, choosing her words carefully, 'we can always work together. We'll be doing it on my project, and then, if you *do* decide to cast me in one of *your* films, there'd *be* no separations. And we both know that if there's one thing that's bad for a marriage, it's separations. Especially in this town.'

'We've never been apart,' Larry said confidently, 'and we have a great marriage.'

'That's probably why. Togetherness is what's important. You see all these divorces taking place. Usually it's because one person's off on location, and their partner's not with them. I want to be here for you all the time, Larry, but I also want to act. I have to be true to myself, don't I?'

'Yes, my darling,' he said. 'I understand.'

When they walked into the restaurant, Taylor was shocked to see that Oliver had brought a date: a young, pale girl with lank yellow hair, a blank expression and a nipple ring – quite evident through her almost see-through silky top. Taylor wondered if it was the same girl she'd spotted lying naked on his mattress the day she'd surprised him. And if it was, would the girl remember seeing her? Oh God, how stupid could this guy get?

'Mrs Singer,' Oliver said, playing his part properly. 'Nice to see you again.'

'Please call me Taylor,' she said, shooting Larry a look as much as to say, *Why has he brought his girlfriend with him?*

'I will,' Oliver said. 'This is Kimberly.'

'Hi, Kimberly dear,' she said, suddenly feeling incredibly old.

Larry didn't seem to notice anything was amiss as they settled into a booth and ordered the famous Spago smoked salmon pizza.

'We're happy you're on board, Oliver,' Larry said. 'This could turn out to be an exciting project. As you know, Taylor's been trying to get it going for some time, but the writers she chose to work with have been too . . . what's the word I'm looking for?'

'Cautious?' Oliver suggested.

'Yes, that's it, cautious. The script has to have more edge.'

'A dash of Tarantino,' Oliver said.

'Let's not go that far,' Larry said. 'We don't want violence.'

'Of course,' Oliver agreed, not about to argue with the great Larry Singer.

'*I'm* planning to direct,' Taylor said, asserting herself. She did not appreciate them discussing her script as if she wasn't there.

'Have you directed before?' Oliver asked.

As if the little prick didn't already know. 'No,' she said, giving him a dirty look.

'Could be a mistake,' Oliver said.

She felt her cheeks flush with anger. '*What?*' she said tightly.

'I know what Oliver means,' Larry interjected, oblivious to his wife's mounting fury. 'Playing the lead *and* directing on your first outing – it's too much responsibility. Plus it'll make it a lot tougher for the studio to commit.'

'Yeah,' Oliver said, playing kiss up. 'You're right, Larry.'

Taylor could not believe that the two of them seemed to be in cahoots. Was this fair?

'Wait a minute,' she said curtly, 'this is *my* project, and *I* plan to direct *and* star.'

'Yes, honey, I know,' Larry answered soothingly, 'only wouldn't it be safer if you concentrated on acting this time out? Especially as I'm coming on as executive producer. I'll hire a director I know I can control, and that way you'll be in on everything.'

'How 'bout me?' Oliver said, with a cheeky grin. 'I'm *dying* to direct.'

'I don't think so,' Taylor said, her tone icy.

'Let's not get into that now,' Larry said, adjusting his glasses, which had an annoying habit of sliding down his nose. 'First we get the script right, *then* we decide on a director.' He leaned forward, full of enthusiasm. When Larry committed to a project he was one hundred percent involved. '*Now*,' he said, 'here are some of my ideas.'

The only positive thing about having Lynda Richter in the house was that Nicci had managed to find out the truth about Evan and his previous fiancée. Yes, he'd been engaged to a script girl from one of their movies, just as Brian had said.

'So what went wrong?' Nicci asked Lynda, trying to sound as casual as possible.

'She was after his money,' Lynda said. 'I could tell it the moment I set eyes on her. She moved into the house and changed things – which, as you can imagine, did *not* please me. She actually *sold* a piece of furniture I'd bought, and Evan *never* saw the money.'

'You mean she lived *here*?' Nicci said, startled. 'In this house?'

'For six months. It wasn't until *I* came out here that I was able to show him what she was up to.'

'How long were they together?'

'Over a year. Surely Evan told you?'

'Oh, yes,' Nicci said quickly, 'but, you know Evan, he doesn't like talking about personal stuff.'

'My Evan,' Lynda said fondly. 'He was always a sensitive boy.'

Nicci decided this was even worse than she'd thought. Not only had Evan not mentioned the girl, but they'd been together for over a year, *and* she'd lived in his house for six months. The same house Nicci was in now.

She couldn't believe that he'd kept it a secret. She was confused and angry, and couldn't *wait* to confront him in person.

In the meantime, what was she supposed to do about his mom? Lynda apparently didn't know anyone in L.A. All she wanted to do was hang around the house changing everything and annoying the help.

'Uh, listen,' Nicci said, 'my dad's in town, and I'll be having dinner with him tonight.'

'Where are we going?' Lynda asked.

'Sorry?'

'Where are we going?' Lynda repeated. 'Somewhere nice?'

Nicci frowned. 'Uh . . . you can't come with us,' she explained. 'I haven't seen my dad in two years, so I need to spend time with him by myself.'

'Oh,' Lynda said, frosty-faced. 'I see. You're leaving me alone here, are you?'

'We'll do something together tomorrow,' Nicci promised.

'If you're sure you can spare the time,' Lynda said caustically.

I spared the time last night, Nicci thought. *Took you to Hamburger Hamlet and you nagged your way through* two *hamburgers and a giant slice of chocolate cake. I'm certainly not subjecting Antonio to that kind of torture.*

'Of course I can,' Nicci said sweetly.

And she couldn't wait to leave the house.

Chapter Thirty-two

A fleet of limos was waiting at the airport to greet Lissa and her entourage when they flew into Vegas.

'You'll come in the car with me, Michael,' she said, as they got off the plane.

Four white stretch limos were lined up, all emblazoned with the name of the hotel in gold along the side. Michael climbed in the first one with Lissa. The interior was carpeted with white rugs, and white and gold leather-upholstered seats.

A pretty girl in a Millennium Desert Princess Hotel uniform immediately offered them champagne and caviar.

'Too early in the morning for me,' Lissa said, smiling slightly.

'Me too,' Michael said, feeling uncomfortable, like some kind of consort. But then, on the other hand, he had to remember he was working. This was strictly work, and he shouldn't take it any other way.

The silence that had started on the plane lasted all the way to the hotel. Michael was damned if he was going to break it, and Lissa didn't say a word.

Rick Maneloni, the manager, was waiting to greet her at a private entrance. He was Mister Slick, all dressed up in a shiny blue suit with brown, moussed hair, and heavy matching eyebrows. He wore a lot of macho gold jewellery, and carried a small silver phone. 'Miz Roman,' he gushed. 'Lissa – if I may call you that. We are delighted to welcome you to the Desert Millennium Princess. It is our pleasure to have you here, and anything you need – anything at all, twenty-four hours a day – please feel free to summon your personal concierge.'

'I have a personal concierge?' Lissa asked.

'Two. They'll be waiting in your suite, which we will escort you to right now. You must be tired from your journey.'

'Hardly,' she murmured. 'L.A. is only an hour away.' She indicated Michael. 'This is Mr Scorsinni, my personal security. I'd like him to be close.'

'Certainly, Miz Roman. We have our own excellent security here for you, but it's quite understandable that you travel with your own.'

'And my other people, you'll take care of them?'

'We have the entire Penthouse One floor reserved for you, Miz Roman,' Rick said. 'I do believe you'll find the accommodations adequate. You have your own roof-top swimming pool, a miniature golf course and, of course, a sauna and gym.'

'Of course I do,' she murmured.

Then they were all whisked into a private elevator and taken to the top floor.

The view from the Penthouse was astounding. The whole of Las Vegas was laid out before them.

'Wait until you see the view at night,' Rick boasted.

'I'm sure it's magnificent,' Lissa said.

'Mr Walter Burns, the owner of the hotel, wondered if you would care to dine with him and his wife tonight, bringing whoever you like.'

'I'll let you know,' Lissa said.

This was the first time Michael had been in her company where she was treated like the megastar she was. It made him realize all the more how far out of her league he was.

He strolled over to Chuck. 'You do know she requested either myself or Quincy to come along on this trip,' he said. 'I understand you're usually in charge of her personal security, and I respect that. I also know you've been doing a first-rate job, so I hope you don't think I'm invading your territory.'

'No worries,' Chuck said. 'I work for her *all* the time. Havin' you around don't bother me.'

'You're sure?'

'Listen, man,' Chuck said, shrugging, 'whatever she wants, she gets. She's the star, okay?'

'Yeah,' Michael agreed. 'She's the star.'

'Everyone can get settled,' Lissa announced. 'I'm planning to relax today, so all of you go off and do your own thing. Danny, please be sure to deal with the clothes when they get here, make sure the jewellery is put in the hotel safe, and double-check that everything's set for tomorrow's rehearsal.'

'Yes, Miz Roman,' Danny said, almost bobbing a curtsy. He was desperate to explore Sin City.

'Michael,' she said offhandedly, 'I'm sorry I can't give you time off.'

'I wasn't expecting it,' he replied evenly. 'I'm here to watch out for you, right?'

'So,' she said, 'do you want to watch out for me at dinner?'

'Where?'

'The owner of the hotel has requested dinner with me. I'm certainly not going by myself. Let's say we'll meet here at eight o'clock.'

'Got it. In the meantime,' he said, handing her a pager, 'if you need me, buzz – I'm in the room next door. And, Lissa, don't go anywhere on your own.'

'I wasn't planning to.'

'I'll see you at eight.'

He spent the rest of the day playing solitaire on a computer in his room. He thought about phoning Carol, then decided against it. It was enough that he was seeing her on Monday night.

In his mind he went over what he was going to say to her. Yes, he'd be there for her. Yes, he'd pay financial support for the baby. Yes, he wanted to be part of the baby's life, but he did not plan on continuing with their relationship. It wasn't fair to either of them.

He wondered how she'd accept it. The truth was he didn't really care – that's the way it was going to be.

At seven o'clock he took a shower and put on a clean white shirt and a Charvet tie – a gift from a grateful client. Next he took out his dark blue Armani suit, his one big extravagance. Wearing the suit made him feel like a million bucks – which he didn't have and never would.

He started thinking about why Lissa had wanted him to accompany her to Las Vegas. She had Chuck, and there was all the security in the world at the hotel, but no, she'd insisted he come too. Maybe she was playing some kind of weird movie star game with him, and even though they were both aware of being attracted to each other, it couldn't possibly go anywhere. And if she thought he was about to be a weekend fling, she was very much mistaken.

Contessa Bianca de Morago looked like Sophia Loren – elegant, beautiful, and definitely over sixty. Antonio was as handsome as ever – he hadn't changed a bit.

'My *cariño*!' Antonio said, grabbing Nicci in a huge embrace as they met in the lobby of the Peninsula Hotel. 'I wish to present my wife, the Contessa Bianca de Morago. Bianca,' he added formally, 'this is my daughter, Nicci.'

Bianca smiled and proffered a languid hand. Nicci was dazzled by the size of the huge diamond solitaire ring on her engagement finger. Obviously *not* a gift from Antonio, who certainly didn't have that kind of money.

'Hi,' she said, still checking the woman out so she could give a full report to Lissa.

'Antonio has told me much about you,' Bianca said, in a deep, throaty, accented voice. 'It is a pleasure to come to California and finally meet you.'

'Uh, thanks,' Nicci said, mentally adding up the cost of the diamonds this woman had on – discreet earrings, a firebird brooch, an impressive bracelet, and the ring. Nicci reckoned Bianca was standing there in over a million dollars' worth of jewels.

'We leave your car here,' Antonio announced. 'Our driver will take us.'

Nicci had booked a table at Spago – not her usual hangout, but she'd thought it was the place they'd want to go. She was right – even Bianca had heard of the famous restaurant.

Somehow Nicci felt strangely shy in the presence of her father. Maybe it was because she hadn't seen him in two years. 'How's Adela?' she asked, inquiring after her stern Spanish grandmother.

'The same,' Antonio replied airily. 'Difficult.'

Nicci thought about Lynda. Nobody could be as difficult as her soon-to-be mother-in-law from hell.

'And Lissa?' Antonio asked, as they walked outside to a discreet black town car complete with a uniformed driver. 'Your dear mama is well?'

'She's getting divorced,' Nicci blurted.

'I heard.' Antonio sighed. 'Poor Lissa – she never has luck with men.'

'I guess she didn't have much with you,' Nicci said, unable to stop herself from making a sly dig.

Antonio laughed. Nothing seemed to faze him, with Bianca and her money by his side, he owned the world.

They all got in the car.

'Have you been to L.A. before?' Nicci asked the Contessa.

'This is Bianca's first trip to America,' Antonio said. 'I am to show her the sights. After L.A. and your wedding, we visit the Grand Canyon and Niagara Falls.'

'Antonio! Those are totally tourist places.'

'I know, I know,' he said, gazing fondly at his wife, 'but my Bianca wishes to see them.'

Bianca smiled – she had very big teeth. 'I read about such places in school,' she said. 'That was a long time ago, now I must see for myself.'

'Tomorrow we fly to Vegas,' Antonio said. 'We have chartered a plane, and I have tickets for Lissa's show.'

'You do?' Nicci said, wondering how Lissa would take the news.

'I thought Bianca should visit the gambling capital, and it will be nice to see your mother's show. Perhaps you will alert her that we are coming.'

'I'm sure she'll be surprised,' Nicci said.

'Yes, I'm sure she will,' Antonio said. 'I would love for my Bianca to meet her.'

Nicci nodded blankly, wondering what kind of a trip *he* was on.

'You wish to come with us?' Antonio asked.

She shook her head. 'No, no, I can't. I have a bachelorette night going on this Saturday. My friend, Saffron, is throwing me a magical mystery tour – it'll be awesome.'

'A bachelorette night?' Bianca questioned. 'Surely that is something only men do?'

'No, in America girls do it too. You know, we'll be like goin' out and gettin' wild – eyeballing crazy strippers and stuff.'

'You look at female strippers?' Bianca said, obviously shocked.

'No, male ones.'

'You have male strippers in America?' Bianca inquired, quite startled.

'They have many things in America you know nothing about,' Antonio said, taking her hand.

Over dinner Nicci learned more about the Contessa. She had been married for forty years to a captain of industry, and when he'd died a year ago, he'd left her his fortune. She and Antonio had met at a party, and apparently fallen in love. She had three grown children, all of whom had never left Spain.

Nicci wondered how they felt about her marriage to Antonio, who was at least fifteen years her junior.

Bianca seemed nice enough, and that pleased Nicci because it was about time Antonio had some stability. And not only was he getting stability, he was getting money too.

The evening passed quickly. On the way out, Nicci stopped to say hello to her mother's friends, Taylor and Larry Singer, who were dining in the neighbouring booth. Sitting with them was Kimberly, a friend of hers from high school.

'Hey, Kim,' she said.

'Hey, Nic,' Kimberly said, jumping up.

'What's the deal?' Nicci asked.

'New guy,' Kimberly whispered. 'He's a hottie.'

Nicci took a discreet peek at Oliver. 'Cute,' she whispered back. 'What are you doing with the Singers?'

'He's writing a script for them.'

'Cool.'

'I'll see you Saturday,' Kimberly said.

'You're coming?'

'Wouldn't miss it!'

'Can't wait!'

Lynda was still up when Nicci got home. She had decided to reorganize Evan's closet, and his clothes were lying around everywhere.

'You shouldn't do that without asking Evan,' Nicci said. 'He's very particular about his stuff.'

'When you know Evan better, dear, you'll realize I do a lot of things he doesn't have time to do for himself,' Lynda said in a patronizing voice. 'I'm sure, over time, I can train you to help.'

Nicci shook her head in amazement. Brian was right. Lynda Richter was a piece of work.

After the pool man had dropped Gregg back at his car, he loaded the boxes into the trunk. Then he set off for the recording studio, where he was paying a young, black producer an exorbitant amount of money to record his latest composition. *I should've called it 'Bitch'*, he thought as he drove to the studio, *and dedicated it to her*.

He was well aware that timing was everything, and soon he'd be running out. He had to cash in on his publicity, take that fifteen minutes and shove it up everyone's ass.

Belinda was in agreement that he should do everything he could. 'Maybe I can perform it on your show,' he suggested, expecting her to jump.

'*I* don't decide what goes on,' she answered. 'My producer does.'

'You mean if you said you wanted me on, singing my song, he'd say no?'

'We're not a musical show, Gregg.'

'It's a no-lose segment,' he argued. 'The guy that got away. The public'll eat it up.'

'I'll bring it up at the next production meeting.'

'You do that,' he said, more than a little irritated.

He was getting bored with Belinda, she was the kind of woman who needed servicing, and he didn't feel like being the in-house service stud. Especially when he wasn't getting anything back.

At the studio he flirted with the girl behind the

reception desk, an ex-groupie with cock-sucking lips and bitter eyes.

'What studio am I in today?' he asked.

'Studio three, Gregg,' she replied.

'See you later, then,' he said, heading up the stairs, filing her away for another day.

He'd hired the producer he was working with when he and Lissa were still together. Teddy was not at the top of his game, but he was on his way. Gregg reckoned that Teddy could easily become the new Baby Face: he had edge, something Gregg needed. Teddy was costing him money he didn't have, so he had to make sure the deal he was working on with the tabloid came through. Fortunately, Teddy was not bugging him for money.

'Ran inta your old lady the other day,' Teddy remarked when he came in.

'Yeah? Where was that?' Gregg asked, walking over to the coffee-maker and pouring himself a cup.

'The Domingos' party. Thought I'd see you there, man.'

'I had something else going on,' Gregg said, livid because he hadn't been invited.

Naturally, all of Lissa's dear, close friends had dropped him the moment he'd left her. Okay with him, he'd never liked any of them anyway. Kyndra was an overblown diva with a fat ass. Taylor was an ambitious bitch busy playing professional wife. And Stella was too assertive and tough for her own good. As for James, no words could describe him. Gregg had always loathed Lissa's *best* friend.

'It was a happenin' party,' Teddy offered.

'Yeah?' Gregg answered, completely disinterested. The last thing he wanted to hear about was a party he hadn't been invited to. 'Let's get to work here, I haven't got all day.'

By the end of their session, he felt pretty high. One

more time and they'd have it down. *Wouldn't it be something*, he thought, *if this song makes me a star? Anything's possible. How would Lissa react to that?*

He drove home and was annoyed to see cars in the driveway. Belinda had a lot of friends, and was constantly entertaining. He didn't like being looked over and inspected. *And here he is, folks – the new stud on campus. Fuck that shit.* Unfortunately, until he had money, there was nothing he could do about it.

He circumvented the living room and went straight upstairs, carrying Lissa's boxes, which he placed in the master bathroom.

Belinda's bedroom was all chintzy and girly, much too fancy. She didn't possess the class and style of Lissa. Belinda was nothing but a ballsy woman who'd made it by climbing over everyone, and probably crushing a few men on her way.

Before he had a chance to open any of the boxes, Belinda was on the house intercom summoning him. She'd obviously spotted his car in the driveway.

'Gregg, honey, can you get on down here? I want you to meet someone.'

Oh, yeah, that's right, Belinda – call me like I'm your pet dog or something.

Who did she want him to meet now? Her grandmother? Her cousins? Her coterie of Hollywood wives?

He walked into the living room and came face to face with Deidra Baker.

'Honey,' Belinda said, 'this is Deidra – she's going to be my personal shopper at Barneys, and since your birthday's coming up in a couple of weeks, I thought you could go in and choose yourself an outfit. Deidra will help you pick it out.'

He stared at Deidra.

She stared back at him.

They both decided they would not acknowledge that they knew each other.

He thought of her nipples and got the stirrings of a hard-on.

She thought of the way he'd walked out on her and the cruel things he'd said, and decided that revenge was long overdue.

'You clean up nicely, Michael,' Lissa said lightly, when he walked into her suite at eight o'clock precisely. 'I like your suit.'

'Thanks,' he answered. 'And you – well, I know you don't want me to tell you that you look beautiful, but if I could, that's what I'd be saying now.'

'I was thinking,' she said, not acknowledging his compliment, 'if you don't want to come with me tonight, I can always take Fabio or Danny. They'd be happy to escort me.'

'Lissa,' he said pointedly, 'in case you've forgotten, I'm here to look after you.'

'Oh, yes, you are, aren't you?' she said, adding a curt 'You'll look after me until it's time for you to run.'

'Huh?' he said.

'You know what I mean,' she said, wishing she hadn't brought it up. It made her look needy, and that's the last thing she was.

He didn't appreciate her attitude. 'Shouldn't we clear something up before we go downstairs?' he said, determined to get it out in the open.

'And what would that be?' she asked.

'I've tried to say it to you before, Lissa.'

'Go ahead,' she said, in that same cool tone she'd been using lately.

'We've, uh . . . got this kind of unspoken thing going on between us, and we both know it. We also know it won't lead anywhere, so what's the point?'

'What's the point of anything, Michael?'

He began rubbing his chin, something he always did when he got agitated. 'Y'know, Lissa,' he said forcefully, 'I can't allow myself to get all screwed up over you. I'd like to do my job, make sure you're safe, and if I can do that, we'll be fine.'

'I'm glad you feel that way, because *I* feel exactly the same.'

'Good.'

'Do you want to take a look at the view before we go?'

'I already saw it,' he said irritably, because he had a feeling she wasn't listening to a word he said. 'My room has the same view.'

'I mean from the terrace. Come, it's quite spectacular,' she said, walking out to the terrace, which was like an exotic plant-filled garden with a thirty-foot lap-pool in the centre.

He followed her out. The view *was* spectacular, a panorama of sparkling lights encompassing the entire strip.

'Isn't this something?' she said, walking to the edge. 'I'm telling you, when they build hotels in Las Vegas they don't play around.'

'It's certainly different from where I come from,' he said.

'What do you think?' she murmured, turning to him.

He could smell her perfume and it was driving him insane. He had to summon every inch of will-power he possessed not to kiss her. 'I think we should go to dinner,' he said.

Walter Burns was a granite-faced man in his late sixties. Tall and broad-shouldered, he had a full head of silver hair, manicured nails and a wary expression. When he spoke, his voice was so soft and raspy that most people had to lean closer to hear him. His wife, Evelyn, was the definitive Barbie-doll type – a top-heavy bleached blonde who wore figure-revealing clothes, flashy jewellery and hooker shoes. She was pushing forty, but dressed twenty.

Walter had left his same-age-as-himself first wife in order to pursue Evelyn, who had once been a famous showgirl. They'd been married for ten years and had no children.

It had been Evelyn's idea to find out if Lissa Roman would be prepared to do a one-night show to celebrate the opening of the Desert Millennium Princess. The new Vegas hotel was a giant amongst a tower of shining giants that had been erected over the last ten years, including the Mirage, the Rio, the Bellagio and the Hard Rock.

Walter Burns's business ventures were spread across America. He owned casino-hotels in several states, but this was his first foray into the Vegas area. He had a couple of investment partners, but he was the main man.

His tenth wedding anniversary to Evelyn was coming up, and his present to her was getting Lissa Roman to appear for one night. Quite a present, considering it was costing him three million dollars. Although to a man such as Walter Burns, three million dollars was like three hundred dollars to anyone else.

Evelyn had dressed for dinner in a low-cut, sequined cocktail dress, cut down to the rise of her butt at the back. Huge sapphires and diamond earrings adorned her ears to match the sapphires and diamonds on her fingers and wrists.

'I'm so excited,' she confided to her husband, as they set off to meet Lissa. She had a slight Brooklyn accent, a sweet personality, and adored her multi-billionaire husband, who regularly popped Viagra to keep his twenty-five-years-younger wife happy. 'This is the best present ever!'

Lissa had no idea she was a present as she travelled down in the elevator with Michael beside her. She'd decided to enjoy herself, forget about Gregg, and throw herself into her show. She certainly had no intention of getting involved with Michael Scorsinni. He lived in a fantasy world if he thought she was even entertaining the idea.

'This is like a mini-vacation for me,' she remarked, as the elevator made its descent. 'It seems I'm always working.'

'This *is* work,' he pointed out. 'You're rehearsing tomorrow, then you've got your show on Saturday.'

'It's hardly the same. I'm not locked in the recording studio, or making a video. I'm not even on location. This is my idea of freedom, and I like it. Tomorrow will be fun. I have a great group of dancers, and I love working with them. You've never seen my show, have you?'

'No, I haven't.'

'You'll be surprised.'

'You couldn't surprise me, Lissa.'

'I couldn't?' she asked, an amused expression in her blue eyes.

'I don't think so.'

'Hmm . . . we'll have to see.'

He laughed. One thing he was sure of, being in her company was never dull.

Walter and Evelyn Burns turned out to be a surprisingly entertaining couple. Walter was gruff and full of interesting stories, while Evelyn played his perfect foil – the dumb blonde who knew how to play it. She worshipped Lissa, gazing at her adoringly most of the night. She even offered to give her the sapphire and diamond ring off her finger.

Lissa politely declined.

'My wife's your biggest fan,' Walter announced, when Evelyn tottered off on her four-and-a-half-inch heels to visit the ladies' room.

'I'm flattered,' Lissa said.

'Yeah,' Walter rasped. 'It's why we were so anxious to get you to open the hotel for us. And, let me say, I'm damn grateful you agreed, otherwise my life would've been crap.'

'I wasn't aware of the back story,' Lissa said, smiling. 'I'm glad I said yes.'

'Your show's all sold out,' Walter offered.

'Good,' Lissa said. 'That means you'll make money.'

'Not with what we're paying you, my dear,' he said, with a snake-like smile.

Michael kept quiet during dinner. He didn't think it appropriate to join in, although Lissa insisted on trying to include him.

After dinner, Walter wondered if they wanted to gamble.

'You must,' Evelyn insisted. 'I'll teach you to play craps. Walter says I'm a natural!'

'We *let* her win,' Walter said, straight-faced. 'Keeps her happy.'

'How dare you?' Evelyn squealed. 'It's a skill. And if there's one thing I have, honeybun, it's skill.'

A photographer appeared shortly after they'd finished, and Walter respectfully asked Lissa if she'd mind posing for a few pictures with Evelyn.

'Not at all,' Lissa said.

Michael had noticed how easy and calm she was with people – there was certainly an extremely kind side to her character. She wasn't like some of the other stars he'd dealt with, most of whom were extremely difficult.

'I'll pass on the gambling tonight,' Lissa said. 'Maybe after the show tomorrow you'll teach me how to do it.'

'Oh, honey, *my* pleasure,' Evelyn said, still star-struck. 'And since you were admiring my shoes earlier, I'm having several pairs sent to your room tomorrow. What's your size?'

'Oh, no, please don't,' Lissa said.

'Honey, when you want something in *our* hotel, you can bet your sweet ass you'll get it.'

'My wife speaks the truth,' Walter said. 'Anything you want, anything at all, call me.'

On their way back upstairs Lissa said, 'You were very quiet tonight.'

'I wasn't quiet,' Michael answered, 'I was watching out for you.'

'You could've been more friendly towards them.'

'I'm not your date, Lissa,' he pointed out.

'I know that,' she said.

'What did you want me to do?' he asked, exasperated. 'Make conversation? Those aren't my friends, I have nothing in common with them. The guy's a multi-billionaire, for crissakes – you think he has anything to say to me?'

'Oh, Michael,' she sighed, 'you're too sensitive.'

'Never been called *that* before.'

'By the way,' she said, her eyes bright, 'you keep implying that I wanted you to stay the other night because we were probably going to indulge in some crazy one-night stand. Well, let me tell you, that's not what I had in mind at all. I needed a friend, and if you think there was anything else going on, you're very much mistaken.'

'I'm glad you cleared *that* up,' he said, as they reached the door of the penthouse suite.

'Good night, Michael,' she said. 'I'll see you in the morning at eight.'

He waited for her to ask him in. She didn't.

Hey, maybe he was imagining this whole thing.

Feeling somewhat dejected, he returned to his room.

Chapter Thirty-three

Friday morning Eric Vernon was on alert. Only one more day and he still had much to do. He went over his checklist, making sure he'd forgotten nothing. Most important were his getaway plans once he had the ransom money. Everything was in place – passport, driver's licence, social-security card, two new credit cards taken out under his new name. Several thousand dollars in traveller's cheques – money left over from his San Diego bank heist – an airline ticket to the Bahamas, bookings for several different flights.

Yes, he could say goodbye to Eric Vernon in seconds. All he had to do was stop being him.

'We'll meet at the park,' Eric said over the phone to Arliss.

'What?' the skinny man replied.

'The park.'

'What park?' Arliss asked.

'Near the school. You know where I mean.'

'Can't we meet at the bar?' Arliss whined.

'I don't care for the way Sam watches us.'

'Sam don't watch us,' Arliss said.

'Yes, he does,' Eric said.

'The park seems an odd place t' meet.'

'Not so odd if we do it at four in the afternoon. Make

sure the others are there. Tomorrow's the day, and remember – no screw-ups.'

Seeing the group in daylight was certainly a shock. Eric knew they were a seedy-looking bunch, but he hadn't realized quite how bad they were. Arliss the weasel, with his thin, pointed face and straggly hair. Big Mark, a huge bear of a man with an unbalanced craziness reflected in his beady eyes. Little Joe, short and fat and quite stupid. Davey 'The Animal', snorting and wheezing, his ferret face cunning and greedy.

'We'll get together at noon tomorrow,' Eric announced. 'At the building. Davey, you'll bring the car. Joe, you'll have the chloroform. Mark, you'll bring yourself.'

'The guys an' me was talkin',' Arliss ventured.

'You were?' Eric said.

'We think we should be gettin' somethin' up front,' Arliss said boldly, while the other three nodded their agreement.

'Will you explain to me how I can give you something up front before I get the ransom?' Eric said, his cold eyes daring them to argue.

'A grand each,' Big Mark said. 'Good-faith money.'

Eric turned on him. 'You dumb fucks,' he said, his tone icy. 'How do you expect me to give you money I don't have?'

'How'd *we* know ya don't have it?' Davey wheezed.

'Yeah,' Little Joe agreed, his eyes popping.

'I'm walking away,' Eric said.

'What?' Arliss whined.

'Walking,' Eric said, making a calculated move to pull them back in line.

'Where to?' Little Joe asked.

'Away from all of you.'

'What about the job?' Arliss asked.

'Fuck the job,' Eric said. 'And fuck you, too.'

He started to walk away. The four men conferred, and within seconds Arliss came running after him. 'All right, no hard feelings, we'll wait for our money.'

Until hell freezes over, Eric thought.

And he turned around and rejoined the four misfits.

Chapter Thirty-four

Watching Lissa rehearse was a revelation. Michael knew she was talented, but he'd had no idea of the kind of dynamic stage presence she possessed. Her show lasted an hour and fifteen minutes, and she sang and danced her way through everything, from wild dance numbers to torchy ballads, all with different changes of outfit and punishing routines.

She rehearsed in sweats in the morning, broke for lunch, then did a full sound check and dress rehearsal.

Sitting in the theatre watching her, Michael was more than impressed. She was an amazing woman who deserved everything she had, because she sure as hell worked hard for it.

The day was hectic. There were so many people running here and there, so many egos, and Lissa was at the centre of it all.

Chuck came over and sat beside him for a while. 'She's somethin', huh?'

'She sure is,' Michael said. 'You've been with her for how many years?'

'Five,' Chuck said.

'What was the husband like?' Michael asked, trying to keep it casual.

'One look at the dude an' I got a bead on his game,' Chuck replied. 'He treated her badly. Lotta screamin' goin' on most of the time. Dunno why she took it as long as she did.'

The words 'comfort zone' sprang to mind. Michael had seen a shrink for a short time after he'd been shot in New York. The woman had explained something to him that he'd found very interesting. 'People always revert to their comfort zone,' she'd told him. 'If you were raised by a violent mother or father, then somehow it seems quite normal to you if your partner treats you badly, because that's your comfort zone.'

It made a lot of sense. He started wondering about Lissa's childhood and why she hadn't said much. Not that she owed him any explanations.

A buffet lunch was set up on long trestle tables. Lissa sat amongst her dancers, back-up singers and various other people connected with her show.

Michael walked over to Chuck. 'I've arranged a meeting with hotel security,' he said. 'I'd like you to be there.'

'Sure,' Chuck said. 'Tomorrow's gonna be a bitch. The press'll be crawlin' all over her, she's got her friends comin' in from L.A., the fans'll go freakin' crazy, an' she's gonna be strung-out about the show.'

Later in the afternoon, Lissa sat in her dressing room while Fabio experimented with various hairstyles.

'I told you, when I do the third number I can't have those extensions falling in my eyes,' she said patiently. 'It's too much hair, Fabio.'

'I'll think of something,' Fabio assured her, dancing around her chair. 'My golden lady has to outdazzle Las Vegas!'

Her cellphone rang and she answered it. 'Yes?'

'Mom?'

It was Nicci. 'What's up, sweetie?' she asked.

'You won't believe *this* one,' Nicci said, sounding breathless.

'Try me.'

'I had dinner last night with Antonio and his new wife.'

'You did?'

'Antonio still looks *amazing*.'

'What's his wife like?'

'Old-fashioned glam in a kind of European way.'

'What does *that* mean?'

'Well . . .' Nicci said. 'She's much older than him and – oh, yeah, she was wearing a diamond the size of Cuba. I suppose she's *sort* of beautiful.'

'So far all I get is old and rich.'

'No,' Nicci said, giggling. 'She seems nice, too.'

'Uh-huh,' Lissa said, remembering how completely infatuated she'd once been with Antonio. That was when they were both young and carefree. Running off to Vegas and getting married had seemed such a romantic thing to do at the time.

'They've chartered a plane and they're coming to see your show,' Nicci announced.

'There's no more tickets,' Lissa said. 'It's a sell-out.'

'He has his own tickets,' Nicci said. 'His own car and driver, *and* a solid gold Rolex.'

'Seems Antonio finally got everything he wanted.'

'Anyway, he *is* my dad, so can he please get a backstage pass and have her meet you?'

'Nicci . . .'

'*Please*, Mom. For me.'

'Okay, okay,' Lissa said, relenting. 'Where will they be staying?'

'At your hotel.'

'Tell you what,' Lissa said, kind of intrigued at the thought of seeing Antonio again, 'there's a party after the show, I'll make sure they get an invitation.'

'You're so cool.'

'Thanks.'

'And another thing—'

'What now?'

'Evan's mom is driving me completely nutto. The woman's obsessed.'

'With what?'

'Her son, of course.'

'Oh dear.'

'I know, it's such a bummer. So I was like thinking – *she* wants to see your show, and if I put her on a plane, could *she* get a ticket and an invitation to the party too?'

'Charming,' Lissa said, 'sticking her on me.'

'Well, you *are* gonna be kind of related.'

'But there are no tickets left, and I'll be too busy to entertain her.'

'This is a dire *emergency*!'

'Okay, I'll try.'

'It'll save me from like *totally freaking*,' Nicci said gratefully.

'As long as I can do that,' Lissa said drily, thinking that Nicci was definitely inclined to over-exaggerate.

'How's rehearsal?'

'Easy. You know I love performing live.'

'Okay, Mom. Thanks. I'll speak to you later.'

Lissa put down the phone pleased. It seemed that since Gregg's departure, she and Nicci were definitely growing closer.

Belinda liked morning sex. Gregg didn't.

Belinda liked sex in the shower. Gregg didn't.

Friday morning Gregg serviced her in the shower and waited for her to leave for work.

Once she'd gone, he jumped back into bed, clicked on the TV and watched a western movie. It wasn't until Patrick phoned to find out if he'd collected the boxes that he remembered.

'Yeah, yeah, I was just going through them,' he said. 'Haven't come across anything juicy yet, but you'll be the first to know.'

He hung up on Patrick and reluctantly made his way into the master bathroom. There they were, piled high – Lissa's private boxes.

He opened the first one, marked 1975. She would've been fifteen, a year before she left home.

The box was filled with mementoes – cards, old pens, a coin or two, and photos. He picked up a photograph of Lissa standing with a skinny boy outside a small house. She was a beauty even at fifteen.

Then he noticed the diary. It was one of those pink diaries, with a tiny lock and a miniature key hanging off the side. He picked it up, opened it and started to read. She had girlish scrawly handwriting that was difficult to decipher.

January the 1st: Got a cold. Ate lukewarm soup.
January the 2nd: Bumped into Skeet. He's a creep.
January the 3rd: Horrible chicken for dinner. Ugh!
Went to movies with Jenna. Saw 'Jaws'. Scary!

And so on and so forth.

Half way through he got bored and put the diary down. Then he began picking out specific dates. Her birthday. Christmas. Easter. Valentine's Day. Every entry was all about what she ate and what movies she'd seen.

He shoved the diary back into the box along with her other mementoes, and went to the 1974 box. The usual stuff, plus another diary, this time a yellow one. He unlocked it and read the same kind of thing.

There was nothing here. Why had he thought there might be? She'd been this little high-school girl living in a small town like thousands of other girls across America. Only Lissa was different: she'd run away from home and became a star.

Just as he was about to put the yellow diary down, he noticed that every so often there was a page entry with nothing but a red exclamation point. Obviously it was some sort of code.

He checked through the diary to see if there was any way of deciphering what it meant. On the back page, written out quite a few times was, 'I hate her! I hate her! I hate her!' – and next to each 'I hate her!' was a red exclamation point.

Gregg couldn't figure it out.

He reached for another box and took out her diary for that year. The same thing. The entries were all about food, movies and school, and every so often another red exclamation point. In the back of the diary, once again, there was a list of 'I hate her!' with red exclamation points next to the words.

He counted the number of days where the red exclamation points appeared. Over the year there were thirty. And the 'I hate hers' were written out exactly thirty times.

Who was *her*? And what did it mean?

He decided he'd better run it by Belinda. Right now she was the brains in the family. He was merely the talent, in every way.

'I can get you a ticket if you're sure you want to go,' Nicci said, finding Lynda in the laundry room.

'I certainly do,' Lynda replied, folding sheets, 'and *you* should come with me.'

'I can't,' Nicci said, wondering how the maid would react to Lynda redoing the laundry. 'It's my bachelorette party, and my friend's having a celebration for me.'

'Celebration of *what*?' Lynda snapped.

'My marrying your son.'

'Bachelorette party.' Lynda snorted. 'I would think

you'd have better ways to spend your time. Brian wanted to throw a bachelor night for Evan, and he refused. I told him it was archaic. You should be thanking me, dear. Nasty strippers thrusting their goods in your intended's face – disgusting!'

'We don't do anything like that,' Nicci said innocently. 'We go out to dinner, all us girls, and, y'know, quietly exchange thoughts.'

'That sounds more like it,' Lynda said, holding up a pillowcase to make sure it was clean enough.

'Anyway,' Nicci said, 'I talked to my mom, and she'll arrange a ticket for you. So, if you *want* to go, I'll call the travel agent and—'

'No need,' Lynda interrupted. 'I have my own travel person who deals with my mileage. Just tell me how I collect my ticket when I get there. After all,' she said pointedly, 'it's lonely for me sitting here in an empty house. And I'll be back in time to greet Evan when he arrives home on Sunday.'

Nicci gave a sigh of relief. *Thank God*, she thought. *Alone at last, and not a moment too soon.*

'When will you go?' she ventured.

'In the morning, I suppose,' Lynda said.

'Or how about tonight?' Nicci suggested. 'Then you could get a cab to take you on a tour of Vegas. Have you been there before?'

'Evan and I were there together,' Lynda said. 'Some convention to do with theatre owners. Evan was treated wonderfully. It was when he was engaged to that awful girl. *She* came, too.'

'What did you say her name was?' Nicci asked casually.

'Julia something or other,' Lynda sneered. 'Common as dirt, came from nowhere.'

Not only was Evan's mother an unbearable, bossy, interfering woman, she was also a snob.

Fortunately she chose to take an afternoon flight. Nicci offered to drive her to the airport, but she preferred to go by cab.

As soon as she was gone, Nicci raced into the kitchen, and promptly rearranged all the pots and pans that Lynda had carefully reorganized, then she put Shaggy on the stereo as loud as possible, jumped into the swimming pool naked, and swam twenty lengths. After that she felt a lot better.

Next she started trying to figure out what to wear for her party. Something wild, because it was bound to be that kind of night.

She tried to reach Evan. His phone was off.

She thought about calling Brian. Did she really have any reason to?

Yes. He was the only one who understood about Lynda, and what the woman was putting her through.

He answered on the second ring.

'What're you doing?' she asked.

'In bed with a gorgeous redhead,' he said.

'No, you're not.'

'Why d'you doubt me?'

'Got a feeling.'

'How are you, kiddo?'

'She's gone.'

'Gimme the scam. Didja kill her?'

'I've sent her to Vegas to see my mom's show,' Nicci said, giggling.

'How'd you manage that? Didja put a magic rocket up her ass?'

'I wish!' They both laughed. 'I can't reach Evan,' Nicci said. 'Where is he?' There was a silence. 'Oh, *what?*' she said. 'He's screwing the script girl again – Julia? Is that it?'

'What're you talking about?' Brian said, obviously not getting the joke.

'What're *you* so uptight about?'

'I'm not.'

'Are you flying back with Evan on Sunday?'

'I was thinking of hopping a plane tonight.' A beat. 'You doin' anything later?'

'I'm planning on an early night.'

'Can I stop by?'

'No.'

'Why?'

''Cause.'

''Cause what?'

''Cause . . . I dunno.' A double beat, then she relented and said, 'I suppose . . . if you want to.'

'It'll probably be late.'

'Like how late?' she said, her heart starting to pound at the thought of seeing Brian again.

'Eight or nine. Is that too late?'

'No more raves?' she said warningly.

'Don't do that any more. You were my last fling.'

'I was?'

'We could go to dinner, though. I know a cosy little lobster place at the beach.'

'One of your make-out spots?'

'Could be. Wanna try it?'

'Only if we take *your* car.'

'Did you get yours fixed yet?'

'No.'

'I'll pay if the insurance doesn't.'

'What a sport!'

'See you later, babe.'

What are you doing? she thought, the moment she hung up. *What the hell are you doing? You're getting married to his brother, and now you're going to dinner with him?*

This was insane.

And yet, for some crazy reason, she couldn't wipe the smile off her face.

*   *   *

'I wish you'd think about coming with us,' Taylor urged. 'There's room on the plane. I've already asked James.'

'Yes,' Montana said. 'But have you asked Larry?'

'It's not *his* decision, it's *yours*,' Taylor said. 'And, anyway, there's no animosity between the two of you, is there?'

'I've got a suspicion I always made Larry a little nervous.'

'Why would you think that?'

'I'm sure I don't have to explain to you, Taylor. You're *married* to him.'

'If you've never seen Lissa's show, it's a must,' Taylor said enthusiastically. 'She's sensational on stage.'

'She's sensational in the flesh, too,' Montana said, with a smile.

Taylor shook her head. 'Uh-huh – Lissa doesn't swing both ways.'

'Do *you*?' Montana asked, looking at her boldly.

'Uh . . . I . . . no,' Taylor replied, quite taken aback, although she had experimented way back in college.

'Just f–ing with you,' Montana said, laughing at Taylor's discomfort. 'You do know it's very fashionable today.'

'And you *do* know that I'm married to Larry Singer.'

'All the more reason.'

'Think about coming,' Taylor said. 'We could go gambling, shopping, have a sauna and a facial – it would be a really relaxing weekend for you.'

'I'll think about it,' Montana promised. 'When are you off?'

'Tomorrow,' Taylor said. 'And we're flying back Sunday morning, so it'll be twenty-four hours of pure relaxation. What more could you ask for?'

Montana smiled. 'I can think of a few things.'

Evan and Brian ran into each other at the entrance of the small hotel where the crew and cast were staying in Utah. Brian had a bag slung over his shoulder.

'Where are you going?' Evan asked.

'Huh?' Brian said.

'It looks like you're going somewhere,' Evan said.

'Back to L.A.,' Brian said. 'You can handle everything here.'

'We didn't discuss this,' Evan said.

'Got some scenes I need to work on,' Brian said. 'Can't concentrate here – too much going on.'

'You're going back to L.A. so you can party,' Evan said accusingly.

'Speaking of partying,' Brian said, putting his bag down, 'I've been meaning to talk to you about that.'

'What?'

'Remember when you warned me to stay away from Abbey?'

'Yes.'

'So now I get it. You didn't want me anywhere near her 'cause *you* had plans.'

'What're you talking about?' Evan said, stony-faced.

'Hey, bro, it's one thing when *I* fuck around, 'cause *I'm* not planning on gettin' married.'

'You're full of it,' Evan said. 'You always have been, and you always will be.'

'You should've seen Abbey's face yesterday when I told her you were engaged. Man, she didn't like it at all. You gotta learn to be more up front.'

'You know what you are? You're a fucking asshole!' Evan yelled.

And before anyone could stop them, right there in front of the small hotel, they were at each other's throats.

Late afternoon, Michael and Chuck took a security meeting with the guards from the hotel and went over everything.

'Lissa Roman received a death-threat letter shortly before leaving L.A.,' Michael informed them. 'We don't

345

think it's anything serious, but we can't take any chances.'

The head of security at the hotel was an ex-FBI agent. He assured Michael that everything was under control. 'When she's on stage, there will not be a second when someone's eyes aren't on her,' the man said.

'That'll be me,' Michael said. 'And I'm glad to hear that everyone else will be watching too.'

He went back to rehearsal to see if Lissa was finished for the day.

She was sitting in a chair, clad in a towelling robe, drinking Evian from the bottle.

'Tired?' he said.

'Delightfully exhausted,' she replied.

'We should get you back to your suite so you can have a good night's sleep before tomorrow.'

'I'll see,' she murmured.

'You'll see what?'

'I'll see what I want to do later.'

Fabio and a couple of the dancers accompanied them back to the suite.

'You can go,' Lissa said to Michael. 'I'm in good hands.'

'I'll be next door. Buzz if you need me.'

'I will.'

'You're in for the night then, huh?'

'I think so. And if I'm not, you'll be the last to know.'

'That's not funny, Lissa,' he said sternly. 'Don't forget about the letter.'

'Oh, please,' she said dismissively. 'Do you know how many of those I've had? Hundreds in my time.'

'Hundreds, huh? And you're still here. Amazing what they *can't* do to you.'

'I'm indestructible,' she joked. 'Didn't you know?'

He was seeing a whole new side of her. She obviously loved performing – it definitely made her more relaxed and easy-going.

He went to his room, which, although smaller than hers, was certainly luxurious. It featured a king-size bed, a panoramic view, a marble bathroom, and a mini bar stocked with everything imaginable.

Great. He had temptation staring him in the face. The good thing was he hadn't been tempted in ten years, and he wasn't about to start now.

He noticed the red light blinking on his phone. He picked it up and listened to his messages. One from Quincy, hoping that everything was progressing smoothly. Then a sexy female voice – 'Hi, Mr Scorsinni – Michael. This is Cindy. You might remember me from the plane. I was wondering if you'd like to see Las Vegas. I could show you the sights. So . . . I'll call you later.'

He remembered the blonde – tall and sexy. Perhaps she was exactly what he needed.

Back in L.A. Taylor simulated the sounds of love-making. Only she wasn't making love to a man, she was naked under a thin sheet and Sonja Lucerne's hands were all over her. Watching was a full crew.

Taylor was totally turned on. Montana had assured her that when the scene was cut together, you wouldn't see anything she might regret later. 'You've got to let yourself go,' Montana assured her. 'I can promise you won't be sorry.'

Sonja obviously trusted Montana implicitly, so Taylor decided she would too.

Sonja's hands were gentle and insistent at the same time. The way they caressed Taylor's breasts was like nothing she'd ever experienced before. Feather touches, but oh, so effective. The scene required her to have an orgasm. As far as she was concerned, there was no acting involved.

Montana and the crew were suitably appreciative, rewarding them with a round of applause as soon as Montana called, 'Cut.'

Taylor sat up, her cheeks glowing, her skin tingling with pleasure. It was then that she noticed Larry standing near Montana, an angry look on his face. Oh God, why hadn't he told her he was coming today? She would have put him off, told him to visit on another day. This was ridiculous – knowing Larry, he'd be absolutely furious. Why the hell hadn't anyone warned her he was present?

The wardrobe woman came towards her with a robe. She slid into it and belted it tightly.

'That's a wrap for today, everyone,' Montana called. 'Thanks again.'

Taylor attempted to compose herself. She knew she must look flushed, and she also knew that Larry would probably recognize the signs of sexual excitement written all over her face. 'Honey,' she said, rushing over to him, 'you should've told me you were coming.'

'I thought I'd surprise you,' he said with a grim expression.

'You certainly did that,' she said, grabbing his arm. 'Come on, let's go to my trailer.'

His expression was getting more uptight by the second. And why not? He'd just seen her making love to a woman, and seemingly enjoying it a lot.

He followed her into her trailer. Once they were inside and the door was closed, he said, 'Taylor, do you understand what that looked like out there?'

'I know exactly what it looked like, darling,' she said, attempting to placate him. 'However, Montana has assured me that she edits in such a way that you don't really see anything. It's all subliminal.'

'Are you *crazy*?' he said, his voice rising. 'Do you have any idea what they can do with that footage if it gets out? And how about the out-takes and the footage she *doesn't* use? You're screwed, Taylor. You should never have allowed yourself to be put in that position.'

'Too late now,' she said. 'I've already done it. That was the final love scene.'

'You *bet* it was the final love scene,' he said angrily. 'How stupid can you get?'

'You seem to forget that I was performing an acting role, Larry, a perfectly legitimate *acting* role.'

'Your naïveté amazes me,' he said. 'You've been in this business long enough to know better.'

'Why are you so upset?' she asked, finally losing it. 'Does seeing two women in bed together make you feel threatened?'

He stared at her as if she'd hit him. Then he turned and marched out of the trailer.

Larry had *never* walked out on her before.

Oh, God, maybe she'd gone too far. She dressed quickly, ran to her car and instructed her driver to get her home as fast as possible.

'I can't figure anything out,' Gregg said.

'What is there to figure out?' Belinda asked.

'Lissa's old diaries, they're all about movies, boys and food.'

'Sounds typical,' Belinda said.

'Yeah, but there're also these red exclamation points all over the place. I know it means something.'

'She's probably marking the dates of her period,' Belinda said. 'Girls do that.'

'Thirty or more times a year?'

'Maybe she was getting laid,' Belinda said, chuckling. 'I used to have secret signals like that. Every time I sucked a boy's dick I'd put a star in my diary. Something my mom wouldn't understand if she ever read it.'

'She didn't like sex that much when we were married, why would she do it all the time when she was a teenager?'

'Girls will be girls.' Belinda sighed. 'You want *me* to read the diaries?'

'Yeah. Patrick says I gotta come up with something juicy if I wanna score the big bucks.'

'I'll take a look. In the meantime, when are you picking out your birthday present?'

'Tomorrow. Where did you find that woman?'

'Barneys always give me a personal shopper and Deidra's new. I like dealing with new people, they're easier to work with.'

Belinda lined up three of Lissa's old diaries and began checking them out. 'What's all this "I hate her" crap?' she asked.

Gregg shrugged. 'That's what I don't know. They match the red exclamation points.'

'You're right,' Belinda said. 'It is some kind of code. Hmm . . . did you go through the rest of the stuff?'

'Naw, it's all junk.'

'Maybe not.'

'You do it. I'm bored.'

'Oh, so now I'm working for you – is that it?' she said tartly.

'You do it,' he said, 'an' I'll tongue your pussy till you scream for me to stop.'

She gave a dirty laugh. 'Dream *on*! I'll *never* ask you to stop.'

Gregg went back into the bedroom, lay down on the bed, switched on the TV and found a ball game. He enjoyed watching sports, it was pure, mindless entertainment – the best kind. He also enjoyed making a bet or two, but he didn't have the money.

'Hey, Belinda,' he called out, 'you got a bookie?'

'No,' she answered. 'Why?'

'I wanna place a bet.'

'Don't *you* have one?'

'I owe him.'

'Can't help you, honey.'

Screw her! The sooner he got out of this house, the better. He was beginning to feel stifled. It was so fucking boring and she was way too old for him. Everything belonged to her, nothing was his. He couldn't even make a fucking bet.

He wished he had some coke. Teddy had given him some primo coke at the studio. He'd snorted a few lines and it had made his voice sound amazing. Belinda didn't do drugs of any kind. How boring could one person get?

An hour later, Belinda walked into the bedroom. 'Guess what?' she said, looking very pleased with herself.

'What?'

'You're about to become a very rich man.'

Chapter Thirty-five

Michael ordered a bacon sandwich and a Caesar salad. Then he lay down on the bed, switched on the TV and channel-surfed, waiting for the fight to start on cable. He thought about Carol and the baby. And then about Lissa, and how much he was attracted to her. He must've dozed off, because a loud knocking at the door woke him up.

'Who's there?' he called out.

'Room service.'

He got off the bed, opened the door, and standing outside was Cindy, holding aloft a bottle of champagne and a tray of hors d'oeuvres. In civilian clothes she was even prettier than she'd appeared on the plane.

'Hey,' he said, surprised but not displeased.

'I'm room service,' she said, sauntering into his room and putting down the tray and the bottle. Then, catching him off-guard, she turned around and threw her arms around his neck, kissing him full on the lips.

This was too fast for Michael. He immediately removed her arms and backed away. 'What's going on?' he asked suspiciously.

'I'm a present from the hotel,' she said blithely. 'They're very concerned about keeping their guests happy.'

'Are you *serious*?' he said, thinking that Vegas was definitely a crazy place.

'No,' she said, with a slight smile. 'It's just that you're a *very* sexy man. And I figured if you're in Vegas with nothing to do tonight, why shouldn't we do nothing together?'

Something didn't ring true. He was used to women throwing themselves at him, but not this rapidly.

'Shall I open the champagne?' she offered. 'It's Cristal.'

'I don't drink,' he said, rubbing his chin.

'Oh, so you're being a *good* little boy?' she teased, shooting him a provocative look. 'I prefer naughty ones myself. Should Mommy spank you?'

'I'm not into that either.'

'Hmm . . .' Cindy said. 'You wouldn't be involved with the star, would you?'

'What's the deal here, Cindy?' he asked, deciding he'd had enough. 'You a hooker?'

'That's nice, isn't it?' she said indignantly. 'A girl always *loves* that question. No, I am *not* a hooker. I'm simply out for a good time, and you look like a good time.' Then she was all over him again, throwing her arms around his neck and nuzzling his ear.

It occurred to him that she was indeed supplied by the hotel. This seemed like a set-up.

'You know what?' he said, pushing her away again.

'What?'

'I'm not in the mood.'

'You're not?' she said, giving him a long, smouldering stare. 'Is there anything I can do to *make* you in the mood?'

'Yeah.'

'And that would be?'

'Go home.'

'God, you're boring!' she exclaimed, not used to rejection.

'Listen,' he said, 'you are a very attractive girl, and I'm sure you're well paid, only this is too strange for me.'

She shrugged. 'I'll probably get fired because of you.'

'How's that?' he asked, trying to figure out if Walter Burns had sent her – or maybe she was a gift from Rick Maneloni.

'I'm supposed to keep the hotel guests satisfied at all times. Our motto is "From the plane to the tables and back to L.A. – satisfaction all the way."'

'I'm not a gambler, Cindy.'

'No, you're a babe,' she said, licking her lips. 'Most of the guys I get to entice are usually fat and old or Japanese.' She gave him another sexy look. 'C'mon, Michael,' she coaxed, 'you wouldn't want to get a girl fired, would you?'

For a split second he was tempted. Jesus Christ, he was a man, after all. Then again, did he really want to hate himself in the morning?

He picked up the bottle of champagne and handed it to her. 'I'll keep the snacks,' he said. 'How's that?'

She shook her head in amazement. 'You don't know *what* you're missing.'

He opened the door and steered her outside towards the elevator. As he did so, Lissa emerged from her suite, catching the action immediately. A girl leaving his room clutching a bottle of champagne, it didn't look good.

'I was paging you,' she said coolly.

'Didn't hear the buzz.'

'There must be something wrong with your pager.'

'I'll be right there,' he said, embarrassed at having been caught.

Caught doing what? Exactly nothing.

He pushed Cindy into the elevator, went back into his room, grabbed his jacket, and made his way to Lissa's suite.

She was pacing around the living room. 'Is it too much to ask for your full attention while we're here,' she said, 'or do you have to get laid immediately?'

'It's not what it looks like,' he replied, realizing how lame that sounded.

'Do you *know* how many times I've heard those words?' she said. 'From *all* my husbands.'

'What was I *supposed* to do? Cindy turned up at my door, compliments of the hotel.'

'Cindy turned up at your door, did she? How convenient. Did *you* buy her the champagne, or perhaps she brought it with her?'

'Brought it with her, and I'm telling you, she was paid for by the hotel. Got a hunch they like making their guests happy.'

'Hmm . . . you get a real live hooker, and *I* get a dozen pairs of hooker shoes,' she said, almost smiling as she indicated a row of brightly coloured, outrageous new shoes lined up against the wall. There were at least twenty pairs.

'Jeez!' he said.

'Yep,' Lissa joked. 'Evelyn came through.'

'She sure did.'

'Y'know, Michael,' Lissa said restlessly, 'I'm beginning to feel like I'm cooped up in an ivory tower – Vegas style. I was hoping that we could sneak out somewhere, just you and me.'

'Where did you have in mind?' he asked, thinking she was hardly a movie and a hamburger type of woman.

'How about one of those funky downtown casinos where I can play the slot machines without getting stared at?' she suggested, eyes gleaming. 'Do you gamble?'

'Gave it up when I ditched drinking. Addictive habits are not for me.'

'I understand. So you can watch.'

'Thanks.'

'C'mon, Michael,' she said persuasively. 'Let's do it.'

'If that's what you want.'

'Well . . . I'm sure you wouldn't appreciate me going out by myself, would you?'

'I get it, Lissa. I'll organize a car.'

'No! The whole point is to *sneak* out of here, take cabs, act like a couple of tourists. I'm so *tired* of being treated like a star.'

'I'd better tell Chuck.'

'Why? Can't you handle me?' she asked, her blue eyes challenging him. 'You think you'll get in trouble if it's only the two of us?'

'Sure, Lissa,' he said sarcastically. 'I can see you're big trouble.'

'Then let's go, Michael. It'll take me two minutes to put on my disguise.'

'You have a disguise?'

'It's a killer,' she said, with a wicked grin. 'Just you wait!'

How could he say no to her? The problem was that she'd managed to get under his skin with a vengeance and he *wanted* to make her happy.

He hurried to his room, picked up some money and then his gun, just in case. Five minutes later he returned to her suite.

She was standing there in a short dark wig, tinted granny glasses, jeans, a denim shirt and sneakers. 'Do I look like a small-town hick?' she asked, twirling around in a circle.

'You sure as hell don't look like Lissa Roman,' he said, thinking she looked like a little kid about to play truant.

'That's good, isn't it?' she asked anxiously. 'It means no one will recognize me.'

'Okay, here's the plan,' he said, getting into it. 'We'll take the service elevator down, walk through the casino and out the front entrance. All you gotta do is hold my hand, keep your glasses on, and pretend you're my wife.'

'Your wife, huh?'

'Hey, if we're going on an adventure, we gotta play the parts.'

She dazzled him with her smile. 'I like it, Michael.'

This, he decided, was much more interesting than being with the tall, sexy blonde.

'So, the wicked witch has cast her bad, bad spell on you, huh?' Brian said.

They were sitting in a small restaurant on the beach, drinking frozen Margaritas, sharing a giant lobster and a large dish of french fries.

'I'm sorry to say this about your mom, Brian,' Nicci said earnestly, 'but she's a walking, talking monster. How did *you* manage to turn out so normal?'

'Oh, so now *I'm* the normal one,' he said, laughing. 'I thought you said I was a total fuck-up.'

'You're normal, apart from the fact that if it walks and breathes and looks vaguely human, you fuck it.'

'Who told you that?' he said, chewing on a succulent piece of lobster. 'My brother?'

'Every time I see you you're with a different girl.'

'Don't you get it?' Brian said sarcastically. 'That's 'cause none of them are as good as Mommy.'

She started to laugh. 'You are so totally full of it.'

'Yeah, well, it's gotten me through life,' he said, downing his second Margarita. 'Y'know, while Evan's busy making all the business deals and bringing the moguls to their knees, *I'm* the one who's writing the scripts and getting them on the screen.'

'I thought Evan helped with ideas,' she said, reaching for a french fry.

'Is that what he told you?'

'Kind of.'

'We do make for a good partnership,' Brian said thoughtfully. 'I'm creative, he's the business brain. Unfortunately, the rest of his growth was stunted by Mom.'

'You know, I got your mom to tell me about Julia.'

'You did, huh?'

'She said Julia was common.'

'Common! Jeez! That woman lives in a different era.'

'Tell me about it. *I*'m the one she's currently living with.'

'You gotta get Evan out from under her influence, Nic,' he said, his face serious. 'Otherwise, you're gonna end up in *deep* shit.'

'Uh-huh,' she said, leaning her elbows on the table. 'Y'see, Brian, here's the thing . . . I'm, uh . . . beginning to have some doubts.'

'Then don't do it,' he said casually. 'Don't marry him.'

'How can I not?' she exclaimed. 'Everyone's *expecting* me to. My dad's even flown in from Spain.'

'It's your grave you're headin' for, babe.'

'That's a nice, cheerful remark.'

'I tell it like it is.'

'At least Evan's a good guy,' she said, trying to convince herself. 'I mean, he doesn't screw around on me, he's—'

'Yeah? *What?*' Brian said tersely.

'Well, he's – he's always there.'

'That sounds like a lot of fun ten years down the line. Even five. And how d'you *know* he doesn't screw around?'

'Can you imagine *Evan* doing that? He won't even do drugs, there's *no way* he'd screw around, I know it.'

'You do, huh?'

'Yes, I do,' she said stubbornly, quite unnerved by Brian's cavalier attitude.

He summoned the waiter and ordered another drink. 'Wanna go to a rave?' he asked casually.

'No, thank you.'

'You're sure?'

'Positive.'

He grinned. 'One of these days you'll be *beggin'* me t' get you outta the house.'

'No, I won't.'

But even though she said it with conviction, she wasn't at all sure.

Lissa and Michael covered Vegas from one end to the other. She held onto his hand and allowed herself to act like a non-famous person. It was exhilarating.

'I cannot remember having such a good time in years,' she said, bright-eyed, as they headed into yet another downtown casino. 'These places are so grungy. I'm finally seeing America.'

'I wouldn't say this is typical America,' Michael said, amused.

'I guess not. Hmm . . .' she said, observing the action. 'There sure are a lot of fat people in Hawaiian shorts and "I love Mom" T-shirts.'

'You only *think* they're fat 'cause everyone in L.A. is thin.'

'Ah, yes, L.A.,' she said, grinning, 'capital of the body beautiful. To some people working out is a religion.'

'I bet *you* look good naturally.'

'Not true,' she said, shaking her head. 'I spend plenty of time at the gym doing all the things that keep me looking good. I practise yoga and Pilates, and sometimes I starve myself to squeeze into something stunning.'

'That's 'cause you're a movie star. You have to.'

'How about you, Michael?' she said. 'You look as if you work out.'

'Gotta be fit in my job.'

'Can we go play another slot machine?'

'Lissa,' he said sternly, 'you've lost two hundred dollars on the slots.'

'Do you *know* what they're paying me tomorrow for one show?'

'I've heard a rumour.'

'So I can lose two hundred dollars, can't I?'

'I should be getting you back to the hotel.'

'Why?' she said, taking off her glasses and staring at him.

'You've got a heavy day tomorrow,' he said. 'And put those glasses on, someone will recognize you.'

'I promise I'll leave soon, but first,' she said, putting her glasses back on, 'do *you* see what *I* see?'

'What?' he said, hoping it wasn't another cash machine.

'An all-you-can-eat-for-ten-bucks buffet,' she said triumphantly.

He shook his head. 'You're a nut.'

'Takes one to know one,' she said, grabbing his hand and pulling him towards it.

'I give up.'

'Excellent,' she said, smiling broadly. 'Let's go eat.'

'So anyway,' Nicci said, thinking that she might be talking too much, but unable to stop, 'my dad married this much older woman, and he seems pretty happy. She's mega-loaded, y'know, Big Buck City.'

'Hey, *I* could go for big bucks,' Brian said.

'You've got your *own* big bucks,' Nicci said.

'How d'*you* know?'

She grinned. 'I saw them when you got out of bed that fateful morning.'

'Ooh!' He burst out laughing. 'You're a *bad* girl.'

'Not really. The truth is that since I've been with Evan, I've turned into a *good* girl. I used to be a wild child.'

'Yeah?'

'I was into – you show it to me, I'll try it. Drinking, drugs, staying out all night.'

'Sounds normal to me.'

'I lived in Europe during most of my growing-up years.'

'That must've been interesting.'

'It was.' She sighed wistfully. 'Y'know, I was kind of looking forward to settling down with Evan.'

'You were?'

'Yes. Only I'm *not* about to settle down with him *and* his mom.'

'Don't blame you,' he said. 'D'you want dessert?'

'Anything chocolate.'

'You read my mind.'

'So, Brian,' she said anxiously, 'how often do you think she'll visit?'

'Hasn't he told you?'

'What?'

'She's planning on living with you.'

'Oh, come *on*.'

'I'm serious, Nic. She says she can't take the New York winters any more, so she's moving somewhere warm. And that somewhere warm is good old L.A.'

'I know you're teasing me,' she said, horrified at the thought.

'Marry him and you'll see.'

It was almost midnight when Lissa and Michael arrived back at the Desert Millennium Princess. They stood outside for a minute watching the incredible water displays and Lissa's name displayed in giant neon lights.

'How does it feel seeing that?' he asked.

She stared up at the flashing lights. 'Like I'm a fraud who's getting away with a scam.'

'How can you say that?'

'It's easy.'

'And you've been a star for how long?'

'Too many years.' She sighed, as they entered the hotel.

'Time to play wife again,' Michael said, taking her hand in his.

'Oh, my God!' she gasped, as they made their way through the crowded casino. 'You see that guy sitting at the blackjack table? The handsome one with the woman loaded in jewels.'

Michael glanced over. 'What about him?' he said.

'That's Antonio. He and I used to be married. He's Nicci's father.'

'I should be getting home,' Nicci said. 'Big night tomorrow.'

'I offered bro a bachelor night,' Brian said, clicking his fingers for the check. 'Got turned down flat.'

'You *see*?' she said triumphantly. 'He's *totally* faithful to me.'

'Keep on believing that, babe, and I've got a lovely piece of real estate for you in Iceland.'

She stared at him, sensing that something was wrong. 'Are you trying to tell me something?'

He shook his head. 'Not at all.'

'It seems that maybe you are.'

'You've got chocolate on your chin.'

'I do?'

'Here.' He leaned across the table and wiped her chin with his napkin.

'Thanks,' she said.

'Let's go,' he said abruptly, 'before I'm forced to take advantage of you.'

'Oh, like you could,' she said scornfully.

'*I* think I could.'

'You do, huh?'

'You're easy.'

'I am *so* not.'

'We'll see.'

'Suck it up, Brian.'

'Oooh, baby, you sure know how t' turn a guy on.'

'I'm having the *best* time,' Lissa said, skirting the table where Antonio was busy playing blackjack.

'Lissa,' Michael said warningly, 'be careful. He's likely to recognize you.'

'My best friend wouldn't recognize me,' she said, edging closer to the table where Antonio and his wife were sitting. 'Hmm . . . that must be the woman he married. She's older than him, *much* older. He still looks great, though, doesn't he?'

'I got no clue what he looked like before.'

'He has that kind of sexy European thing going,' she mused. 'He'll never grow old, not Antonio. Besides, he's only a few years older than me. Actually, he's about your age. Let's see now,' she said, giving Michael a quick once-over, 'who looks the best?'

'C'mon, Lissa,' he said, wishing she'd get off the ex-husband kick. 'It's past midnight.'

'I don't *feel* like going upstairs. I'm not tired.'

'You're on your way,' he threatened. 'Even if I have to carry you.'

'Promises, promises,' she murmured.

'Do you realize what you've got going on tomorrow?'

'Yes,' she said. 'You keep on reminding me.'

'Which is a good thing.'

'No, it's not, I want to hang out and people-watch.'

'Why?' he said, unable to control a twinge of jealousy. 'You still got a thing for your ex?'

'Are you *crazy?*' she said, laughing. 'Antonio was twenty years ago.'

'Twenty years, huh? And you haven't seen him in all that time?'

'No, after I divorced him he went back to Europe. Our only contact was Nicci. She split her time between the two of us.'

'Upstairs, Lissa.'

She mock-saluted. 'Yes, *sir.*'

'You really do look funny,' he couldn't help saying.

'Are you sure *cute* isn't the word you're searching for?'

'That too.'

They made it to the service elevator and up to her suite without anyone knowing.

'Come in and have a drink,' she said at the door.

'Why are you always asking me if I want a drink, when you know I don't drink?' he said, perplexed.

'Habit. Anyway, you're never tempted, are you?'

'I think I've told you before, will power of steel.'

'Yes,' she said flirtatiously. 'I noticed.'

He couldn't help smiling. There was something about her that he found irresistible. Especially in the wig and the glasses, when all she had going for her was a sensational body and an abundance of charm. 'I'd better check out your room,' he said, following her into the huge suite.

She took off her granny glasses and removed the short wig, shaking out her platinum hair. 'Wow! That feels better.'

He walked around checking out the bedroom, bathroom, kitchen and powder room. 'You're all safe and sound,' he said. 'And remember, I'm right next door.'

'Yes, Michael,' she said, her blue eyes watching him.

'And I'm a real light sleeper,' he added.

'So am I,' she said.

'Well . . . uh . . . I'll say good night,' he said, moving closer without even realizing he was doing so.

'I guess you should,' she murmured, taking a step towards him.

And as if it was meant to be, they fell into a kiss, neither of them aware of who made the first move.

Lissa experienced a rush of excitement. Her heart began beating incredibly fast. She had not intended this to happen, but now that it had, she was not about to stop it.

Michael felt as if he was coming home. He couldn't get over the warmth of her soft lips drawing him in, making him feel welcome and alive.

She touched his cheeks with her hands, and he

experienced a desire so strong and powerful that all the warnings he'd given himself meant nothing, and he knew he had to have this woman. It didn't matter that she was rich and famous. It didn't matter that he had a pregnant girlfriend back in L.A. and that there wasn't a chance in hell of this working out. Nothing mattered except the two of them being together.

'Michael.' She murmured his name very softly. 'Michael . . .'

He caressed her breasts through her denim shirt, then feverishly began unbuttoning it as she thrust her body towards him.

Her hand snaked down to the hardness between his legs.

'Don't!' he said sharply, worried that he'd blow it and come like a thirteen-year-old getting his rocks off for the first time.

She understood and left him alone, concentrating on kissing him with such intensity and yearning that he could barely breathe.

After a few minutes he unhooked her bra, releasing her breasts, marvelling at how perfect they were, touching them, stroking her satiny skin, bending his head to suck her erect nipples.

'You are so . . . goddamn . . . beautiful,' he muttered, picking her up and carrying her into the bedroom.

He had a thirst for her that nothing could quench. Her craving for him was equally intense.

And before long they were making slow, sensuous love, falling into each other's rhythms, transporting themselves to a place where only the two of them existed.

Chapter Thirty-six

Riding to the airport in Claude's Rolls-Royce, James kept his conversation clipped and to the point, an indication of his extreme displeasure at Claude's behaviour.

'What *is* the matter with you?' Claude finally burst out. 'You're actin' like a prima donna with a stick up her ass.'

'*You* should know all about sticks up people's asses,' James muttered.

'Cut it out,' Claude said warningly. 'So I stayed at the beach house, big deal.'

'You stayed at the beach house with that Latin slut,' James hissed. 'And what *really* annoys me is that you did not even have the courtesy to invite me to watch.'

'You're so English,' Claude said, in a put-down voice. 'What kick is there in cheating if *you*'re sitting there watching?'

'We *used* to do everything *and* everybody together,' James reminded him, with a toss of his head. 'Now I see you wish to fly solo.'

'Christ!' Claude exclaimed. 'You're turning into a jealous queen.'

'*Me?* Jealous?' James said imperiously. 'I beg to differ. Let us not forget, dear Claude, that *I* am twenty-one years your junior. Therefore, if *anyone* should be jealous, that someone should be *you*.'

'Oh, stick it up your crack,' Claude said, just as the Rolls pulled into the private airport.

'It's a damn good job you have your own plane,' James said huffily.

'Yeah, yeah, yeah,' Claude said. 'Love me, love my plane.'

Since Larry was a stickler for being on time, he and Taylor were already aboard. Everyone exchanged the appropriate amount of kisses.

'I hate Vegas. I don't know why we're doing this,' Larry muttered to his wife.

'For Lissa,' Taylor answered calmly. 'She's one of my best friends. And you know you like her.'

'I certainly wouldn't do it for anyone else.'

He'd been in a bad mood ever since he'd visited the set and caught her in a heated love scene with Sonja Lucerne. When she'd arrived home that night, he'd been pacing around the house in an agitated state.

'I meant what I said, Taylor,' he'd informed her. 'You shouldn't allow yourself to be put in that position. Your actions affect both of us.'

She was through with listening to his complaints. 'Y'know, Larry, cast me in one of your movies if you don't want me appearing in anything else.'

'Isn't it enough that I'm getting your film off the ground?'

'It might have been two years ago,' she'd retorted. 'You've certainly taken your time helping me.'

'That's not true,' he'd objected.

'Yes, Larry, it is.'

The next morning they were still hardly speaking. They got in the limo and sat in silence. What Taylor didn't know was that when she'd asked Larry to go back upstairs to pick up her jewellery pouch, which she'd left in her dressing room, he'd inadvertently come across Oliver Rock's cheque made out to her and dated days before he'd introduced them. Something was going on, and this weekend Larry was determined to find out what that something was.

'Nice plane,' Taylor said to Claude, admiring the upholstered leopardskin seats and black lacquer furniture.

'I recently had it redecorated,' Claude said. 'Unfortunately, it's too rock 'n' roll for James.'

'Actually I find the décor perfectly tasteless,' James said in his best 'I-am-a-snob' voice. 'However, what does *my* opinion matter?'

'The next plane I buy, *you* get to decorate,' Claude said magnanimously. 'How's that?'

'Thank you *so* much,' James said haughtily. 'You're *so* generous.'

Claude looked at his watch. 'Where's Norio and Kyndra?'

'Surely you don't expect Kyndra to arrive promptly?' James snapped.

'I had my assistant tell her we were leaving an hour earlier than we told everyone else. They should be here any time now.'

True to form, five minutes later Kyndra, thinking she was an hour late, swept onto the plane looking extremely glamorous in an all-white outfit. 'Oh, my God!' she wailed. 'Dramas! Dramas! How do I manage? Because I'm *me*, that's how. I'm forced to do *everything* myself!'

Norio was right behind her. 'The diva overslept,' he said drily. 'Sorry, guys.'

'Who are we waiting for now?' Claude wanted to know.

'Seth and Stella,' Taylor said. 'They're usually on time.'

Claude took another look at his watch. 'The pilot has clearance, I'd like to get moving.'

'I'll call her,' Taylor said, taking out her cellphone.

Stella picked up, sounding panicky. 'Yes? Yes? *What?*'

'Where are you?' Taylor asked. 'We're all waiting.'

'I'm giving *birth*!' Stella screeched. 'We're at the hospital now. Oh . . . my . . . God! What an experience!'

'She's giving birth,' Taylor announced to everyone.

'I didn't even know she was pregnant,' Claude said.

'She's not,' Taylor said. 'It's complicated. *Her* eggs, *Seth*'s sperm, mix them up in a blender, shoot 'em into a surrogate, and there you have it.'

'Does that mean they're not coming?' Claude said.

'Let me ask. Okay, Stella, sweetie, calm down,' Taylor said, speaking into the phone. 'Are you flying to Vegas with us?'

'I can't run out on my twins the moment they're born. Or can I? It's not as if I have to *feed* them or anything. I guess the surrogate looks after them for a few weeks, right?'

'How do *I* know, Stella? I've never had a baby.'

'I'm sure it's all taken care of. And I wouldn't want to let Lissa down.'

'So you *are* coming?'

'Yes, only we'll never make the plane – unless you can wait an hour?'

'Sorry,' Taylor said. 'Claude's anxious to go now.'

'Does that mean we'll have to fly commercial?' Stella wailed.

''Fraid so.'

'Damn!'

'They're coming later,' Taylor said, clicking off her phone.

Claude picked up the intercom and spoke to his pilot. 'We're ready. Let's go.'

Across town, Gregg sat with Belinda and Patrick in Belinda's over-decorated living room.

'Reckon I can get you fifty grand for this story,' Patrick said.

'That's good,' Belinda said.

'Not good enough,' Gregg interjected.

'Whaddaya mean, not good enough?' Patrick questioned. 'You gotta remember the high-price days are way over.'

'The stuff I've come up with is worth at least a hundred,' Gregg said, deciding that he didn't like Patrick, and he certainly didn't trust him.

'A hundred grand?' Patrick exclaimed in shock. 'Who're *you* shittin'?'

'Go back to the people who make the money decisions and see what *they* have to say,' Gregg said, playing it close. 'In the meantime I'll shop around.'

'You don't wanna do that,' Patrick said quickly.

'Then I'd appreciate a decision by this evening,' Gregg replied. 'Otherwise I'll start shopping.'

'Jesus Christ,' Patrick said disgustedly. '*I'm* the one put you up to this.'

'Then come up with a hundred grand and the story's yours,' Gregg said smoothly. 'That's only fair, isn't it?'

He caught Belinda's eye. She gave him an imperceptible nod, as much as to say, 'You're doing the right thing.'

He wondered if she expected to share the money with him. Chance would be a fine thing. He wasn't sharing one dollar, even though it was Belinda who'd discovered the notebook filled with Lissa's heartfelt confession.

And what had she confessed?

The sins of her parents.

Belinda had unearthed a small black notebook with a large red exclamation point on the front. Inside, it was filled with what appeared to be a short story about a girl. Only it was quite obvious the girl was Lissa.

The story started off:

I am fifteen years old and I hate my parents. I hate them because they are cruel and unloving. Ever since I was eight years old they have touched me, both of them, my mom especially. At night they come to my bedroom, and she touches me all the time, then she makes my dad come and help her. I hate her! I hate her! I hate her! One of these days I would like to kill her. But before I do, I must get away, because if I don't go, I will kill both of them. I'd like to do that. I'd like to see them suffer, as I have. My innocence was ripped away from me when I was eight. Now I'm fifteen, and I'm leaving soon. If I don't go, I will kill myself, or I will kill them.

When Gregg had first read it he was shocked, and it took a lot to shock Gregg Lynch. Then it all began to make sense. So *that*'s why Lissa was so fucking self-obsessed and needy: she'd been abused as a kid. Well, tough shit, nobody had it easy.

Belinda had summoned Patrick, who'd immediately come running over. 'This'll up the ante,' Patrick had said, rubbing his hands in glee.

Now they were haggling over money.

Gregg stood up, indicating that the meeting was over.

Patrick reluctantly took off, promising to phone before the end of the day.

'They'll pay,' Gregg said, when he'd left.

'You think so?' Belinda said, not quite so confident.

'I *know* so.'

Waking up with Michael beside her was exciting and exhilarating. Lissa rested on one elbow and stared at him. He was a beautiful man, not only good-looking, but kind and caring and a sensational lover. She touched his face, gently stroking the faint stubble around his chin. Then she fingered the scar on his chest, a souvenir of his days as a New York detective.

He stirred in his sleep. She removed her hand, not wishing to disturb him. It was only six a.m. and he'd had a hard night.

A smile played around her lips. Something magical had taken place last night, a true connection of two people reaching out and finding each other. It wasn't simply sex or a one-night stand. It was something extraordinarily special, something to be nurtured.

And how did she go about nurturing a man like Michael Scorsinni? He wasn't an actor or a performer. He didn't want anything from her professionally. He was his own person. Strong, independent, not the kind of man who would enjoy basking in her limelight. For his own reasons, Michael would not want that at all.

She lay there worrying about how she was going to act when he awoke. It was crucial that she didn't make him nervous. And how not to do that when she had her big show coming up, and all the attention would be on her? Sometimes it wasn't easy being famous.

She ran her fingers lightly over his chest. He stirred again, and this time began to wake up.

'Good morning,' she said softly.

'Good morning, you,' he said, opening his eyes. 'Am I dreaming?' he added, which was a good sign.

'No,' she said happily. 'And guess what? We weren't even drunk. Well, you wouldn't be, would you? But all I drank last night was Evian, so we don't have that excuse.'

'I didn't know we needed an excuse,' he said, stretching lazily.

'No,' she said, shaking her head. 'We certainly don't.'

'By the way,' he said, yawning, 'I should mention that you look absolutely beautiful without makeup. Why do you wear all that gunk on your face?'

'Now, now, Michael,' she chided, 'it's too soon to start trying to change me.'

'Change you? Nobody could change you,' he said warmly.

'That's true,' she said, smiling.

'C'mere,' he said, reaching for her.

She fell into his arms willingly, and soon they were

making rapturous love again, slowly, leisurely, as if they had all the time in the world.

When they were finished, she fell asleep wrapped safely in his arms.

They awoke to a ringing phone. Lissa stretched out, picked up and listened to a frantic Max. 'Where are you?' he demanded.

'Where am I supposed to be?'

'In Penthouse B. I have eight camera crews waiting to interview you.'

'Sorry, Max. I must've overslept,' she said guiltily. 'Give me twenty minutes.'

'Dammit, Lissa,' Max said brusquely, 'we're on a tight schedule here.'

'Calm down, I'll be there.' She hung up and turned to Michael. 'I feel a crazy day coming on. I hope you understand.'

'Like I wouldn't?' he said.

'And for the record, I want you to know this.'

'What?'

'No way are you Rebound Man. I was attracted to you the moment we met.'

'Isn't that nice?' he said, grinning. ''Cause I walked into my office that day, took one look at you, and it was all over.'

'Really?' she said, delighted.

'Would I lie?'

'You'd better not.'

He sat up in bed. 'There's stuff I gotta tell you about, Lissa. It's not great.'

'Hmm . . .' she murmured, feeling quite light-headed. 'Now what could it be? Perhaps a criminal past you're dying to reveal to me?'

'Not exactly.'

'Then whatever it is, it'll have to wait until later. You'll be with me all day, won't you?'

'By your side. Only it's not a smart move to let people know about us.'

'Why?' she asked, quite prepared to tell the world.

''Cause it's too soon. It won't make you look good.'

'I guess that means today you're my bodyguard?'

'Just call me Kevin,' he said, laughing.

She stretched and smiled. 'Last night was . . . special. I want to make sure you know that.'

'For me, too, sweetheart,' he said, wondering how he was going to tell her about Carol and the baby.

'Y'know, Michael,' she said softly. 'It's almost as if we were . . . destined to be together.'

'How's that?'

'Well, we were thrown together by circumstances, weren't we?'

'I guess you could say that.'

'If I hadn't decided to dump that lying, cheating husband—'

'One thing you should know about me, Lissa,' he interrupted. 'I will *never* lie to you.'

'Promise?'

'Forever,' he assured her.

'I hope so,' she said, her clear blue eyes staring into his.

'C'mon,' he said. 'Time to get up.'

'I'd better call Fabio and have him fix my hair,' she said, suddenly remembering Max sitting in a room with eight camera crews waiting to interview her. 'Poor Max, I think if I don't move fast, he'll have a major breakdown!'

To Nicci's amazement, Brian behaved like a perfect gentleman. After their lobster dinner at the beach, he'd driven her back to the house, dropped her off, and hadn't even tried to kiss her good night.

She was deeply disappointed. She'd wanted to ask him in, but didn't, because she knew it wasn't the right thing to do. 'So, I'll see you,' she'd said, a touch forlornly.

'Yeah, you will,' he'd said.

'Probably before the wedding, I hope.'

Damn! She'd had her opportunity with Brian and blown it.

What kind of opportunity was it anyway? He wasn't interested in her, he was treating her like she was his kid sister.

In the morning she called Evan. 'I'm planning on coming to the airport to meet you,' she said.

'Not necessary,' he replied. 'I'm flying in with two of the actors. The studio's sending a car.'

'Don't you *want* me to meet you?'

'It's better that I see you at the house.'

'Your *mother* will be at the house.'

'So?'

'We need to talk, Evan,' she said, determined to clear some things up. 'Over the last few days stuff has been getting kind of out of whack between us.'

'That's because you're nervous about the wedding.'

'I am so *not*.'

'Yes, you are. My mother said she thinks you're overexcited.'

'I don't give a shit *what* she says,' Nicci said, furious that Lynda was talking about her with him.

'Don't speak about my mother like that.'

'Your *mother* is who we have to talk about. It seems you're more interested in what *she* says and does than me.'

'Don't be ridiculous.'

'I'm not,' she said stubbornly.

'All right, we'll discuss it when I get back tomorrow,' Evan said, cutting her off. 'I've got to go now.'

Something about him sounded different, and she couldn't pinpoint what it was.

She had a strong urge to phone Brian. And why not?

She had the whole day with nothing to do except get ready for her bachelorette night, so she picked up the phone and called him.

'Am I catching you in bed with a blonde?' she asked, only half joking.

'Hey, yesterday was a redhead, today you've got me with a blonde. The miserable truth is I'm by myself. Ain't that the pits?'

'Why are you by yourself?'

'"Why?" she asks,' he said ruefully. ''Cause I was with *you* last night. Remember?'

'Oh, yeah.'

'No time for a date.'

'Sorry.'

'Bet you're not.'

'Uh . . . Brian?' she said impulsively. 'Wanna go for breakfast?'

'Don't you do *anything* but eat?'

'C'mon,' she said persuasively. 'I've only got a couple of weeks left as a free person. May as well make the most of it.'

'How did we suddenly become friends?' he asked, sounding puzzled.

'Dunno,' she confessed. 'It must've happened the night we were naked in bed. I think we'd better discuss how we're *never* telling Evan about that night.'

'By the way,' he said, 'I've been meaning to tell you.'

'What?'

'You have a sensational body.'

'Oh *pu-lease!*' she said, almost blushing.

'And I'm an expert.'

'Expert. *Sure.* Save those corny lines for your parade of girlfriends.'

'Where d'you wanna go for breakfast?' he asked.

'I was thinking pancakes.'

'You really *are* my kinda girl.'

'I am?'

'If only you were blonde and stacked.'

'Screw you!'

'I'll pick you up in ten minutes.'

'Is he out of the house?' Patrick asked.

'Yes,' Belinda replied, cradling the phone. 'I sent him to Barneys to pick out a birthday present.'

'Generous of you.'

'I can afford to be, can't I?'

'If this deal flies, you sure can. I got the magazine up to a hundred an' fifty grand from a hundred, which, as you know, was their original offer. Since your boyfriend wants a hundred, you and I get to split the other fifty. The magazine'll pay me, an' I'll cut him a cheque. Sound like a go?'

'Oh, yes,' Belinda said. She failed to see why she shouldn't score off this. Gregg was not paying rent, and the two times they'd gone out to dinner he'd said he was short of cash and she'd picked up the check. This way she could recoup her expenses and more besides.

'We'll let him sweat a bit,' Patrick said. 'Then I'll get back to him around six, an' tell him I made the deal.'

'And *I'll* persuade him to accept it.'

'Anything for an old flame, right, Belinda?'

'Not so much with the old.'

'How old *are* you?'

'That's for God to know, and everyone else to speculate.'

Saturday morning Eric Vernon left his apartment, took a trip out to LAX, hired a storage locker, and placed his one suitcase in it. Then he drove back to town, stopping at Denny's to devour a hearty breakfast. Eggs over easy, bacon and toast, two cups of coffee and a glass of orange juice. He needed his strength.

Next he went to the building to meet Arliss, where he checked everything over one final time. He'd already driven by Nicci's boyfriend's house a couple of times. Yesterday the woman who'd been staying there had taken a cab to the airport. This was good news: Eric had been worried about someone else being in the house. Now he had a clear shot. Or, rather, Big Mark and Little Joe did because he was sending *them* in to snatch her. He'd wait in the car. It was safer that way. And Eric did not plan on taking any chances.

Arliss was nervous. His face kept on twitching, and his bony hands were shaking uncontrollably.

'You'd better keep it together,' Eric warned him. 'This'll all go down smooth if you handle yourself right. What are you getting in a panic for?'

Arliss chewed on a strand of greasy hair and wiped his nose with the back of his hand. 'Dunno,' he muttered.

Eric was totally at ease. As far as he was concerned, everything was right on track.

Chapter Thirty-seven

T he Desert Millennium Princess had arranged suites for all of Lissa's guests.

'This place is over the top,' Larry said snappishly, exploring their lavish suite. 'It's too extravagant for its own good.'

'Each hotel they build has to be more outrageous than the next,' Taylor replied. 'Otherwise people wouldn't come here.'

'They come to Vegas to lose their hard-earned money, not to sit in a hotel room,' Larry said. 'The poor schmucks.'

'Those poor schmucks are the same people who go see your movies, Larry. This is their other form of entertainment, their fantasy land.'

'The place is a monument to vulgarity,' he said contemptuously.

'I'm sorry about yesterday,' Taylor said, thinking it was time she dealt with her husband's bad mood. 'I was acting and I have to admit that I enjoyed it. Only now that you're helping me with my film, I'll be in control of what I do.'

'You looked like a lesbian in that scene, Taylor,' he said accusingly.

'I was *playing* a lesbian, Larry,' she pointed out, wondering how someone so smart could sometimes sound so prejudiced. 'And can we please *drop* the subject?'

'Let me ask you something,' he said.

'Yes?'

'Are you pleased I've hired Oliver Rock to work on your script?'

'I'm pleased you've hired *someone*,' she said, wondering what he was getting at now. 'If *you* think he's good, I'm sure it'll work out.'

'Did you ever meet him before?'

'What?' she said, startled.

'Did you *know* Oliver before I brought him to the house?' Larry repeated.

She was silent for a moment, trying to decide what to say. Had Oliver mentioned that they knew each other before? Could he be *that* stupid?

'Why would you think I might've met Oliver before?' she asked, deciding to bluff it out.

'No reason. I'm simply asking.'

'It seems rather a strange question, Larry.'

'I suppose it does,' he said. 'Think about it. Maybe you ran into him somewhere and don't remember.'

'I'm sure I didn't,' she said vaguely, thinking that she'd better call Oliver pronto and find out if he'd said anything. 'Claude wants us all to get together for lunch at Spago in Caesar's,' she added, briskly changing the subject. 'He's sending a car at one o'clock. Lissa is meeting us there.'

'And what are we supposed to do for the rest of the afternoon?'

'I thought I might visit the hotel spa. Why don't you come with me?' she suggested. 'You'll love all that pampering.'

'I'll pass,' he said, shaking his head. 'I have work to do. I'll stay in the suite.'

'No gambling? We could play roulette, blackjack, craps.'

'No, thank you, Taylor,' he said stiffly. 'I prefer to stay here. Gambling is for idiots.'

* * *

Lissa sailed through her TV interviews with a serene smile on her face. Max had already instructed the journalists that they could not mention Gregg Lynch. All but one of them obeyed the rule. Lissa didn't mind. 'I don't wish to discuss my personal life,' she'd said politely, 'so, if you'll excuse me . . .' And she'd stood up and left the journalist sitting there.

'You handled that very well,' Max informed her.

'I'm glad you're pleased.'

'I'm always pleased with you, Lissa,' he said fondly. 'You're my favourite client. Oh, yes – and here's a copy of the *L.A. Times*,' he said, handing her the newspaper. 'Your interview came out well.'

She took the paper, then glanced around for Michael. He was standing close by looking incredibly handsome. She wanted to blow him a kiss – anything to let him know she was thinking of him. But she controlled herself because she knew he was right: it was best not to let people know about them. Not yet anyway.

Once she was finished with the interviews, Michael escorted her to the hotel's impressive large theatre where she was due to do a final sound check.

'I thought about you all morning,' she whispered on their way over.

'You too.'

'I can't wait for later, Michael.'

'No more slots?'

'No more anything except us together.'

'That suits me.'

Danny was waiting at the theatre. 'I won last night!' he announced proudly. 'Can you imagine?'

'That's great, Danny,' Lissa said. 'How *much* did you win?'

'Five hundred dollars,' he said excitedly, then remembering his place, he switched into assistant mode. 'Everyone's here. They all arrived safely and are settled in their respective

381

suites. Mr Fallow said they are expecting you for lunch at Spago. I told him you wouldn't have much time to spend with them.'

'Thanks, Danny,' she said. 'Tell James I'll get there around one fifteen. And please double-check on everyone's seats for tonight. Oh, yes, and add the name of Nicci's future mother-in-law, Mrs Richter, and Mr and Mrs Antonio Stone to the party guest list.'

'Yes, Miz Roman,' he said, wondering how soon he could get back to the casino.

She couldn't decide what to do about Michael and lunch. If she introduced him to the group they'd all know – especially James. It was best if he didn't sit with them.

'Michael,' she said, 'do you mind being at another table with Chuck during lunch?'

'Why would I mind?'

She shrugged. 'I'm following *your* rules. You said we shouldn't tell people about us, and if my friends see us together, believe me, they'll know.'

'Don't worry about it,' he said. 'I'm happy to stay in the background. As long as you're safe, that's all that matters to me.'

'Later,' she promised. 'After the show and the party, we'll be together.'

'I'm not sure I can wait that long.'

'Try,' she said, squeezing his hand.

'Watch it,' he warned. 'Someone might see.'

'What does it matter?'

'It matters, Lissa. You gotta remember your public image. Your husband is busy mouthing off about you everywhere he goes. You don't want people thinking you've jumped into bed with the first man who comes your way.'

'Oh – are you the first man who came my way?' she said teasingly. 'I might inform you that every bachelor in Hollywood has been calling me for weeks.'

'Now they can lose your number, right?'

She smiled. 'Oh, yes, Michael. Definitely.'

Gregg gave his car to valet parking and strolled into Barneys, where he requested Deidra.

It didn't take long for her to appear.

'So,' he said, checking her out, 'you're a personal shopper now. Is that an upgrade?'

'Yes, it is,' she said crisply. 'And I see *you*'ve upgraded to Belinda Barrow. Or should I say downgraded?'

'Now, now, don't be bitchy.'

'I'm not being bitchy, merely truthful,' she said, hating the sight of him. 'It beats me how you can go from superstar to a hack television reporter who's been around a hundred years.'

'Belinda's a nice lady.'

'I hardly think the word *lady* applies. She acts like a stuck-up bitch when she comes in here.'

He hadn't come to Barneys to listen to Deidra complain about his current girlfriend.

'What am I buying today?' he asked.

'How much does *she* want to spend?' Deidra retorted, her lip curling.

'I was thinking an Armani suit, a couple of silk ties, and maybe two or three Brioni shirts,' he said. It was about time Belinda spent some real money on him.

'Let's go upstairs,' Deidra said, 'and I'll get you set up.'

She soon had him settled in a fitting room, while a sales assistant brought him several suits to try on.

Once the suits were hanging in the room, Deidra dismissed the assistant. 'I'll call if I need you, Jeff,' she said, pulling the curtain closed.

'I was thinking about you the other day,' Gregg remarked, taking off his pants.

'What were you thinking?' she asked, removing the Armani suit pants from their hanger.

'I was thinking about those nipples of yours, and how much I miss them.'

'I see.'

'I see,' he mimicked. 'Gonna play it cool with me, Deidra? Is that it?'

'You played it pretty *cold* with me when you walked out that night,' she said accusingly.

'I was drunk and upset. Didn't realize what I was doing. Sorry.'

'*Are* you?' she said.

'Come over here,' he said, 'and I'll *show* you how sorry I am.'

'How'll you do that?'

'Get down on your knees, put my dick between your tits, an' I'll give you my best apology.'

The moment Lissa arrived at lunch, she sensed an atmosphere. 'Hi, everybody,' she said, sitting down. 'I'm so pleased you all made it.'

'Wouldn't miss it,' James said, very uptight.

'Only for you would I come to this place,' Larry said, also uptight.

'Stella's not here yet, she's giving birth,' Taylor announced. 'She's flying in later.'

'Is it twins?'

'Yes.'

'You mean she's leaving her babies to come here?'

'Stella is not exactly Earth-mother two thousand and one,' James sniffed.

'I can't imagine Stella playing mommy,' Taylor said. 'I'm sure she'll hire a house full of nannies.'

'How are rehearsals going?' Claude asked.

'Terrific,' Lissa said warmly. 'It'll be different from my

last show. I've added a couple of numbers I think you'll like.' She sipped a glass of apple juice. 'What do you think of the hotel, Claude?'

'Quite impressive,' he replied.

'Vulgar,' James said, shooting Claude a spiteful glare.

'I'll have to introduce you to the owner,' Lissa said. 'He's throwing the party after the show. His wife is quite a character. She had on these hooker shoes the other night, and when I admired them, she sent me twenty pairs!'

'Does she wear lots of jewels?' Kyndra drawled.

'Loaded with them.'

'Do you think if I admire them, she'll hand me a necklace or two?'

Everyone laughed, breaking the tension.

'You look particularly glowing,' James said, moving close to Lissa and talking quietly. 'Is that dancer still in your troupe? The good-looking Italian?'

'You mean Sergio? Yes, he's still there. Why?'

'Straight or gay?'

'What is this? A game?'

'I'm simply asking.'

'Sergio is straight.'

'I see. Hmm . . .'

'What does *that* mean?'

'It means you're looking very sort of I've-just-had-great-sex-ish.'

'Y'know, James,' she said, laughing. 'You really do have the wildest imagination.'

'Do I now?'

She glanced over at the nearby table where Michael was sitting with Chuck. Their eyes met for an instant. She smiled. He smiled back. God, if she didn't have her show tonight, she'd blow off everything and spend the day with him.

* * *

'Stop calling me,' Saffron said warningly.

'Why?' Nicci said.

''Cause you're only trying to pump me about tonight. Wear something sexy and shut up.'

'What are *you* wearing?'

'It doesn't matter what *I'm* wearing.'

'Then tell me what time kick-off is?'

'It's a surprise. Now, will you *stop* calling? I'm not talkin' to you today.'

The moment Brian swung by to take her to breakfast, she felt better.

'Hi,' she said, running out of the house to meet him. He looked hot in jeans, a denim shirt and a baseball cap.

'Is this Miss Appetite of the Year?' he asked, grinning.

'Breakfast is the most important meal of the day,' she informed him.

'Sure. And, according to you, so is lunch, tea *and* dinner.'

'I spoke to Evan,' she said, jumping into his Porsche.

'What did he have to say?'

'He sounds weird. Not like his usual self.'

'Yeah?'

'I offered to go to the airport and meet him tomorrow. He told me not to bother, he's flying in with a couple of the actors.'

'Which ones?'

'He didn't say, but apparently the studio's sending a car and I guess he wants to ride with them. I told him we had to talk about his mom.'

'How'd he take that?'

'He didn't sound pleased.'

'He's not gonna like it, Nic.'

'I don't care if he does or not,' she said defiantly. 'This is something we have to discuss, otherwise – what was it you said? Oh, yeah, I'll be like *digging* my own grave.'

'Y'know,' Brian remarked as they headed down the hill, 'you're ruining my sex life.'

'What're you *talking* about?'

'I'm spending more time with you than I am chasing pussy.'

'Nicely put. Anyway, I'm certainly not like *forcing* you to spend time with me.'

'Yes, you are.'

'How's that?'

''Cause – I gotta be truthful – I *like* spending time with you. You're different.'

'Different how? I got horns?'

'No, you're easy to get along with. Y'know, some of the girls I take out have no conversation. It's like when their tits get inflated, their brains get smaller.'

'You're obviously dating the wrong kind of girl.'

'Maybe you can find me someone like you.'

'Like me, huh?' she said, pleased.

'Yeah, you.'

'I'm an original.'

'That's what I thought.'

'Where are we going for breakfast?' she asked, as he raced his Porsche along Sunset.

'The beach,' he said. 'I know a great little place for waffles.'

'I can't stay out long,' she warned. 'I've gotta get back and prepare myself for my big evening.'

'No problem,' he said, failing to tell her that the beach he was taking her to was in Santa Barbara.

Deidra's nipples were as chewable as ever, Gregg had missed them. Being with her in the fitting room at Barneys was quite an erotic experience. The first thing he did was unbutton her blouse, unclip her bra, and bury himself in Nipple City. He had a genuine hard-on, not the half-hearted sort he managed with Belinda.

Deidra was into it, he could tell. Oh, yeah, he certainly had a magic touch with women. After the way he'd spoken to her, he'd thought she'd never have anything to do with him again. But no, here she was, begging for more. Women! He'd never met one he couldn't nail if he put a little effort into it.

Deidra was building him to a nice climax as she massaged his penis. Slowly did it. He had to admit he'd missed her seasoned touch.

'I'm nearly there, baby,' he muttered. 'Get down on your knees. Put my cock between your tits.'

'Hold that thought, Gregg. I'll be right back.'

And before he could stop her, she ran out of the dressing room.

'Where are you going?' he yelled. 'I'm almost coming, for crissakes!'

And then he heard her strident cries. 'Rape! Rape!' she shouted. 'That son-of-a-bitch just tried to rape me.'

As soon as Taylor arrived at the luxurious spa, she reached for a phone and called Oliver. 'Did you say anything to Larry about us meeting before he entered the picture?' she asked, in a low voice.

'No way,' Oliver said. 'Why d'you ask?'

'Because Larry said something, and it seemed odd. Are you *sure* you didn't mention that you'd seen the script before?'

'Whaddaya think I am – a moron?'

Yes, she thought.

'He's probably fishing,' Oliver said.

'For *what*?' she said waspishly. 'I never give him cause to be suspicious.'

'That's good, then.'

'I suppose so.' A beat. 'Anyway, as soon as I get back we'll sit down and go over the script. I know you don't think much of it, but it does have great potential.'

'Larry wants me to work with *him* on it, Tay.'

'He does?'

'Isn't that what you wanted?'

'Not if he's taking over completely.'

'It's good for you. We'll get the script right, then you'll move in and play the lead.'

'This is *my* movie, Oliver,' she said vehemently. 'Mine!'

'You were always bitching about Larry not helping you,' Oliver pointed out.

'Okay, okay,' she said impatiently. 'I'll talk to you when we get back. And by the way . . .'

'What?'

'Next time you come out with us, kindly don't bring a date.'

'It's cool if I have a date. Larry won't get suspicious.'

'Larry is *not* suspicious,' she said irritably. 'He made a stupid remark for no reason. And if he *were* suspicious of me, it certainly wouldn't be about someone like you.'

'Thanks!'

'Don't mention it.'

Thank God she was at a spa. If there was one thing she needed, it was to immerse herself in an afternoon of total pampering.

It was almost four thirty when Brian dropped Nicci back at the house. They'd spent a wonderful day together, both of them enjoying it immensely. They'd had lunch at a seafood restaurant on the beach in Santa Barbara, wandered around the shops, browsed the bookstore and record store, where Brian had insisted on buying her a stack of CDs.

Then they'd raced home, because she'd suddenly realized it was getting late, and any moment Saffron might be picking her up.

Now, as he pulled up outside the house, she was reluctant to say goodbye.

'Have fun tonight,' Brian said. 'Try not to get too wasted.'

'I'll try,' she said. 'Can't promise.'

'And remember, no touching the strippers.'

'No touching, huh?' she said, grinning.

'It's not allowed,' he said good-naturedly.

'Who says?'

'Me.'

'Oh, you do, huh?'

'Maybe one light touch.'

'Do I have your permission?'

'Go for it, Nic.'

'I guess I'd better get moving,' she said, still reluctant to leave him.

'Yup.'

'Uh . . . Brian.'

'What?'

'I'm definitely thinking of breaking it off with Evan.'

'Don't let *me* influence you.'

'You're not,' she said quickly. 'It's just that I think I'm gonna tell him we should wait until I'm like *twenty*. I mean, this obsession with his mother and everything – it's scary.'

'Maybe you shouldn't trust Evan as much as you do.'

'What does *that* mean?'

'Listen, Nic, I feel real close to you lately, and it's shit if you go walking into something with your eyes closed. So . . . watch out for yourself.'

'Like how?'

'Ask Evan about Abbey.'

'Who's Abbey?'

'The actress in our movie.'

'Abbey *Christian?*'

'That's right.'

'Are you saying—'

'I'm not saying anything. All I'm telling you is to ask Evan.'

She felt a shudder of apprehension. Abbey Christian was a movie star. If Evan was having a thing with her, there was no way she could compete. Who wanted to anyway?

'This is too strange for me, Brian,' she said, not prepared to get into a long discussion. 'I'm having fun at my bachelorette party tonight whether I'm getting married or not.'

'What time does Evan arrive tomorrow?'

'He didn't say.'

'Call me if you wanna do the breakfast thing again. This time I promise we'll stay in L.A.'

'What're *you* up to tonight?' she asked.

'Trying to figure out whether I should have the blonde, the redhead, or the brunette,' he quipped. 'I'd better get on the cell.'

'You've forgotten Miss Russia,' Nicci said, playing along. 'She certainly had lust in her eyes every time she looked your way – which was every second!'

'If I didn't know any better,' he said, laughing, 'I'd think you were jealous.'

'Oh, *pu-lease*,' she said scornfully. 'Your ego grows bigger every time I see you.'

'And that's not all,' he said, with a sly wink, helping her out of the car with her packages. 'If you get home and it's past midnight, call me.'

'Huh?'

'You can call me any time,' he said, getting back into his car. 'I wanna hear about your evening.'

'I'll do that.'

She stood and watched him as he sped off.

Brian Richter. It was time she faced up to the truth. *He* was the one she really wanted.

She was marrying the wrong brother.

As Brian drove off, he failed to notice the battered old green Chevrolet parked a few feet down the street.

Nicci didn't see it either as she ran into the house, carrying her packages and singing quietly to herself. She felt great – excited and happy. Brian had that effect on her.

Eric Vernon watched in sullen silence as Nicci entered the house. He'd been sitting in the car with Big Mark, Davey and Little Joe for two and a half hours. The stench was unbearable. Didn't any of them ever take a shower?

'Who are we waiting for?' Big Mark kept on asking. 'And where is she?'

'She'll be here,' Eric said, determined to remain calm. Because if the bitch didn't show, his plan would be shot to hell.

When she finally arrived home, Eric nudged Big Mark into action. 'That's her,' he said. 'Wait till the Porsche has left, then go do it.'

'She looks young,' Little Joe mumbled, peering out the car window. 'Didn't know we was snatchin' a young one.'

'She *is* young,' Eric said. 'She's young and strong, which means nothing will happen to her if you all do your job right.'

'Who is she?' Davey asked. 'Must be somebody rich living up here in this fancy neighbourhood.'

'Of course she's rich,' Eric said scathingly. 'I wouldn't be snatching her if she wasn't, would I?'

God, they were morons. He couldn't wait to be rid of them.

Big Mark and Little Joe got out of the car and headed for the house. Big Mark pulled a stocking mask over his heavy features, while Little Joe soaked a cloth pad in chloroform.

Eric watched the street to see if there were any nosy neighbours observing. As far as he could see, it was deserted. It wasn't as if the houses were next to each other, they all had spacious grounds and trees around them. Besides, the house was up in the hills and quite remote.

In minutes his plan would be put into action.

He took a deep breath. It wasn't long before he'd be a rich man.

As soon as Nicci slammed the front door, the doorbell rang.

What does Brian want now? she thought, dropping her purse and packages on the floor. *More stories about Evan?*

She flung open the door.

A man stood there in a stocking mask. A man so large and frightening-looking that she almost cried out.

For a moment she was paralysed, then, as she attempted to slam the door on him, his large foot jammed it open, and before she could stop him, he pushed his way inside the house and grabbed her in a choke-hold.

Next he placed a chloroform pad over her mouth and nose, and she felt her world crumbling as she fell into a deep unconscious state and slumped helplessly to the ground.

Chapter Thirty-eight

The Mahoneys had lived in their apartment for thirty-two years. It wasn't a luxurious place, but the sturdy brown building had withstood earthquakes, floods and riots. Mrs Mahoney, a happy soul, worked as a cleaner to a rich family in Sherman Oaks. Mr Mahoney lived off his pension and stayed home a lot watching TV. They had no children, never felt the urge. They did have a cat, a small yappy dog, a parrot, and two fish.

On Saturday afternoon, Mrs Mahoney emerged from her apartment and came face to face with two policemen, one white and one black. With them was the ruddy-faced man who owned the bar around the corner.

'Morning, Sam,' Mrs Mahoney said, recognizing him immediately. 'What're *you* doing here?' She stared at the two cops. 'And what're *they* doing here?'

The small yappy dog started to bark, tugging at the bottom of the white cop's trousers. He attempted to kick the dog away.

'Lookin' for Pattie,' Sam said. 'She ain't been in for two days. Not like her. No phone call, nothin'. I tried reachin' her. Started thinkin' there coulda bin foul play, so I called the cops.'

'Foul play?' Mrs Mahoney said, eyebrows rising. 'I've never heard of such a thing. In *our* building?'

'You don't happen to have a key to this apartment, do you, ma'am?' the black cop asked, indicating the apartment across the hall from the Mahoneys.

'No,' Mrs Mahoney said. 'I don't care for that girl. She's too noisy, and she drops garbage in the hallway.'

'She's a slag,' Sam said, 'everyone knows that, but we still gotta find out why she ain't come to work.'

'Where can we reach the janitor?' the white cop asked.

'My husband has a key to all the apartments,' Mrs Mahoney said. 'Why? Are you going in?'

'Yes, ma'am.'

'Aren't you supposed to have a warrant or something?'

'You've been watching too much TV,' the black cop said. '*Law and Order, NYPD*?'

Mrs Mahoney went back into her apartment and interrupted her husband, who was busy drooling over Pamela Anderson on a *Baywatch* rerun. 'They want to get into the apartment opposite,' she said. 'Where's the key?'

'Why they going in there?' he grumbled.

'Something about the woman who lives there not showing up at work.'

Reluctantly, Mr Mahoney heaved himself off the couch, walked into the bedroom and grabbed a bunch of keys from the top of his dresser. 'They're numbered,' he said, handing them to his wife.

She took them out to the cops, and stood there while they opened the door.

As soon as the door swung open, her little dog darted past everyone and raced into the apartment. It immediately started barking and scratching at the closed bathroom door.

Gingerly, the cops entered the apartment, followed by Sam and Mrs Mahoney.

'What's that smell?' Mrs Mahoney asked. 'It's disgusting.'

'Dunno,' Sam said, sniffing the air like a bloodhound.

'She must be away,' Mrs Mahoney said. 'I haven't heard that loud music she plays lately.'

The cops exchanged glances. They checked out the small living room and kitchenette, peered into the bedroom, and finally they turned to the closed bathroom door, where the dog was still furiously scratching.

'I got one of my feelings,' the black cop said.

'Yeah,' the white cop agreed. 'Me too. Sometimes I hate this job.'

They opened the door.

Pattie was hanging from the shower rail, tethered by her wrists. She was naked and covered in dried blood. Her throat was slit.

Chapter Thirty-nine

And so they poured into Las Vegas for the official opening of the Desert Millennium Princess Hotel and Lissa Roman's show. There was the big action star, who'd spent his entire life pretending to be straight. The innocent-looking *ingénue*, who was into whips and chains. The TV executive, who screwed around on his wife with the stars of his shows. The mother-daughter combination, who'd double-teamed their way to the top by blackmailing certain studio executives. The hot young actor hopelessly addicted to crack cocaine. The skinny TV actress with a bad case of bulimia. The other skinny TV actress with an even worse case of anorexia. And the madam, whose little black book was worth more than anybody would care to guess.

Lights, music, action. When Lissa Roman hit the stage, it was a major event. The audience was jam-packed with celebrities all jostling for the best seats.

Lissa made her entrance on a golden swing, wearing a daring red catsuit slit down to her navel. With her platinum hair and gorgeous face she looked like she could conquer the world. The audience went crazy as her dancers surrounded her for the opening number.

Standing by the side of the stage, Michael watched her in wonderment. He was trying to be logical about everything, but the truth was that he'd fallen hard, and what was he planning to do about *that*? Right now everything was fine, but maybe he *was* Rebound Man, and maybe she *was* going to regret the fact that she'd taken him into her bed.

Christ! Carol was pregnant in L.A., Quincy would shake his head, and Amber . . . well, he didn't even want to think about what Amber would say.

Anyway, what was he worrying about? Lissa would probably say goodbye the moment they hit L.A. So he may as well take it for what it was – a weekend romance. Exactly what he'd tried to avoid.

He checked with the rest of security via his two-way radio. Everything seemed to be under control. The more he thought about it, the more likely it seemed that it was Gregg who'd sent her the threatening letter. It was exactly the kind of attention-getting stunt he'd pull. What an asshole he must be.

Fabio grabbed Michael as he walked past. 'Isn't she divine?' Fabio gushed. '*The* most *beautiful* woman. *The* most *talented*. Isn't she *unbelievable*? She *belongs* to her public, see how they love her.'

That's all Michael needed to hear. He was sleeping with a woman who belonged to her public. Great.

The show went by fast, and since the audience was in such a frenzy, screaming and stamping for more, Lissa performed three encores.

When she finally came off she was coated in a thin film of sweat. Two dressers rushed to attend to her. Michael hovered outside her dressing room next to Danny, who held the official guest list of who was allowed in and who wasn't.

He'd already checked out her dressing room, which was huge – bigger than his entire apartment in L.A. There was the inner sanctum, then there was a large reception room where tables were loaded with caviar and champagne for her visiting guests.

James and Claude were the first to appear.

'Hello, Mr St Lucia,' Danny grovelled, almost bowing as he ushered them in.

'Who was that?' Michael asked.

'The tall one is Madam's *best* friend,' Danny confided. 'And the other gentleman is Claude St Lucia, the record mogul.'

Michael found Danny's choice of words quite archaic. Who used the phrase 'record mogul'?

He recognized a few of the celebrities as they began filtering in. The very pretty Britney Spears, James Woods with a young date, singing star Al King, Lucky Santangelo, Dennis Hopper, Lara Flynn Boyle, Nick Angel, Hugh Grant. A mixed bag all paying their respects.

It made Michael realize how much he was *not* a part of her world. There was no way this could be anything other than a one or two night fling. No way at all.

And yet . . . he didn't regret anything.

'I'm in jail,' Gregg yelled over the phone.

'*What?*' Belinda said.

'I *said* I'm in fucking *jail*,' he repeated, at full shout. 'Get me a fucking lawyer.'

'What are you doing in jail?'

'That's a stupid question.'

'Do you want to tell me?'

'For crissakes, later. Just get me the fuck out.'

Belinda put down the phone and immediately called Patrick. 'I think we might have another hot story,' she said.

'I'll be right over.'

Lissa recovered from her show in the inner sanctum, attended by her dressers and Fabio, who began putting her back together, fussing with her hair and makeup as she changed into a slinky black dress. She felt exhausted and triumphant and happy, and she wished she could share her happiness with Michael.

Soon she was greeting the well-wishers and accepting congratulations before being whisked off to her party, which was in the Desert Millennium Princess's Infinity Room – a circular rooftop space with an unbelievable view of Las Vegas.

Surrounded by her friends, she looked around to see if she could spot Michael. Surely he was watching her? After all, it *was* his job.

Stella was carrying on about her twins. Taylor was confiding that Larry had finally agreed to help her with her movie. Kyndra was talking about the clothes Lissa had worn in her show, and how she was planning on using the same designer. And James was busy complaining about Claude.

Then she saw Michael, and everything stopped for a moment.

She caught his eye. They exchanged secret smiles, and she couldn't wait for the party to be over.

Nicci's eyelids fluttered and very slowly she began to regain consciousness. Her throat felt dry and parched and her eyes were stinging. If this was Saffron's idea of a joke, she was not amused.

She was lying on a filthy blanket in a windowless, dimly lit room. The light was coming from a weak naked bulb hanging from the high ceiling. Her limbs felt stiff and lifeless and she had a strong urge to throw up.

Shivering, she hugged her arms across her chest. It was freezing, and all she had on was a skimpy tank, low-rider jeans and combat boots.

Shit! Saffron had gone too far this time, and she wanted to put an end to it *now*!

* * *

'Lissa!'

'Antonio.'

It was a touching reunion as they faced each other after twenty years of separation.

'Allow me to present my wife, the Contessa Bianca de Morago,' Antonio said.

'It's a pleasure,' Lissa replied, shaking the Contessa's rather limp hand. 'So, Antonio,' she said, turning to her ex-husband, 'you finally did it again.'

'It took me a while,' Antonio said, flashing his whiter than white teeth. 'And now I have my beautiful Bianca beside me.'

Lissa checked the woman out. As Nicci had said, she was obviously very rich and much older than Antonio. But still, if he was happy that was the main thing, because in spite of their rocky past she bore him no ill will, and he *was* Nicci's father.

'You look wonderful, Antonio,' she said. 'You haven't changed a bit.'

'Nor have you, my exquisite one,' Antonio said. 'And your show – it was divine.'

Bianca nodded her agreement. 'You are so . . . how do I say it? Energetic?'

'Yes, I guess you could say that,' Lissa said, with a slight smile. 'It's a hard show to do. My saviour is that I have a magnificent troupe of dancers around me, and they make me look good, which is what's important.'

'So modest,' Antonio said fondly. 'My little Lissa, how well you have done.'

'I met your daughter,' Bianca said, toying with a thick diamond bracelet clamped around her wrist. 'She is lovely.'

'Yes, she is,' Lissa agreed, smiling proudly at Antonio. 'We did one thing right, didn't we?'

'We certainly did,' Antonio replied.

'She looks like you,' Lissa allowed.

'Ah, but she has *your* lips,' he said, his eyes lingering on the mouth he'd once known so well.

'Is this your first trip to America?' Lissa asked, turning to Bianca.

'It is,' Bianca replied, her mammoth diamond ring catching the light. 'And I am very happy to see amazing sights such as Las Vegas.'

'This isn't typical of America,' Lissa said, remembering her discussion with Michael about everyone being fat. 'You'll have to spend time in L.A. Bring Bianca up to the house, Antonio. I'll throw a dinner for the two of you.'

'That would be very generous of you, Lissa,' he said.

She couldn't help wondering if he was still the same old womanizer he'd always been. Probably. Leopards never changed their spots, and neither did Antonio.

And as they stood talking, Lynda Richter bore down on them. An imposing woman in a bright orange patterned dress and rhinestone-studded spectacles. 'I'm introducing myself,' she said in a loud voice. 'Lynda Richter. Evan's mother. Your soon-to-be son-in-law.'

'Oh,' Lissa said politely. 'Nicci's told me all about you.'

'Seems like a nice enough girl,' Lynda said, her voice getting louder. 'Too independent, but that'll change when they're married.'

'It will?' Lissa said, frowning.

'I must say that your show was quite something,' Lynda continued, oblivious to Lissa's frown. 'I don't know where you get the energy at your age to do all those things you do on stage. You must have been an acrobat in another life.'

'Not quite,' Lissa said, hardly warming to the woman. 'I'd like to introduce Antonio and Bianca. Antonio is Nicci's father.'

Lynda peered at Antonio, noting his Mediterranean complexion. 'Are you foreign?' she asked.

'Foreign?' Antonio said, puzzled.

'Antonio is Spanish,' Lissa said.

'I didn't know that,' Lynda said. 'Evan never told me there was mixed blood in the family.'

'Well, now you know,' Lissa said. How dare she make a thing about Antonio being Spanish? What kind of attitude was that?

'I'm here by myself,' Lynda announced. 'So, since we're going to be relatives,' she added, holding onto Antonio's arm, '*you* can look after me.'

Lissa was rescued by James. 'Meet my new friend,' he said, with an imperious toss of his head.

'And who might that be?' Lissa asked, noting the trim young blond man standing beside him.

'This is Kane, the magician.'

'Hi, Kane,' Lissa said.

'Kane is headlining at the Rio,' James announced. 'We have a mutual friend, so I looked him up, and here we are.'

'Where's Claude?' Lissa asked, remembering James's vow to get his revenge.

'Who knows?' James said with a dismissive shrug. 'And quite frankly, my dear, who cares?'

Michael circled the party, his eyes ever alert. He would never be able to fit into this kind of lifestyle. All these high-powered people, the women dripping in diamonds and dressed to the hilt, the men talking business deals and movie grosses. It was a whole different scene.

A couple of the women came on to him. One was an extremely thin TV actress whom he immediately recognized. 'And who are you?' she asked, giving him an appraising once-over with her flinty eyes.

'Security,' he said.

'You can check *my* security any time you want,' she said, with a thin smile. 'What are you up to later?'

'Busy,' he said.

'Are you turning me down?' she said, surprise written all over her pointy face.

Why was it that whenever he said no to a woman she got insulted? 'I'm afraid so,' he said. 'Got a wife and three kids at home.'

'Oh,' she said. He waited for her to add, 'You don't know what you're missing,' but she was too smart for that.

Ignoring him, she walked away on the lookout for her next victim.

'I'm leaving,' Larry said.

'It's still early,' Taylor said. 'We're in Las Vegas, Larry. Can't we play the tables?'

'I'm going back to the suite. Are you coming with me or not?'

This was not the Larry she was used to. This Larry was bad-tempered and remote. She knew what she needed to do. A session in the bedroom put a smile on his face every time.

'It seems a shame that we're only in Vegas for one night, and you're anxious to get back to the suite,' she said, touching his arm.

'You don't have to come,' he said flatly. 'You can go gamble with your friends. I don't care.'

'No, no – of course I'm coming with you,' she said quickly. 'I'll run over and say goodbye to Lissa.'

'Whatever you want, Taylor.'

I want to know why you were asking me about Oliver, she thought.

Lissa was surrounded by people. It took Taylor a while to get close to her, and when she did, she asked if she was flying back with them the next morning on Claude's plane.

'I think I'll spend an extra day here,' Lissa said off-handedly. 'I've got things to take care of.'

'The show was sensational!' Taylor enthused. 'I can't say it enough times. You deserve everything you get.'

'Thanks, Taylor.'

'And I'm truly sorry about what happened with you and Gregg. The good news is that he'll fade away, and you'll go onto bigger and better.'

I already have, Lissa thought.

Larry was waiting by the door.

'Are you all right, honey?' Taylor asked, as they headed for the elevator. 'You seem rather quiet.'

'It's funny you should ask,' he said, 'because I'm *not* all right.'

'You're not?' she asked, full of wifely concern. 'Do you think you're coming down with something?'

'No, Taylor. I'm beginning to see the light.'

'And what light would that be?' she asked, wondering what he was talking about.

'Allow me to show you something,' he said, fishing in his pocket and producing the cheque Oliver had given her. 'What's this?' he asked, waving it in front of her.

'Never seen it before,' she lied.

'It's made out to you, and it's signed by Oliver Rock.'

'Really?' she said vaguely. 'I can't imagine how that happened.'

'Taylor, you don't seem to get it. This cheque is dated *before* you even met Oliver. Why was he giving *you* money?'

'I . . . I have no idea.'

'It was in your drawer. I found it when you sent me back for your jewellery.'

'I don't appreciate you snooping through my things,' she said, trying reverse psychology.

'I wasn't *snooping*. The cheque was lying there. So what do you have to say about it? Because if *you* can't explain it to me, perhaps Oliver can.'

'Oh dear, you've caught me.' She sighed, thinking that she'd better come up with a fast explanation. 'You see, Larry, I didn't want to spoil your surprise, but, um, an agent set up a meeting with me and Oliver a while ago – *before* he made his big score. The truth is, he *did* look at my script and hated it. I didn't want to tell you, because you were so pleased about hiring him. I paid him a small amount for an evaluation, and since he didn't do any work on the script, I asked for my money back. That's all there is to it.' A short pause, then, 'What did you think? That I was having an affair with him?'

Larry stared at her. 'Why didn't you tell me before?'

'I should've. I was being stupid.' She took his hand. 'Now, *please*, can we go back to our suite, climb into our sumptuous oval bed with the mirrored ceiling, and let me show you *exactly* how much fun Vegas can be?'

Eric Vernon sat in a poky, smelly room with Arliss and Little Joe. There was nothing much in it except a few chairs, a big wooden table and a TV. Big Mark had gone to work and would return later. Davey was getting rid of the car.

So far, all had gone smoothly, and Eric was satisfied. Although now was the time he could not afford for anything to go wrong.

For a moment there it had been touch and go as to whether Nicci would come home or not. As much as Eric had studied her movements and routines, there was always a wild card. Brian Richter had turned out to be the wild card – sniffing around the girl like a dog in heat.

Finally Brian had brought Nicci home, and Eric had experienced an inward sigh of relief, because it wouldn't do to let the morons he was stuck in the car with suspect that he'd been nervous she wouldn't show.

Surprisingly Big Mark and Little Joe had handled the snatch like professionals. They'd had her in the trunk of the car within minutes. And when they'd reached the building, Big Mark had carried her in through the gloomy and deserted underground car park without a hitch.

Now they had her locked in the room Arliss had set up. And all Eric had to do was contact the bitch mother and demand the ransom.

With any luck he'd be on a plane within twenty-four hours.

Chapter Forty

Detective Fanny Webster had been stuck with an unfortunate name. Christened Frances, she'd been called Fanny from a very early age. It was okay as a kid, but now as a homicide detective, and one of great repute, she hated her name.

Fanny was a skinny woman in her forties, with a Jennifer Lopez ass – another thing she hated – and swollen ankles. She had short, reddish hair that always looked as if it needed combing, clothes that always seemed to need pressing, and a big friendly smile. Her smile was her greatest asset. It drew people in, persuading them to tell her everything.

The one thing Fanny hated more than anything else was violence against women. And she saw it all the time. The wife beaten to death with a baseball bat. The girlfriend shot in the head. The little kids, sexually abused and tortured. Fanny had never grown immune to violence, and the day she inspected Pattie's body hanging from the shower rail in her bathroom with her throat slit, she felt nothing but sadness.

What was it that drove people to commit such fiendish acts of violence? She didn't know, but she certainly knew that she was very adept at catching them.

The first thing she did after her team went to work was question everyone in the apartment building. Nobody seemed to know anything, including the Mahoneys.

'You heard no screaming? Saw no strangers coming in the day before yesterday? Nothing like that?' Fanny asked, making notes in a weathered notebook.

Both of them shook their heads. 'I usually have the TV turned up loud,' Mr Mahoney admitted. 'My hearing's not as sharp as it was.'

'I see,' Fanny said. 'And you, Mrs Mahoney? Did you hear anything unusual?'

'No,' Mrs Mahoney said. 'Except—'

'Yes, what?'

'Well, somebody did ring my doorbell.'

'Who was it? Do you know?'

'It was a man. He was asking for Pattie.'

This was exactly the kind of information Fanny was looking for. 'Do you happen to know who it was?'

'I'm not nosy,' Mrs Mahoney said, a touch priggishly. 'Nobody would call me a nosy neighbour, because as far as I'm concerned, people have to do what they have to do, and it's not my place to interfere. But . . . I did take a look through the peephole.'

'You did?'

'Yes, and I saw the man.'

'Can you describe him?'

'He had one of those forgettable faces. And he was sort of medium height and build, with brownish hair. I didn't think anything of it, because,' Mrs Mahoney lowered her voice, 'she *has* had gentlemen callers before.'

'A lot?'

'No. She was mostly alone, always playing her music too loud. She worked in the bar around the corner, you know.'

'Yes, I do know that, Mrs Mahoney. Sam's the one who put out an alert she was missing.'

'Nice man, Sam,' Mrs Mahoney remarked. 'We don't go in his bar much, but since it's around the corner, we try to pop in on special occasions.' She lowered her voice again.

409

'He has topless girls working there. *She* was one of them. I don't think that's right, do you?'

'I'm meeting with Sam shortly,' Detective Webster said. 'If I showed you some pictures, do you think you could recognize the man who was here?'

'I might,' Mrs Mahoney said, puffed up with her own importance. 'Does that mean you want to take me down to the station and show me a book of mug shots?'

'Perhaps,' Fanny said. 'You've been very helpful. There's nothing else you can think of that's unusual?'

'No, that's all. I was wondering why he rang *my* bell. Of course, they're not marked downstairs. I've told my husband he should mark them, but he never gets around to it. Too busy watching TV.'

'I know what you mean,' Fanny said, giving her the friendly smile.

'Men,' Mrs Mahoney said. 'They're a lazy lot.'

'Right,' Fanny said. She was actually a lesbian, so she couldn't care less whether men were lazy or not.

She checked in on her team again. The photographer and the fingerprint boys had done their job, so had the DNA expert. Everything had been done that had to be done, and the body had already been taken away. There would definitely be an autopsy on this one.

Fanny wandered around the small depressing apartment. Pattie was into old-fashioned music. There were several Neil Diamond and Barry Manilow CDs. She was not exactly up to date with her musical tastes.

Fanny picked up a picture of Pattie with a tall boy in a Marine uniform. Brother or boyfriend? Who knew? Who cared? Did Pattie have anyone who cared about her?

Now Fanny had the job of calling the parents if they were still alive.

Methodically, she went through the kitchen drawers, finding nothing of interest. Then she spotted a trash bin jammed in next to the fridge. She emptied out the contents. The usual paraphernalia. Dirty Kleenex, chocolate wrappers, an empty Sparkletts bottle, two Diet Coke cans, and some crumpled pieces of paper.

Fanny smoothed out the papers on the table. There were several drafts of a letter to someone called Eric. And, judging by the tone of the letters, Eric was someone that Pattie had obviously liked a lot.

Eric . . . The name stuck in Fanny's mind. She had a strong suspicion that he might be the man she was looking for. Now all she had to do was find out where he lived, and she'd bring him in for questioning.

That shouldn't be too hard, should it?

Chapter Forty-one

Exhaustion swept over Lissa like a wave. She'd had enough. She managed to catch Michael's eye and signal that it was time to leave. He headed towards her at the same time as Evelyn and Walter Burns. They all reached her together.

'Fabulous!' Evelyn enthused. 'Fabulous! Fabulous!' She was clad in a too-tight red cocktail dress, black fishnet stockings, four-inch, red ankle-strap shoes, an abundance of rubies, and a long sable stole. 'Did you get my present?' she asked anxiously.

'Thanks so much,' Lissa said, wondering how she was supposed to dispose of twenty pairs of hooker shoes.

Walter began telling her how sensational he thought her show was.

Evelyn turned to Michael. 'Did *you* get my present?' she asked, in a low voice, a mischievous smile playing around her over-glossed lips.

'Your present?' he questioned.

'Cindy,' she said, winking. 'I know you're supposed to be working, but a little hanky-panky never hurt anyone, and Cindy deserved a treat.'

So *that*'s where Cindy had come from. 'Oh, yeah – thanks.'

'Thanks! Is that all I get?' she said, edging nearer and giving him a sexy look.

This was all he needed, the wife of the owner of the hotel coming on to him. He'd met men like Walter Burns before – Walter would think nothing of crushing anyone he thought disrespected him.

He quickly turned to Lissa. 'I'm afraid I've gotta get you out of here,' he said. 'You have a phone interview to Australia in your suite.'

'I do?' she said.

'Max arranged it.'

'Oh, yes, right,' she said, catching on.

'I thought I was teaching you to play craps,' Evelyn wailed. 'I promise you'll win.'

'Another time,' Lissa said.

'Maybe later?' Evelyn questioned, ever hopeful.

'I'll let you know.'

It took Michael twenty-five minutes to move her through the crowded room towards the door. Everyone wanted a piece of her. Men *and* women.

They finally made it to the private elevator. Once the doors closed, she sighed with relief. 'It's over!' she said. 'Thank God!'

'I don't know how you do it,' he said.

'Stamina,' she answered, smiling. 'Besides, it's what I've always done, I'm used to it.'

'I don't mean the show, I mean socializing with all those people.'

'Some of them are nice,' she said, leaning forward and pressing the stop button. The elevator ground to a halt between floors.

'What are you doing?' he asked.

'Fulfilling the fantasy I've been imagining all night.'

'And that is—'

'*You*, Michael,' she said softly, reaching over to touch his face. 'Why wait until we get upstairs?'

He was instantly hard; she had that effect on him.

413

'Hey,' he said, reaching up and blocking the tiny security camera with a packet of book matches. 'Who am I to argue?'

And then they fell into each other's arms, hungry for everything they could get.

Saffron was in a mild fury. How many times had she told Nicci about the bachelorette night? How many times had she warned her to be prepared for anything?

And now here she was, standing outside Nicci's door with a limo filled with three girlfriends ready to rock, and Nicci was nowhere in sight.

'Dammit!' she complained. 'Where *is* the bitch?'

Kimberly jumped out of the limo and joined her at the front door. 'Maybe she went for a swim and drowned,' she said helpfully. 'Her car's here, so she must be in the house . . . or the pool. Whatever.'

Saffron threw Kimberly – a friend from high school – a withering look, ever since she'd been dating that writer guy she'd become even more stupid. Saffron wished she'd gone with her original idea and invited gay guys only. They were far less trouble and double the fun.

Still . . . perhaps she *should* check the pool.

Trailed by Kimberly, she walked around to the back.

Pool. Empty.

A glass door overlooking the pool was unlocked, so she let herself into the house and began calling Nicci's name. Then she did a quick check of the house. Nobody home.

House. Empty.

By the front door she discovered a shopping bag full of CDs from a record store in Santa Barbara. And next to it Nicci's purse, containing her wallet with everything in it, driver's licence, credit cards, money, phone, a picture of the two of them with Lulu.

Something wasn't right, Nicci never went anywhere

without her purse; it was like her security blanket. If she didn't have her phone and credit cards, she claimed she couldn't function.

'Where d'you think she is?' Kimberly asked.

'Dunno,' Saffron said. 'But I got a weird feelin' somethin's not right.'

Danny was tired, however, he was not too tired to hit the casino again when the party was finally over. Why waste time sitting in his room when he could be out experiencing exciting adventures in Las Vegas?

He sat at the roulette table until he'd lost the five hundred dollars he'd won the night before. Then, depressed, he left the table and reluctantly went upstairs.

He wasn't in his room five minutes before the phone rang. Lissa had not wanted any direct calls going to her suite, so everything was routed through him. He picked it up, and a muffled voice mumbled words he couldn't make out. 'What?' he said impatiently. 'Speak up.'

'Get me Lissa Roman.'

'I'm sorry, who is calling?'

The voice got louder. 'This is an emergency regarding her daughter.'

'An emergency?' Danny said officiously. 'In that case you can tell me. I'm Miz Roman's personal assistant.'

'Get me Lissa,' the muffled voice repeated. 'Otherwise Nicci will die.'

'Oh, my God,' Danny said, his heart jumping into his throat. This was obviously a matter for security. 'Wait a minute,' he said into the phone, and on the other line he buzzed Michael's room. There was no answer.

Damn! What should he do now? He didn't want to wake Lissa, she'd be asleep by this time, and yet . . . He was not equipped to deal with such a call, he needed advice. He tried Chuck's room, also getting no answer.

Wasn't one of them supposed to be on duty looking after her? This was a horrible situation to find himself in.

He picked up the phone again, taking it off hold. 'Who are you?' he asked, his voice quavering.

'It doesn't matter who I am,' the muffled voice said. 'If she's not on the line when I call back in fifteen minutes, Nicci's one dead girl. And no cops – if anyone calls the cops, believe me, she's gone.'

Taylor had a little trick she played on Larry – she'd been doing it for the last year. Before any kind of sexual activity, she handed him a glass of fine brandy, and unbeknownst to Larry, in the amber liquid, she crushed a Viagra pill.

It worked like a charm every time. Half an hour later he was ready to go all night. And *he* thought it was because of her that he was suddenly Mr Virile. Taylor did not consider this duplicity. She considered it helping out a man who was sexually very insecure.

Fortunately she'd brought the blue diamond-shaped pills with her, and while Larry was in the bathroom, she poured them both a glass of brandy from the mini bar, crushing the pill into his. Then she changed into a peach negligee with a plunging neckline and daring slit to her thigh. Larry was into visual stimulation.

When he emerged in his pyjamas, she tried to hand him his drink. 'Don't want it,' he said brusquely.

Which presented her with a dilemma. She could still get him hard, but not rock hard the way the Viagra made him, and unfortunately, he wouldn't have any staying power.

This was not good. Tonight she wanted the sex to be special.

'Come lie beside me,' she murmured, lounging back on the circular bed.

'What?' he replied, still in a bad mood.

'Come over here, Larry, and let's relax.'

He did so, and once more she handed him the glass of brandy. This time he took it, and she toasted him with hers, clinking glasses. 'We should celebrate you becoming involved with my movie,' she murmured. 'It's exciting for me, and I know you'll probably think I'm crazy, only it's kind of *sexually* exciting too.' As she spoke she allowed the strap on her negligee to slip, exposing her left breast. 'The thought of us working together is making me hot, Larry,' she whispered. 'Hot and sexy. Maybe it's time to play one of our games.'

Their games were another device she used to keep Larry interested. She would pretend to be someone else, and he'd do the same. She'd noticed that when he adopted the role of the plumber or repairman, he could become quite aggressive.

'I think I'll be a Vegas hooker tonight,' she said lightly. 'How about you? What will your role be?'

'I'm not in the mood for games, Taylor,' he said. But she could tell he was weakening.

'It doesn't matter,' she said, turning on her side, revealing even more flesh. 'We can lie here, watching ourselves in the overhead mirror, and enjoy our drinks.'

He sipped his brandy, his eyes straying towards her exposed breasts.

Hmm . . . she thought. *Not in the mood for games, huh? Give me half an hour and you'll be all mine.*

Claude St Lucia was not a man to be trifled with. As far as he was concerned, James's behaviour was unacceptable. Running all over the place with that magician person. Flaunting him in front of their friends. It was humiliating.

Claude left the party and went to his suite, where he immediately contacted his pilot. 'We leave in an hour,' he said. 'Have the plane ready. I'll meet you at the airport.' Then he called one of his assistants in L.A. 'I'm coming back tonight,' he informed the young man. 'Alert Mr and Mrs Singer, the Domingos, and the Rossiters. Tell them if they wish to fly back with me to L.A., they should be at the airport in an hour. If they prefer to stay, I understand.'

'Where will I find them?' the assistant asked.

'That's for you to discover,' Claude said, and hung up.

James and he had been together for ten years.

He was beginning to get the feeling that ten years was long enough.

'You'd better tell her, and you'd better do it the moment you get back to L.A.,' Abbey Christian said, swinging her long legs off the bed and prancing across the room quite naked.

'I can't tell her the moment I walk into the house,' Evan objected, staring at Abbey's buff body. 'We're supposed to be married in two weeks.'

'So I found out,' Abbey said, a bitter twist to her America's-sweetheart mouth. 'When *were* you going to tell me, Evan? Or was it your plan to string me along until I finished your movie?'

'Since Nicci isn't here, I didn't think I had to deal with it until I got back,' Evan explained.

'She's *living* in your house,' Abbey exploded, her small nipples disturbingly erect. 'You're *supposed* to be getting married in two weeks, and you didn't *think* you'd have to deal with it?' Her voice rose even higher. 'It's a good job Brian filled me in, isn't it?'

Evan could kill his goddamn brother. If there was one person who should have understood, it was Brian. But no, as soon as Brian found out, he'd run straight to Abbey and blabbered about Nicci. If Brian hadn't done that, Abbey would never have known. They would have got back to L.A. and he would have eased out of the affair, because he *did* want to marry Nicci – she was a far better candidate than Abbey Christian, who was a movie star, a coke-head *and* a lunatic.

Evan was having the greatest sex of his life. But great sex did not make Abbey a suitable bride.

Now Brian had ruined everything. Probably because he was pissed off *he* wasn't banging her. And to hold the movie together, Evan had been forced to pretend he was dumping Nicci and staying with Abbey. Fortunately, she hadn't mentioned marriage.

If his mother ever got an eyeful of Abbey Christian, she'd throw a fit. Abbey was a total raving nymphomaniac.

'Once you've told her, you can come stay at my beach house for a few days,' Abbey decided. 'You don't want to be around while she packs up and gets out.'

'I *have* to go back to my house,' he said. 'My mother's there.'

'What's *she* doing in your house?' Abbey asked rudely.

'She flew out for the wedding.'

'Well, send her back to where she came from,' Abbey snapped, used to getting her own way.

'I can't send my mother back,' he objected. 'I haven't told her the wedding's off.'

'Fucking *tell* her,' Abbey said, walking into the bathroom. 'Or *I* will.'

'No, Abbey. I'll do it myself.'

They were leaving the Utah location tomorrow, and after that they had six weeks of shooting in L.A. Six long weeks, and he'd better string Abbey along until then, otherwise she'd cause chaos, and he couldn't risk any delays on the movie.

What to do about Nicci, that was the problem. He might have to postpone the wedding. Yes, to save the film he might just have to do that.

In the meantime, he may as well take advantage of the phenomenal sex.

* * *

'Hi – Brian?'

'Yeah?' he said, picking up the phone. 'Who's this?'

'Saffron. Nicci's friend.'

'Oh, hi,' he said, wondering what she wanted.

'Remember, we met at the dinner party up at your brother's house?'

''Course I do. Why aren't you out with Nicci? I thought this was your big celebration night?'

'That's why I'm calling. I thought Nicci might be with you.'

'Why would she be with me? She's been carrying on about her bachelorette party all week.'

'That's what I don't get,' Saffron said, sounding puzzled. 'I'm at the house now and she isn't here.'

'What do you mean, she isn't there? I dropped her off late this afternoon.'

'You did?'

'Yeah,' Brian said. 'She was all excited.'

'She's not here now. I went around the back, and let myself in. Found her purse.'

'So?'

'Nicci never moves without her purse. And it's lying on the floor by the front door.' A beat. 'Brian, I kinda got this premonition that something bad has happened.'

'No way.'

'Then where is she?'

He thought for a moment, remembering their conversation about Evan. 'She might've gotten on a plane and gone to see Evan.'

'You think?'

'That could be it,' he said. 'She was upset about some shit between them.'

'Can you check it out?' Saffron asked. ''Cause this isn't like Nicci, she wouldn't hang me up.'

'I'll call Evan right now and get back to you.'
'Thanks. I'll be waitin'.'

'So,' Lissa said, 'what was it you wanted to tell me this morning, Michael?'

They were lying in bed, comfortable and relaxed. Not only had they made love in the elevator, but they'd also made out in the living room *and* the bedroom. Now they were sharing a huge dish of vanilla ice cream with strawberries and chocolate sauce on the side.

'There *is* something I need to tell you,' he said, loath to break the mood. 'It's something that happened before us, if there *is* such a thing as us.'

'Of course there is,' she said, dipping a strawberry in the chocolate sauce and feeding it to him. 'Whatever you might think, this is *not* a weekend fling.'

'I hope not,' he said, 'although watching you tonight, I couldn't help thinking how far apart we are.'

'Far apart how?'

'Everything.'

'Hmm . . .' she said, reaching for another strawberry. 'Do you enjoy going to movies?'

'Yeah.'

'Watching ball games?'

'I'm a big Lakers fan.'

'What kind of music are you into?'

'I'm easy.'

'You see,' she said triumphantly. 'We're *totally* compatible. Occasionally I have to work, the rest of the time I'm completely there for you doing all the things *you* like to do.'

'You're a sweetheart,' he said.

'I'm not such a sweetheart. I'm just happy I found you.'

'You found *me*, did you?' he said, raising a cynical eyebrow.

She smiled. 'Sorta. Kinda.'

'Anyway,' he said, wanting to get the bad news over with, 'd'you remember I mentioned I was about to give someone the break-up speech?'

'Yes,' she said, dipping her finger in the chocolate sauce.

'Well, here's the deal – just as I was getting ready to tell her that we were definitely over, she suddenly informs me she's pregnant.'

'Pregnant,' Lissa repeated dully. This was the last thing she'd expected to hear.

'It's mine,' he said. 'I'll take a blood test, of course, but I know it's mine.'

She was silent for a moment, filled with mixed feelings. Why did this have to happen now? Why couldn't anything go smoothly? 'What will you do?' she asked.

'Carol doesn't want anything from me, not even financial support, although I *will* support the baby,' he said, reaching for a cigarette. 'Do you mind if I smoke?'

'Go ahead, poison yourself.'

'You see,' he said seriously, 'Carol and I are over, so it's not a problem, is it?'

'Depends what you regard as a problem,' she said coolly, trying to figure out how she really felt.

He stared at her intently. 'I had to be up front with you, Lissa, didn't I? No secrets.'

'I appreciate your honesty,' she said, 'and I know it's not an easy situation for you, especially in view of what happened before with Bella.'

'Right,' he said, lighting up. 'But being here with you has made things so much better.'

'I'm glad,' she said softly. 'Because I have a feeling you and I were meant to be.'

'Yeah?' he said, trying not to blow smoke in her direction.

'Yes,' she said. 'But if we're going to keep seeing each

other, we can't keep it under wraps. We have to be out in the open.'

'I got a hunch you're not a hot dog and movie kind of girl,' he said. 'Too many people bugging you for your autograph.'

'I think you're forgetting.'

'What?'

She couldn't help smiling. 'My famous disguise.'

'Oh,' he said, grinning. '*That*'ll be a kick, going out with you in your wig and glasses. I can just see me taking you over to Quincy's and saying, "Hey, meet my new girlfriend. She's a little strange." '

Lissa started to laugh. 'There *will* be problems,' she warned. 'However, *I* think we've got a lot going for us.'

'I dunno,' he said unsurely. 'You're famous, you live in a different world from mine. And now there's this baby thing.'

'We can deal with it, Michael. I promise we can. And as far as *we're* concerned, well, you're not like Gregg. He wanted everything from me, even expected me to make him a star. We did not have a healthy relationship. But you and me—'

'I hate to interrupt,' he said, 'but I can hear someone hammering at the door.'

'I put a "Do Not Disturb" on the phone *and* the door,' she said. 'Who would dare disturb me?'

'I'm sure someone's knocking,' he said, getting out of bed and reaching for a hotel robe. 'I'll go take a look.'

'You have a great butt,' she said playfully. 'Why is it that men always have better butts than women?'

'Hey, *you*'ve got nothing to complain about,' he said, walking through the living room to the door of the suite.

Somebody *was* banging on the door and calling, 'Lissa! Miz Roman, I have to speak to you. It's Danny! It's urgent!'

Jesus! Here he was in a robe and Danny was outside the door.

He hurried back into the bedroom. 'It's your assistant,' he said. 'Should I see what he wants? He's yelling about it being urgent.'

'What can be so urgent?'

'Who knows? Maybe you'd better go yourself.'

'You're right,' she said, jumping out of bed and reaching for her own robe. 'If Danny catches you here, he'll tell everyone. You stay put, I'll be right back.' She hurried to the door and flung it open. 'Danny,' she said crossly. 'What the *hell* are you doing here? It's late and I was asleep, and in case you haven't noticed, there is a "Do Not Disturb" on my door. This better be *very* important.'

Danny almost fell into the living room. 'It is,' he said. 'Somebody's threatening to kill Nicci.'

Chapter Forty-two

'She's awake,' Little Joe said.

'How do you know?' Eric asked.

''Cause I took a gander through the peephole.'

'What's she doing?'

'Sittin' on the mattress,' Little Joe said, scratching his head. 'She's pretty,' he added. 'What's her name?'

'It doesn't matter what her name is,' Eric said guardedly. 'You'd better get some sleeping pills down her. We need to keep her sedated.'

'How'm I supposed t' do that?' Little Joe whined.

'Your problem,' Eric snapped. 'That's what you're getting paid for.' He was so sick of this group of losers. And glad that he'd made the decision not to pay them. They didn't deserve shit.

Arliss had gone to pick up food. Big Mark wouldn't return until later when he finished work. Davey was due back any minute.

In the meantime, Little Joe better take care of her, because Eric sure as hell wasn't going anywhere near her. He didn't want her picking *his* face out of a line-up if it ever came down to it. 'Get moving,' he said to Little Joe. He wanted him out of the way before he made the second phone call. If any of them suspected the kind of ransom he was demanding, they'd want more.

Not that it made any difference, because what they were getting was absolutely nothing.

Nicci couldn't believe that Saffron would pull a stunt like this. It was the most bizarre thing she'd ever heard of. And any moment now, some horny stud dressed up as a prison guard would come walking in and start taking it off.

Damn! This was *so* not a good idea. She was freezing cold and starving hungry, and she could cheerfully *murder* her inventive friend. This was *way* over the top.

When the door was pushed open, she was prepared. It could be George fucking Clooney or Brad fucking Pitt, and she'd tell them to put their fucking clothes on and get lost, because she'd *had* it.

It wasn't George or Brad, it was a short, pop-eyed man, in brown trousers and a sickly maroon sweater. And he looked nervous as hell.

'Jesus!' Nicci said. 'If you dare take one item of clothing off, I am *so* kicking you in the balls!'

The man's expression was stunned.

'Tell Saffron the game is *over*,' she said, getting up and heading for the door.

Little Joe was galvanized into action. He might be short, but he was strong. He stopped her at the door, blocking her way with his sturdy bulk.

'Get out of my way,' she said threateningly. 'I don't care *how* much Saffron is paying you, the game is *fucking* over!'

'That's not nice language for a girl,' Little Joe said. 'You go back over there.'

She attempted to push past him.

'Get back over there,' he repeated, his eyes almost popping out his head.

'Don't you fucking tell *me* what to do,' she said angrily. 'I've had enough! Doesn't anyone understand English?'

'This is n-not a game,' Little Joe stammered.

She made another move to push past him. This time he shoved her so hard that she fell back across the room.

'You'd better stay quiet,' he warned, his eyes still popping alarmingly. 'Eric won't like it if you make a fuss.'

She picked herself up, shocked. 'Who's Eric?'

'The boss,' Little Joe said. 'We do what *he* says, an' you do what *we* say.'

'Where's Saffron?'

'There's no Saffron,' Little Joe said. 'You're our prisoner, but not for long.'

'Your *prisoner*?' she said, feeling fear for the first time. 'What *is* this?'

'You've been kidnapped,' Little Joe explained. 'And when they pay, Eric will let you go.'

'*What?*'

'Don't be nervous,' he said, staring at her exposed strip of stomach between her brief tank top and low-rider jeans. 'You're pretty. Nothin' to worry about.'

'Oh my God!' she gasped, suddenly feeling dizzy. 'I think I'm gonna throw up.'

Brian reached Evan, who was not at all happy to hear from him. 'What do you want?' he said nastily.

'I'm looking for Nicci,' Brian said.

'Very funny,' Evan said.

'No, really. Is she there?'

'Of course she's not, and I can't talk now.'

'Why? You in bed with Abbey?'

'None of your business, Brian.'

'Hey, you should be thanking me – I'm calling to give you a heads up. Nicci's probably on her way there.'

'What're you talking about?'

'Saffron came by to pick her up for her bachelorette night and she was gone. We think she's on her way to see you.'

'Christ!' Evan said. 'Are you serious?'

'Unless you know where she is.'

'Shit!'

'Call me when she gets there,' Brian said. 'Saffron's worried.'

'What's *she* worried about?'

'In case Nicci's *not* on her way to you. We don't know where she is.'

'She probably flew to Vegas to see her mother.'

'No. She was with me all day. When I took her home she was all excited about her night out with Saffron.'

'What was she doing with *you* all day?'

'We had breakfast, that's about it.'

'Breakfast took all day?'

'We drove to Santa Barbara.'

'Jesus Christ, Brian,' Evan complained, 'do you think you can keep your hands off *my* fiancée?'

'Sure. I'll keep my hands off her, when *you* keep your hands off Abbey.'

'Fuck you,' Evan said.

'No,' Brian said. 'Fuck *you!*' And he slammed down the phone. A few minutes later he called Saffron. 'She's not there,' he said. 'She could be on her way.'

'I'm phoning Lissa in Vegas,' Saffron said. 'I got a bad feeling, Brian.'

'D'you want me to come over?'

'Yeah – I'm still at her house.'

'I'll be right there.'

'Cool. I'll see you in a minute.'

Patrick arrived at Belinda's and headed straight for the bar.

'What do you think?' Belinda asked. 'Is it time to call a lawyer?'

Patrick was chuckling to himself as he fixed himself a Jack Daniel's on the rocks. 'You sure know how to pick 'em,' he said.

'What's *that* supposed to mean?' Belinda inquired, wondering why her ex-boyfriend was in such a jovial mood.

'I've just come from the police station,' Patrick said, downing a shot. 'Guess what Gregg was arrested for?'

'What?' she asked curiously.

'Attempted rape.'

'Rape?' she said blankly.

'Yup,' Patrick said, laughing aloud. 'Your boyfriend was caught with his pants down.'

'Who was he trying to rape?' Belinda asked, shocked.

'Remember that personal shopper you fixed him up with?'

'Deidra?'

'She's the one,' he said, happily swigging Jack Daniel's. 'Seems your boyfriend attacked her in the dressing room at Barneys. Can you friggin' believe it?'

'No, I can't,' she said, sitting down on an overstuffed couch.

'Yeah, she ran out of the dressing room screaming rape, an' someone called the cops. She pressed charges, an' now he's in jail. I've got a photographer on stand-by and the story is all set to go. Forget about that crap with Lissa's diary. This is bigger and better.'

'Better than twenty-five grand?' Belinda asked.

'Sure,' Patrick said, sitting down beside her. 'You'll make plenty, 'cause I'm cuttin' a deal for you to tell everything.'

'What is *everything*?' she asked, alarmed.

'Bedroom details of your life with this loser.'

'I can't do that, Patrick,' she said, thinking of the ramifications. 'I'm a public figure, I'm on TV, for crissakes.'

'Here's the sweet thing,' Patrick said, edging closer. 'The story won't come from you. It'll be a series of quotes from a close friend, someone who'll come up with all the details. So, *you*'ll be clean, *we* get the money, an' the story flies. I've already spoken to Deidra – I'm buying her story, too. This is *very* sweet, darlin'.'

'Patrick,' Belinda said admiringly, 'you're such an operator.'

He planted a quick kiss on her cheek. 'Takes one to know one.'

'Fix *me* a drink,' she said, with a smile. 'I never thought Gregg was a keeper. He *was* good in the sack, though.'

''S good as me?' Patrick asked, with a cocky leer.

'According to *you*,' Belinda said, still smiling, '*nobody*'s as good as you.'

He snickered. 'Listen,' he said, 'here's the problem. If you bail him out, he'll try t' come here, an' I don't think you want that. So you gotta act like the disgusted girlfriend an' dump him. We'll stash his luggage at a hotel. I'll spring him, an' tell him the bad news. In the meantime, you'd better change your locks.'

'He doesn't have a key.'

'Always knew you were a smart one.'

'This could be another hoax,' Michael said, pacing around the room. 'Like the death-threat letter.'

'You think so?' Lissa asked hopefully.

'We'll soon find out,' he said, desperate for a cigarette. 'Where is Nicci tonight?'

Lissa tried to think clearly. 'It was her bachelorette party, so she'll be out somewhere with Saffron.'

'You got Saffron's number?'

'No, but Kyndra will have it.'

'Okay, we've got to stay calm here. Danny, have all calls re-routed to this room.'

Danny nodded, white-faced.

'Lissa,' Michael continued, 'you have to realize that this could turn out to be nothing. The important thing is finding Nicci and talking to her.'

'Yes,' she said weakly. 'I understand.'

'She'll be fine. I'm sure of it.'

'What if she's not?' Lissa asked, starting to panic. 'What if somebody's got her?'

'It's unlikely,' Michael said. 'Danny, get on the phone and find out Saffron's number. Use line two. Meanwhile, I'll try reaching Nicci. You have her number?'

Danny nodded.

'Lissa, I want you to take a few deep breaths and try to relax. I've dealt with situations like this before. The main thing is to stay in control.'

Danny was already on the phone to Kyndra, getting Saffron's number.

'The man who called told Danny he'd get back to you in fifteen minutes,' Michael said, glancing at his watch. 'That's in approximately four minutes' time. I'm putting you on speaker-phone, Lissa. You'll listen to what he has to say, and we'll take it from there. Can you do that?'

'You're almost sure it's a hoax, aren't you?' she whispered, her face pale.

'Yes,' he said, trying Nicci's cellphone.

A girl's voice answered.

'Nicci?' he said, relieved.

'Who's this?'

'You don't know me. I'm Michael Scorsinni – your mother's security. She wants a word with you.'

'This isn't Nicci, it's Saffron.'

'Saffron, can you put Nicci on? Lissa wants to speak to her.'

'I don't know where she is.'

'Isn't she with you?'

'No, she's not, and I'm kinda worried.'

'About what?'

'Well, I'm at her house – we were supposed to go out tonight – and when I arrived to pick her up, she wasn't here. Brian thinks she might have flown to see Evan, only

I'm not so sure 'cause she didn't take her purse an' she never goes anywhere without her credit cards and phone. I'm on her cell now. I heard it ringing an' I ran to pick up. Something weird is going down.'

Michael felt a sinking in the pit of his stomach. This was no hoax. Something bad had happened. 'Keep that phone with you, Saffron,' he said. 'We'll get back to you.'

'Do you know where she is?'

'We're finding out.'

'Who was that?' Lissa asked, as soon as he put the phone down.

'Saffron . . . Now, don't get alarmed.'

'Where's Nicci? Why isn't she with her?' Lissa asked, the colour draining from her cheeks.

'Saffron thinks she might've flown to see Evan.'

'How do we find out?'

'Where is he?'

'On location in Utah.'

'Danny,' Michael said, 'check the airlines. See if she was booked on a flight.'

'Why would she run out on her own party?' Lissa asked. 'She was looking forward to it, that's all she's been talking about.'

Michael shrugged. 'Beats me.'

Danny was totally confused. What with the threatening phone call, and now coming in and finding Lissa and Michael in their robes, he didn't know what to make of it all. 'I'll go check the airlines,' he said, leaving the room.

When the phone rang, Michael put it on speaker and handed the receiver to Lissa. 'Stay cool,' he mouthed.

'Hello?' she said.

'Is that Lissa Roman?' a muffled voice asked.

'Who is this?' she asked, as calmly as she could.

'I'm calling about your dear daughter.'

'Where is she?'

'Don't worry, she's safe, and she'll *stay* safe as long as you come up with what I want.'

'What *do* you want?'

'Two million dollars,' the muffled voice said. 'Cash. And I want it within twenty-four hours or Nicci dies. And . . . if you call the FBI, the cops, or anyone else, she dies anyway. I'll get back to you with instructions. You'd better start getting the money together. That's if you ever want to see your daughter's face again.'

Chapter Forty-three

Just as Taylor had Larry exactly where she wanted him – primed and ready to go – the phone rang.

Taylor was furious at the interruption. Why hadn't she remembered to put a hold on all calls?

Larry reached for the phone, listened for a moment, then said, 'Yes, we'll be there.'

'Where?' Taylor asked, as he hung up.

'Claude's flying back to L.A. tonight. If we're at the airport in an hour, we can go with him.'

'I don't want to go with him,' Taylor said stubbornly.

'*I* do,' Larry replied. 'I hate it here.'

'But, darling,' she crooned persuasively, 'we were just starting to enjoy ourselves.'

'We can enjoy ourselves in L.A.,' he said, getting off the bed.

Oh, great! Now he'd have a major erection on the plane, where it would do her absolutely no good.

'Why can't we stay?' she asked.

'Because this place is tacky, Taylor,' Larry replied, already starting to dress. 'And I told you, I hate it here.'

'Well, I don't,' she murmured.

'Be ready to leave in fifteen minutes. I'll call a car.'

'Whatever,' she said sulkily. 'Are Seth and Stella coming?'

'I have no idea. Call their room.'

'I will.' She tried to reach the Rossiters: there was no answer. Then she tried the Domingos: no answer in their room either.

'They're probably all in the casino,' she said.

'What a waste of time,' Larry said. 'I can't wait to get out of here.'

So much for a night of sensual sexual pleasure. Taylor wondered if Larry's discovery of Oliver's cheque had anything to do with him wanting to leave. Was he still suspicious?

Absolutely not. There was no way he could imagine her having an affair with someone like Oliver Rock.

Downstairs in the lobby they ran into James and his new friend.

'Where are you going?' James asked, noting they were carrying their hand luggage.

'Back to L.A.,' Larry said. 'Aren't you coming?'

'Why would *I* be coming?' James drawled. 'I'm on my way to play baccarat.'

'While *you*'re playing baccarat,' Taylor said, 'Claude is waiting at the airport. He's taking off tonight.'

James's lips tightened into a thin white line. 'He is?'

'Yes,' Taylor said. 'Surely you knew?'

'I imagine he forgot to tell me,' James said, refusing to react. 'Have you met my friend, Kane, the magician?'

'Nice to meet you, Kane,' Taylor said, getting the picture. 'Any message for Claude, James?'

'Yes,' James said, in a crisp English accent. 'Tell him to go fuck himself.'

'Christ!' Gregg said, bitching and complaining all the way as he walked out of the Beverly Hills lock up. 'It took you goddamn long enough.'

'Sorry, mate,' Patrick said, his eyes darting this way and that, searching for his photographer. 'Had to get the bail money together.'

'Where's Belinda?' Gregg asked.

'May as well give you the bad news,' Patrick said. 'She doesn't want you back. You're on your own, mate.'

And at that precise moment, the photographer Patrick was looking for appeared and sprang into action, catching every nuance of Gregg's outraged expression.

Finally Nicci got it. This was no joke.

When she'd started to struggle with the short man, he'd run out of the room, slamming the door in her face and locking it so she couldn't get out.

Shit! she thought, looking around. *I really am a captive.*

There were no windows, a stone floor, a big old heavy door, a rickety cot with a stained mattress in the corner, an old blanket and a bucket. She was screwed.

How had this happened?

She shut her eyes for a moment, trying to summon all the strength she could. *Don't panic,* a little voice whispered in her head. *Stay calm. You will get out of this.*

The short man with the pop eyes had tried to force some pills into her mouth. She'd kicked him in the balls and the pills had scattered on the ground. If she'd been quicker, she might have reached the door before him, but he was fast for such an unfit-looking man. Strong and smelly, too. She wrinkled her nose in disgust.

Kidnapped. It seemed like a plot from a movie. No wonder she felt so sick, they'd obviously used something to put her out.

She remembered the big man coming to her front door and grabbing her. After that it was all a blank until she'd woken up here.

Who were they going to demand the ransom from? Her mom? Her dad? Did this have anything to do with Antonio and his rich new bride?

She was so cold she could barely think straight. The

bleak room was freezing, and the effects of the chloroform had made her feel quite sick.

She sat on the side of the filthy cot and tried to figure out what to do next.

Claude was already aboard when Taylor and Larry arrived at his plane.

'This was rather a sudden departure, wasn't it?' Taylor commented, settling into a seat.

Claude nodded abruptly. He did not wish to discuss it.

She wondered if she should impart James's message, then decided it wouldn't be a good idea.

Larry sat down and buckled up. She still hadn't got him where she wanted him. Sex would have done it but, no, he'd had to insist they fly back to L.A. with Claude.

'Anyone else coming with us?' Claude asked.

'We have no idea,' Taylor said, reaching for a magazine.

'Five minutes,' Claude said, 'and then we're leaving.'

'Fine with me,' Larry said. 'The sooner we leave this place, the better.'

'Where the fuck are you taking me?' Gregg asked, as Patrick drove along Sunset. 'And where d'you think that fucking photographer came from?'

'Beats me, mate,' Patrick said. 'Those bastards pop up everywhere.'

'Yeah,' Gregg said.

'I took the liberty of bookin' you into a hotel,' Patrick remarked. 'I got your stuff in the trunk.'

Jesus Christ, Gregg thought, *is this becoming a pattern, women throwing me out?* 'I want to talk to Belinda,' he said.

'Naw, you don't wanna do that,' Patrick said. 'She heard about the rape thing, doesn't wanna talk to you.'

'I didn't try to rape the bitch,' Gregg said angrily. 'Between you and me, I knew her before.'

'You did?' Patrick said, keeping his eyes on the road.

'I was *fucking* her, for crissakes,' Gregg admitted, 'and when I walked out on her, she was pissed. This crap is her way of getting revenge.'

'What's her name again?' Patrick asked casually.

'Deidra,' Gregg said disdainfully. 'She's some little cunt who works at Barneys. Used to be a salesgirl there.'

'Really?' Patrick said, making a mental note of Deidra's name so he could approach her for a story. 'How long were you banging her?'

'A few months. It was when Lissa and I were together. Then she started nagging like they all do, so I dumped her. And I might've said a few choice things she didn't like.'

'You screwed *her*, now she's screwin' *you*,' Patrick said, with a morbid chuckle.

'Damn right,' Gregg said, glad that someone understood the truth. 'I'm sure when I explain it to Belinda she'll understand.'

'The way *I* heard it,' Patrick ventured, 'Belinda introduced you to the girl at the house, an' you didn't know her then.'

'What was I *gonna* say?' Gregg said, totally pissed off. 'Oh, yeah, *I* know Deidra, we used to get it on. That would've gone down well.'

'I'd let Belinda cool off if I was you,' Patrick advised. 'Wouldn't try to contact her now.'

'What's happening with the paper?' Gregg asked. 'Did they come up with my price?'

'We're gonna have to put that on hold, mate, this shit has stirred up the waters a bit.'

'Doesn't anybody get it?' Gregg complained. 'I've been set up.'

'I'd call your lawyer as soon as possible,' Patrick suggested.

'You mean Belinda didn't get me a lawyer?' Gregg said, outraged.

'No, mate. I bailed you out myself.'

'Shit!' Gregg said. 'Women! You can shove 'em up your ass with bells on.'

Abbey was painting her toenails. She was nude, of course. Once the door closed, Abbey was always nude. And why not? She had quite a body.

'Were you ever a nudist?' Evan asked, wondering how he was going to tell her that Nicci might be on her way.

'No,' Abbey said, giggling. 'Can you imagine what those places must be like? All those saggy tits and hanging balls.'

'I was thinking, it might be a good idea for us to stay in *your* room tonight,' Evan said.

'Why?' she said. 'I'm perfectly happy here.'

'I got a call that Nicci might be on her way to see me.'

'Your *fiancée* Nicci?' she said, almost spilling the bottle of nail polish.

'That's the one.'

'Why is *she* coming here?' Abbey asked, a spiteful glint in her eyes.

'We haven't been getting along on the phone,' Evan explained, 'so she's probably coming to find out what's going on.'

'Good,' Abbey said, with a vindictive smile. 'You can tell her about us.'

'I will,' he promised. 'Only *you* shouldn't be in the room.'

'And why's that?'

'Because it's not a good idea.'

'*I* don't see anything wrong with it.'

'I'd prefer it if you weren't here.'

'Tough,' Abbey said, with no trace of her famous smile. 'It's you and me now, Evan. I'm in on everything. And,' she added, giving him a baleful glare, 'if you're too *scared* to tell her, *I'*ll do it.'

Evan had a strong suspicion that Abbey was going to be hard to shake.

'I think we should call Antonio,' Lissa said, her blue eyes filled with worry.

'The fewer people who know about this, the better,' Michael said. 'When the man calls back, you'll tell him that under no circumstances can you come up with the money unless you speak to Nicci first. It's very important.'

'I still think we must get Antonio here,' she said, desperately trying to stay calm. 'He *is* her father.'

'The main thing is to talk about how we should handle this,' Michael said. 'Do you want me to contact the FBI?'

'No,' she said sharply. 'You heard what he said. I'll pay the ransom, Michael.'

'Do you have two million dollars lying around in cash?'

'Of course I don't,' she said, her eyes filling with sudden tears. 'I was thinking we should go to Walter. This *is* a casino, they'll have the cash. I'll ask Walter to pay me – after all, he owes me three million so he can't argue.'

'There's no way we can bring Walter in without telling him,' Michael argued.

'I'll say it's personal.'

'The man's not a fool, Lissa, he'll suspect something's going on.'

'Then we'll bring him in on it,' she said determinedly. 'I *have* to get the cash, Michael.'

'I understand, but first you must speak to Nicci.'

'Why?'

'I don't mean to sound morbid, but how do you know he's even got her? And that she's all right?'

'What're you saying?' she asked, trying her best to stay on top of the situation without falling to pieces.

'I'm saying,' Michael said, speaking slowly, 'that we have to receive proof of life. Otherwise, there's no deal.'

Saffron and Brian hung out in the living room of Evan's house trying to figure out what could've happened.

'Nicci's not in Vegas,' Saffron said.

'She's not with Evan either,' Brian said, 'although she could be on her way.'

'Then all we can do is wait.'

'That's about it,' Brian said, getting up and walking around the room. 'You got a joint?' he asked restlessly.

'Sorry,' Saffron said, thinking she should call her babysitter and tell her she might not be back.

'I think I know where Nic keeps her stash,' Brian said, going in the bedroom. He found a bag of marijuana and some cigarette papers pushed to the back of her bedside drawer. Quickly and expertly he rolled a joint, then returned to the living room.

'Do you think it's *likely* she flew off to see Evan?' Saffron asked.

'I spent the day with her,' Brian said, taking a deep hit because he needed it. 'She was having doubts about the whole wedding scene.'

'She was?'

'Nic's a great girl,' he said, offering Saffron a hit. 'She deserves better.'

'Yeah,' Saffron said knowingly. 'I hear you two had quite a time the other night.'

'Yeah, we did. She's not only great-looking, she's also nice and fun to be with. Totally different from the girls I usually date.'

'Am I gettin' a clue you're interested?' Saffron asked, raising an eyebrow.

'C'mon,' he objected. 'She's *engaged* to my brother.'

'I didn't ask that. I asked if you were interested.'

'How do I know? She's very young.'

'Oh, like you're so old? Thirty – right? The same age as good old Evan.'

'I guess that's not so old, huh?'

'You *do* like her,' Saffron said triumphantly.

'Yeah, I do. So whaddaya goin' t' do – shoot me?'

'No way, man, I think it's cool.'

'Anyway,' he said, moving on, 'there's something about Evan I think you should know.'

'Go ahead.'

'He's screwing Abbey Christian.'

'Holy shit!' Saffron exclaimed. 'If Nicci knew this, she'd *definitely* be on the next plane to confront him.'

'Well . . . I kind of alluded to it.'

'Why'd you do that?'

''Cause I didn't think she should marry someone she wasn't sure about. And since she said she was having doubts, I gave her a hint.'

'The good news is we now know where she is,' Saffron said. 'On her way to beat the crap outta your bro.'

'You think?'

'*I* feel much better,' Saffron said. 'Let's call the hotel an' have them contact us the moment she arrives.'

'Good idea.'

'So, Brian,' Saffron said, grinning. 'Tell me how you *really* feel about our girl? I'm dying to know.'

Chapter Forty-four

Arliss returned with a brown bag of greasy hamburgers and several cartons of soggy french fries. Davey was back, so the only one missing was Big Mark.

'I got six burgers,' Arliss announced, face twitching. 'One for her.'

'This isn't a restaurant,' Eric said, hating being confined with this bunch of cretins. 'She gets nothing. I want her weak. I don't need her getting strong and trying to escape.'

'She can't escape,' Arliss boasted. 'I made that room escape-proof.'

'She's strong,' Little Joe volunteered. 'She kicked me in the nuts.'

'You shouldn't get that close,' Eric warned.

'You told me to give her the pills,' Little Joe said, foraging in the bag for a burger.

'Did you get them down her?'

'Yes,' Little Joe lied. 'It was all I could do to run outta the room an' lock the door.'

Arliss wheezed with laughter. 'This is *so* easy,' he crowed. 'We gotta do it again. It's like money for nothing.'

'Easy for *you*,' Little Joe said, sweating. '*We*'re the ones who grabbed her. Me and Big Mark.'

'And you did well,' Eric said.

'What happens next?' Arliss asked.

'All in good time,' Eric said. 'First they have to understand that she's gone, next they need to know that to get her back they'll have to pay.'

'How're you gonna swap the girl for the money?' Little Joe asked, tomato ketchup and hamburger juice dribbling down his chin. 'They could call the cops.'

'No,' Eric said. 'I told them no cops or the girl dies.'

'Dies?' Arliss said, jumping up in alarm. 'We're not gonna *kill* anybody.'

'Yeah,' Little Joe joined in. 'You never said nothin' 'bout that.'

'Because it won't happen,' Eric said calmly, his face impassive.

'What if they don't pay?' Davey asked, making snorting noises in the back of his throat.

'They will,' Eric said. *And if they don't*, he thought, *the girl dies.*

When Michael called, Antonio was not in his room.

'Do you know what Antonio looks like?' Lissa asked Danny, who'd returned with the news that he could not locate Nicci's name on any flights from L.A. to Utah.

Danny bobbed his head, anxious to do whatever he could to help. This was such a distressing situation, he hated seeing his princess so sad.

'Okay,' Michael said. 'Walk through the casino and see if you can find him.'

'He plays blackjack,' Lissa added. 'He'll probably be at one of those tables.'

'And, Danny,' Michael said, 'not a word to anyone about this. Do you understand? We're involved in a very dangerous situation, and anything you hear in this room can go no further.'

'What do I tell Mr Stone?' Danny asked.

'Tell him that Lissa has to speak to him about Nicci. If he doesn't seem inclined to leave the table, then add that it's urgent.'

'I'll go right now.'

'Can you trust him?' Michael asked, as soon as Danny left.

'Yes,' Lissa said. 'He's very trustworthy and loyal. He's worked for me for six years.'

'You're *sure* we can trust him?'

'Yes, Michael,' she said wearily. She was very close to falling to pieces, the pressure was becoming intense and she wasn't sure she could handle it.

Michael got up and put his arms around her, holding her close. She began to cry. 'Oh, God, Michael,' she sobbed, 'what am I going to do?'

'It'll be okay, baby,' he said, rocking her back and forth. 'I promise you, it'll be okay.'

'It will?' she asked.

'Here's the deal,' he said. 'First we have to find out she's okay. Then you'll pay the money, and we'll get her back. As soon as we're sure she's safe, I'll catch the motherfucker.'

'Thank God you're here with me.' She sighed. 'I don't know what I'd do if I was by myself.'

'I'll *always* be here with you, Lissa,' he said, holding her close. 'There's no getting rid of me now.'

She hugged him. He was so strong and big and handsome. Somehow she knew she would always feel safe with him beside her.

Nicci could swear someone was watching her. She'd noticed a crude peephole in the door, and whenever an eye blocked it, she could tell.

'Whoever you are,' she yelled, 'I'm ready to get the hell out of here. If you let me go right now, I won't press

445

charges. I swear to God I won't. 'Cause you *do* know that kidnapping's a federal offence. So, whoever you are, you'd better let me go.'

She jumped up, ran over and gave the locked door a hearty kick. The eye vanished.

'Asshole,' she muttered to herself.

She wasn't frightened, she was angry. She'd removed the filthy blanket from the cot in the corner and wrapped it around her shoulders for warmth, although she still couldn't stop shivering.

She wondered if she could make a run for it the next time someone opened the door. Perhaps there was only one guy – the short, fat, smelly one. Then she remembered the other one, the big scary man in the mask who'd burst into the house and grabbed her. Where was he now? A couple of years ago she'd taken a self-defence course with Saffron. Unfortunately she could hardly remember anything she'd learned. *Kick 'em in the balls*, that was the main thing. And yet it hadn't seemed to bother the little runt who'd tried to force the sleeping pills down her throat.

She looked around for the pills and discovered three of them on the floor. They were Halcion, a strong sleeping pill. A cockroach scampered past, grazing her hand, and she almost screamed.

Fuck! she thought, staring at the pills. Is that what they're trying to do to me? Keep me sedated so I won't cause any trouble?

She kicked the door again. 'Help!' she yelled. 'Help! Somebody help me! I'm trapped. Get me out of here. *Help! Help!*'

Instinctively she knew it was no good, her cries could not be heard. Wherever she was, she had a horrible feeling it was in a totally isolated place.

* * *

Danny skirted around the casino, searching for Antonio Stone. He'd seen him at the party and knew he would recognize him. He checked out the blackjack tables, and finally spotted him sitting at a table with his wife.

Danny was not sure how to approach, but since this was an emergency, he did it boldly. 'Excuse me, Mr Stone,' he said, coming up behind him.

'Don't bother me now,' Antonio said, waving him away. 'I'm busy.' He had a stack of chips in front of him and seemed to be enjoying himself.

'Mr Stone,' Danny persisted, 'I have a message from Miz Roman about your daughter.'

'Not *now*,' Antonio repeated, as the dealer dealt him a card. 'Ah! Blackjack!' he crowed. The dealer pushed another stack of chips towards him. It was only then he turned to glance at Danny. 'What is it?' he asked impatiently.

'Miz Roman would like you to come to her suite.'

'Who is this, darling?' Bianca asked, leaning over.

'Something to do with Nicci,' Antonio said. 'Lissa wants to see me.'

'You cannot leave now – you're winning,' Bianca pointed out.

'It's very urgent,' Danny interjected.

'Can't it wait until tomorrow?' Antonio said bad-temperedly.

'No,' Danny replied. 'It's about Nicci.'

Reluctantly, Antonio rose from the table. 'You stay here and play for me,' he told his wife. 'I'll be right back.'

He followed Danny to the elevator, and then to the suite. By the time they got there, both Michael and Lissa were dressed.

'*What* is so urgent?' Antonio asked, entering with plenty of attitude. 'I was being very lucky for once.'

'It concerns Nicci,' Lissa said, 'and whatever I tell you has to stay in this room.'

'What has she done now?' Antonio asked, implying by his tone that whatever Nicci did was always a drama.

Michael stepped forward. 'We think she's been kidnapped,' he said. 'They're asking for a two-million-dollar ransom.'

Eric left the building to make his third call. He drove a few blocks away and used a pay-phone. He realized it was possible they might be able to trace his calls, so the first two he'd made on a cheap cellphone he'd purchased under an assumed name, but this time he'd decided to call from somewhere different. Besides, he did not want Davey, Arliss and Little Joe listening to him. They still had no idea who Nicci was. They thought she was simply a kid with rich parents who'd pay to get her back. Little did they know how famous and successful her mother was.

He made the call short and sweet. 'Delivery of the money will take place in L.A.,' he said, 'so get back here fast. Give me a number where I can reach you. At eight a.m. you'll get further instructions.'

'I have to speak to Nicci,' Lissa said quickly, 'or there'll *be* no money.'

'She's not here,' Eric said.

'I have to talk to her,' Lissa repeated. 'Otherwise, no ransom.'

'You'll speak to her in the morning,' Eric said, furious that she'd asked. 'Have the money ready then. No delays. This is my last call until then.'

Everyone in the room listened to the call. Lissa, Michael, Antonio and Danny.

'It's not good that he didn't put her on,' Michael said. 'Although he did say he'd allow her to speak to you in the morning, so that's something. He must be keeping her somewhere else. He's going out to use a phone, probably afraid we'll put a trace on it.'

'We can't risk her life,' Lissa said. 'Don't you agree, Antonio?'

He nodded, his expression sombre.

'I'm thinking,' Lissa said, 'that I should meet with Walter Burns to see if he can arrange to give me the cash.'

'Who is Walter Burns?' Antonio asked.

'The owner of the hotel,' Michael said.

'Then it is an excellent idea,' Antonio said. 'I am not in my country, Lissa, otherwise I would help.'

'I know,' she murmured.

'You must tell me if there is anything at all I can do.'

You can offer to pay half the ransom, Michael thought, but didn't say it. It wasn't any of his business. 'I'll go call Walter,' he said. 'Maybe he'll see you now.'

Lissa nodded. 'Please do that, Michael.'

Michael left the room and Antonio took her hand and whispered words of comfort. She put her head on his shoulder and let it rest there.

'You'd better go back to your wife, Antonio,' she said, after a few minutes. 'There's nothing else we can do until tomorrow.'

'We'll keep you informed,' Michael said, coming back into the room. 'And it'll be better if you don't say a word to anyone – including your wife.'

Antonio nodded, kissed Lissa on both cheeks and embraced her. She noticed that his embrace felt puny next to Michael's. 'Stay strong, my beauty,' Antonio said. 'I am here if you need me.'

'Thanks,' she murmured.

And then Antonio was gone.

Walter and Evelyn Burns' living quarters made Lissa's penthouse suite look like a pit-stop. They had created a magnificent twenty-five-thousand-square-feet home on the top floor across the other side of the hotel. The five-bedroom penthouse featured rooms with sixteen-foot-high ceilings, delicate rare-wood mouldings and Italian marble floors. Venetian glass chandeliers were everywhere. Picassos and Matisses hung on the walls, and there were many Italian rococo mirrors. Walter and Evelyn obviously enjoyed looking at themselves.

Walter greeted them, resplendent in a red and black smoking jacket, with black silk pants and slippers monogrammed in gold with his initials. He was smoking a large Cuban cigar. Evelyn was nowhere in sight.

'Come in, come in,' he said, welcoming them. 'What can I do for you at this late hour?'

Lissa was so upset and unnerved she could barely speak. 'Michael,' she said, 'you tell him.'

'Unfortunately, we have a situation,' Michael said, clearing his throat. 'A situation that cannot go beyond these four walls.'

'If there's one thing I understand,' Walter said, 'it's situations. Believe me, I am a man you can trust.'

'I'm sure,' Michael said, getting right to the point. 'Miz Roman's daughter, Nicci, is being held for ransom.'

'Is your daughter in Vegas?' Walter asked. 'Because if she is, she'll be found immediately. Nothing goes on in this city that I don't know about.'

'It didn't happen here,' Michael said. 'It happened in L.A.'

'What are their demands?' Walter asked, stubbing out his cigar.

'Two million dollars in cash.'

'So I thought,' Lissa said, her words tumbling over each other, 'that you could give me the cash as part of my payment.'

Walter nodded thoughtfully. 'Do you have any idea who's taken her?'

'No,' Michael said. 'We found out late tonight. A call came through, and the man on the phone threatened to kill Nicci if the FBI or the cops are brought in. Lissa wants to pay.'

'I need your help,' she said, appealing to Walter. 'I have to get my daughter back safely.'

Walter and Michael exchanged glances. They both knew what the other was thinking.

'Well,' Walter said, puffing on his cigar, 'this is unusual. Of course, I understand the situation, and if you wish to be paid in that fashion, I *can* arrange it. However, I never recommend paying kidnappers and, believe me, I've had my share of threats.'

'What would *you* do?' Lissa asked.

'I wouldn't call in the FBI, they're useless,' Walter said. 'I have my own people who use the latest European technology. When he phones again, we can put that into action.'

'He's calling tomorrow at eight a.m.'

'Where?'

'L.A.,' Michael said.

'I have people in L.A.,' Walter said.

'So you will help me?' Lissa asked.

'My wife loves you, Lissa. She would want me to do anything I can to help you. So I'll arrange for you to get the cash. And when your daughter is safe, I'll make sure the perpetrators of this crime are caught and punished. We have our own way of punishing people.'

'You do?' she said unsurely.

'They've got your daughter, Lissa, and they're holding her for ransom,' he said harshly. 'Surely you want to see justice done? In this country people talk about criminal justice. And that's what it is – justice for the criminals. I take care of things my way.'

'I see,' she murmured.

'Now,' he said, all business, 'I must organize the cash and instruct my pilot that we'll be leaving early. We'll fly to L.A. together. Trust me, Lissa. Everything will work out.'

She looked at Michael. He nodded his reassurance. At a time like this it wasn't a bad thing having a man like Walter Burns in your corner.

Chapter Forty-five

Big Mark staggered into the building drunk and belligerent at three o'clock in the morning.

Eric glared at him, he was angry. 'I warned you I didn't want any activity around here at night,' he said. 'If the cops saw you coming in here late at night, they'd be interested in finding out what you were doing.'

'Not my fault,' Big Mark grumbled. 'The club was jumping, an' I couldn't get away. I'm the friggin' bouncer.'

'I told you to say you were sick and take off early,' Eric said.

'Couldn't do that,' Big Mark said, burping loudly. 'I stopped by the bar on my way to work,' he added. 'There's been a freakin' murder.'

'Who got murdered?' Little Joe asked.

'Pattie,' Big Mark said.

'*Our* Pattie?' Arliss asked.

'Yeah,' Big Mark said. 'The poor bitch had her throat slit. Right in her own apartment. They found her last night. She'd bin dead a couple of days.'

'Holy Mother of Christ!' Arliss said, crossing himself. 'Who did it?'

'Nobody knows,' Big Mark said. 'She was hangin' from the shower rail in her own bathroom.'

'Jesus!' Davey snorted.

'That's what yer get for runnin' around with yer tits hangin' out,' Big Mark said, laughing rudely. 'Where's the girl?'

'Asleep,' Little Joe said. 'I just took a look.'

'*I'*m goin' down there,' Big Mark said.

'No!' Little Joe said sharply. 'She's asleep.'

'That's what we should all try to do,' Eric said. 'Get some sleep before tomorrow.'

'Did yer reach her parents?' Big Mark asked.

'Yes,' Eric said. 'They'll be coming up with the money soon.'

'How much're you asking?' Arliss inquired.

'If you must know, a hundred thousand.'

'A hundred thousand!' Big Mark exclaimed. 'And we're only getting ten each?'

'Figure it out,' Eric said. 'By the time you've all been paid, I'll have less than half left.'

'We deserve a bigger cut,' Davey muttered.

'I haven't got the money yet,' Eric said flatly. 'And don't forget who set this up. I gave up my job to follow the girl. It wasn't easy. Ten thousand dollars is a lot of money, you should be grateful.'

'A hundred thousand dollars,' Big Mark muttered belligerently. 'An' yer gettin' over half?'

'It's *my* scam,' Eric pointed out. 'Come up with one of your own, and you can take half too.'

Big Mark staggered out of the room. 'Gotta take a piss,' he mumbled. 'I'm thinkin' 'bout this.'

'Shockin' about Pattie, ain't it?' Arliss said, quick to move off the subject of money. He hadn't told Big Mark, Davey and Little Joe that his payout was twenty-five thousand. They wouldn't like it and that was too bad. He deserved a bigger cut because he was the one who'd put everyone together and supplied the location. Without him this entire scam wouldn't've come to pass. 'She liked you,' he added, turning to Eric. 'She was always watching you.'

'Was she now?' Eric said. *And look where it got her.*

'I liked her myself,' Arliss said. 'Only she didn't wanna know about me.'

'I can't imagine why,' Eric said, staring at the skinny man with the long greasy hair and the nervous facial tic. Like any woman would have anything to do with Arliss Shepherd. Ha! That was a laugh.

Nicci had fallen into an uneasy sleep when she heard the door open. It wasn't until a large hand started stroking her hair that she sat up with a start and began screaming.

'Shut the fuck up,' said a deep voice.

And there he was, sitting on the edge of the cot, the big, ugly, frightening man she'd seen at her house. The one who'd grabbed her.

'What do you want?' she asked, shrinking away from him, trying to keep the fear out of her voice.

'Thought yer might need company,' he mumbled, breathing whisky fumes all over her.

'I don't,' she said, her eyes darting towards the door, which he'd left open.

'No need t' be pissy,' he said, his big hands reaching out to touch her breasts.

'I'm thirsty,' she gasped, squirming away from him. 'I need water.'

'What do I get for a drink?' he leered, his big hands continuing to fondle her.

Kicking this one in the balls probably wouldn't have any effect – he looked like he was made of cement. God, he was a hulking beast of a man. Big hands, huge feet, a Herman Munster head. 'Please,' she said, pushing his hands away. 'I'm sick. I need water.'

'Fuck!' he mumbled. 'Yer remind me of those girls who come drivin' up in their fancy cars an' their sexy outfits, treatin' me like I'm nothin'. Starin' right through me like

I'm no one. "We're on the list," they say as they shove past me an' shake their tight little pussies all the way inta the club.'

'What club?' she asked.

'Never you mind,' he said, his big hands moving down to the zipper on her jeans.

'Leave me alone,' she yelled, kicking out. 'Can't you see I'm sick?'

'Yer too good fer me, is that it?' he said, getting nasty.

Suddenly she heard a voice behind him. 'I told you she was sleepin'. You shouldn't be in here.'

Thank God! It was the short man coming to her rescue.

'Jus' seein' if she wants anythin',' Big Mark slurred, backing off.

'Eric would be mad if he knew you came in here.'

'What the fuck?' Big Mark mumbled. 'He ain't the boss a' me.'

'You'd better leave her alone,' Little Joe warned. 'Nobody wants trouble.'

'Who said I was makin' trouble?'

'You're in here, aren't you?'

'Aw, piss off.'

'You want me to tell Eric?'

'What're we in – *school?*' Big Mark said, burping loudly. 'Run an' tell Eric. I reckon we should dump him an' keep all the money ourselves. *We*'re the ones did the job.'

'He's gotta *get* the money first,' Little Joe pointed out. 'He knows how to do these things.'

'Somebody's gotta watch him,' Big Mark said. 'I don't trust the bastard.'

Nicci realized she now knew who two of them were. Eric, who was probably the mastermind. And although she didn't have a name for the giant, he'd revealed that he worked in a club. Sounded like he was a bouncer. He was big enough and rough enough.

'I need some water,' she repeated weakly.

'I'll get you water,' Little Joe said. 'C'mon,' he said, grabbing Big Mark's arm. 'Go sleep it off.'

'Shit,' Big Mark said, lumbering out of the room. 'Nobody gets t' have any fun 'round here.'

Once the big man was gone, Little Joe turned to her. 'You hungry?'

She shook her head. The thought of food was sickening.

'I got you a burger,' he confided, 'only the boss wouldn't let me bring it to you.'

'Thanks,' she murmured.

'If anyone asks 'bout the sleepin' pills,' he continued, 'say you took 'em – okay? You help me, an' I'll help you.'

'Will you help get me out of here?' she asked, hoping to appeal to his better nature.

'Can't do that.'

'They're not going to hurt me, are they?'

'Naw,' Little Joe assured her. 'Why'd you think that? Your folks'll pay the money, an' we'll let you go.'

'When?'

'Tomorrow, the day after.' He groped in his pocket and came up with a couple of stale cookies. 'Here,' he said. 'I saved these for you.'

She took them from him, wondering if she could make a dash for the door.

'It's no good tryin' to run out of here,' he said, reading her mind. 'This building is locked up tight. You'll be trapped in it, then we'll catch you again, an' Eric'll punish you. He's a cold one. Not like me – I got compassion. See, I even know words like compassion.'

She nodded. Everything she'd ever heard about kidnapping came to mind. *Make friends with your abductors. Force them to realize that you're a person, and then they won't hurt you.*

'What's your name?' she asked.

'Oh, no,' he said. 'Can't tell you that.'

'Thanks for the cookies. If you could get me some water, I'd be grateful.'

'I'll come back,' he said. 'Gotta see where Mark went.'

Now she had two names. Eric and Mark. Eric was the mastermind, and Mark worked as a bouncer in a club. She knew she had to hang onto every detail.

Little Joe left, locking the door behind him. He was back a couple of minutes later carrying a paper cup filled with water. She gulped it down.

'I'll be in to check on you in the morning,' he said. 'Don't mind the rats an' roaches, they can't do you no harm.'

She shuddered. Maybe he *would* help her.

Chapter Forty-six

Lissa and Michael left the hotel at five a.m. with Walter Burns, who brought along Rick Maneloni, the hotel manager. Rick carried the bag containing the money.

As they boarded the Desert Millennium Princess plane, Michael was surprised to see that Cindy was still on duty. She gave him a cool look. 'Morning,' she said. He barely acknowledged her. He'd spent a sleepless night looking after Lissa, who was holding up well considering the circumstances.

They'd sent Danny on ahead, warning him not to alert anyone about what was going on. Michael had called Quincy and filled him in. 'Stay by a phone,' he'd said. 'I'll be in touch if I need you.'

Going to Walter Burns for help had been a good move: the hotel owner was turning out to be a useful ally. It was reassuring to have the support of what was obviously a far-reaching organization.

Everyone slept on the short flight into L.A. Everyone except Michael. He watched over Lissa, wanting nothing more than to take her in his arms and protect her. She looked so young and vulnerable. How he hated the son-of-a-bitch who was putting her through this torture.

Shortly before landing, Walter conferred with him. 'I've been involved with this kind of case before,' Walter said.

'Me too,' Michael said.

'Then we know what we're dealing with.'

'Yeah, the unknown,' Michael said.

'There's a team set up near her house,' Walter said. 'They'll track the eight a.m. call and find out where it's coming from. As soon as he tells her where to make the drop, my men will fall into position. They're professionals of the highest calibre.'

'What do you think our chances are of getting Nicci back safely?' Michael asked.

'I'm a gambling man,' Walter replied. 'Fifty-fifty.'

'That's not very good odds.'

'If this was Italy, they'd have sent Lissa an ear by now.'

The first thing Brian did when he surfaced on the couch in Evan's house was call his brother. 'Did she get there?' he asked.

'No,' Evan replied. 'Thanks a lot, you've turned Abbey into a nervous wreck.'

'I don't think anyone could turn Abbey into a nervous wreck,' Brian said. 'Give her some coke to start the day, that's what she needs. What're you doing with her anyway?'

'None of your goddamn business,' Evan said.

'Does this mean that Nic's up for grabs?'

'No, it doesn't. I'm thinking of postponing the wedding. Nicci and I will be married a couple of months later. I can't allow our movie to get fucked up.'

'That's big of you, Evan,' Brian said. 'The movie first. Your bride second.'

'Anyway, where *is* Nicci?'

'I'm glad you're finally concerned.'

'What do you mean?'

'She's vanished. She's not in Vegas with her mom, she's not with you.'

'So where is she?'

'Nobody knows.'

'Call me if you hear anything.'

'Your concern is touching.'

Saffron was asleep on top of the bed. He shook her awake, then went into the kitchen and made coffee. A few minutes after that he tried calling Lissa in Vegas and was informed she'd checked out. He looked at Saffron and shrugged. 'I dunno what to say. This is a bummer.'

'Do you think we should call the police?' Saffron asked.

'First we should talk to Lissa. I'll call her house.'

He did so, and Danny answered.

'Has anyone seen Nic?' he asked. 'Did she go to Vegas?'

'Miz Roman knows where she is,' Danny said.

'Thank God!' Brian exclaimed. 'So where is she?'

'Miz Roman will contact you later. She asked me to tell you and your brother not to worry.'

'That sounded weird,' Brian said, hanging up.

'What?' Saffron asked.

'Some shit about they know where she is, only they're not saying, and we shouldn't worry.'

'At least she's okay,' Saffron said. 'I'm heading home, and later I'm telling Nicci *exactly* what I think of her, putting us through this crap for nothing, that's cold, man.'

'Yeah,' Brian agreed. 'I guess we'll find out why she did it later.'

Larry was up long before Taylor. Not only was he up, but he was on the phone to Oliver Rock before seven.

Oliver was still sleeping. 'Yeah?' he managed.

'Do you jog?' Larry asked.

'Who's this?' Oliver mumbled.

'Larry Singer. I'm asking if you jog?'

'I've been known to,' Oliver said, stifling a yawn.

'Then get your ass out of bed. I'm coming by to pick you up.'

'What time is it, man?'

'Don't worry about the time. We need to talk.'

'Yeah, sure,' Oliver said, imagining that this was the way Larry Singer did business. Shit! And he hadn't even glanced at Taylor's crappy script since Larry's involvement.

Larry was already dressed in his jogging clothes. He walked back into the master bedroom and took a long look at his sleeping wife. After staring at her for a few moments, he left the room, went downstairs, got into his car and set off to meet Oliver.

Larry Singer had made a very important decision.

Upon arrival in L.A., everyone went straight to Lissa's house. She'd already alerted Nellie and sent Chuck on ahead with Danny to make sure everything was in order. They knew something was going on, but had not been filled in.

'We'll be in meetings all day,' Lissa informed Nellie, when they arrived. 'Please keep the coffee coming.'

'Yes, Miz Lissa,' Nellie said, wise enough not to ask questions.

Nicci slept in fits and starts, shivering all the while. When she awoke in the early hours of the morning, she was extremely hot, and knew she probably had a fever.

Great. How could she fight her way out of this dungeon if she was ill?

Little Joe came in early, bringing her a piece of dry bread and more water. She wondered if they'd drugged the water to keep her sedated. She was so thirsty that she gulped it down anyway.

'I'm getting sicker,' she informed him. 'I'm freezing cold one minute and burning up the next.'

Little Joe felt her forehead with his clammy hand. 'You might have a temperature,' he conceded.

'I do,' she said weakly. 'I know when I'm sick.'

'The boss is coming to see you,' Little Joe said. 'You gotta speak on the phone. He'll tell you what to say. You'd better not mess with him.'

'Who'm I speaking to?' she asked wearily.

'Your mom or your dad. One of 'em.'

'Oh,' she said.

'Your daddy must be rich,' Little Joe added, ''cause the boss is askin' for a hundred thousand bucks.'

Is that all I'm worth? she thought. *A hundred thousand.* Lissa would have her out of here in no time.

When Eric was ready to make the call, he slipped a stocking mask over his face and entered the windowless room. He hadn't wanted to have any contact with the girl at all, but the money cow had forced him into doing so.

'You'll tell your mother you're all right,' he said. 'And that's *all* you'll tell her. Understand?'

'Yes,' Nicci muttered, wondering why he was wearing a mask and the other two weren't.

I know your name, she thought. *You're Eric. And now I know what you look like. I can't see your face, but I can describe your body and what you're wearing. Once I'm out of here, they'll catch all of you, and you'll be locked away. Forever I hope.*

When the phone rang at exactly eight a.m., everyone was ready. Once again the call was on speaker-phone. Walter had reiterated his assurance that with the sophisticated equipment his team of people used, they'd be able to trace the call as long as Lissa got him to stay on the line long enough.

'You have to keep him talking,' Michael drilled into her.

'I'll try,' she said.

The first thing the muffled voice wanted to know was if she had the money.

'Yes,' she said. 'Now let me speak to my daughter.'

'I'm putting her on now.'

'Nicci?' Lissa said, desperate to hear her voice.

'Mom?'

'Are you okay, sweetheart?'

'Pay them, Mom, and they'll let me go.'

'Where are you?'

Before Nicci could answer, the phone was snatched away from her.

'I'll call back in five minutes,' the muffled voice said. Then the line went dead.

'Was that long enough to trace it?' Lissa asked anxiously.

'No,' Rick replied. 'You need to keep him talking longer.'

'Lissa,' Michael said, taking her hand, 'when he calls back you've got to pretend you don't understand when he gives you instructions for the drop-off, 'cause that's what he'll do next.'

'He will?'

'Yes. He knows you've got the money, so he'll be hot to get it. Don't forget, he's as nervous as you are.'

'I'll do my best,' she said faintly.

Five minutes later the phone rang again. Lissa tried to draw her words out, even saying, 'Hello?' in a slower tone.

'Satisfied?' the muffled voice said. 'Do you have the money?'

'I do.'

'Cash?'

'Yes.'

'They'd better be clean bills, because if they're not, I'll come back for the girl, and this time she won't be so lucky.'

'You'll have to tell me where to meet you.'

'You're not meeting *me*,' the man said. 'I'm not *that* stupid. And I hope *you*'re not stupid, because if you've brought in the FBI or the cops, you'll be very sorry indeed.'

'How are we going to do this?' she asked, speaking as slowly as possible. 'And how do I know I'll get my daughter back?'

'You'll have to trust me.'

'How can I trust you when I don't even know you?'

'There's no other way,' he said. 'Give me your cellphone number.'

'Just . . . just a minute,' she said. 'Hold on, I have to get it.'

'You don't know your own number?'

'I recently changed all my numbers. I'll get it. Don't go away.' She stayed off the line as long as she could before coming back with the number. Out of the corner of her eye she saw Rick giving her a thumbs-up.

'Okay,' the man said. 'Here's what I want you to do. Walk out of your house right now, get in your car, and drive towards the beach. I'll contact you with further instructions.'

He hung up and she put the phone down, her hands shaking.

'The call was coming from a pay-phone in the valley,' Rick said. 'Our guys are on it.'

'They can't do anything until I have Nicci,' Lissa said. 'Promise me.'

'Don't worry,' Walter said. 'Nobody makes a move without instructions from me.'

'What do you think, Michael?'

'I think you did great,' he said, encouraging her to stay strong. 'You were calm, in control. Now we'll go out to your car, and you'll do as he says.'

'You can't come with me. If he sees someone else in the car, it could endanger Nicci's life.'

'I understand, Lissa. They've put a device in your car that'll pick up everything you say. I'll be able to hear you, so you'll keep me informed.'

'Where will you be?'

'Close enough that you'll feel safe and he'll never know.'

'Are you sure?' she asked, turning to him, her beautiful face creased with worry.

'Yes, Lissa, I'm sure.'

'Oh, God!' she said. 'This is such a nightmare.'

'Don't worry,' Walter said. 'Between all of us, we'll get your daughter back safely. That's a promise.'

'Are you sure?' she repeated, turning to Michael again.

'Positive, sweetheart,' he said.

But in his heart he wasn't sure at all.

Chapter Forty-seven

Eric had a plan. The plan was to get into his car, pick up the ransom, and head straight for the airport. He couldn't care less what happened after he got the money. If he'd had the time, he would've torched the building with all of them in it, including the girl. They were useless human beings – every one of them.

Arliss and his friends were slouched around the room when he returned from his second phone call. It stank of sweat, urine and unwashed bodies. How he despised them. 'I'll be leaving shortly,' he said. 'When I return, we'll sit here and divide up the money. After that, you're on your own.'

'What about the girl?' Little Joe asked. It was apparent that he'd become her primary caretaker.

'You'll drive her up into the hills and let her loose,' Eric said. 'She can find her own way home.'

'How long're you gonna be?' Arliss asked, picking his teeth with a used matchstick.

'A few hours,' Eric said.

'Why so long?' Big Mark wanted to know.

'I have to lead them on a dance,' Eric explained. 'If I get caught, we end up with nothing. They think they're meeting me at one place, when they get there, I tell them to go somewhere else. And so on and so forth. It takes time to do this properly.'

'One of us should come with you,' Big Mark said.

'No,' Eric said. 'This is the most dangerous part of the operation. They get me, and whoever I'm with goes down too.'

'Yes,' Arliss agreed. 'He's better off alone.'

'How'd we know he's comin' back?' Big Mark asked.

Eric threw him a look of shocked surprise. 'You think I'd run out on you four?' he said. 'You'd find me, and my life wouldn't be worth shit. I'm no fool.'

'He's no fool,' Arliss said, echoing him.

No, I'm not, Eric thought. *But you four certainly are.*

Big Mark didn't look too sure. He was suffering from a massive hangover, and the thought of riding around with Eric didn't exactly appeal to him. But still . . . once Eric had the money, how could they trust him to come back?

'I'd better drive with you,' he said. 'For insurance.'

'You want insurance?' Eric said, turning on the huge hulk of a man. 'Here's your fucking insurance,' he said, digging in his pockets and producing his social-security card, driver's licence and two credit cards. 'Does that make you happy?' he demanded, throwing them on the table. 'Keep them until I return. *Jesus!*'

'So when y' get back, we're lettin' the girl go, is that it?' Little Joe asked.

'Yes,' Eric said. 'If all goes smoothly and I have the money.'

'You'll have it,' Arliss said, his face twitching.

'And don't leave here until I return,' Eric warned. 'It's important that you all stay out of sight until this is done.'

Morons, he thought. *Dumb, stupid, imbecilic morons.*

At least they'd served their purpose.

Eric left the building and got into the black Ford he'd rented the day before. Then he entered the freeway and drove all the way to the Hollywood exit, before doubling back to Farmer's Market.

He parked across the street on Fairfax, and called Lissa. 'Turn around and come to Farmer's Market on Fairfax,' he said. 'When you get there, park your car, leave the bag with the money on the passenger side, don't lock the doors, get out and walk across the street. Keep walking for fifteen minutes. If you look back, your daughter dies. Do you understand?'

'Yes,' she said.

'Good. When I'm sure all the money is there, you'll get Nicci.'

'Where will she be?'

'She'll find *you*.'

'How can I be sure?'

'You'll just have to trust me.'

When Lissa finally arrived, he noted that she was not being followed. He immediately picked up his cellphone again and called her. 'More instructions,' he said. 'Stay in your car, make a U-turn out of there and head down Wilshire towards downtown.'

'I thought you wanted me to park the car here and leave the money in it,' she said, confused.

'No. Keep driving. I can see you, so you'd better make sure you follow my instructions. And do *not* use your phone. I'm watching you, bitch.'

'What is it you want me to do again?' she asked.

'Get onto Wilshire and drive downtown.'

She repeated his words and looked around to see if she could spot Michael. She couldn't, but she knew he'd be close by, he'd promised he wouldn't let her out of his sight.

She did a U-turn out of Farmer's Market and set off down Fairfax. Her heart was beating so fast she could barely think straight.

This was an impossible situation to be in. Where was Nicci? Was she all right? She must be so scared by now.

Random thoughts kept running through her head. Antonio had wanted to come to the house. She'd told him no, and asked him to wait at his hotel for news. As Michael had said, the fewer people involved, the better. Then she started thinking about who could be doing this to her. Was it Gregg? She wouldn't put it past him. He'd turned out to be a truly evil man, and she hated him.

Oh, God! If only she could wake up from this ongoing nightmare.

When she reached Wilshire, she turned left, heading downtown, anxiously awaiting further instructions.

The moment the phone rang again she grabbed it.

'Do you have the money?' the man asked, no longer bothering to disguise his voice.

'Yes,' she said.

'Where is it?'

'In a bag on the floor next to me.'

'Pick the bag up and put it on the passenger seat. Then unlock your doors and open the passenger side window.'

'But—'

'Shut up, *bitch!* If you want to see your daughter again, you'll do exactly as I say.'

'Here's some water,' Little Joe said.

Nicci was lying on the cot, her head felt like it was exploding. She grabbed the paper cup and drank the water.

'How d'you feel?' he asked.

'How do you *think* I feel?' she responded. 'Lousy. When are you letting me out of here?'

'Everything's under control,' Little Joe said. 'Your parents are gonna pay. Eric's gone to collect the ransom now. With any luck, you'll be free in a few hours.'

'I'm very sick,' she mumbled feverishly.

He leaned over her and felt her head. She was burning up. 'Try t' sleep,' he said. 'You can't do nothin' else.'

'Do you realize what kind of crime kidnapping is?' she muttered.

'We won't hurt you,' he said. 'We're lettin' you go.'

'When?' she asked, shivering uncontrollably.

'Soon,' he assured her.

Larry Singer walked into Oliver Rock's place unannounced.

Oliver was standing in the bathroom cleaning his teeth. 'Shit, man – you scared me,' he said, when Larry appeared behind him.

'Don't you lock your door?' Larry asked.

'What for?' Oliver said. 'If they wanna get in around here they'll just kick the door in.'

'Nice neighbourhood,' Larry said. 'Are you ready?'

'Where do you want to jog?' Oliver asked.

'Where do people usually jog around here?'

'Down on the boardwalk,' Oliver said.

'Fine,' Larry replied. 'Let's go there.'

They headed out of his apartment.

'We can walk,' Oliver said. 'That's the advantage of living at the beach.'

'Yes,' Larry said. 'I've often thought of buying a beach house. Taylor wants me to.'

'Do it,' Oliver said. 'You can run on the sand, get away from the smog. It's cool, man.'

'I'm sure,' Larry said.

They reached the boardwalk, which was surprisingly crowded for so early in the morning. There were plenty of joggers, people on roller-skates, scooters and bikes, and various transients recovering from a night out in the cold. The sun was already shining and the surf looked most inviting.

Larry began to jog slowly. Oliver fell into step beside him.

'You know, Oliver, you're very young,' Larry remarked, 'and I know you've recently scored a big deal with your first screenplay. However, I thought I should warn you about this town.'

'Yeah?' Oliver said.

'Never cross the wrong people.'

'How's that?' Oliver asked.

'It's an old cliché – but honesty *is* the best policy.'

'Yeah, yeah,' Oliver said. 'That's what my dad always says.'

'Your father's a very nice man,' Larry said. 'He has integrity. That's a very important quality to have if you want to survive in this business.'

'I got integrity,' Oliver said.

'Have you?'

'Oh, yeah.'

'Integrity and drugs don't mix,' Larry said. 'You should stop doing drugs.'

'Hey, man, all I do is smoke a little weed once in a while, that's not exactly doin' drugs.'

'Don't forget the coke,' Larry said. 'It's all over the tip of your nose.'

'What?' Oliver said, embarrassed. He rubbed his nose with the back of his hand.

'It's not smart to do drugs in this town,' Larry said. 'Too many people end up out of control. You saw what happened to River Phoenix. And he was just the beginning. Christian Slater. Robert Downey Jr. They've all had their experiences. You don't want to put yourself in that position, you have to stay in control.'

'Yeah, yeah, I *get* it,' Oliver said. He was already out of breath, which pissed him off because Larry was almost thirty years older than him, and was obviously in much better shape as far as exercise was concerned.

'Another thing,' Larry said.

'Yeah?' Oliver said, thinking, *What is this? Fucking lecture hour?*

'You don't sleep with other men's wives.'

Uh-oh, Oliver thought, keeping his eyes fixed firmly ahead. 'Huh?' he managed.

'You heard me,' Larry said, cool as a block of ice. 'You don't sleep with other men's wives. Especially mine.'

'I dunno what you're—'

'Please!' Larry interrupted, and stopped jogging. 'Taylor has told me everything.'

'Aw, shit!' Oliver whined, bending over because he was experiencing a nasty cramp. 'Why'd she do that?'

'My wife is an honest woman,' Larry replied, 'and since I'm friendly with your parents, I thought I'd give you a chance to explain yourself. When was the last time you and Taylor were together?'

'Hey, listen, man, I'm sorry. I dunno how it happened. She told me you weren't into sex and, uh . . . Jesus, I mean, it wasn't something I was gonna keep doing. Neither was she.'

'That's all right, Oliver,' Larry said calmly. 'I understand you both had your reasons. When *was* the last time?'

'A couple of days ago, man – but, you know, it wasn't any big deal. We both knew it was over.'

'You've already said that.'

'Yeah, well, I know. Hey, listen, you're bein' real cool about this, and uh . . . I'm kinda surprised she told you, 'cause she didn't want you to know. But we'd already decided we weren't gonna do it any more out of respect for you.'

'Respect for me, huh?' Larry said.

'Anyway, man, maybe we should discuss the script, get into that.'

'Yes, Oliver, maybe we should. You see, I've decided to go with another writer.'

'You have?'

'I wouldn't want you to overburden yourself. You recently sold your first script and I think you should concentrate on that. I don't wish to take up your valuable time.'

'Hey,' Oliver said, blinking rapidly, 'if it's 'cause of me and Tay – I told you, it's over.'

'Yes,' Larry said, staring at him. 'You're right, Oliver. It's over.'

Shit! Michael thought. *He's changing the dance. I should've known it was too easy.*

As Lissa made a U-turn out of Farmer's Market, he hung back, making sure whoever was tracking her didn't realize she was being followed.

He was pretty good at it, considering trailing people was part of his profession. He was always able to stay far enough away from his target so that they never realized he was behind them.

Still, he couldn't let Lissa out of his sight. Who knew what kind of maniac this guy was?

What the kidnapper wasn't aware of was that her car had a speaker device connected to his car, so she could fill him in on everything.

She'd already told him that whoever was following her was somewhere nearby.

Michael continued to hang back. As long as she kept up a dialogue with him, he'd know exactly where she was without being on her tail. That way, the kidnapper would be between her car and his, and when the man instructed her where to leave the money, he'd be right there.

It was a game.

And Michael knew exactly how to play the game.

Walter Burns prided himself on never being taken advantage of. He'd put together teams of people across the country who looked after his interests. And his interests were many. Nobody got away with anything. If he was owed money, they paid. If anyone attempted extortion in any way, they also paid.

Lissa was unaware that they'd placed a tracking device in the bag containing the money. Whoever the kidnapper was must be foolish to think he could get away with two million dollars. Maybe if he'd asked for fifty thousand he might've pulled it off. But no, greed always pulled people under, and made them lose out in the end.

Walter liked Michael Scorsinni. He was obviously a man who knew what he was doing. Walter already suspected he was in bed with Lissa Roman, but so what? It was good that she had somebody around her who could take care of her. Walter was thinking that when this little caper reached its rightful conclusion, he might offer Michael a job. Meanwhile, his people had called him from the valley to inform him that they'd explored the area where the phone call was made, and come up with two possibilities. One was a large warehouse building that seemed to be deserted, and the other was a rundown apartment building in the same neighbourhood.

'We're carrying out a search of both places,' Rick Maneloni informed him.

'Good,' Walter said.

Rick Maneloni had worked for Walter for many years. He'd started off doing menial jobs in Chicago, until finally rising to manage Walter's flagship hotel in Vegas. Trust. That was Walter's motto. *Surround yourself with people you can trust.*

There was two million dollars in cash in a bag in Lissa Roman's car, and he wanted it back. He also wanted Nicci, her daughter, back. And if all went according to plan, he'd get the money *and* the girl back safely.

Nobody crossed Walter Burns and got away with it.

Chapter Forty-eight

Detective Fanny Webster questioned Sam, the bar owner, for the second time. 'Okay,' she said patiently. 'Let's go over this again. You've told me about a man called Eric who frequents the bar. You don't know his last name or where he lives. But you *do* know he was on his way to see Pattie two days ago. In fact, that would be the day she was killed. And the way I look at it, he would be our prime suspect.'

'Pattie liked him,' Sam said. 'He said somethin' about owin' her money. Strange guy, moody, dead-fish eyes. Kept to himself. Except—'

'Except what?' Fanny asked.

'He was always hangin' with Arliss an' Little Joe, and another coupla guys who come in here. I think they was planning somethin'.'

'What kind of something?'

'They was always huddlin' together. The day Eric asked where he could find Pattie, I said, "What're you up to?" He never told me nothing – never wanted t' talk to me, just those other guys.'

'How can I reach them?'

'Dunno,' Sam said, blowing his nose on a cocktail napkin. 'This is a place where nobody asks questions.'

'Can't you come up with anything at all? What does this Arliss character do?'

'Works as a caretaker in some old building.'

'Where?'

'Off Ventura, way down. Dunno what street.'

'That's all you can tell me?' Fanny asked, flashing him the friendly smile in case it would elicit more information.

'I don't ask questions,' Sam said. 'People wouldn't come here if I did.'

'Okay,' Fanny said.

'I *do* know where Big Mark works,' Sam offered.

'Who's Big Mark?'

'One of them guys I mentioned.'

'So where does he work, Sam?'

'At a fancy club on Sunset where rich kids hang out. It's called . . . let me see . . . yeah, it's called the Place.'

'Thanks, Sam, you've been a big help.'

Sam beamed and wondered if she'd go out with him. She had a lovely smile.

'Oh, yeah,' he said. 'I just remembered somethin'.'

'What?' she said.

'Arliss's last name.'

'You did?'

'Yeah, it's Shepherd – like the dog.'

'Okay, Sam.'

By the time Larry returned home, Taylor was up practising Pilates on the machine he'd recently bought her for their gym.

When Larry walked in, she stopped stretching and reached for a towel. 'You were out early this morning,' she said, throwing the small towel around her neck. 'Where did you go?'

'Jogging,' he said. 'At the beach.'

'The beach,' she said, surprised. 'You should've woken me. I would've gone with you.'

'Taylor,' he said.

'Yes,' she answered, still doing stretches.

'You look very lovely this morning. Getting back to work seems to agree with you.'

'Thanks, darling,' she said. 'I'm so pleased you think that.'

'I do.'

'So,' she said, smiling, 'what would you like to do today? I'm all yours. No more work until tomorrow. So maybe we could drive down to Shutters at the Beach for lunch, even spend the night. Or just stay home. I'm all yours, whatever you want.'

'I'll tell you what I want, Taylor,' he said, his plain face rather serious.

She looked at him expectantly. 'Yes, Larry, what?'

He was silent for a moment before speaking, and then his words came across loud and clear. 'I want a divorce.'

Little Joe worked in a hospital, so he knew when something was wrong, and there was definitely something wrong with Nicci. Her fever was rising alarmingly.

'The girl's sick,' he said to Arliss.

'Sick?' Arliss said. 'How's that?'

'She's got a high fever. I think she needs to go to a hospital.'

'You're such a friggin' moron,' Big Mark said. 'We can't take her to a hospital. How stupid can you get?'

'Then we'd better sponge her down. Her temperature's going up.'

'What d'you do? Carry a thermometer with you?' Big Mark said rudely.

'I work in a hospital,' Little Joe pointed out. 'I know these things.'

'You work with a bunch of loonies,' Big Mark said disparagingly.

'I'm tellin' you, she's sick,' Little Joe insisted, 'an' we'd better do somethin' about it.'

'No. *You*'d better shut the fuck up,' Big Mark said. 'And don't bother lookin' in on her again, 'cause you're a loony too.'

'When Eric gets back, we'll drop her outside a hospital,' Arliss said. 'How's that?'

Little Joe nodded. He wasn't at all sure.

Driving down Wilshire, Lissa was aware that her hands were shaking. She tried to steady her nerves, think clearly and stay in control. 'Michael, if you can hear me,' she said, barely moving her lips in case she was being watched, 'I've put the money on the seat as he requested.'

The traffic was not heavy. She checked her rear-view mirror, wondering which car the kidnapper was in. Her phone rang again and she grabbed it.

'Get into the left-hand lane,' the voice instructed, 'and when you get to the next red light, stay there until I tell you to move. Whatever happens, do not react.'

She veered into the left lane, her heart pounding. Up ahead the light was green. She drove through it, watching for the next one – which was changing to red as she approached. She came to a stop.

And then everything seemed to happen at lightning speed. A car pulled up alongside her. The driver reached out his arm, put it through her passenger window and snatched the heavy bag from the seat. Then the car raced off at top speed.

'Michael!' she yelled, totally stunned. 'He's taken the money. He's in a black Ford. It's ahead of me on Wilshire.'

Immediately her phone rang. 'I'm on it,' Michael said. 'Turn around and go back to the house.'

'What about Nicci?' she cried. 'Where is she?'

'I'll get him,' Michael said. 'And then we'll find out where Nicci is. Don't worry, Lissa, I won't come home without her.'

479

* * *

Eric shot off along Wilshire, making a fast right. He *had* the money. He had the goddamn money!

With one hand, he unzipped the top of the bag, checking out the stacks of bills.

Bingo! He'd finally made the score he'd always dreamed of.

Now that Lissa was out of the picture, Michael could do what he had to do, nail the son-of-a-bitch and find out where Nicci was.

The kidnapper had the money, but who knew what he'd done with Nicci?

Michael concentrated on keeping him in sight. It was a matter of life and death.

'She's gettin' worse,' Little Joe announced to the group.

'What d'you mean?' Arliss asked.

'I'm tellin' you, she's worse now. Freezin' one minute, burnin' up the next. She needs medical help.'

'Well, she ain't gonna get it,' Arliss said. 'You know that.'

'What if we dropped her off at a hospital?' Little Joe suggested. 'Nobody would be any the wiser.'

'Are you fuckin' *nuts?*' Big Mark exploded. 'Course they would. *She*'d tell 'em.'

'What're we gonna do?'

'I'll come take a look at her,' Big Mark said, lumbering to his feet.

'No,' Little Joe said. '*I*'m takin' care of her. I'll give her more water.'

Meanwhile, Nicci was completely out of it. She felt as if someone had poisoned her. Her stomach was cramping, and her skin was breaking out in angry red blotches. Suddenly she began to vomit.

She was too sick to get up and reach the bucket.

She didn't care. She just wanted to die.

*   *   *

As Eric raced down the Santa Monica freeway, he managed to transfer the stacks of bills into an empty Nike bag he'd purchased the day before. As soon as he'd achieved that, he took the original bag and flung it out his window. It landed on the side of the freeway. That done, he got off the freeway at the next exit and began taking surface streets to the airport, constantly checking his rear-view mirror to make sure he was not being followed.

It seemed to be all clear. A sense of triumph swept over him. He began to whistle to himself, thinking, *how smart can one guy get?*

When he'd taken out Eric Vernon's driver's licence, social-security card, and credit cards, and left them with the morons at the warehouse, that had been his way of saying goodbye to them *and* Eric Vernon.

He was Norman Browning now.

Nobody would ever see Eric Vernon again.

Michael's head was pounding. There was nothing more tedious than following a vehicle while trying to avoid the person in the other car knowing you're right behind them. Especially when that person was the kidnapper who was now carrying a shitload of money and had everything to lose.

Michael relied on his instincts to tell him which way to go, and he was usually right.

The black Ford was way ahead of him. He had a strong suspicion it was heading towards the airport, which meant that the man in the car probably wasn't about to release Nicci.

Shit! He'd have to grab the son-of-a-bitch and force it out of him. If he'd harmed Lissa's daughter in any way, he would certainly live to regret it.

*   *   *

Rick Maneloni, accompanied by three of Walter Burns's men, reached the warehouse ten minutes before Detective Fanny Webster drove up with two squad cars. They were looking for Nicci. And she was looking for Arliss Shepherd who, she thought, would lead her to Eric Vernon. Once Sam had remembered Arliss's last name, it didn't take long to track him down. And he had a record, which Fanny found quite interesting.

Walter Burns's men made short work of getting into the building. They stood in the old reception area, and listened for noise. The sound of a TV came from along the hall.

Rick signalled that they should go in that direction. When they reached the room, one of the men kicked the door open. Arliss, Big Mark, Davey and Little Joe were sitting around watching a ball game.

One of Rick's men pulled a gun and pointed it at them. 'I suggest you don't move, motherfuckers,' Rick said. 'Where's the girl?'

Big Mark sprang into action like an angry bear, hurling himself towards them. 'Shoot the dumb son-of-a-bitch,' Rick ordered.

The gun exploded, blowing a hole in Big Mark's leg. He screamed in pain and fell to the ground.

Arliss, Little Joe and Davey shrank back in terror.

'Where's the girl?' Rick repeated, as Big Mark lay on the ground, moaning.

'She – she's down the hall,' Arliss stammered. 'H-here's the key,' he said, throwing it in their direction.

'You dumb cocksuckers,' Rick said, shaking his head. 'Did you honestly think you could get away with this shit? You,' he said to Little Joe, 'take us to her.'

Little Joe scurried to oblige, leading them down to the basement, and along a dark musty corridor to a locked door at the end. With trembling hands he opened the door.

Nicci was sprawled on the floor, unconscious.

* * *

Eric pulled his car kerbside, jumped out, grabbed the bag containing the money, and hurried into the airport. He glanced behind him. Nobody following. Easy! Two million dollars, a new identity, and he'd be on a plane to the Bahamas within minutes.

He strode briskly over to the check-in desk and presented his ticket.

'I think that flight might be closed,' the woman behind the desk said.

'It can't be,' he said. 'My mother's very sick, and it's imperative I make that flight. Please do something.'

'Let me check,' she said, picking up a phone. She spoke for a few seconds, then said, 'Gate seventeen. You can make it if you hurry.'

'Please alert them I'm on my way,' he said. 'I have to be on this plane.'

'I will,' she said. 'Hope your mom gets well.'

He ran over to the security checkpoint. He'd left his gun in the rental car, so he had no problem getting through. Before putting the money in the bag, he'd insulated it with magazines and old sweaters. It was snug and safe, and nobody knew it was there except him.

He hurried down the walkway towards gate seventeen, waving his boarding pass as he approached.

Just as he was about to present it to the gate clerk, a voice behind him said, 'Excuse me, sir!'

He turned around. A tall, dark man stood there.

'Yes?' he said.

'We're conducting a series of random security checks today. You'll have to accompany me.'

'I can't,' he said angrily. 'I'll miss my plane. My mother's sick, and I have to catch this flight.'

'I'm sorry, you'll have to come with me.'

'Fuck *you*,' Eric said, and thrusting his boarding pass at

483

the surprised gate agent, he began running down the narrow corridor towards the plane.

Michael started to follow him.

'I'm sorry, sir,' the gate agent said, blocking his way. 'You must have a boarding pass.'

'This is an emergency,' Michael yelled. 'Police business.'

'Show me your badge.'

'I don't *have* a fucking badge,' he said, and pushing past her, he raced after Eric.

He got to him before he reached the plane. 'You low-life son-of-a-bitch!' he shouted, grabbing his shoulders and spinning him around. 'Where is she?'

'I don't know what you're talking about,' Eric said blankly.

'You *know* what I'm fucking talking about. Where's Nicci?'

'If you don't let me get on this plane, you'll never know, will you?' Eric said, an evil look on his face.

'You wanna fucking *bet?*' Michael exploded, slamming him against the side wall.

Eric wished he'd kept his gun, because if he'd had it with him, he would've blown this cocksucker's head off. This cocksucker who was just about to ruin everything.

With a sudden show of strength he fought back, kneeing Michael in the groin and gouging at his eyes like a madman.

Michael responded with a swift kick to Eric's knees, forcing his legs to buckle under him, throwing him off balance so that he sprawled on the ground, still clutching the bag containing the money.

His hate-filled eyes stared up at Michael. 'You'll never find her,' he said, 'because she's fucking *dead.*'

Epilogue

Walter Burns's tentacles of power stretched in many different directions. And because of his enormous power, he was able to squash the story about the kidnapping of Lissa Roman's daughter, much to everyone's relief.

Of course, when the case came to trial, it would be impossible to keep it quiet, but in the meantime, everyone had a few months to recover.

Lissa got her money *and* her daughter back. She was ecstatic about having Nicci safely home. She couldn't care less about the money.

Nicci spent a few days in the hospital, recovering from extreme dehydration and an allergic reaction to chloroform. If left unattended, she probably would have died.

Evan rushed to her bedside, his mother beside him. He'd finally realized there were some things more important than a movie.

'I'm happy to see you,' she told him, while Lynda hovered outside, 'but here's the thing, Ev, I've changed my mind. I don't want to marry you.'

'What're you *talking* about?' he said, quite shocked. 'I'll admit I had an affair with Abbey, but it didn't count. It was a last-minute fling.'

'I'm sure that's exactly what it was, Evan. Only you and I, we were not meant to be together.'

Bitter about the break-up, Evan resumed his affair with Abbey. It was a big mistake. She drove him crazy with jealousy and alienated his mother, who flew back to New York in a huff.

By the time they got married in a quickie ceremony in Mexico, he was a broken man.

Six weeks later they were divorced. And since she'd refused to sign a pre-nuptial, Abbey Christian – in the true Hollywood bitch-on-wheels tradition – walked away with half his money.

A month after that, Nicci and Brian ran off to Las Vegas and were married by an Elvis impersonator.

Nicci grinned at Brian. 'You've made my dreams come true!' she exclaimed. 'Elvis *and* you. What a wild combination!'

Laughing, he raced her to the limo. 'I always knew there was somebody as crazy as me,' he said. 'And now I've finally found you.'

'Oh, yeah,' she joked. 'But you sure did a lot of looking before I came along.'

'Hey,' he said. 'Got it out of my system, didn't I?'

'You'd better. No more blondes, redheads *or* brunettes.'

He threw up his hands. 'I'm done!'

'You bet your sweet ass.'

They spent their honeymoon white-river rafting down the Colorado river, followed by a trip to the carnival in Rio.

And when they got back they bought a funky house on Bluejay Way above Sunset, and settled into really getting to know each other.

It was a trip. A trip they were both into one hundred percent.

*   *   *

Saffron met a guy, another stud. His uncle was a TV producer, who decided that Saffron was exactly the girl he was searching for to star in his new TV series.

The stud didn't last.

The TV series did.

Taylor and Larry Singer were also divorced. And Taylor was also entitled to half her successful and respected husband's money. But what good was half of Larry's money, when she'd lost her standing in the Hollywood community?

No longer Mrs Lawrence Singer, she was just another Hollywood wife.

Oliver Rock's million-dollar movie was finally produced and became the cult hit of the year. He gave up drugs and concentrated on his work.

Oliver Rock had aspirations to be the Larry Singer of his generation.

Arliss Shepherd and his three cohorts, Big Mark, Davey and Little Joe were all arrested on kidnapping charges.

Their ringleader, Eric Vernon, was nailed by Detective Fanny Webster for the murder of Pattie, the waitress from Sam's bar.

Eric sat in prison and brooded about what he would do when he got out.

Eric Vernon, a.k.a. Norman Browning, had big plans.

After a week's 'absence makes the heart grow fonder', James and Claude got back together. James presented himself at the house one day as if nothing had happened.

Claude was out in the lavish grounds tending his tomatoes in his state-of-the-art greenhouse, Al Green blasting on the sophisticated sound system. 'What are *you* doing here?' he inquired.

'I've reached a conclusion,' James announced.

'Yes?'

'Well . . .' James said, walking up behind his partner and placing his hands on his shoulders. '*Your* magic is *so* much better than his.'

Patrick's lurid cover story in *Truth and Fact* was a hit with the hungry public. The magazine had its biggest circulation of the year. Belinda's imaginary best friend was quoted liberally, while Deidra recounted the sorry story of her almost rape by Lissa Roman's ex-husband.

Patrick and Belinda rekindled their off-on again romance. There was nothing like a shitload of money to bring two people together.

Gregg found that nobody wanted to know him. His record came out and was a flop. The money he got in the divorce settlement did not last long. He invested it all in technology stocks and soon lost everything – including his Ferrari. He was finally reduced to appearing in a soft-core porno movie with an actress whose silicone tits completely obliterated his presence on the screen.

So much for stardom.

Antonio and the Contessa de Morago returned to Spain and Bianca's fortune. Every day Antonio thanked God that Nicci had survived her terrible ordeal. Antonio considered himself a lucky man: his daughter was safe, and he was married to a woman who could keep him in the style he'd always craved.

Shortly after returning to Spain, he met a twenty-five-year-old female bull-fighter, and fell in lust.

Antonio would never change.

Carol's pregnancy turned out to be a false alarm. 'I'm so sorry,' she told Michael.

'That's all right,' he said, relieved and yet strangely disappointed at the same time.

For a moment he considered giving her the speech, and then he thought better of it. Carol was a nice woman, she deserved the truth. So he told her about Lissa and their affair, and she thanked him for being so honest.

They parted friends.

Lissa and Michael fell in love. Happily, deliriously in love as if it was the first time either of them had ever experienced such an emotion.

'I'm taking a year off,' Lissa informed him. 'I want us to be together, so we can do whatever we feel like doing.'

'I don't know . . .' he said unsurely. 'You have a major career to take care of. And we—'

'Yes, I know,' she interrupted. 'We live in different worlds, lead different lives, you've told me a hundred times.'

'I have?'

'Yes, Michael. Now when are you going to realize that you can't get rid of me?'

'Like I would want to.'

'Maybe you would. I'd better warn you, I'm not easy.'

'Did I mention that I wasn't either?'

'Well,' she said, with a cunning smile, 'you were pretty easy in Vegas. I had the whole thing planned, you know.'

'You did, did you?'

'Uh-huh. Yeah,' she mused. 'I'd say you were pretty easy.'

'Tell you what,' he said.

'What?' she said.

'Go put your disguise on and let's catch a movie.'

'No,' she said. 'I have courtside seats for the Lakers. And . . . I'm going as myself.'

'Courtside? Are you kidding? They're impossible to get.'

'You see,' she said triumphantly, 'there are *some* advantages to being me.'

'Oh, yes!'

'We're not hiding any more, Michael. We're coming out, so prepare yourself for an onslaught of press.'

He pulled her into his arms and kissed her. 'I got a strong suspicion I've been fighting this for too long,' he said. 'So . . . here's the deal. From this day on – I'm all yours.'

'You are?' she said, her blue eyes gazing into his.

'I am.'

'And about time, too,' she said, smiling. 'Because that's *exactly* what I've been waiting to hear.' A beat. 'Oh, yes, and one other thing.'

'What?'

'You – are going to be a daddy. So . . . I guess you'd better start getting plenty of sleep, 'cause *I*'m not leaving my bed at four a.m.'

'You're not, huh?' he said, beaming.

'No way.'

'Then I'll just have to marry you and turn you into an obedient wife.'

'Me?'

'Yes, you.'

'Forget it, Michael. I'm not the obedient-wife type.'

'And . . . I wouldn't have it any other way.'

'No, you wouldn't, would you?'

And they fell into each other's arms, blissfully happy.

They were a perfect match.